SALTWATER
Cowboy

I0563175

ASHLEY
MCCONNELL

For anyone learning to live gently,
to trust the timing,
and to bloom right where they're planted.

Playlist

SALTWATER
Cowboy

CHAPTER 1

I HOPE YOU'RE HAPPY NOW

Rose

I
F LOOKS COULD KILL, THE COUPLE SITTING AT THE OTHER END
of the bar would've been dead thirty minutes ago.

They're so in love. Hugging. Kissing. Brushing shoulders. Laughing.

Disgusting.

Four hours ago, I was that kind of hopelessly in love. Now, I'm sitting at a dingy airport bar, shooting eye daggers at a couple just living their lives. They say your world can change in an instant—I used to think that was just a cliché. But after today? Finding out my ex-boyfriend was dead would've been easier to stomach than the bomb he dropped on me.

I press my elbows against the worn wooden bar, my head sinking into my hands. The tears I've been bottling up claw at my throat, threatening to break free.

Keep your shit together.

Don't cry in an airport bar.

You're not weak.

I shook off the emotions and poured the rest of the red wine down my throat, swallowing it with the lump that formed when I sat down alone. It burned as it went down, the only feeling I had in my body at the moment. I felt numb. This is not how I saw my afternoon going when I woke up this morning. I had so much hope for the future, and now I have… nothing. I haven't even had a chance to process today's events.

"*You're just… you're just too hard to love, Rose.*" The words played on a loop in my head. Each time, it ripped my heart further to shreds.

"Hello?" The bartender waved her hand in front of my face.

I snapped out of the dark place I was heading. "Hm?"

"I asked if you wanted another glass." She nodded towards my empty wine glass.

"Oh. No, thank you. Just the check would be great." I offered a pitiful attempt at a smile.

The quicker I pay, the faster I can get the hell out of Seattle. The bartender slid the check over to me and I slapped my debit card down. My nails bit into my palms as I waited for her to come back so I could get out of this claustrophobic bar. I don't know why all the restaurants in these god-forsaken airports are the size of a New York bodega, but I needed fresh air.

I can't breathe. I need to get out of here now.

"Have a safe flight and enjoy your trip." Her words were flat as she made eye contact with another patron and handed over my card.

"Thanks." What if I wasn't going somewhere fun? What if I were going to my Aunt Lucille's cat's funeral? Yes, that was an actual family affair I narrowly avoided earlier this year. My family celebrated everything—even death.

I shoved my card into the depths of my tote bag and made a beeline for my gate, small suitcase in tow.

The woman at the check-in desk earlier thought I was crazy as I loaded up three massive suitcases.

"Moving?" The older woman with kind eyes asked.

A humorless laugh came out of my mouth. "More like running away."

I found my gate before locating the wine, so I could remove one bit of stress. I couldn't miss this flight. The events of this morning have rattled me to my core. I don't even know who I am anymore. I glanced down at my watch; I had twenty minutes before my boarding group was called. I could either sit amongst my fellow passengers or buy some snacks at the convenience store.

Snacks will always win. Any type of sour candy is my guilty pleasure and after the day I've had, I deserved a damn treat.

My eyes scanned the wall of snacks that would probably kill me early, but I didn't care. At this point, my world had been turned around. The script of the life I thought I was about to have has been turned upside down. My stomach sank as I automatically reached for a chocolate bar, Thad's favorite. The familiarity of what I had hit me like a ton of bricks. I no longer had to think about "us"...now it was just me.

I haven't been alone for the better part of two years. I don't know how to be alone. Which, in itself, sounds so sad. I am a thirty-two-year-old woman who has lost my sense of identity. I don't even know what I like to do on my own.

I shook off the suffocating thoughts and grabbed a bag of sour Skittles before heading to the checkout. There was a couple in line in front of me. My blood boiled. I guess I was past the first stage of grief and have moved onto the second—anger. The sugary sweet couple paid, and I moved up.

I'm not sure when airports implemented self-checkouts, but I wasn't mad about it. The less I had to interact with people today, the better. Just because I'm in a foul mood doesn't mean I need to take it out on innocent bystanders trying to enjoy the beginning of their trip.

I swiped my card and tossed my snacks in my bag, ignoring the man who told me to have a good day as I walked out the door. Usually, I try to be friendly, but I think that version of me died a few hours ago. The blood coursing through my veins now had a chill.

Thankfully, the gate agents had already started the boarding process so that I could escape this suffocating city.

"Boarding group two!" The agent spoke into the microphone.

Two more groups to go.

"Group three!" Another large swarm of people made their way to the line.

Once the group had subsided, she called group four. It was finally my turn to make my way to the line and get the hell out of here. I queued up and counted down until it was my turn to scan my boarding pass. The scanner turned green as I held my phone up to it, almost to freedom.

"Have a great flight!" The gate agent chirped.

I offered a small smile. I quickly took inventory of everything, ensuring I had my bag and suitcase, and turned back once more before I stepped onto the gangway.

Maybe it's naivety, but I thought Thad was going to come running towards me like they did in the movies. I had fully convinced myself that he didn't mean what he said earlier and was going to come to Wippowa with me. It's silly of me to think that someone who had told me they loved me for years would move with me like he had said. I couldn't help but think the last two years of my life were a complete sham.

As I stepped onto the plane, the air was dry. My throat immediately turned into the Sahara desert, and I regretted not buying a seven-dollar bottle of water at the airport convenience store with my nine-dollar bag of candy.

Fifteen A. I repeated it over and over, checking each row. I dropped my tote bag in my seat and braced myself to lift my suitcase. When I packed it yesterday, I loaded it to the brim with the items I wouldn't be able to live without if the airline lost my luggage. I didn't think I would be the one lifting it.

My dad always said to lift with my legs, so that's what I did, hoisting the bag into the overhead bin. I'm not sure if it was the rage coursing through my now-icy veins, but it was surprisingly easy.

I threw myself down in my aisle seat, becoming painfully aware of the vacant seat next to me—the seat Thad was supposed to be sitting in. I'm usually a nervous flyer, so this was pretty much my version of hell. I thought the glass of wine I had would help, but I guess it amped up my anxiety. I've gone three decades and have never flown by myself—strategically, of course.

I buckled my seatbelt and put my headphones on, tuning out the world. My head rested on the back of the seat, and I prayed for sweet, sweet sleep. I wanted to forget today. I wanted to forget the last two years of my life and pretend like it never happened.

My phone buzzed; it was a text from my best friend, Blythe. She packed up and moved to Wippowa Island, Georgia, a few years ago and is now married with a step-daughter and is pregnant with their first little boy.

> Blythe: Have a safe flight. Can't wait to
> see you guys soon!

My heart sank as I typed a reply. I couldn't tell her that only one of us was going to be at the airport terminal.

> Rose: Can't wait for a hug.

That's part of the reason Thad and I were moving—I wanted a fresh start, and I wanted to be with my best friends when they added a new bundle of joy to their family. There were moments that I refused to live through via video calls and photos. I wanted to be there for them. I wanted to be the fun aunt who gave them messy, yet thoughtful, gifts for the holidays. I wanted to be there for all the milestones.

Seattle no longer had anything to offer me. The well had run dry. My parents didn't even live there. It was time for me to move on. Painfully, but move on.

I switched my phone to airplane mode before Blythe could reply and rested it face down on my lap, letting my "Good Vibes Only" playlist help me tune out the world. The weight of the day melted away as I dozed off to sleep before the plane even took off.

A slight tap on my shoulder jolted me back to reality.

"Miss?" The flight attendant rudely woke me up. Surely it was illegal to touch a passenger. *Maybe…*

I unsuctioned my headphones from my ears. "Yes?"

A burly man towered behind her.

"This man," she shifted to the side and pointed towards him, "is sitting in that middle seat. Would you mind getting up?"

I yanked my headphones down around my neck. "That's impossible. I bought that seat."

"But it's empty..." the bronzed-skinned woman observed.

"Someone was supposed...never mind. I paid for it." I shot back. Was it too much to ask just to be left alone?

"Please, rest assured, we will refund your ticket."

Being reimbursed for Thad's ticket would certainly help in the grand scheme of financial things.

"Oh-kay." I stood up and moved into the aisle so this titan of a man could wedge himself into, arguably, the smallest seat of the row.

A muffled "thanks" wafted my way as he squeezed by.

I plopped back down in my seat and resituated my headphones back over my ears. Here I was thinking I'd be sitting next to my boyfriend, but now I'm alone and sitting next to a stranger who is taking up the entirety of my right armrest. I paid for it, and damn it, I'm going to use it.

Keeping my eyes locked on the seat in front of me, I propped my elbow up on the armrest and shoved. Very unladylike of me, but I could not care less in this moment.

"I'm sorry, ma'am," my new row-mate apologized.

Even though my headphones were on, no music was playing. I pretended like I didn't hear him.

He tapped my knee. My word, his hands are massive.

Why does everyone keep touching me today? My body language is practically screaming "fuck off."

I grabbed the right headphone and glanced in his direction. "It's fine."

"There was a mother and daughter in the back. I offered to change my seat so they could sit together."

Why this guy didn't just sit in the seat either the mother or daughter was sitting in was beyond me.

"I didn't ask." I shot back, immediately regretting my attitude.

This guy was trying to do a nice thing; he didn't need to be dealing with my nonsense. "Really, it's fine."

Out of my peripheral vision, the giant man sat back in his seat. Conversation successfully avoided.

With my headphones secured once more, I scrolled through my playlist of songs that would put me in a good mood. There was no way they would work today.

Even though this trip was starting on the wrong foot, I still held onto a little bit of hope that the salty air of Wippowa Island would heal my salty mood.

When Thad and I visited last year for Blythe and Charlie's wedding, there wasn't a doubt in our minds that we would move. I was between odd jobs, and Thad worked from home, so why wouldn't we live in a sleepy little beach town? It has always been my dream to live on the coast, so this was the perfect time. How funny it all is now in hindsight.

The flight attendants gave the safety demonstration, and I barely paid attention. If this plane went down, I would accept my fate and become a shark's late lunch.

This move has become a divine comedy—for the universe, not me.

CHAPTER 2

SOMEONE LIKE YOU

Rose

PONDERED LIFE'S BIGGEST QUESTIONS AS THE FLIGHT ATTENDANTS made their final pass down the aisle, checking seatbelts and giving practiced smiles.

Before Thad, I spent years chasing fulfillment, waiting for something—*anything*—to make me feel whole. Losing my job a few years ago pushed me into teaching yoga, a side gig that turned into a three-year career in the same sunlit studio. At first, I thought it would be my purpose, the thing that finally brought me joy. But when it became something I dreaded, something that drained me instead of filling me, I felt lost. Like I'd wasted all those years on something that was never meant to last.

And that was the worst feeling.

Did I still love practicing yoga? Absolutely. Would I ever open my own studio? *Hell no.* That dream had died a long time ago.

When we first started dating and I had been let go from my corporate accounting job, Thad insisted on taking care of me financially. I had done a pretty good job investing my money, so I knew I would be okay for a while, but he insisted on paying for all of my stuff, down to my toilet paper. He's an Investment Banker and cleared over two hundred and seventy-five thousand dollars last year, a number he considered low.

When people saw us together, they didn't think it would work. He was this suave, analytical man, and I wore boho dresses and taught yoga. On paper, it shouldn't work, but we were different. He was the calm to my storm, and I was the sunshine on his rainy day. We balanced each other out.

The day I broached starting the yoga studio with him, he told me no. I had proposed it as a business venture, and I just needed a little capital to get started. I mentioned I wanted it to be a loan so I could pay it back. Thad told me it was a stupid idea and there were already too many around Seattle. I tried to refute his shootdowns, telling him that the type of yoga I practice isn't a saturated market and there were plenty of people looking for the classes I could offer. He scoffed at me and moved on to the next topic.

My heart sank.

I guess everyone was right—we wouldn't work. Two people so different would never work.

My shoulders tensed, and my right eye started twitching again. Which, a quick Google search said, was probably stress-induced. Just two major life changes happening at the same time and going horrifically wrong.

The thought of the wheels lifting off the ground turned my palms sweaty. I like to be firmly planted with my feet on the floor, so this was horrifying. When I booked these tickets, I thought I would have an emotional support person here, but alas, I do not.

"Flight attendants, prepare for takeoff." The pilot's voice came over the intercom.

No.

The plane started to move and I thought I was going to be sick. For me, taking off is the worst part. For nervous flyers like myself, the whole takeoff process is a tease. You start moving slowly and then stop. Then when you think it's another move, then stop, BAM— you're hurtling through the space time continuum. No one could convince me that hurdling through the air at over five hundred miles per hour was a speed a human should go. I doubt the Wright brothers ever anticipated their little invention going that fast.

We went left. Then right. Then there was a long pause. We don't like the long pause.

My hands rubbed nervously over my shorts before they gripped the armrests for dear life. My knuckles were white.

My poor attempt at a breath hitched in my throat. As the wheels lifted, the weight of the world barreled down on me, and my stomach dropped.

"You alright?"

I ignored the muffled question to my right and kept my eyes squeezed shut. This guy was way too chatty for me. Didn't he learn about stranger danger? I could be a Black Widow ready to prey on my next victim and he's over here asking if I'm okay.

My lungs filled with stale air in a desperate attempt to calm my nerves. A few years ago, my therapist taught me how to do these deep breathing exercises, and she claimed they would "regulate my nervous system." I can attest that my system was still very nervous, and this breathing technique was doing absolutely nothing. Instead, I focused on the repetitive melodies ringing through my ears.

What felt like a lifetime later, we hit cruising altitude, and my vice grip on the armrest let up a bit. I finally felt like, for the moment, I was safe and dug through my bag to grab my snacks. I popped a sour red Skittle into my mouth, and my teeth cried for mercy. Out of reflex, I squinted and scrunched my nose.

The first sour candy is always the worst; after that, I adjust and can eat an entire resealable bag in one sitting.

"Those are the best," the mountain sitting next to me noted.

The absolute last thing I wanted to do was converse, but I ignored him enough already. I paused my music and slid the right headphone down.

"What?" I pretended I didn't hear him.

He nodded towards the candy on my tray. "Those are awesome. I mean, I'm more of a chocolate kinda guy, but those are a close second."

This man was way too chatty for me. I just wanted to eat my candy in peace and get off this plane.

"The orange ones are my favorite," He shared.

I grimaced. I had a vehement dislike for those. When I was seven, I choked on an orange Skittle. A quarter of a century later, and I still eat around them. You tell me you wouldn't still be a little wary of the thing that tried to kill you as a youth.

Traumatized.

Why is he talking? This man is an open book. One I didn't want to read.

On any other day, I would've indulged him and tried to carry on a conversation. Today, I wanted to feed all men to the alligators in Georgia. Except the pilot, he could stay—as long as he gets us to Wippowa safely. Then he goes to the gators with the rest of them.

"Those are the worst ones." I countered.

"Agree to disagree. Orange flavored anything is superior to whatever the red flavor is."

This man's southern drawl was thicker than molasses. I would dare to say thicker than Blythe's husband Charlie—and that's saying something because he's a country boy through and through.

I finally made eye contact with him. "The orange Skittles taste like toilet bowl cleaner."

"Do you often taste toilet bowl cleaner?" A ghost of a smile danced on his lips.

If this was his way of flirting, he was horrible at it, and I was certainly not in the mood.

"All the time." I hit my limit on conversing. My headphone slid back over my ear, and his chatter went away.

I rifled through my bag in a desperate attempt to find my book. Surely that would keep Mr. Orange Skittles quiet. An open book was the universal sign that the person didn't want to be disturbed—they wanted to get lost in a fictitious world and forget about whatever it was that was plaguing their everyday life.

Why do I always overstuff my bags, making it impossible to find anything? All of my closest friends are so organized—then there's me. I thrive in chaos.

"That's a full bag if I've ever seen one. Do you have your life in there?" Orange observed.

This guy is tap dancing on my last damn nerve. We were barely at the halfway point of this flight, and I was ready to ask if I could go sit in the cargo hold just to get away from him. I thought it was common knowledge that everyone is just trying to get from point A to point B and doesn't want to have random conversations with strangers.

Thankfully, my hand found my book at the bottom of my bag. I had just started getting into reading again. When your best friend owns a bookstore, you read. I typically read romances because they're relatable; however, when I got to the check-in desk, I switched them out. I went from a swoony rom-com to a thriller.

I shoved my bag back under the seat in front of me and focused my attention on the book. I was barely into the second chapter when out of my periphery, I saw Orange Man look at my book.

"Whatcha reading?"

I glared at him, refusing to remove my headphones once again. I'm in the midst of a mental breakdown, and he wants to make small talk.

He motioned for me to remove my headphones. I shook my head in response. Mr. Orange slumped back in his seat.

"A thriller where a fiancée brutally murders her soon-to-be husband after finding out he cheated on her and then goes on the run." I piped up.

The look of absolute horror on his face was hilarious.

"That's…dark," he observed.

"No shit."

The guy pointed towards my phone. "You're not listening to anything."

"Again—no shit." I inhaled sharply. "Do you think maybe I just don't want to talk to you? First, I put my headphones on, and you still talked. Then I opened a book with my headphones on, and you're *still* talking to me."

My words had a bitter edge to them.

"I'm sorry. I just—"

I held up a hand, not giving him a chance to respond.

"Noted."

The goliath next to me finally took the hint and put his own headphones on. I sneakily watched as he unlocked his phone—his wallpaper was of the most incredible sunset—and listened to country music. This man wasn't doing anything to break the country boy stereotype. His accent was so pronounced it sounded fake, and it was already grating on my frayed last nerve.

The next hour was peaceful. Well, as peaceful as it can be when you're reading a book about murder thirty-two thousand feet up in the air. I had finally convinced myself that I was going to make it safely to Wippowa and would figure my life out. Right now, I'm just going to get lost in this book. One that I was sure wouldn't have a happily ever after.

At this point, I don't even know if I believe in love. Love is just an emotion; I like things that are logical. If you had asked me earlier today if I believed in love, you would've received an emphatic yes. I think I was just stupid and blinded by the thought of it all.

Did I ever really love Thad?

Did he love me?

Were we happy?

Why didn't he want to continue living life together?

I found myself absentmindedly running my fingers over my bare left ring finger. The space once occupied by a promise ring for the past six months now felt empty—a quiet reminder of something lost, as if a piece of me had vanished along with it.

"Passengers, please prepare as we start to make our descent down into Wippowa." The pilot's voice came back over the intercom and I fully removed my headphones. "The weather is currently an unseasonably sixty-four and raining. Hope you packed a jacket!"

Of course, I would be in shorts and a T-shirt. It was supposed to be mid-to-high seventies and sunny. I looked at my pale legs and sighed. Even the weather in normally sunny Wippowa was reflecting my foul mood. I was optimistic that I would be able to sit outside and parse through my thoughts, all while getting a good tanning session in.

All my life, I felt my best when I was tan. My blonde hair gets blonder. The small gold ring hugging my left nostril shines beautifully against my skin. I feel like a brand-new person, hence why I thought *we* were moving.

We had planned the perfect life. We were going to rent an apartment until we figured out which lot we wanted to buy and then build our dream home on it. Thad was going to be close to an airport for work travel. I was going to try to start my yoga studio up again. We were going to get married, surrounded by our closest family and friends. Everything was going to be perfect.

Except perfection doesn't exist.

The plane bobbled, pulling me out of my self-wallowing. This is it. This is how I die. The plane is going down.

I gripped the armrests for dear life, my breath hitched in my throat.

The plane dipped again and I thought this was it for little old me. Maybe Thad would feel bad if he found out I died alone on this plane.

"Sorry, folks! Just a little bit of turbulence. We should be out of it soon. Please be sure your seatbelts are fastened." The pilot tried to ease the nerves of the passengers—well, passenger. Everyone else on this plane was acting like nothing had happened. We nearly plummeted to our deaths. Twice!

Am I being a little overdramatic? Maybe. But flying alone is my biggest fear. Thad would remind me that having him with me would do absolutely nothing if the plane went down. I always countered that it just made me feel better.

Maybe I was being silly.

"Are ya gonna make it?" The thick southern drawl sitting next to me asked.

My eyes met his.

"Unsure." That was all I could muster up.

"Do ya wanna hold my hand until we land?" He extended what I would classify as a goddamn tiger paw. His hand was massive.

I shook my head, unable to find more words. My anxiety shot through the roof. My heart raced. Deep breaths weren't working. My ears started to ring. The walls felt like they were closing in on me. My life was crumbling around me.

My head pressed up against the back of the seat. My chest rose and fell at a rapid rate.

"Ma'am?" Mr. Orange piped up again.

I rolled my head to the right and looked at him. Maybe focusing on something else would help me come out of this anxiety attack. "Are ya alright?"

I swallowed hard before nodding my head. I could lie to a perfect stranger without consequence.

"I only ask 'cause your eyes are redder than a strawberry in the middle of June."

Reflexively, my hand brushed away a tear. In the midst of my panic attack, I hadn't realized I started crying. The tears I had expertly held in all afternoon had started flowing, and I wasn't sure they would turn off. My mom always teased me that once the waterworks turned on, I couldn't stop until I heard a joke.

"Can I do anything to help you?"

I offered up a pathetic smile. "I'll be fine."

My stomach sank as we started the descent into Wippowa airport. I hadn't even admitted it to myself that my boyfriend… ex-boyfriend…didn't want me anymore. Now I have to tell my two closest friends that I'm single and unlovable.

That cuts deep.

"It sure doesn't look like it."

I snapped back to the present. I wiped my eyes and straightened up, pushing the clouds in my head away for the moment.

"A joke might help." I capitulated, wringing my hands.

"A joke?" He confirmed.

I nodded. "Anything will do."

"Challenge accepted." A wide grin spread across his face. "Why was the whale sad?"

I raised a shoulder, not sure where on earth this joke was going to go.

"It lost its porpoise."

A corner of my mouth lifted.

"Did it help?" This man was suddenly self-conscious about his dad joke.

"Yeah." The lie rolled effortlessly off my tongue.

"Flight attendants, please prepare for landing."

I kept my hands folded in my lap and my eyes shut tight as I braced for landing. The wheels smashed the runway, and we all jolted forward. My hammering heart realized we were in the clear and started to slow back down to normal range. I rested my heavy head in my hands, bracing against my knees.

"See, you made it, trooper."

I didn't respond to the titan's remarks, reaching for my phone, turning off the airplane mode. No messages came through—not that I was expecting any, but I still held out hope that Thad would see the error in his ways and follow me.

"That's a nice picture." Mr. Orange commented, looking at my home screen. It's a photo of Thad and me at his company's holiday party last year. During the few years we were together, we always attended all the fancy black-tie events he had to go to, but never did I feel as beautiful as I did on that day back in December.

"I should probably change it," I answered honestly, my eyes glued to the screen that went dark.

"You're right. You should crop the douchebag out."

The corner of my lip lifted slightly. This guy didn't know my story, but he was spot on with his character evaluation of Thad from a picture.

"I should change it, regardless." My heart sank at the thought.

The cabin door was opened, and everyone started filing out. I stood once the row in front of us had started to make their way to the exit.

"Do you need help with your carry-on?"

I reached up and grabbed the too-full suitcase. "I've got it," I paused. "Thank you, though."

"No problem." He tipped his baseball cap brim towards me.

My legs immediately started carrying me towards the exit, the bag of orange Skittles in my hand. I spun on my heel and handed the bag to Mr. Orange. Better to give them to someone than throw them away.

"That's really kind of you." I heard him stop walking behind me. "Sorry, I never caught your name."

I kept walking.

Blythe: I tracked your flight and saw you landed a few minutes ago. I should be there in fifteen minutes.

Thankfully, the Wippowa airport isn't huge, and I was able to make it to baggage claim quickly. I said a silent prayer on the way down here that my row-mate hadn't checked a bag because I was at wits' end and one more awkward interaction with that guy would've sent me into a tailspin.

I watched as the first of my big suitcases made its way around the conveyor belt. I reached up and grabbed it. The second wasn't too far behind. Then the third came rolling around.

The three large suitcases, the one small one, and a massive tote bag were going to be a challenge to get out the door. By sheer willpower, I managed everything.

Now I'm here—outside an airport terminal—with all my belongings waiting, once again, for my life to begin.

CHAPTER 3

EXILE

Rose

I HAVEN'T BEEN TO WIPPOWA WHEN IT WASN'T WARM AND sunny. The lack of humidity was alarming, and the amount of rain being dumped from the sky was a pretty accurate representation of how many tears I had to let out as soon as I was home.

Where is home?

A cool breeze blew through Arrivals, and I shuddered. I thought I had left the cold in Seattle, but that didn't seem to be the case.

A gray pick-up truck rolled up, and a wave of relief washed over me. *Blythe*. It's been my safe space since we became friends at work. From that fateful day six years ago, we've been each other's ride or die.

When Blythe called and told me her vacation had turned into a move to Wippowa, I felt the gamut of emotions. I was sad we wouldn't be able to have coffee dates anymore, but I was thrilled she followed her heart and started fresh—hell, she needed it after all she went through.

Blythe parallel parked in front of me and raised an eyebrow through the windshield. The "where is Thad" look. She sprinted around the truck to me, enveloping me in the biggest hug she's ever given me. I melted into it, finally feeling safe.

"I missed you so much!" Her arms wrapped around my

shoulders, pulling me closer. The familiar smell of her perfume wafted, and I felt like I was where I needed to be, albeit alone. She pulled me even closer than I thought possible. It was only then that I felt her slightly protruding stomach.

"I missed you more," I admitted into her neck. I stepped back and held her at arm's length. "You're glowing, Bee."

"I'm happy someone thinks so. Wren told me the other day that I was looking haggard. She's eight, how does she even know what that means?" A wide smile spread across Blythe's face.

I offered up the best fake smile I could muster. "That's my *nephew* in there."

"Your nephew, who is currently tap dancing on my bladder."

"Ladies, save your greetings for later. Load your car and get moving." The airport attendant scolded.

Blythe lowered the tailgate, and I set my suitcases in the bed before closing it up and making my way to the passenger's seat.

"So," Blythe broke the silence a few minutes into the drive back to her house. "Do you want to tell me why Thad isn't here, or is that a conversation for later?"

My eyes didn't leave the road ahead of us. "Later." I paused, fighting back the tears. "Definitely later."

"One question," Blythe piped up. "You don't have to give me any details until you're ready, but is there anything I can do for you?"

"Only if you want to go to jail with me for murder." I tossed back. "But I don't think that's a good idea. You're with child. Poor little guy shouldn't be an accomplice in our shenanigans."

Blythe laughed, "Fair enough." Her eyes met mine as we pulled up to the red light. "There's nothing else I can do for you?"

I shook my head. "Thank you, though."

I let the silence hang in the air. I knew Blythe wouldn't pressure me into talking until I was good and ready. Hell, I was still trying to make heads and tails of what happened.

The gravel under the tires as we pulled into the driveway pulled me out of my thoughts and back into reality. No matter how foul my mood was, I was going to have to pretend like nothing was wrong when I saw—

"Auntie Rose!" Wren, Blythe and Charlie's eight-year-old daughter, came sprinting out of the house and towards the car.

"Wren, it's raining. Get back up here!" Charlie called from the covered front porch; the rain pummeled the windshield.

As the truck came to a stop, Wren was already jiggling the door handle, trying to see me.

Blythe nodded, and I opened the door for the kid.

"I missed you!" Wren climbed up into my lap to get out of the rain. Her little arms wrapped around my neck, and I could cry then and there. I wish I still had her level of innocence. Back then, the only things I had to worry about were what birthday parties I was invited to and what toppings I wanted on my pizza.

"I have so many new documentaries we can watch together! Do you like seahorses? Mom said you like seahorses. Grammy, you know my grammy, got me some new ones and I was waiting to watch them with you." The kid rambled on, holding my face in her hands.

Blythe stifled a laugh. "Wrenny, Auntie Rose has had a *really* long day. Why don't we help her bring her things inside?"

"Okay!"

Charlie lifted her off my lap and pointed her in the direction of the house before taking a look in the backseat. "Where's…?"

Blythe shot her husband a "shut up" glance.

"Suitcases are in the truck bed?" Charlie immediately changed the subject.

I nodded glumly.

"You ladies get in the house, and I'll grab your bags."

Blythe blew him a kiss before turning the engine off and exiting the truck. I followed suit, slinging my bag over my shoulder. She met me at the front of the truck, and she wrapped her arm around my shoulder, pulling me close.

"Whatever happened with he who shall not be named, doesn't matter. We're here for you."

I rested my head on her shoulder as we walked into their house.

The coastal home that was typically spotless had stuff everywhere. It looked like they were renovating the entire house.

"Sorry for the mess, we're putting the finishing details on the living room, and Charlie hasn't put anything away yet."

"It's just in case I need it again," he muttered, rolling two of my suitcases through the door.

"Do you *still* need the ladder?" Blythe questioned, clearly annoyed by the mess.

He shrugged haphazardly, "I might."

Blythe gave him an exaggerated eye roll. Being pregnant has made her even more sassy.

We moved from the cluttered entryway towards the stairs.

"Rose, we have the guest room made up for you. I'll just put your suitcases in there." Charlie was trying to tread carefully. I mean, I don't blame him. Not only does he have to deal with a pregnant wife and a sassy as hell daughter, but now he has a best friend whose life has been upended.

I offered the smallest smile, "Thank you."

He disappeared up the stairs.

Blythe's eyes met mine; sympathy flooded them. "Why don't you go take a bath? I picked up some bath bombs at the farmer's market last weekend. They smell nice."

Today's weight hit my shoulders. I was exhausted. My body ached. Emotionally I was done for. My heart physically hurt—so much so, I Googled what a heart attack would feel like.

I just wanted to lie down and sleep. At least if I were asleep, I wouldn't have to think.

When I didn't respond, Blythe spoke again, "Do you want a hug?" She outstretched her arms.

I shook my head. "I think a hug would probably open the floodgates at the moment so a bath might be the best option."

She nodded slowly before placing her hand on her stomach. "Are you hungry?"

My stomach grumbled but the thought of eating right now made me feel sick. "No."

Blythe cocked an eyebrow, "You're telling me that if I had extra pasta with some of my world-famous marinara sauce, you *wouldn't* have it." She feigned horror.

I shot her a pointed look. "You temptress."

She popped a shoulder, "I just know you and if I don't make sure you eat while you're sad, you'll lie in bed and rot."

Blythe took a step towards me and held my shoulders in her hands. "Whatever happened has happened. What matters is how we move on from it. Whenever you're ready to talk about it, you know I will be all ears."

She always knew what to say to make a shitty day better. "All I want to do is get wine drunk with you. Little dude in there needs to hurry up so I can have a glass of wine with his mom again."

"Soon. But, in the meantime, Charlie got me some nonalcoholic wine so we could drink together."

The corner of my mouth lifted, "That's adorable." I started up the stairs. "Be nice to him. He's a good man."

"Since when do you take his side?"

I stood at the top of the stairs. "I'm fair."

"That's one of the many things I love about you," Blythe called up. "You know where everything is. There are extra towels under the sink. Take your time."

At least someone still loves me.

The floorboards creaked under my feet as I made my way down the long hallway to the guest bedroom. I took in the room as the door creaked open—I was here alone. We were only going to stay with Charlie and Blythe for three nights before our new apartment was ready for us to move into. The thought of moving into that place alone and single crushed me. How am I supposed to move into a place that was supposed to represent our future when all I had left was our past?

I tossed my bag onto the bed and unzipped my suitcase, filled with my comfiest clothes. As I pulled out each item, memories surfaced like ghosts from the past. The sweater on top—I had worn on my second date with Thad, the night we went ice skating. The denim overalls—those were from his work picnic. Every piece of clothing was a relic of us, each one carrying a weight I wasn't ready to bear.

My heart ached even more than before, the pain settling deeper with every memory woven into the fabric of my past.

Frustrated, I rummaged through the suitcase, desperate to find something—anything—that didn't remind me of Thad. My fingers finally landed on a pair of worn-out leggings and an oversized college t-shirt. *Good enough.* Without a second thought, I grabbed my toiletries case and headed to the bathroom, needing a moment to breathe—or cry.

I tucked away the toiletries I didn't need into the cabinet, then rummaged through a drawer in search of the bath bombs Blythe had mentioned. My fingers skimmed over neatly folded towels and spare toothpaste, but the bath bombs were nowhere to be found.

There was a slight knock on the bedroom door. "Auntie?"

Wren.

I crossed the room and pulled open the door, only to find my favorite little human standing there, a triumphant smile on her face and a bath bomb clutched in her tiny hand.

"Mommy said she forgot to put this in your bathroom." Wrenny sniffed the purple ball in her hand before holding it out to me. "I don't know what smell it is."

I took it from her and inhaled. "I think it's lavender."

She scrunched up her nose. "I don't know what that is. It smells like the perfume Grammy wears." Then, as if struck by a brilliant idea, she perked up. "Do you want one of my Mickey ones instead? It smells better."

I stifled a laugh. "I like how this one smells, but thank you. That's very sweet of you, Wrenny."

"Okay!" She spun toward the door, then glanced back. "Is Thad coming?"

The question hit me like a punch to the stomach. My breath stalled, my mouth suddenly dry. "No."

"Cool! Then I get to spend more time with you." And just like that, she was gone in a flash, leaving me standing there with my heart in my throat.

The sweet relief the bath provided was next-level. Was I still a shell of a person? Absolutely. But the warm water and the soothing scent of lavender wrapped around me, loosening the tension I'd been carrying all day. And the second I sank into the heat, the dam broke. The tears I'd fought so hard to hold back finally spilled over, each one carrying a weight I could no longer bear.

Blythe would never judge me—I knew that. But the thought of facing my closest friends, of admitting that the man I had spent years defending was exactly who they always said he was? That felt unbearable. From our very first date, they warned me.

Thad is selfish.

He's an asshole.

He doesn't care about anyone but himself.

And every time, I had an excuse. Every time, I smoothed over his rough edges and made him seem softer than he was.

Now, I had to look them in the eyes and say they were right. That, after all the years I spent believing in him, he told me, without hesitation, that I wasn't worth following across the country.

As if everything else wasn't enough, this just added insult to injury.

CHAPTER 4

HARD TO LOVE

Rose

STUDIED MY REFLECTION IN THE MIRROR. MY BLUE EYES WERE bloodshot and glassy; my skin was blotchy from crying. My nose was stuffy, and I could feel the weight of the jet lag crashing over me. Between the emotional wreckage of this morning and the exhaustion, I was done. There was no way I was going to go downstairs and pretend everything was fine. No way could I sit at a dinner table and smile, acting like nothing had changed. Once the floodgates had opened, there was no shutting them.

The depression was settling in, a heavy, suffocating weight. I felt small. *Unworthy*. Unworthy of love. Happiness. Joy.

I pulled on the clothes that held no memories, no reminders of the past, and opened the bedroom door. Charlie was just closing the door to the room next to their bedroom.

We locked eyes.

"Hey," he said, his voice softer than usual.

"Hi."

"Wren mentioned Thad's not coming. You gonna be alright?"

I shrugged, the motion small and defeated. "Maybe."

Charlie surprised me, pulling me into a hug—a gesture I never would have expected from him. I went rigid in his arms, not used to physical affection from him. When I met him, he was a stone wall.

"We're here for you."

I pulled back slightly, blinking in disbelief. "You're hugging me."

"You looked like you needed one. So shut up and accept the offering."

His words shattered the fragile hold I had left, and the water-works came rushing back. I buried my face into his shirt, the tears pouring out uncontrollably as I sobbed, clinging to him for some kind of comfort.

"Blythe!" Charlie called down the stairs.

"Yeah?"

"Help!" Charlie capitulated.

"What's wrong?"

"Rose is getting snot all over my shirt."

I heard Blythe set whatever she had in her hands down and hurry up the stairs. By the time she reached us, she was breathless, but the concern in her eyes was clear.

I pulled my head from Charlie's chest and turned to face her.

"Oh, sweetie," Blythe whispered, pulling me into her arms. "Do you want to go outside?"

I nodded, the sadness too heavy to put into words.

Blythe poked Charlie's chest. "You're in charge of making sure the pasta sauce doesn't burn. Don't get distracted like you did last time."

She turned towards me and rolled her eyes, "Last time I asked him to do that, he nearly burnt the kitchen down."

We made our way down the stairs to the covered front porch. The rain had started to let up to a pour, so we were thankful for the roof. Blythe sat down on the rocking chair closest to the door, and I took the one next to her.

"How are you feeling?" I collected myself enough to ask.

"No, ma'am. We're not talking about me right now. Stop deflecting."

I sat there in silence, my mind racing, unsure how to even begin explaining why Thad wasn't here. My anxiety started to claw at me, and I found myself nervously picking at the cuticle on my left thumb.

It was as if Blythe could sense my struggle, because, without missing a beat, she broke the stillness.

"We don't need to talk. You just needed some fresh air."

"I don't even understand what happened." My eyes fell to my hands in my lap. "Where I went wrong…"

I struggled to find the right words. No words to describe the heartbreak. No words to capture the gut-wrenching feeling of being told the person you love doesn't love you back. No words for the sheer agony of continuing with my move, pretending like my entire world hadn't just imploded twelve hours ago.

Blythe shifted beside me. "Is there anything you want to do tomorrow? It's supposed to be nice out."

"No," I said quickly, my voice sharper than I intended. I inhaled deeply, steadying myself. Then, finally, I let the words fall out. "Thad's not coming… at all."

She nodded slowly, "Okay."

I could see the wheels turning in her head, trying to piece together what had happened. But true to who she was, she didn't push. She just sat there, offering quiet support, and I appreciated that more than I could put into words.

A sob slipped out.

Blythe let out a sharp breath. She pinched the bridge of her nose, her expression a mix of frustration and concern. Anyone close to me would say I'm not a crier. I get angry. I shut down. But I rarely, rarely, cry.

Today was one of those impossible days—one where I cried twice with no end in sight.

"He had valid reasons for not coming," I said instinctively, rushing to his defense.

Blythe's brows shot up. "Oh? Was work too important for him to leave? Another celebrity gala? A yacht club meeting? Maybe a last-minute getaway to the Maldives?"

I opened my mouth, but nothing came out. I had no words. Only the truth I wasn't ready to face.

"What was his excuse this time, Rose?"

It took everything in me to force out four words. Four words that felt heavier than they should have.

"I'm hard to love."

The moment they left my lips, my stomach plummeted. I could have died right then and there. Saying it made it real, solid, unshakable. It wasn't just a whisper in the back of my mind anymore. It had weight. It existed outside of me now.

Blythe's face fell. "You're what?"

A rumble of thunder cracked overhead, making both of us jump. The rain pelted against the windows, filling the silence between us.

Blythe just stared at me, mouth slightly open. And then—"That is the stupidest thing I've ever heard."

I shrugged.

"Do you want to talk about it?"

I wiped at my damp cheeks and lifted one shoulder in a half-hearted gesture.

Blythe softened. "You don't have to if you're not ready. But just so we're clear—that's not true. You're in a house surrounded by three people who love you very much. Your niece thinks the sun shines out your ass."

"The feeling is mutual."

Blythe tilted her head. "Do you want to eat dinner?"

I shifted in my chair, restless. "Can we talk first?"

"We certainly can. I'll be right back."

She disappeared into the house, leaving me alone with my thoughts. I stared off toward the road, willing Thad to appear—maybe on a white horse, like in the stories. Except Thad didn't know how to ride, and he hated anything that might ruin his clothes.

Back in fourth grade, I was fearless. One of the boys dared me to dig for worms, and I did it—dressed in my Sunday best, no less. It became the talk of the school. A little girl in a frilly dress, hands covered in dirt, grinning like she'd won something. But as I got older,

I let that part of me slip away. The city girl took over. Instead of chasing adventures, I chased routines. By my teenage years, yoga had become my controlled space, where I could breathe.

Blythe returned a moment later, carrying two glasses filled with deep ruby liquid.

"One for you," she said, handing me a glass before settling back into her chair. "And one for me."

I smiled faintly. "You always know what helps."

"I know." She smirked, then motioned toward my glass. "Now, take a long sip of that and tell me what happened."

I took a breath, gripping the stem of the glass tighter. "It all started first thing this morning."

Blythe's brows lifted. "This all went down today?"

I nodded, and the weight of it settled in my chest all over again. "I was in the middle of taking the key off my keychain…"

CHAPTER 5

LAST KISS

Rose

Yesterday

"THAD, ARE YOU READY TO GO?" I CALLED INTO THE BATHROOM. I gave myself a final look over in the mirror, brushing my hand over the black silk of the bodice of my dress. No matter how many galas Thad and I went to, I never felt like I belonged there. He was so well-spoken and proper, and I was the polar opposite. I didn't know how to have a conversation without cursing. I would much rather be sitting on our couch in sweatpants, having take-out, than being here. This was Thad's thing, not mine.

Small talk would be the death of me.

"I'm just putting on my shoes. I'll be ready in a minute." He called back.

I tossed my shawl over my shoulders and grabbed my clutch. Do you know how hard it is to go from a bottomless pit of a tote bag to the world's smallest clutch?

"You look stunning, my darling." Thad complimented. He grabbed my hand and twirled me around.

"Thank you," I beamed.

His phone buzzed. "The limo is outside. Ready to head out?"

"Sure am."

Thad led the way down from our apartment to the main entrance. He tapped his foot impatiently as we stood in the cooler night air.

"Where is this asshole?" His tone was sharp.

"It's fine. We still have plenty of time." I consoled.

"The guy said he was down here, and *clearly* he is not."

Thad tapped aggressively on his phone, calling the limo driver. "Where are you?"

Pause.

"Oh."

Pause.

"Thanks." He turned to face me. Thad pointed to a white SUV to the left. "He's over there."

I followed him without a thought. He led, and I followed. I was *always* the follower.

"It's a thirty-minute drive there, so we should still be early enough to walk the carpet they have set up.

"What is this gala even for?" My head cocked involuntarily.

"This one..." Thad pulled out his phone and checked his email. "It's not a gala, just a dinner."

My shoulders relaxed.

He continued scrolling. "This is for the Great Tits Foundation."

My eyes bulged, "*Excuse* me?"

Thad looked at me like I had five heads. "The Great Tits."

My brows shot up, "That clarified nothing."

"Great Tits...like the bird. My grandfather was a big fan of the bird and started this foundation during his retirement. My parents host an annual event. They didn't host one last year because they were grieving in Malta after he passed away."

The bird, you uneducated fool.

I bit the inside of my cheek, holding back a smile. "Right. For the Great Tits."

We sat quietly. Thad looked out the window while his left hand held my right. His thumb mindlessly rubbed the top of my hand.

"This is a big night for your family. Are your parents anxious?"

I finally broke the silence twenty minutes into the drive to the event space.

Thad shrugged, "No idea. I've not spoken to them in a few months."

"I thought you said you spoke with them the other night, when you were working late."

"Oh yeah, you're right. Totally forgot about that call." His eyes never left the window.

I couldn't help but feel like I caught him in a lie. "Can I be honest?"

"Of course, my love." Thad's eyes finally pulled away from the window and met mine. "What's on your mind?"

I took a deep breath. "This is my first time meeting your parents. What happens if they don't like me?"

"They are going to love you." Thad comforted.

I glanced down at the promise ring he had given me for Christmas last year. It was a large cushion cut deep blue sapphire surrounded by small diamonds. I'm not a showy person, but Thad insisted everyone know I was taken, even though he wasn't ready for marriage.

I debated taking the ring off and putting it in my purse for safekeeping. If this was some sort of family affair, I didn't want to answer any questions from a nosy grandma.

Just as I got lost in my thoughts, the SUV came to a stop. "Mr. and Mrs. Carter, we have arrived."

"Oh, we're not married." Thad quipped…a little too quickly.

My heart sank. Was the promise ring to placate me? Even though I never mentioned marriage, he's always been the one to bring it up.

Thad opened the car door and got out, extending a hand to help me down.

"Thank you," I smiled at him before placing a kiss on his cheek.

"Are you ready to walk your first red carpet?"

I nodded before lacing my arm in his. We walked to where the carpet started, which was roped off. There were a handful of photographers taking both staged and candid photos.

"Mr. Carter, Miss Solace, over here!" A photographer waved his hand, encouraging us to look his way.

He took a few photos and we moved on to the next. It was like this for a good fifty feet. All of this for a bird… wait until I tell Blythe about this tomorrow.

With the end of the carpet steps away, an older couple walked up to us. His parents. My stomach flipped.

I extended a hand politely, "Mr. and Mrs. Carter, I'm Rose. It's very nice to finally meet you."

If I didn't know better, I would think Thad is embarrassed to be seen with me around his family. We've been together for years, and there was always an excuse for why I couldn't meet them.

"Rose," I could've sworn his mom's nose turned down on me. "It's nice to meet you." Her eyes ran up and down my dress.

"You as well." I locked eyes with her.

"Rose, it's a pleasure to meet you." His dad broke the awkward gaze.

"Likewise, sir."

Thad rested his hand on the small of my back.

"What do you say—should we head inside?" Thad spoke up.

As we stepped through the massive doors into the ballroom, my jaw hung open. By Thad's definition, this might "just be a dinner," but this was the fanciest "dinner" I've ever been to. My gaze swept around the room, taking in all the feather décor.

Feathers everywhere.

"Would you like a drink, my love?" Thad whispered against my ear, realizing I had stopped walking.

I looked at him, relief washing over me. With a drink in my hand, I could sip it occasionally to avoid awkward conversations. "That would be great."

He grabbed my hand and led us over to the bar. My eyes scanned the wall full of top-shelf liquors, locking in on a bottle.

"What would you like, miss?" The bartender came up to us immediately.

"Can I please have a glass of Blanton's? Neat."

"Why don't you get one of the specialty cocktails on this list. My parents picked them." Thad offered.

"It's nothing against these," I gestured toward the menu. "I just know what I like. If I ordered one of those fancy drinks, I'd waste half of it. But a glass of good bourbon?" I leaned back slightly. "That's a sure thing. One glass, and I'm set for the night—nothing wasted, nothing left behind."

He rolled his eyes, "Whatever you'd like. But you can tell my mother why you're not having her Tequila Mockingbird, the Blue Jay Breeze, or the Falcon Fizz."

Because they sound overly sweet and are stupidly named. I kept the comment to myself.

I sighed heavily, scanning the menu. I made eye contact with the bartender. "Can I please have the Tequila Mockingbird instead?"

I knew I could stomach it—for the most part

My stomach rolled at the thought of tequila. In college, tequila and I were the best of friends. Now ten years removed, we're not on speaking terms.

His lip twitched in disgust. "Absolutely. It's currently made with tequila, but if you wanted to substitute the bourbon, it would be good as well."

I appreciated his suggestion, "Oh! Yes, please."

Surely that would make the sweet drink a little more palatable.

"And for you, Mr. Carter?"

"I'll have the Tequila Mockingbird as well, just as it was intended, with the tequila."

"I'll have those right up for you both."

I watched as all the attendees slowly started filtering into the ballroom, understanding why Thad wanted us to get here early—so he could socialize and welcome people to the event.

"Mother did a fantastic job decorating, didn't she?" Thad was mesmerized by the venue.

This all seemed so ostentatious for a bird event. Time to lie to save face. "Yeah, it's stunning."

"I'm always amazed by the events she's able to throw together. One day, I hope we can start a foundation and host events like these. Wouldn't that be such a delight?"

I forced out the fakest smile I could. "Absolutely."

Please let our drinks be ready.

"Here are those drinks. Please have a taste and let me know if they are up to your standards." The bartender slid our drinks across the bar towards us.

The first sip hit, and I could tell the extra ingredients they put in this weren't necessary; the bourbon alone would've sufficed. "Mine is delicious. Thank you for switching the tequila for bourbon."

"My pleasure." He turned to face Thad, "And yours, sir?"

"I think it could use a bit more tequila."

The bartender nodded. "Let me make that adjustment for you."

He took the glass back and added another splash of tequila before handing it back to Thad. "Let me know if that's better."

Thad took a sip and nodded slowly, "Much better."

"Thank you, sir!" I cheerfully added.

"My pleasure. Come back if you need anything else."

I smiled and waved as we made our way over to a crowd of people. The only two that were even remotely familiar were Thad's parents.

Thad said his hellos, presumably, he knew these people. "Everyone, this is my lovely girlfriend, Rose." He turned to face me, "Rose, you met my parents earlier. These are the Bennetts, our family friends since before I was born. And this is my sister, Priscilla."

I shook everyone's hands. "It's very nice to meet you all. Thank you for having me. This is a beautiful event."

We stood there, and Thad chatted with everyone for a bit. Since I didn't have anything to add to the conversation, I took in all the décor. Not only was this place decked out in feathers, but there were also creepy fake birds everywhere. Each table had a bird cage with a fake bird inside.

Standing here so out of place, I wished it was a Gala for actual Great Tits—boobs, not the bird. At least then I would feel like I belonged. I've been told on a few occasions that mine are pretty spectacular.

"Good evening. If you could all make your way to your seats, we can get this wonderful event started." A faceless voice came over the speakers.

Thank goodness. It felt like it had been four hours when, in reality, it had barely been forty minutes.

"I'm going to run to the restroom and I will be right back." I handed Thad my drink.

Did I need to go to the bathroom? No. Was I going to have two minutes to myself? Yes.

He beamed at me, "I'll wait right here for you."

I headed to the bathroom and stood at the sink, taking in my reflection. The woman looking back at me wasn't an accurate representation of who I am. This was a mask. I always wore my metaphorical mask at these types of events.

The door started to open, and I darted into the open stall.

"She's just so…plain. I thought Thaddy would've picked someone a little more glamorous." I heard Priscilla say.

"I know. Did you see how ugly her dress is? She couldn't have found something fancier to fit the occasion?" Mrs. Carter shot back.

I shouldn't be overhearing this. It's a good thing I'm in the bathroom because I'm going to be sick.

"Absolutely hideous." There was a pause. "I can't believe Thad is moving across the country for *her*. He should just stay here."

My head was spinning, out of all the things that I thought could go wrong tonight, being shit on by my boyfriend's mom and sister wasn't on that list.

Thankfully, they were just touching up their lipstick—or at least that's what it looked like through the crack in the door. Once the door closed, I counted to thirty and followed suit, trying to play off that I hadn't overheard them talking.

I made my way back to the ballroom, and Thad was patiently waiting for me right where he said he would be.

"Ready to head to our seats?"

I nodded, "Yeah."

He paused before walking further. "Are you okay?"

Fake smile mode activated.

"I am! My feet just hurt. I should've picked a more comfortable option."

The black stilettos I shoved my feet into were probably drawing blood at this point.

"If it's any consolation, they look amazing." He wagged his eyebrows and grabbed my hand, leading me over to the table closest to the small stage. "You'll sit there."

He pulled the chair out for me, which was draped in a blue cover. I sat down and he sat next to me.

Priscilla sat to my right, and I could feel the daggers she was throwing my way. I kept my eyes locked on the blue bird in the cage in front of us. At events like these, I felt a lot like that bird—dead inside and in a cage where everyone could see me.

Mrs. Carter got up from her chair, made her way to the small stage, and took her spot in the middle with a microphone.

"Good evening, everyone. Thank you so much for being here. After having to cancel last year, we at the Great Tits Foundation wanted to make this year even bigger and better. We have a wonderful night planned for all of you. To kick off the event, we do have an announcement." She paused dramatically as the crowd gasped. "As you all know, my father was the Chairman for over thirty years. After his passing last year, we've been on the hunt for a replacement. After much consideration, we would like to announce that my son, Thad Carter, will be stepping into the Chairman role of the Great Tits Foundation."

My mouth hung open and I looked at Thad.

"For real?" I mouthed.

He nodded.

"Son, would you mind coming up here to say a few words?" His mother asked into the microphone.

Thad got up and went to the center of the stage. As soon as he was up there, his mom wrapped him in a tight hug. He took the microphone from her hand.

"Hello, I am Thad Carter. I'm the grandson of George, the founder of this incredible foundation. I'm honored to be your new Chairman." There was a round of applause and cheers. "Today we are here ..."

My stomach knotted and I blacked out. Thad knew about the new position, why didn't he tell me?

CHAPTER 6

BEFORE YOU GO

Rose

Earlier Today

MY ALARM BLARED. "HAPPY MOVING DAY!"

I rolled over to find Thad's spot in the bed empty.

"Babe?" I called out, still snuggled under the blankets.

No response.

"Thad?"

Nothing.

I checked my phone and saw a text from him.

Thad: Went for a run.

> Rose: Okay! I'll have coffee ready for you.

I swung my legs over the edge of the bed as the realization hit me. Last night was the last time I would ever sleep in this room.

Thad and I had agreed—it made financial sense to keep the Seattle apartment and rent it out. The cost of living in Wippowa was much cheaper, so the bed would stay. Most of the furniture would. Thad said we'd start fresh when we got there. Everything would finally be *ours*, not just his.

I studied my reflection in the mirror, the exhaustion from a restless night evident in the dark smudges under my eyes. Today was, by all accounts, the biggest day of my life.

Last night's event had been... interesting. Beyond the not-so-lovely conversation I'd overheard—one I couldn't stop replaying—I kept circling back to the same thought. Why hadn't Thad told me about being placed in a leadership role for the Foundation? It wasn't bad news. It was actually great news, which made his secrecy even more confusing.

Still, despite the unanswered questions, a weight had been lifted. With this move finally here, I felt lighter, freer.

Telling my parents about Wippowa had been a moment I'd braced myself for, expecting concern or hesitation. Instead, they were ecstatic. *Ecstatic*. Not at all the reaction I had anticipated. But when I asked why, they simply said they were ready for their own change. My move was the push they needed. They were selling their house, buying a camper, and setting off to travel the country. They'd always dreamed of it, and now, they were making their dreams a reality.

It's never too late to follow your dreams.

I finished getting ready, moving through the apartment with a newfound awareness, drinking in the details one last time. The way the morning light poured through the massive windows. The steady hum of the city below. The kitchen island where I sat for breakfast while Thad got ready for work.

My eyes landed on the little table I'd bought after teaching my first yoga class, back when I still loved yoga. Back when I still loved living in Seattle.

When Thad finally walked in, his face was flushed, his movements unusually stiff. He ran a hand through his hair, a telltale sign—he was nervous.

"Good run?" I asked, zipping up my final suitcase.

"Yeah. I'm going to go shower." He didn't make eye contact, just made a beeline for the bathroom.

I ran my fingers over the key on my keychain, hesitating before slipping it off. Letting it go felt like the end of an era—because it was. My time in the Emerald City had run its course. I'd had a good run here, but this was it. A chapter closing. A life left behind.

I placed the key on the smooth marble counter, the soft *clink* echoing in the empty space. Turning, I took in the apartment one last time—the high ceilings, the sprawling windows, the memories woven into every corner.

Against the entryway wall, seven suitcases stood neatly in a row, packed with only what we couldn't bear to leave behind. I traced my gaze over them, a quiet realization settling over me. Three decades of life, reduced to three large suitcases. It was strange how little we truly needed in the end.

Thad came out of the bathroom looking less nervous than he did when he got home. A wave of relief washed over me.

"I'm ready to head to the airport whenever you are. I think I saw the car downstairs waiting for us." I leaned up and pressed a kiss to his cheek.

"Let's start rolling the suitcases down." Thad rolled two of mine while I rolled the other large one and my carry-on.

I paused in the doorway, taking everything in one last time. A lump formed in my throat. "Goodbye, apartment. You've served us well."

We rode the elevator silently, anxious butterflies fluttering around my stomach. Thad handed off the suitcases to the driver and I did the same.

I started to head back upstairs to grab the remaining three suitcases.

"Where are you going?" Thad asked, eyebrows scrunched.

"To help you carry the last ones down." It was a statement but it came out more like a question.

"No need." He took a step towards me and grabbed my cheeks in his hands.

I cocked my head, "Alright. I'll just wait here."

"Rose, I'm not coming with you to Wippowa."

Record scratch.

"Do you have a business trip?"

He shook his head, "No."

"Do you need to finish stuff up here? I know we talked about renovating the bathroom…"

"Sweetheart, I'm not moving to Wippowa."

My mind raced. Of all the things that could have gone wrong today, Thad not coming with me wasn't even on my radar.

I'd worried about the plane being delayed. I'd imagined the horror of getting explosive diarrhea mid-flight. I'd even considered the sheer inconvenience of forgetting my toiletries. But *this*? This had never once crossed my mind.

My boyfriend wasn't coming with me.

"But why? Just last night you said you couldn't wait to start a foundation together and throw lavish events. What changed?"

"I'm the Chairman of the foundation now, I need to be based here."

My skin went cold. "But you knew about that before and never said anything."

"I was waiting to see if your little moving idea actually stuck. You know how you are—sometimes you get something in your head, swear you're going to follow through, and then… you don't."

"We rented out the apartment. We *can't* stay," I argued, grasping at anything that might hold weight.

"I'll call the leasing company and tell them we've changed our minds. We'll stay."

My heart sunk; tears pricked at my eyes. "But I don't want to stay."

"You know you're better off here." Thad stated plainly.

"You're just going to let me go alone?" My pulse drummed in my ears. I gripped my purse strap for dear life.

"No, I came down here with you to talk you out of it. We have such a good life here. What more could you want?"

What more could I want? I want a life where I don't live in an apartment. I want space. I want a life where I'm near my best friend and her family that I adore. I want to find my passions.

A life I love.

"Living here is suffocating, Thad." I drew in a sharp breath. "You don't understand how much shit I've gone through in my life. All of the things that were on track to go right that went catastrophically wrong."

I could tell I struck a nerve—the softness in his face vanished, replaced by something sharper, harder. His expression darkened, anger flickering behind his eyes like a lit match.

"You mean getting fired for running your mouth to your manager?" He shot back. I don't know what got into him, but he has never talked to me like this before.

"Thad, you know he was out to get everyone. He fired me because I took an extra five minutes for lunch."

"Whatever you say."

"This city has nothing to offer me anymore. It's time to start fresh." I replied honestly, quietly.

"Is that why you're moving to a podunk town in Georgia, where you already know people? That doesn't sound like starting over to me. That sounds like you're trying to piggyback off your best friend's life—which is pathetic."

His words had bite. We've been talking about this move for the last year and he's been onboard the whole time. I don't know what changed.

"It's not as small as you think. There are ten thousand people that live there. Over one million people visit every year."

He tossed me jazz hands. "Big whoop."

"What has gotten into you?"

"My life here is better than it could be anywhere else. I have a great job. I'm near my family." He put his hands on my shoulders. "I'm a Chairman, Rose, at thirty-three. I've got it fucking amazing here. I'm staying put." He paused. "And I want you to as well."

"We've made plans. We have found an apartment to rent. Blythe and Charlie are excited for us to be close to them. Wren—" I couldn't even finish the thought without the tears falling.

"She's a kid. She'll get over it."

"Thad, she's my niece. I love her like she's my own." My fists balled at my sides.

"But she's not. She's not even Blythe's. Charlie had that kid out of wedlock."

A flush of red bloomed in my cheeks, warmth creeping up my neck before I could stop it.

"You cannot talk about her like that." I said through gritted teeth.

He scoffed. "So overprotective."

"I'm overprotective about people I love." I rolled my shoulders back, squaring my shoulders.

"I know and I love that about you." His eyes softened and lowered to mine. "I really think you should stay. You could go back to school if you don't want to get back into accounting. You can get a real job again."

Confusion crossed my face. "You told me I should pursue teaching yoga instead of going back into Corporate America. Why are you flip flopping on everything now?"

"I knew the whole yoga thing wouldn't last—you get bored too easily." Thad shrugged. "Honestly, I'm surprised you didn't bail on the move too."

"You thought I was going to bail?"

He nodded smugly.

"Why would I do that? I've put so much time and effort in to making this smooth."

"Yeah, but I thought it was only a little project for you to manage."

I felt like I was going to be sick. "Do you have any faith at all in me, Thad? Or has all of this," I waved my hands in the air. "been you patronizing me?"

"I mean, I know you can do amazing things…" He trailed off.

It was clear he didn't have anything else to say that he wouldn't immediately get put in the doghouse.

"You don't believe in me."

"You're just so hard to love, Rose."

My heart shattered, crashing to the ground like a delicate wine glass knocked off the counter—fragile, broken, and impossible to piece back together.

Thad stood there, stunned—caught off guard, like he hadn't expected me to see right through his patronizing façade.

I stared back, wide-eyed, my fingers tightening around the car door handle.

"Where are you going?" he called after me.

"Home."

A soft laugh drifted through the air, but I refused to look back.

"Before you go, I'm going to need the ring back."

Without a word, I slipped it off my finger and pressed it into his palm. Cold. *Final.*

The driver pulled away from the curb, and I watched as everything I'd ever known faded into the distance.

Numb. My entire life—my entire *plan*—had just blown up in my face.

CHAPTER 7

DIE FROM A BROKEN HEART

Rose

Present

"SO THAT'S HOW WE ENDED UP HERE."

"He let you leave..." Blythe trailed off, tucking her hair behind her ear.

I nodded, tears spilling over as I dropped my head into my hands.

"I hate him," she said, her voice was sharp with anger.

I sniffled. "I mean... he wasn't wrong. I do tend to abandon ideas."

"Stop defending him, Rose!" Blythe snapped, shaking her head. "You justify everything he says and does. His family talked shit about you, and you just let it slide. The Rose I knew before Thad would've decked him in the face and stood up for herself."

Pregnant Blythe was sassy.

"What happened to the version of you who didn't take anyone's crap? You stood up to our asshole boss when your career was on the line, and you didn't even hesitate."

"I'm still like that," I argued weakly.

"You one hundred percent are *not* like that. You gave up everything you loved for him. A guy. The one thing you swore you'd never do."

"I still have hobbies."

Blythe shot me a knowing look. "Name one."

"Yoga."

She scoffed. "That's work. And if you remember, Thad talked you out of opening your own studio. He was manipulating you. Can't you see that?"

I picked at my cuticles. "Maybe I should've stayed."

"Oh my God." She threw up her hands. "You're just proving my point! Whoever you've become in the last two years… that's not the best friend I know and love. Moving here is the best thing you could've done."

Her voice softened. "I just want you to be okay. I want the real Rose back."

"I'm broken," I whispered, my eyes locking onto a floorboard. My voice cracked, betraying me.

Blythe grabbed my hands, firm but gentle. "You need to know that you're loved. That you're safe."

I tried to smile, but it fell flat.

"Mom, dinner is ready!"

Wren came barreling through the front door, then stopped short, eyes bouncing between us.

"Auntie Rose, you're crying," she observed. Then, as if it was the most obvious solution in the world, she added, "Do you want to see my turtle? His name is Terry." She tapped her finger on her chin, "I think you met him at mom and dad's wedding."

Wren believed turtles could fix *everything*.

Blythe ruffled her daughter's hair. "Why don't we let Auntie wash her face, and then we'll have dinner?"

Wren nodded, then launched herself into my lap, wrapping her tiny arms around my neck. "I love you."

She wiped away a stray tear from my cheek with her little thumb. "I love you too."

Wren ran inside, leaving just me and Blythe in the quiet, humid air.

"Are you going to be okay?" she asked. "I can bring you a plate if you want to hide out tonight."

I pushed my damp hair out of my face. "I don't know if I'll *ever* be okay again. How could I?" My head lolled back against the chair. "I don't even know where I go from here. I can't step foot in-side that rental—it would be too painful. Too much of a reminder of what could've been. What life was supposed to be." I swallowed hard. "How do I move on from being told I'm a flake? That I'm too hard to love?"

Blythe sighed. "Rose, you're free-spirited. He wanted to tie you down to a life you hated. Did you look hot as hell at every event you went to? Without a doubt. Could I see right through that fake-ass smile? Also yes."

She stood, brushing invisible dust off her leggings. "I think it's time you admit you've been lying to yourself."

She pulled open the door, pausing. "Come in whenever you're ready."

A loud clap of thunder rolled across the water. I clenched my jaw. I hate that she can see right through me.

I'd spent most of my life cycling through friends. No one ever stuck.

People irritated me, their presence grating after too long.

Until fate stepped in, and I ended up working with Blythe. She was my assigned Onboarding Buddy. We went from forced small talk to being glued at the hip in record time, after that first glass of wine hit our systems, we became best friends.

She loves me so much that she quit her job after I was fired. Total badass move, if you ask me.

The disdain I had for those fancy events was next level, but Thad enjoyed them, and I wanted him to be happy. Besides, I still got delicious food and cocktails out of it, so who was I to complain?

It was fine when it was balanced—when most of our nights were spent curled up on the couch, ordering takeout, relaxing. When he was actually home.

Now, I wasn't sure if any of it had been real. Everything felt like a nightmare.

The four of us sat around the dinner table in awkward silence, pasta twirling lazily on forks, glances bouncing between Blythe and Charlie like a secret game of ping-pong.

I kept my eyes on my plate, pushing spaghetti from one side to the other.

Charlie exhaled sharply. "Am I allowed to ask questions here, or am I just supposed to stay in the dark?"

"Thad isn't coming." My voice was flat. I refused to look up.

"No shit. What did that douchebag do?"

"Charlie!" Blythe and I snapped in unison.

"What? He was." Charlie lifted a shoulder, unapologetic.

"Be nice," Blythe scolded.

Charlie turned to me. "Sorry, Rose. I didn't mean it."

A small smile tugged at my lips. "You totally did."

"I did, but the right thing to say here is that I didn't."

Marriage had domesticated him. The once grumpy, broody man I met years ago had softened around the edges, like a well-worn leather jacket.

His expression shifted to something earnest. "Stay as long as you need to get back on your feet."

"I appreciate it." I hesitated. "Almost decked a guy on the plane today."

Three sets of eyebrows shot up—even Wren's.

"You what?" Blythe asked, keeping her tone carefully neutral.

I leaned forward. "I had the aisle seat, and Thad was supposed to be in the middle. Obviously, that didn't happen, so the seat was empty. Right before takeoff, the flight attendant asked if this *behemoth* could sit there. I said no, but she wouldn't take no for an answer."

"So he sat next to you?" Charlie asked.

"Oh, he sat next to me. Chatted the whole flight. Had the fakest southern accent I've ever heard. And, get this—he likes orange Skittles."

Blythe gasped. "Not the orange Skittles!"

"Yep. And when we hit turbulence, I started crying. I was convinced I was going to die, and he offered to let me hold his hand."

Charlie set his fork down. "Rose, you know the odds of a plane crash are one in eleven million, right?"

I narrowed my eyes. "First of all, how did you know that? Second of all, what if I was the one?"

"I read; despite what you two think." He motioned between Blythe and me.

Blythe tapped her fingers against the table. "Sweetie, it sounds like he was just being nice. Did he hit on you?"

I shook my head. "No."

"Then you almost punched a man because he was friendly?"

I nodded vigorously. "All men should become extinct." I paused, glancing at Charlie. "Except you. You don't count."

Charlie narrowed his eyes at me. "Not sure if I should be honored or offended…"

"Take the compliment, Charles."

"Are you about to enter your All Men Suck phase?" Blythe asked, eyes locked on mine.

"Fuc—" I remembered there's a kid sitting at the table. "*Fudge* yeah I am."

Blythe smirked. "Can't say I blame you."

Charlie groaned, dragging a hand down his face. "Here we go…"

Wren, completely unbothered, happily stabbed at her spaghetti. "Mom says all boys are dumb except for Dad."

Blythe pointed her fork at Charlie. "See? Even our child understands."

Charlie huffed. "I feel so appreciated."

"You should." I smirked, reaching for my wine glass. "You made the cut."

Charlie muttered something under his breath before taking another bite.

Blythe leaned in, resting her chin on her hand. "So, what's the next move? You staying here forever? Running off to the mountains to become one with nature?"

I sighed dramatically. "I have no plan. Right now, I'm just a broken woman with her life packed in suitcases and an irrational hatred for orange Skittles."

Blythe clinked her glass against mine. "To new beginnings. And to never trusting a man who prefers orange Skittles."

"I'll stay here for a little while if that's okay. I need to contact the leasing company tomorrow and cancel the lease. I need to find a job. Literally start from scratch."

"You always have a home here." Blythe consoled.

A yawn escaped, my day fully catching up to me. "I think I'm going to go lie down and try to sleep this headache off."

I picked up my plate and left it on the counter, "I'll probably come back for that."

Blythe and Charlie offered sympathetic looks.

"Call down if you need anything," Blythe offered. "And get some rest."

I made my way upstairs and got into the plush bed Blythe had made for me.

Of course, sleep didn't come easy. It never did when my mind was running laps around the same miserable thoughts.

I flipped onto my other side, pulling the blanket tighter around me. The guest room was cozy, but it wasn't *mine*. It smelled like fresh laundry and whatever candle Blythe had burning earlier—something warm, like vanilla and amber.

I exhaled slowly, staring at the ceiling. My heart wasn't just broken; it was wrecked, gutted, torn apart in ways I didn't know were possible. I had every intention of drifting off to sleep, of shutting it all off for a few hours, but instead, I lay there, wide awake, fully convinced I was going to die from a broken heart.

And if I didn't? Well, I'd have to figure out how to survive it.

CHAPTER 8

AWAKE MY SOUL

Rose

BURNED THROUGH AN ENTIRE BOX OF TISSUES, WATCHING AS
the clock dragged itself closer to dawn. The bed felt too big, too
cold—like a hollow space where something vital used to be.

Any excitement I had for this move had vanished somewhere
over the fly-over states, replaced with a crushing emptiness. My life
had been on the brink of something beautiful, and now it felt like
a wasteland. Every plan I had carefully built was gone, scattered
like ash.

At some point, exhaustion finally won, pulling me into a restless, fragmented sleep. My dreams were cruel—flashes of standing
at the altar, waiting for a future that would never come. Ironic, really.

As soon as the first sliver of sunlight broke through the blinds,
I took it as my cue. Lying here wouldn't change anything. I had to
get up.

No point in lying there, staring at the ceiling, waiting for sleep
that clearly had no interest in me. My body felt heavy, but my mind
was wired, stuck in the loop of what could have been.

I threw on a hoodie and padded out to the kitchen, where the
coffee pot was already half-full—Charlie's doing, no doubt. The
smell was warm and familiar, but it didn't bring me any comfort. The

house was quiet—Wren was at school, Blythe was at the bookstore, and Charlie was at the coffee shop.

Pulling a mug from the cabinet, I wrapped my hands around it like it could somehow piece me back together. My life felt foreign now, like I'd been dropped into an alternate reality where none of my plans existed anymore.

And that was the worst part. The vision I had spent years building with Thad was ripped away like it was never real to begin with.

I took a shaky breath. I didn't know what today would look like, but I knew one thing for sure—I had to figure out where I went from here. The first step? Cancelling this lease before the first month of rent is withdrawn from my bank account and I find myself in an even worse predicament.

I glanced at the clock, no one from the apartment complex leasing office would be in the office for a few more hours. To ease an ounce of my anxiety, I typed up a quick email to the leasing agent I had been working with.

Charlotte,

Unfortunately, Thad and I will not be able to rent the apartment. It's a beautiful complex and the apartment itself was a dream, but our plans have changed drastically. Please let me know the procedure for cancellation of our lease. I apologize for any inconvenience this may have caused.

Thank you,
Rose Solace

I hated every moment of this. My body felt heavy—like it was carrying the weight of the world. The weight of the universe rested upon my shoulders. *My* universe. I closed my laptop lid and sat quietly while the slow rain pattered on the window. I stared at my coffee cup, hoping I'd find some answers at the bottom.

Growing up in Seattle, I loved the rain. The rhythmic sound was oddly comforting. The gloominess outside resonated deeply.

An email popped up in my inbox.

Rose,

So sorry to hear about your change in plans! I can take care of everything on our end, we shouldn't need anything from you.

The deposit you placed of the first and last month's rent will be refunded back to your card that ends in -0120. Confirm back if that card is still active and you will be all set!

Charlotte

Hi,

That's great news! -0120 is still the correct card.

Rose

I washed my mug and placed it in the dishwater and made my way back up to my room. At least I was going to have a little more money in my bank account than I had anticipated. I had forgotten about the deposit because we handled that when we signed our least nine months ago.

Nine months ago we planned our paradise. Our forever. And now we're just a fleeting moment in time.

The plush bedding cuddled me as I laid back down. I picked up my phone and stared at my background. Thad and I were so happy. That night was really something special—we laughed until we tried in the limo home, tipsy on expensive champagne. We sloppily walked into our apartment and danced around the living room. It was the perfect night. Now it's nothing but a memory from a relationship that ceased to exist, or did it?

Now reflecting on yesterday's events, Thad and I might still be in a relationship. Did he take me leaving as us being over? Did he just think we were on a break.

I should text him.

Rose: Can we talk?

Every fiber of my being told me that I shouldn't have hastily hit send, but I needed to. I needed to save us.

Thad: What do you want?

Rose: Can we talk?

Thad: You moved. We're done. Nothing to talk about.

Rose: I'll come back home.

Thad: Too late.

My heart splintered into a thousand pieces. My phone slipped from my hands and my eyes slowly closed. My lungs tightened and my heart raced. My fingers cripped the sheets in a panic.

Too late.

I don't know how to be alone with my own thoughts.

It's been the longest and most painful week of my life. I haven't left this bedroom. I only come out to have meals like a moody teenager.

I've had a lot of processing to do this week. I've done a lot of soul searching and…I'm still destroyed.

Hearing that you're hard to love is a hard pill to swallow. Even if there was some truth to it, doesn't mean it didn't slice me open and expose my innermost insecurities. I don't know *how* to heal.

Day faded into night and another day of nothingness turned over.

My eyes were unable to produce anymore tears.

Blythe and Charlie have been respecting my boundaries. Blythe has only knocked once and that was shortly after I received the confirmation from Thad that we were over.

I promised myself last night today I would live life outside of these four walls. The day took a step back into my reality instead of dragging myself from the bathroom to the bed and then back.

My day didn't go according to plan. Thad deleted all photo evidence of me from his online presence and my bed continued to be my safe space. I refused to leave bed—even for food.

Blythe knocked on the door earlier this evening.

"Not now." I mumbled into my pillow watching my comfort show.

"If you want anything, just text me. I can bring it to your door. You won't even know I'm here." Blythe's voice dripped with concern.

"Hi, Auntie." Wren chimed in.

"Thank you. Hi, Wrenny."

My gaze locked on the ceiling. My mind started to race. Blythe and Charlie had been so wonderful letting me stay here. I was being rude.

I grabbed my long-empty water tumbler and slowly creaked open the bedroom door. It was almost midnight on a Wednesday and everyone had to be up early in the morning so I needed to be as quiet as a church mouse. Which is impossible because their dog Marsh is the most vigilant freakin' dog I've ever seen.

I crept down the stairs like a child peeking at presents on Christmas morning before everyone else is awake. I slowly made my way over to the refrigerator and refilled my water.

Tiptoeing through the kitchen, I opened the door that led to the side of the house that had the boat dock. The creaking of the door made me want to abort mission and head back up to my room. I felt like I was sixteen again and sneaking out of the house to go to a party.

The salty air hit my lungs and I breathed deeply. I could breathe.

I made my way down to the dock and sat down, my legs dangling over the edge. I stared out at the ripples in the water. The humid air clung to my clammy skin.

The immensity of the situation hit me all at once. I let the waves of sadness wash over me—bringing all those wounds I fought to push down back to the surface.

My chest heaved as sobs shook through my body. The hollowness in my chest gaping wide.

"Hey," I opened my eyes to see Charlie standing above me. He motioned towards the spot next to me at the edge of the dock. "Mind if I sit down?"

I sat up and wiped my face with my sleeves. "It's your house. You don't need to ask me."

He was uncomfortable. "You seem like you're in the middle of something."

"Don't be stupid. Sit down." I straightened my posture.

We sat there in silence for a few minutes.

"Do you wanna talk about whatever went down with you and Thad?" Charlie finally broke the silence, keeping his eyes on the horizon.

"No." I looked at him, "Why are you out here anyway?"

"This is my thinking spot," he answered honestly.

"What's on your mind, *Charles?*"

"Can I tell you something that you have to swear not to tell Blythe?" his voice was low.

I tapped my chin, "Depends on how much it impacts her."

"It doesn't."

"Then air your dirty laundry out, Hannigan."

"I'm nervous." Charlie's voice was barely above a whisper.

"About?"

"Having another kid. I barely made it out of the newborn phase the first time."

An audible laugh spilled out, "You're kidding me."

His eyes locked on mine, anxiety flooding them.

"Oh my...Charlie, you're serious?" My eyes were wide. "You also had a lot of other things on your plate the last time. This time you have a spouse and Wren will an incredible big sister and help out. Don't stress."

"Thank you for that. I didn't know you were capable of being sweet."

I shot him a look before looking back at the water. "Want me to fill you in?"

"Rose, you know I hate gossip, but this shit has been killing me. Blythe won't say a word. She locked that shit in the vault."

"Buckle up, buttercup..." I trailed off, filling Charlie in on what happened and how my life has become a dumpster fire.

"All that to say, I'm the problem. Not him."

His shook his head and wrapped an arm around my shoulder. "Do you really believe that?"

I lifted a shoulder, "I don't know what I believe anymore."

"I can tell you none of those things are true. You're not a flake, you just find things you're passionate about. You're loved by anyone who knows you." Charlie paused, clearing his throat. "He's not worth anymore of your time. Close the book and move on—to someone who will love you as you are and not force you to go to fancy events that you hated."

"Thanks," I offered a small smile.

"I mean, hell, Rose, his name is Thad. What did you really expect?"

I raised a brow, "You're not wrong."

"He's gonna wind up missin' you. Just wait. And when he comes back with his tail tucked between his legs, tell him to go fuck himself."

"Thanks, Charlie. You're going to give a great pep talk to Wren one day when she gets her heart broken."

"I will sure do my best."

We sat with the conversation hanging in the humid air.

"I just had a thought. Feel free to say no."

"Oh-kay..."

"Why don't you come work at the Coastal Cup? The newest barista we hired is graduating from college and is taking some time off, so we could really use another set of hands."

"Charlie, I—" I interrupted. They were already letting me live in their house for free, I couldn't have them pay me at work.

"You'll be paid the same as all the other employees. There won't be any favoritism. You'll have to help clean the bathrooms like everyone else." He paused, "Plus, it's not us paying you, it's Larry."

"Who's Larry?"

"The guy we hired to do all that HR and payroll stuff. He's a bit of a jack of all trades."

"I don't know…" I trailed off.

"You don't have to decide now." He comforted.

I changed the subject. "Are you happy to be having a boy?"

A wide smile, "Yeah. I am."

"I know this all really sucks for you, but I have something that might cheer you up."

"What's that?"

"The name of your nephew if you're interested."

My heart leapt in my chest, "Abso-freakin-lutely."

"His name is …" Charlie paused dramatically. "Silas Wells."

I burst into tears again and wrapped my arms around his neck. "Come here, you oaf! That's the most precious name I have ever heard."

Charlie was beaming. "We really like it."

"I do, too." I paused, taking in the beautiful evening. "I'm really happy I get to be here for all of this. The thought of missing everything was tearing me apart inside. Finding out Blythe was pregnant over a video call and not in-person sucked. I should've been here. I should've moved here when she asked after she did." I gave a heartless laugh, "Would've saved me some heartbreak."

"All paths lead to lessons learned—both good and bad. What matters is you're here now and don't have to live in the 'what ifs' anymore. Move on from Thad. Start over here in Wippowa. No one really knows you, so it's a clean slate. Take chances. Step outside your comfort zone."

There was a spark of something inside me.

"Maybe."

CHAPTER 9

YOU'RE LOSING ME

Rose

One Week Later

AFTER MY CONVERSATION WITH CHARLIE, SOMETHING IN ME started to shift. I still felt unmoored, like a plastic bag caught in the wind, but I was beginning to surface—stepping out of my room for longer stretches, breathing in the world beyond my own walls.

Most afternoons now, I sit outside with Wren after school, coloring in the soft afternoon light. It's a small thing, but it grounds me.

I'm not healed. The wounds still run deep, raw in ways I don't fully understand. I don't know if I'll ever trust again—hell, if I'll ever love again—but I'm taking it moment by moment. Some days, it feels like I'm drowning. Others, I catch glimpses of something lighter, something that almost feels like hope.

This afternoon, Wren is humming next to me, her legs swinging beneath the picnic table as she presses a blue crayon hard against the page. The sound of it scratches through the silence between us, and for once, I don't mind. It's comforting, in a way.

A small reminder that the world is still moving.

"You should draw something too," she says, glancing at me with expectant eyes.

I hesitate, but she slides a blank page in front of me before I can make up an excuse. "You don't have to be good," she adds, as if she already knows what I'm thinking. "Just do it, Auntie Rose."

A breath escapes me, half a laugh, half something else. I pick up a crayon. The color doesn't matter. The shape doesn't matter. What matters is that, for the first time in a long time, I want to try.

And that's enough for now.

Once dinner was cleaned up, I pulled a shot of espresso and carried it to my room, the rich aroma curling through the air like a small comfort.

I unzipped my suitcases, the sound sharp in the quiet, and took inventory of everything I had brought with me. Now that Thad and I were officially over, most of it felt like dead weight—gifts, memories, reminders of a version of us that no longer existed.

Shoving my headphones over my ears, I hit play on my workout playlist and got to work. For the next hour, I sorted through every item, emptying my suitcases until the floor was covered in carefully constructed piles—clothes, shoes, household essentials, and everything in between.

Then I straightened up, surveying the mess. My gaze landed on a flower pot painted with a single rose, the one my grandma had given me when I was ten. A wave of realization hit me, knocking the air from my lungs. Everything I owned was right here, spread out in front of me. The bare necessities. Just enough to get by.

This move had turned me into a minimalist, though not by choice. Space was limited, and that had forced me to be intentional. No need for a parka in Georgia, which meant I had room for all my water tumblers—something Thad always claimed was a waste of space. My eyes locked onto the stack of forty-ounce tumblers on my dresser. My life might have crumbled, but at least I was hydrated.

Slowly, I started putting my life back together, one small step at a time. Clothes folded into drawers. Shoes lined up neatly in the closet. Dresses hung with care. Water tumblers placed in the kitchen where they belonged. And finally, for the first time since I got here, I unpacked my toiletry bag, setting my skincare neatly in the bathroom cabinet.

I glanced around my space and felt like the thousand-pound weight was lifted off my shoulders. This wasn't just a room anymore. It was mine. It was time I accepted my reality.

I went to close the blinds before bed but paused when I saw Blythe sitting out on the dock, her figure outlined by the soft glow of the moon.

Is that where everyone goes to clear their mind?

Grabbing a sweatshirt, I slipped my feet into my slides and made my way down to her, careful with my steps so I wouldn't startle her. The cooler spring air sent a shiver down my spine.

"Hey," Blythe greeted, not even turning around.

I settled next to her, the wood cool beneath me. "How did you know it was me?"

She let out a soft laugh. "Are you kidding? You act like I don't know the sound of your footsteps after all these years." Then, as if it were the most natural thing in the world, she rested her head on my shoulder.

"Fair enough." We sat in comfortable silence for a moment, the gentle lapping of the water filling the space between us. "What are you doing out here?"

Blythe sat up and stretched before shrugging. "Needed some fresh air. I've been staring at spreadsheets all day, and my eyeballs were starting to hurt."

I nudged her shoulder. "Look who's using her accounting brain again."

She shot me a playful glare. "We hired Larry, but I still have to deal with some of the stuff. I didn't want to do this again." Her last words came out in a dramatic whine.

"At least your business is thriving, and you actually need to balance the books."

"Yeah, I suppose." She gazed back out at the water, thoughtful. "What about you? I saw you moving around your room."

I turned to her, narrowing my eyes. "Blythe Hannigan, were you spying on me?"

A smirk tugged at the corner of her mouth. "Never. But you were dancing in front of your window while doing… whatever it was you were doing."

I twisted around and, sure enough, there was a clear view straight into my room.

"Well," I muttered, shaking my head, "I saw you down here and wanted to check on you."

"Yeah, I'm good. What about you? How are you holding up?"

I exhaled, feeling the weight of it all settle in my chest. "I put everything away, but all that did was make the breakup feel more real, you know? I don't know where to go from here. Staying seems pointless. Going back to Seattle isn't an option. I feel untethered. Like I'm drifting in and out of other people's lives."

Blythe sighed. "Selfishly, I think you should stay. I know this isn't the life you imagined for yourself, but you have people who love you to the ends of the earth. You belong here, Rose. And going back to Seattle? That's admitting defeat. If there's one thing you don't do, it's capitulate."

I rolled my eyes. "You really look for any excuse to use that word, don't you?"

A shit-eating grin spread across her face. "Learned it in sixth grade and never looked back."

"You're a nerd," I laughed.

"You're in my house. Take that back." She paused, then corrected herself. "Well, technically, the house is in Charlie's name, but whatever."

She laid back on the dock, and I followed suit, staring up at the endless stretch of stars. The silence between us wasn't awkward—it never was. It was familiar, easy.

After a while, I finally spoke. "Charlie thinks I should work at the Coastal Cup."

Blythe yawned. "I'm gonna head to bed. If you decide to take us up on the offer, we're heading over to the shop at six."

I groaned. "That's so early."

I stood, extending a hand to help her up. She grabbed it, hauling herself to her feet.

"These Wippowa folks take their caffeination very seriously," she said, stretching her arms over her head. "If we're not open by seven, they're practically beating down our damn door."

I followed her inside, the warmth of the house settling over us like a thick blanket. We climbed the stairs, feet quiet against the wood.

"Good night, Bee," I murmured.

"Nighty night, Rose."

She turned left. I went right.

Back in my room, I flicked off the lights and nestled into my bed. It wasn't home—not yet—but it was warm, my clothes were put away, and for tonight, that was enough.

Still, my mind wouldn't settle. The ache in my chest remained, raw and relentless, like my heart had been ripped out, tossed onto the highway, and run over—again and again.

I stared at the ceiling, thoughts circling like vultures. Should I take the job at the Coastal Cup? Or should I try to find something else?

The guilt gnawed at me. Accepting a paycheck from my friends felt like another layer of dependency, another reminder that I wasn't standing on my own two feet.

I reached for my phone to check if Thad had tried contacting me, but of course, he hadn't. He cut me out of his life like it was the easiest thing in the world. Like *I* was nothing. How do you go from moving across the country with someone to nothing in a span of a few hours?

I rested my head on the plush pillows and employed a tactic I hadn't used since I was a kid—counting backwards from one hundred. The last number I remembered was thirty-three before I drifted off to sleep, still unsure of what tomorrow held.

For the first time in a few weeks, my alarm went off. Despite feeling like I was going to die inside, I got washed up and threw on a pair of jeans and a t-shirt and made my way downstairs. Blythe and Charlie were in the kitchen with a familiar voice. I turned the corner and saw Charlie's mom standing there.

"Good morning," I interrupted, standing awkwardly in the doorway.

"Rose!" Charlie's mom enveloped me in a hug. "It's so wonderful to see you again! How has your move been?"

I nodded awkwardly. "It's great to see you again. Charlie and Blythe have been very hospitable."

"Good!" She patted her son on the back.

"Is this you formally accepting the interim role at the Coastal Cup?" The corner of Blythe's mouth perked up.

"I'd like to take you both up on your offer."

"Oh thank goodness." Charlie added. "We really do need help."

My gaze shifted between the Hannigans. "Just know that I've never made someone else a cup of coffee, so if it sucks, don't say I didn't warn you."

"I'll give you the lowdown. Don't stress." Charlie offered.

"Then consider me your newest barista."

CHAPTER 10

SUNDAY MORNING

Rose

"**A**RE YOU READY FOR YOUR FIRST SHIFT?" CHARLIE ASKED, wiping down the counter.

I looked up at him from tying my apron, my fingers fumbled with the knot. I'm not sure if ready was the right word. Excited? Nervous? Terrified? Maybe all three. "I think so," I admitted, though it came out sounding more like a question.

Charlie smiled, "Trish is going to be training you this morning."

My eyes went wide, "I thought you were."

He shook his head, "I have to run back home. My mom isn't feeling well and is heading to urgent care, so I have to take Wren to school this morning." Charlie rested his hands on my shoulders, "I'm leaving you in the best hands."

I gulped as a young, bubbly brunette walked over to me, extending a hand. "I'm Trish, it's so nice to meet you! Miss Blythe has told me so much about you. It's really cool that you moved here."

"Don't fuck it up!" Charlie called out with a laugh as he walked out the door.

"Thanks for the vote of confidence, *Charles*."

Trish's eyes were saucers, her voice was low. "You called him Charles. No one does that."

"Blythe and I do when he's made it onto our shit list."

The girl suppressed a laugh.

"I've never done this before," I admitted.

Trish grinned, "You'll be just fine! The first rule of working in a coffee shop—look like you know what you're doing, even when you don't."

She gestured for me to follow her behind the counter and the moment I stepped behind the register, the energy shifted. The hum of the espresso machine, the rhythmic clinking of cups, the scent of freshly ground coffee—it was a world in motion, and I had no choice but to keep up.

"Let's start with a tour." Trish moved smoothly through the space, pointing things out as she went. "Espresso machine: your best friend and your worst enemy. Milk fridge, syrups, tea station. Cleaning rags are here, cups are stacked there, and if you ever lose track of anything, just look where the chaos is happening. It's probably there."

I nodded, trying to absorb everything but it was like drinking from a firehose.

"Now, the menu." She slid a laminated sheet in front of me. "Mr. Hannigan—"

I cut her off. "Do you all really call him Mr. Hannigan?"

"Everyone else calls him Charlie, I was just raised by very polite people." Trish answered.

"Noted." I suppressed a laugh. "Sorry for interrupting you."

"The menu has the classics—lattes, cappuccinos, Americanos, cold brew. But customers are rather creative and like to come up with their own concoctions. Last week I had a woman order an oat milk matcha with a splash of lavender. Then the next day, a man ordered a honey cinnamon cold brew."

I laughed nervously but Trish winked, "I promise you'll get the hang of it."

Blythe walked in from the bookstore and sat on one of the barstools at the end of the counter. "How's it going in here?"

"Good! I'm teaching Rose all the things. Would you like a decaf, Mrs. Hannigan?"

Blythe nodded. "Trish, sweetheart, how many times have I told you—just call me Blythe. I promise, you're not being rude." The corner of Blythe's lip perked up, "However, please keep calling Charlie Mr. Hannigan, it makes his skin crawl in his skin and it's hilarious."

Trish turned towards me, "Let's make an espresso shot."

I watched as she moved through the process with practiced ease, loading the portafilter, tamping the grounds with a firm press, and locking it into the machine. A few seconds later, dark ribbons of espresso streamed into the cup. "Golden rule—if it looks like tar or water, something's wrong. Would you like to try before it gets busy?"

"Uhm…" I looked over at Blythe for encouragement and she nodded. *My, how the tables have turned.* "Sure."

I took a deep breath and copied Trish's movements. I pressed the button and the espresso machine roared to life. The little cup holding the shot looked like a watery mess.

Trish looked at the cup and then at me, "What do you think?"

"Um, it looks too watery?"

She grinned, "Let's adjust the grind."

The rest of the morning there was a whirlwind. Customers came in and out like their lives depended on it. I learned how to steam milk without turning it into bubbling lava, how to take orders without panicking, and how to smile at customers even when I had no idea what they were asking for. At one point, I fumbled with the cash register, hitting the wrong buttons so many times that the system beeped in protest.

"Deep breath," Trish murmured, stepping in beside me. "They're just people who need caffeine. You're their hero."

By the time the rush slowed and the day came to an end, my apron was dusted with coffee grounds, my shoes stuck slightly to the floor from a caramel drizzle fiasco, and my brain was spinning.

When I handed a customer their drink and they smiled, saying, "This is perfect, thank you," something settled in my chest.

By no stretch of the imagination am I remotely qualified to be a barista, but I had a patient teacher, a boss that wouldn't fire me, and a strong desire to do a good job.

My first week at the Coastal Cup has flown by. Much to my surprise, I picked up the role quicker than I thought I would. When Trish called out sick this morning, I panicked.

She was my lifeline.

I was nowhere near as good as she is at this job and it's a Friday, also known as the busiest morning of the week.

I wiped down the counter and straightened up the straws while my nerves fluttered about. A wave of relief washed over me when I saw Charlie walk in with his Coastal Cup shirt on.

"Morning, bossman."

He looked flustered, "Hey, Rose."

"What's wrong?" I knew him well enough to know something was up.

"Wren is sick so Blythe is home with her. We need to reach out to the bookstore employees to see if anyone can come in and cover today."

"I can go over there after my shift here."

He unfurrowed his brow. "You wouldn't mind staying a little late?"

A laugh escaped, "Where am I going? Your house."

His shoulders relaxed. "Thank you. I'll help you out this morning and then you can go over to the store after the crowd dies down."

"You were going to lose customers if I was over here alone."

He didn't respond; instead, he started taking care of the cold brew. I went over and straightened up the tables. He was in work mode.

"I think it's really cool what you both have here, Charlie." I broke the silence. "You've formed a sense of community. I didn't tell Bee because it would get to her head, but she was the talk of Seattle when you guys were featured in that travel magazine."

Charlie beamed, "I'm just living the dream."

A lump formed in my throat. I wanted to live the dream, too. I wanted to settle down. To have kids. I wanted the stupid white picket fence. I longed for family movie nights.

I cleared my throat and threw a fake smile across my face. "Guess we should open the doors."

"You ready?" He raised his hand for a high-five.

I slapped it. "Let's do this."

From when the first customer walked in the door at 7:02 until the last walked out at 1:04, Charlie and I were a well-oiled machine. We cranked each order in record time.

We sat down at a table and looked around at the empty coffee shop.

"That was insane." Charlie stated, shock in his voice.

"We freakin' killed that." A grin spread across my face.

"And you said you weren't a barista."

I shrugged a shoulder. "Apparently I'm decent."

"I know we said this was just a short-term thing until our new graduate comes back, but if you want to be put on the team full-time, the job is yours."

My smile faded. "I've gotta go back, Charlie."

He sat up straight. "Why?"

"I'm leeching off you guys." I sighed heavily, the weight of the world returning to my shoulders. "I'm a big girl, I can swallow my pride and go back. Thad might take me back."

"That's the most disgusting thing I've ever heard you say." His eyes met mine. "And I've heard you say *very* inappropriate things. Why are you going to go back to some guy who didn't have the guts to follow you?"

"I was asking him to uproot his life. His family lives there."

His eyes were serious. "And *yours* is here."

"I—" I didn't know how to respond.

Charlie's eyes narrowed. "Are you going to be the one to tell Blythe?"

"She'll understand."

He raised a brow. "Do you really think that?"

I half-heartedly lifted a shoulder. "I don't know. Maybe? I just don't belong here."

"Why not?"

"I almost punched a man on the plane, Charlie. Just for being too nice."

"The guy probably deserved it."

"He did have a really annoying accent." I said matter-of-factly.

"Most of us do."

"I need to try and salvage whatever I can from my life."

"Why are you going back when you've been given an incredible opportunity to start over?"

"I'm scared." It was barely above a whisper.

"You have a place to live. You have a job. Those are the big scary things."

He was right. Blythe and I hated to admit it, but he was usually right.

Charlie stood, his voice was steady. "Make your own decision, but you owe it to yourself."

I didn't respond. Instead, I pushed open the bookstore door, flipped the sign to *Open*, and busied myself tidying up the shelves. It wasn't long before customers trickled in, then more, until the quiet space buzzed with conversation and the rustling of pages. The hours passed in a blur of helping readers find their next favorite book, ringing up purchases, and keeping the store in order.

When the last customer left, I finally sank into my chair, exhaustion settling into my bones. That's when I noticed Charlie standing in the doorway.

"Ready to head home?"

I exhaled slowly. "I just need to straighten up first. Maybe another half hour."

"I'll come in early and take care of it," he said. "You've had a long day—let's go."

Too tired to argue, I grabbed my bag and followed him to the truck.

"Pizza okay for dinner?" he asked as I climbed in.

"Yeah, of course."

As soon as I settled into my seat, my eyelids grew heavy. The weight of the day pressed down on me—physically, mentally. The move back to Seattle lingered at the edge of my thoughts, a quiet but persistent reminder of the uncertainty ahead.

The crunch of gravel signaled our arrival. The truck rolled to a stop, and I stepped out without a word, heading straight inside.

"Rose, how was—oh." Blythe stopped in her tracks. "You look exhausted."

"I am." A yawn escaped before I could stop it. "Do I have time for a quick shower before dinner?"

"Of course. Take your time. Wren won't be hungry for a while."

I trudged upstairs, each step feeling like I was dragging a thousand pounds. Once inside my room, I shut the door and sank onto the plush rug, letting the softness cradle me. My chest tightened, the threat of tears building.

I didn't want to go back to Seattle. I didn't want to admit defeat.

No matter how much Blythe and Charlie reassured me, I still felt like a burden. Even with tips from the coffee shop, it would take forever to afford rent, groceries, utilities. And without a car, everything felt even more impossible.

I could book a flight tomorrow and slip right back into my old life. The yoga studio would take me back. Maybe, if I swallowed my pride, so would Thad.

The thought made me sick.

Shoving it aside, I forced myself up and into the shower.

By the time I returned downstairs, I felt like a new woman. My freshly washed blonde hair was braided, a light coat of mascara lifted my lashes, and though I still had no idea what my future held, at least I looked put together.

"Auntie Rose!" Wren's voice called from down the hall. "Come here!"

I found her in her room, holding up two shirts.

"Can you help me pick an outfit for tomorrow?" she asked.

"What's happening tomorrow?"

"It's *W Squared Day*," she said, as if I should already know. "I think I'm gonna wear jeans, but should I wear my pink shirt with the little flowers or the white one with the sunflower?"

She held up both, and honestly, they were equally adorable.

"I like the pink one."

She nodded vigorously. "Me too. Thanks!"

Without another word, she grabbed my hand, leading me downstairs.

"Mom! Auntie Rose helped me pick out my outfit for *W Squared Day*!"

Blythe smiled. "That was nice of her. Did you say thank you?"

"Yes, Mommy."

"Oh, that reminds me," Blythe turned to me. "Could you take my car tomorrow and drop Wren off at her uncle's house?"

My stomach twisted. I hated driving.

"I could cover for you at the bookstore instead?" I offered, hopeful.

"You know I wouldn't ask you to drive unless I really needed you to. I have to be at the store to meet an author dropping off some signed copies of her book. We're meeting to chat through an event we're hosting for her." Blythe paused, choosing her next words carefully as we walked out the door. "Does it help that it's all country roads? You don't have to touch a highway."

Dang it. That did help.

"I'll do it."

Wren wrapped her arms around my waist. "Thank you, Auntie Rose! You're the best."

My heart swelled. Charlie was right, this is where my family is.

CHAPTER 11

SMALL TOWN BOY

Rose

THERE WAS A LOUD KNOCK ON MY DOOR. I CHECKED THE CLOCK on my nightstand—6:42. Who in the—?

"Auntie Rose, it's time to get up. It's W Squared Day!" Wren opened my door and came bounding into my bed. She grabbed my face with her hands. "Let's go!"

"Wrenny, it's so early."

"I have to be there to feed the goats."

"The what?" I'm still half-asleep, surely I misheard her.

"The baby goats. Uncle Wells feeds them at nine."

"Where are we going?"

"Uncle Wells' farm."

My brain slowly started to put together the pieces. I vaguely remembered Blythe telling me that one Saturday each month, Wren spends the day at her uncle's farm.

"Oh, right."

"Get up. I can't be late!" Wren leapt down and ran back to her room.

I rolled onto my back and pulled the covers over my head. My back sank into the bed. All I wanted to do was sleep in. I vowed I would take a nap as soon as I got home from dropping her off.

With a deep breath, I got up and walked over to my drawers. I grabbed a bra to throw on under my t-shirt and a pair of workout shorts and got washed up, pulling my hair out of the braid it was in all night.

"Wren, I'm ready. I'll be downstairs."

"Okay! I'll be down in a minute."

I strolled into the kitchen. Charlie and Blythe were standing there, guilt all over their faces.

"You didn't tell me she had to be there to feed the damn goats."

Blythe stifled a laugh. "Sorry, might have forgotten to tell you that part."

"I'm napping when I get home." I rolled my head from side to side.

"I'm ready." Wren came into view with the pink shirt I helped her pick, jeans, and little cowboy boots.

A grin spread across my face. "You look adorable."

She gave a little spin. "Thank you."

Blythe turned towards me. "The gas tank is full. I texted you the address. The roads all have speed limits of forty miles per hour or less, so you will be fine."

Charlie held out a freshly brewed cup of coffee. "For you."

I smiled at them both. "Thank you."

Wren and I walked towards the door. "I'll make sure she makes it there alive." I called over my shoulder.

"Have a good time!"

We walked over to the car and got buckled in.

I leaned over the console. "Ready to go?"

"Let's do this!" Wren high-fived me.

I adjusted the seat and mirrors and wiped my sweaty palms on my t-shirt. I pressed start on the directions and saw it said it was an hour away.

Estimated time of arrival: 8:27 A.M.

"Is it okay if I roll our windows down? It's nice out this morning." I asked.

Wren's finger hovered over the button and she raised a brow questioningly.

I nodded. "Go for it."

The thick, humid air wrapped around me, loosening the exhaustion in my limbs. Fifteen minutes passed before I finally settled in, my voice slipping into the familiar melodies of my playlist. I hadn't expected Wren to join in—but somehow, she knew nearly every word.

The country roads stretched before us, a thin ribbon of asphalt winding through marshlands and past towering oak trees draped in Spanish moss. The salty breeze filtered through our open windows, carrying the scent of sun-warmed pine and distant sea air. The sun had just crested over the tops of the oaks, creating a golden haze that danced through the trees, flickering across the road like a silent rhythm.

"So, Wrenny, are you excited to be a big sister?"

I looked in the rearview mirror and she had a grin on her face from ear-to-ear. "Yes!"

"That's very nice of you. I know you're going to be a great sister."

Wren nodded. "I hope so."

We continued on for a little while longer before Wren spoke up again. "We're getting close!" She cheered from the back seat, her excitement bubbling over.

I glanced down at the ETA—two minutes to go.

"I didn't know your uncle lived on a farm."

"Auntie Rose, he has *so* many goats."

"How many?" I questioned.

"Thirteen."

"That's thirteen too many for me." I joked.

"Mhm! I named them all."

"That's really impressive."

I turned left through a white fence and onto a gravel road, the tires kicking up a thick plume of dust that blurred the view ahead.

Are you sure this is the right way?"

"Sure is! Pull right over there." Wren pointed confidently to the right.

I eased the car into park, slid my sunglasses over my eyes, and stepped out.

"You're early!" The deep southern drawl carried across the dust-clouded driveway.

"Uncle Wellsy!"

Wren launched herself into his arms with a hug I don't even get—and she adores me.

I strolled toward them, taking in the way she clung to him, her tiny arms wrapped tight around his neck.

"Happy W Squared Day!"

"Happy W Squared Day, Wrenny."

That voice. It was unsettlingly familiar.

I pushed my sunglasses up onto my head. "Alright, I'll bite. What's W Squared Day?"

Wren let go and turned toward me, ready to explain. But my attention was locked on the man standing in front of me.

I froze. No way.

"Orange Skittles?"

He smirked. "Hey, Sunshine."

The nickname sent a jolt through me. My stomach tightened as I took him in—towering well over six feet, his presence making my five-seven frame feel downright petite. Sharp angles cut across his face, a striking mix of rugged and refined, his jaw shadowed by a beard. But it was his eyes that held me in place—piercing green, like shattered emeralds that saw straight through me. Ink covered both his arms, intricate tattoos shifting as he tipped his cowboy hat.

"Wells Calloway." He extended a hand. "Nice to meet ya."

I felt my exterior go frosty. "Rose Solace."

The irritating man from the plane—the one who spent hours getting under my skin—was Uncle Wells?

"You look like you've seen the sun a bit since you got here." He winked.

He fucking winked.

"Maybe I have," I said coolly.

"Still full of sunshine, I see."

I turned on my heel. "I'm heading home."

"You should help feed the goats!" Wren piped up.

I crouched to her level. "I'm sure you have a fun day planned, but I've got things to do."

"Like what?" Wells asked, all smooth confidence.

I shot him a look. "None of your business."

The irritation from the plane hadn't faded—not one bit.

"It's crazy our paths haven't crossed before. Ya know, with our best friends being married and all."

My hand hovered over the door handle. "You weren't at the wedding."

"So observant." The corner of his stupid mouth twitched. "I was in the hospital having my appendix taken out, if you must know."

I narrowed my eyes. "Convenient."

"Yeah, I really planned that one out," he drawled. "Figured an organ rupture was the perfect excuse to skip the party."

I huffed, crossing my arms. "Well, you missed a good one."

His gaze flicked over me, something unreadable in those green eyes. "I know I did."

I rolled my eyes and yanked open the car door. "Tragic. I'll be sure to light a candle in remembrance of your appendix."

Wren giggled behind me, and I heard Wells chuckle—low and deep, like he was enjoying this way too much. I refused to look back. Instead, I slid into the driver's seat and pulled the door shut with more force than necessary.

As I shifted into reverse, Wells stepped forward, resting a forearm against the open window. "You always run, Sunshine?"

I gripped the steering wheel. "I don't run. I just have better places to be."

"Sure you do." His smirk deepened. "See you soon."

I slammed the car into reverse and pressed the gas, sending a satisfying spray of gravel in my wake. The farther I got from that stupid cowboy hat and infuriating smirk, the better.

But as I sped down the long dirt road, his voice lingered in my head.

See you soon.

Like hell he would.

CHAPTER 12

TAKE ME HOME, COUNTRY ROADS

Wells

WHEN I WOKE UP THIS MORNING, I SURE AS HELL DIDN'T think I'd be running into my mortal enemy from the plane. Well, I'm her enemy, she's not mine.

I'd barely gotten my boots on before Wren came barreling toward me, a bundle of excitement about W Squared Day. And then—there she was. Standing next to the car, arms crossed, sunglasses hiding whatever fire was probably burning in those sharp eyes.

The woman from the plane.

I hadn't expected to see her again. But I sure hadn't forgotten her either.

She'd been nothing but attitude on that flight—stiff shoulders, exasperated sighs, like my attempt at conversation was some kind of personal insult. I was trying to be nice, maybe offer a little distraction, but she looked at me like I'd ruined her whole day just by existing.

And today? No different.

The second she recognized me, she went full ice queen. Like running into me was somehow worse than whatever had already gone wrong in her life.

Which, if I'm being honest? Made this way more entertaining.

"Auntie Rose doesn't like you," Wren observed, watching her speed off in a cloud of dust.

I let out a low whistle. "Nope. She sure doesn't."

"What did you do?"

I shook my head, hands on my hips. "Not a clue, kid." Then I looked down at her and grinned. "You ready to go feed those baby goats?"

"I was born ready!"

Wren was already halfway to the pen before I even got the gate unlatched, her little boots kicking up dust as she ran ahead.

"Slow down, Wrenny," I called, but she was too focused on the small herd of bleating baby goats crowding the fence.

"They're so hungry!" she gasped, gripping the bottle in her hands like it was a golden ticket.

I stepped inside, closing the gate behind me as the goats swarmed around our legs, nipping at the bottles we carried. One particularly bold little guy—white with a black patch over one eye—headbutted my shin like he had something to prove.

"Easy there, bud," I said, crouching to scratch between his ears. "We're getting to ya."

Wren was already crouched down, her tiny hands wrapped around the bottle as one of the smaller goats latched on, sucking greedily. She giggled, eyes wide with delight.

"Uncle Wells, look!"

I grinned, handing off my own bottle to another eager mouth. "Told ya they'd be excited to see you again."

She ran her free hand over the goat's fuzzy head, completely in awe. "I think this one's my favorite," she declared. "Her name is Biscuit."

I eyed the little troublemaker still ramming his head against my boot. "This one's definitely mine," I muttered.

Wren giggled. "He's a troublemaker."

I smirked. "Takes one to know one, kiddo."

W Squared Day is the best day of the month.

Not just because I get to spend time with my favorite person on the face of the earth—don't tell Charlie—but also because, for once, I've got an extra set of hands around here, even if they were the hands of an eight-year-old.

I've been running this place on my own for three years now, and it sure as hell hasn't gotten any easier. Long days, longer nights, and more work than any one person should probably take on. But when Wren looked up at me with those big, hopeful eyes and declared we needed goats—not one, not two, but thirteen of them—well… I never really stood a chance.

So here we are. Just me, my niece, and a whole mess of trouble wrapped in fur and tiny hooves.

We finished up feeding the goats and made our way inside, brushing off bits of hay and dust as we stepped into the kitchen. Wren scrambled up onto a barstool, swinging her little legs under the counter.

I leaned against the island, crossing my arms. "Alright, kiddo. We've got two options for breakfast—whip up some pancakes here, or head into town. What's it gonna be?"

Wren tapped her chin, eyes full of serious deliberation. "Let's make pancakes."

"Yes, Chef."

She giggled, clapping her hands. "I'll be in charge of the chocolate chips."

"Bold move." I grabbed the mixing bowl. "Think you can handle the responsibility?"

She nodded solemnly. "That's my job at home."

After a truly massive mess—flour on the counter, batter splattered on the stove, and at least half a bag of chocolate chips mysteriously missing—breakfast was finally served. We sat side by side at the kitchen island, wolfing down pancakes like we hadn't eaten in days.

Between bites, Wren leaned in, lowering her voice conspiratorially. "Uncle Wells, do you wanna know a secret?"

I raised a brow. "Tell me."

She glanced around, like someone might overhear us in the empty kitchen. "You know Auntie Rose?"

I nodded, already bracing myself.

"Her boyfriend was supposed to move here and didn't."

My fork hovered mid-air as her words sank in. Well, damn. That explained a lot. So that's why she was such a pain in the ass on the plane.

I set my fork down, watching Wren as she popped a syrup-drenched piece of pancake into her mouth like she hadn't just dropped a bombshell. "That... sad."

She shrugged. "Now she has more time for me... and baby Silas when he's born."

I pressed my tongue against the inside of my cheek, debating whether I should pry for more details. But Wren didn't need much prompting.

"She's working at the coffee shop now because she didn't have a job either."

That caught me off guard. Rose didn't exactly strike me as the small-town coffee shop type.

I let out a slow breath. "Wren, you probably shouldn't be telling me this."

She grinned, completely unbothered. "Why not? You're family."

I shook my head, hiding a smirk. This kid was trouble.

After breakfast, we cleaned up the kitchen—well, Wren cleaned up the kitchen, since I was pretty sure the mess was her doing in the first place. But, to her credit, she took it all in stride, humming as she wiped down the counters and placed the dishes into the sink.

Once the chaos was under control, we grabbed our hats and headed back outside. The sun was already climbing higher, casting that perfect morning glow over the farm. It was just another day of getting things ready for the farmer's market tomorrow.

We made our way over to the garden, the air warm but not yet too hot, and I handed Wren a small basket. "Alright, let's get to work. We need some tomatoes, maybe a few zucchinis, and definitely more of those peppers."

She nodded eagerly, already diving into the rows of plants with enthusiasm. Her small hands were quick, picking the ripe vegetables and carefully placing them in the basket. I couldn't help but smile as I watched her move between the rows of greenery. She might've been small, but she was as serious about this farm life as any grown-up.

"Look, Uncle Wells!" Wren held up a giant zucchini like it was a prize. "This one's bigger than my head!"

I gave her an approving nod. "That's the one. Good job."

We worked in the garden for another hour or two, gathering up tomatoes, cucumbers, and a few more herbs. The fresh scent of the earth, mixed with the faintest hint of basil, filled the air. There was something grounding about it all.

After we finished picking everything, we took the baskets to the back porch, where I'd already laid out the table for prepping. Wren handed me each vegetable as I cleaned and cut, sorting everything into piles for the market tomorrow. We both worked in rhythm. Wren shared elementary school gossip as the day slowly stretched on.

By the time the sun started to dip lower in the sky, we had everything ready—baskets packed with fresh produce, neatly labeled, and stacked for tomorrow's sale.

"Good work, kiddo," I said, wiping my hands on my jeans and tipping my hat. "Looks like we're ready for the market."

She beamed up at me, proud of the day's work. "We make a great team."

I ruffled her hair. "We sure do."

As the light faded and the moon started to rise, I loaded Wren up in my truck and drove her home.

"Thank you for a great W Squared Day, Uncle Wells."

"My pleasure, Little Bird. Thank you for your help."

CHAPTER 13

SHUT UP!

Rose

I SEETHED THE ENTIRE DRIVE HOME. THE ODDS OF RUNNING into the irritating guy from the plane were literally a million to one. The last thing I expected this morning was to end up at his house.

I pulled into the driveway and practically sprinted to my room, my bed a beacon of comfort. I yanked off my bra, sinking into the warmth and solace it promised.

I must've passed out the moment I hit the bed. When I finally stirred, it felt like I'd been asleep for days. The light outside had dimmed to a dusky haze, and the quietness in the house made my head spin. My body was heavy, groggy, the kind of tired that seeps into your bones.

I rubbed my eyes, trying to shake off the fog, when a familiar voice drifted upstairs from below.

Wells.

It was faint, but unmistakable—probably dropping Wren off. I could hear the soft hum of his deep drawl, then the sound of the front door clicking shut.

I froze for a moment, unsure of whether I wanted to stay

hidden under the covers or face whatever awkwardness was brewing downstairs.

I waited a few minutes before emerging from my cave.

"Hey," Blythe greeted from the couch, her voice warm with a hint of amusement. I sat beside her. "We weren't sure when you'd wake up from your hibernation."

"Ha-ha," I groaned, moving to the couch. "I didn't mean to sleep that long."

"Clearly, you needed it."

"Is Wren home?"

Blythe nodded. "Yeah. Wells dropped her off a few minutes ago. I think she went out back with Charlie."

"Ah, okay. Wells is gone, right?"

Blythe gave me a puzzled look. "Yeah. Why?"

"You remember the guy on the plane I almost punched?"

She nodded.

"Apparently, it was Wells."

Blythe burst into laughter, almost choking. "You almost punched Wells Calloway?"

"He was incredibly annoying, as you might recall."

Blythe could barely catch her breath from laughing. "What are the odds?" She paused, still laughing. "I totally forgot he mentioned he was in Seattle for his cousin's wedding."

"I hope I never have to cross paths with him again."

"That might be a bit tricky living here."

I exhaled a long, frustrated sigh. "Shit."

"The universe has a funny sense of humor."

"Don't even start with that, Bee."

Blythe leaned back, her eyes twinkling with mischief. "Come on, you've got to admit, this is kind of hilarious."

I shot her a look, my face still scrunched in annoyance. "Yeah, hilarious. I'm going to be dodging him every time I step out of the house."

"Or," Blythe teased, "you could just be normal and talk to him like an adult."

I groaned, collapsing back onto the couch. "I can't even imagine trying to hold a conversation with him. He's one of those people who just—" I threw my hands up in exasperation. "—ruins everything with his existence."

Blythe chuckled, reaching for the TV remote. "Sounds like you're overreacting."

"Me? No way," I shot back, sarcasm dripping from every word. I stared at her, silently wishing for the day to end already. The thought of running into Wells again twisted my stomach into knots, and the way my pulse quickened just thinking about it didn't help. I didn't want to deal with him, not now, not ever.

Suddenly, the back door opened and I froze. I could hear the faint shuffle of footsteps, then the sound of Wren laughing in the yard.

"Is that Wells?" I asked, my voice barely above a whisper.

Blythe peeked out the window. "It looks like he's outside with Wren."

"Are you really this worked up?" she asked, laughing. "Relax. If you're gonna survive living here, you're going to run into him every now and again. He doesn't leave the farm much, so you should be okay."

I slumped deeper into the couch, closing my eyes. "This is going to be hell on earth."

"Come on," Blythe said, nudging me. "It's just one guy. You're a grown woman. You can handle it. You've handled worse."

I let out a sigh, unsure whether I believed her or not. I'm over here trying to move on from the worst day of my life, and seeing Wells was a sharp reminder of what happened the morning before his massive body crammed into the airplane seat next to me.

"Hey, Bee, I'm leavin'!" His deep drawl cut through the air. Wells stepped into view, his presence as undeniable as the evening itself.

"Oh, hey, Sunshine. Didn't expect to see your smiling face again today."

That was it. If he called me *Sunshine* one more time, I was seriously considering decking him.

"I didn't want to see you again," I shot back.

He placed a hand over his heart, his face a picture of feigned injury. "Harsh."

Wells shook his head, a smile tugging at the corner of his mouth. "Anyways, I'm heading out." He placed a hand gently on Blythe's stomach. "See you soon, little dude." Wrapping Blythe in a warm hug, he added, "Is there anything I can bring for the party next weekend?"

Blythe thought for a moment before shaking her head. "I don't think so."

"If something comes to mind, just shoot me a text."

"I appreciate it."

He turned to me, a sly grin spreading across his face. "See you next Saturday, Sunshine."

With a light pat on my shoulder, his touch sent an involuntary shockwave through me—a jolt of repulsion that was anything but pleasant.

Wren's birthday party was next weekend. There went my plan to dodge the Orange Skittles aficionado.

The last week flew by. Between picking up extra shifts at the Coastal Cup and helping out at Sea Reads, the days blended together in a whirlwind. I couldn't remember the last time the days moved so fast—certainly not when Blythe and I were stuck in that drab little accounting department, counting down the minutes until we go free ourselves from the confines of those suffocating walls.

I set an alarm early to help Charlie and Blythe set up for Wren's birthday. By the time I made my way to the backyard, it was already buzzing with activity. Wren and Marsh were running around. Charlie was hanging up the string lights. Blythe was arranging the tables, her hands expertly folding napkins with a kind of grace that made everything look effortlessly perfect.

"Hey," Blythe called, flashing a smile as she straightened a centerpiece. "We're about to start on the balloons."

I jumped in to help, tying ribbons and arranging clusters of colorful balloons, all while trying to dodge the growing tension in my chest.

The weather was perfect—sunshine spilled across the sky without a cloud in sight. The kind of day that made you feel like everything was about to fall into place.

Except it wasn't. Wells just pulled into the driveway and was walking towards us. He was dressed casually, but somehow it still looked like he'd just stepped off the farm. A white t-shirt peeked out from beneath a navy button-down, the sleeves rolled up to his elbows, showing off his forearms. His cowboy hat was nowhere to be seen; instead, he wore a Coastal Cup baseball cap.

"Looks like you're all set," he called out, his voice warm and teasing as he got closer, three large boxes—undoubtedly gifts for Wren—in his arms.

I forced my attention back to the balloons I was adjusting, pretending I didn't notice the way his eyes lingered on me, like he had something more to say but was waiting for me to crack first.

"We're getting there," Blythe said, offering him a smile. "You're just in time to help with the cake."

Wells grinned. "I can't let anyone mess that up."

Charlie and Wells went into the house and returned carefully carrying the box with the sheet cake to the table.

"*That* was a two-man job?" I asked incredulously.

"Your niece would murder me in my sleep if I dropped this cake." Charlie quipped.

Wells went over to help Blythe with a banner and I stood there with Charlie.

"Need help with anything else?" I asked, trying to sound casual as I finished up a cluster of balloons.

Charlie looked over with a grin. "Maybe you can keep Wells from ruining the decorations this time. He thinks 'more is better'— he's already plotting his next disaster."

I rolled my eyes. "Literally anything else."

Charlie's eyes scanned the yard. "I think we're done."

As if on cue, Wells re-appeared at my side, his presence undeniable. "What's up, Sunshine?" His grin was wide, teasing, and I could already feel my patience wearing thin. But I forced a fake smile.

"Just making sure you don't ruin Wren's party." I shot back, my voice laced with just enough sarcasm to get under his skin.

"Out of all the things on my to do list today, ruining this party is not on it."

CHAPTER 14

HERE COMES THE SUN

Wells

ROSE HAD MANAGED TO AVOID ME FOR MOST OF THE AFTERNOON, seamlessly weaving through Blythe's friends while throwing the occasional death glare my way.

If looks could kill...

I had no clue what I'd done to deserve such loathing—whatever happened on that plane must have been catastrophic in her mind. Sure, she moved here fresh off a breakup, but all I did was try to be nice.

Lesson learned: next time, I'll just be an asshole and let the girl sitting next to me cry.

I turned my attention back to Marjorie, Charlie's mom, who is basically my second mother. She followed where my gaze was.

"Have you had a chance to meet Rose yet? She's a delight!"

I hooked a finger over my shoulder. "That girl? The blonde?"

"Yes!" Marjorie cupped her hands together. "Bee's best friend. She was a real hoot at the wedding. She also made me a mean dirty chai latte the other day."

"I've had the real pleasure of meeting her."

She bumped my shoulder, "You should go talk with her. She's single."

"I'm good in that department."

"You like being out on that farm of yours all alone too much. Your mom wanted you to take it over, she didn't want it to take over your life." She cocked a brow. "You're not getting any younger. Just sayin'!"

"Thank you for the vote of confidence."

"Go on, go talk to her." Marjorie pushed me over to the bench Rose was sitting on.

I lifted my hands up as I walked over to her.

Rose's lip curled in disgust. "What?"

"Only over here because Marjorie told me I needed to talk to you." I lowered my hands. "You don't even have to look in my direction. I'm just here so she doesn't yell at me."

"Scared of a five-foot-tall woman, are we?"

"More scared of the five-foot-seven one sitting in front of me." I answered honestly.

Rose looked past me. "How long are you obligated to be over here?"

"Best guess?" I lifted a shoulder. "Five minutes."

She lowered her sunglasses onto her face. "That's a long time."

"You have no idea." I shoved my hands in my front pockets.

"What's that supposed to mean?" She snapped.

Feisty.

"It's evident you hate my guts. Trust me, I don't want to be over here anymore than—"

"You're in the clear." She interrupted.

"What?"

"Marjorie just left." Rose stated plainly.

I turned to walk away.

"You should've just let me cry in peace on the plane."

"Noted." I called over my shoulder, not wanting to engage anymore.

I typed out a message to Charlie. Something I had been considering for the last few days.

Wells: Do you think it's a terrible idea?

Charlie: You've had worse.

Charlie: It's definitely not your best.

Charlie: I don't think it's gonna go over
well. She's got some thick walls built up.

A few years ago, I couldn't get this guy to send a single text.
Now, he's sending three in a row.

I sank into my favorite chair overlooking the wildflower field,
the place where my thoughts always seemed to settle. Ever since my
conversation with Marjorie last week, her words had been circling
in my mind. Inheriting the family farm had consumed every part of
my life, leaving little room for anything—or anyone—else. I tried to
remember the last time I'd been on a date. I searched my memory,
coming up empty. Years, I realized. It had been years.

Years of sitting out here alone. No soulmate. No family. Just me
and the land, stretching endlessly before me. Charlie and Blythe had
been my saving grace, but at the end of the day, when the sky turned
dusky pink and the crickets started to chirp, the loneliness settled
in my chest like an old friend. The days were long. The nights, even
longer. Not that I'd ever admit that to anyone.

My phone buzzed again, another message lighting up the screen.
I didn't need to check to know who it was.

For years, I told myself I was fine on my own. That the farm
was enough. That the rhythm of planting, growing, and harvesting
could fill the empty spaces in my life. But I wasn't so sure. Lately, I
found myself staring a little too long at the horizon, wondering what
else was out there for me.

I exhaled, raking a hand through my hair. Maybe Marjorie was
right. Maybe it was time to let someone in. Or maybe I'd just had
too much beer and was feeling sentimental. Either way, my fingers
hovered over the screen, heart pounding as I finally typed out a reply.

Charlie: But best of luck...

Wells: Can I have her number? I can't find her on social media.

Charlie: You didn't find her because she doesn't want to be found. She hates social media. Thinks it's the downfall of society.

Wells: I don't disagree.

Charlie: You're going to have to be a grown man and talk to her face-to-face.

Wells: She terrifies me.

Charlie: You're scared, but you're still going to proposition her?

Wells: Yes...

Charlie: Suit yourself. She'll be at the coffee shop tomorrow.

Charlie: I'm not involved in this. Whatever the deal is between the two of you, don't bring us into it.

I watched as the sun dipped below the clouds, setting the sky ablaze with hues of pink and orange. Nights like this always made me pause, made me feel like maybe—just maybe—my mom was out there somewhere, painting the horizon as her way of saying hello.

But as much as I loved the beauty of it, the sight always carried a sharp edge. A reminder of what was missing. She should be here, tending to the fields, making the farm thrive the way only she could. This was supposed to be hers. Instead, it was mine. And some days, I wasn't sure I'd ever be enough to fill the space she left behind.

I ran a hand over my face, leaning back in the chair as the last sliver of sun disappeared beyond the trees. No matter how many years passed, the weight of it never lessened—the responsibility, the legacy, the love woven into every inch of this land. My parents built this place with their bare hands, poured their whole hearts into it, and when it became mine, I vowed to do the same.

And I had.

Through early mornings and late nights, through storms that threatened to undo it all, through seasons of doubt and exhaustion, I gave everything I had to this farm. Because if I let it fall apart, it would feel like losing them all over again.

That was *not* going to happen.

I shook off the wallowing, wiped my hands on my jeans, and pushed myself up from the chair. No use sitting out here drowning in thoughts I couldn't change.

Tomorrow would bring a new battle and I was nowhere near ready. But ready or not, the sun would rise, the farm would call, and I'd show up.

I took a quick shower, scrubbing away the dirt and grime of the day before collapsing onto the bed. Exhaustion weighed heavy in my bones, but sleep remained just out of reach. I stared at the ceiling, willing it to come, but like most nights, it never did.

With a sigh, I flicked on the television, letting the familiar hum of a cooking show fill the quiet. When I was a kid, I used to fall asleep on my mom's lap watching these same shows, her fingers running through my hair as the soft voices of chefs filled the room. Back then, it felt safe. Comfortable. Now, it was just something to chase away the silence.

Granger let out a content sigh beside me, his warm body curled up against mine. My trusty sidekick. My only real companion. I reached over, scratching behind his ears as the host on the screen whisked something in a bowl, talking about patience.

Patience.

I huffed out a laugh. If there was one thing I was running out of, it was that.

CHAPTER 15

WHO'S AFRAID OF LITTLE OLD ME?

Rose

DON'T KNOW IF IT WAS THE SHEER EXHAUSTION FROM yesterday or some kind of miracle, but I'd had the best night of sleep in ages. The kind that left me feeling brand new, like I could take on the whole world and still have energy to spare before lunchtime.

By the time I made it downstairs, I was ready before Charlie and Blythe, which never happened. Usually, they were the early risers, already buzzing around with coffee in hand while I dragged myself into the day. But not today. Today, I was ahead of the game. A rare win for me.

Even the torrential downpour outside couldn't dampen my spirits. Rain lashed against the windows, thunder rumbled low in the distance, but inside, I felt nothing but light. Today was going to be a good day, I could feel it.

Blythe and I drove over to the Coastal Cup while Charlie took Wren to school, the steady rhythm of the rain tapping against the windshield. The streets were slick, the sky a heavy shade of gray, the kind of morning that made people want to stay curled up inside with a good book and a hot drink.

"I think it's going to be slow today," Blythe said, glancing out at the nearly empty sidewalks. "Tourist season is winding down, and this weather will keep people indoors."

"I'm okay with quiet," I admitted, stretching my arms. "Yesterday was absolute madness. A slow day sounds like a blessing."

She hummed in agreement as we pulled into the small lot. The cozy glow of the café lights spilled through the windows, promising warmth against the gloomy morning. Maybe it would be a slow day, but sometimes, those were the best ones.

The first two hours crawled by at a snail's pace. I spent most of it curled up on a stool behind the counter with my book, only setting it down when the occasional customer wandered in, ordering a coffee to escape the rain. The hum of the espresso machine and the patter of water against the windows was peaceful in a way I hadn't realized I needed.

I had no idea how much time had passed because I was completely absorbed in my book. Lately, romance had taken a backseat in my reading lineup. With everything that had happened, happily-ever-afters felt more exhausting than comforting. I was deep in my thriller era now—messy breakups, betrayals, and the occasional murder were more my speed. At least in fiction, heartbreak came with a plot twist.

The café door chimed, but I didn't look up, turning another page.

"So you're the bright and shining face the Wippowa folk are talking about."

My blood ran cold.

I didn't have to lift my eyes to know who that voice belonged to. I knew it too well. Knew the way it could crawl under my skin, the way it could unearth things I'd rather leave buried.

"What are you doing here?" I didn't look up right away, my voice sharp as I braced myself for whatever Wells had come to stir up this time.

He laughed, that same cocky smirk tugging at his lips. "What? A man can't support his best friend's thriving business?"

"Save it. What do you want?" I shot back, finally lifting my gaze to meet his. Wells stood there, dressed in what I could only describe as his uniform—a t-shirt, cowboy boots, and a baseball cap, as if he couldn't have looked more out of place in a coffee shop if he tried.

"This is a coffee shop, right?" His grin widened, the kind that made you wonder what he was up to.

"Sure is," I answered, trying to hold my ground.

"I'd like three shots of espresso, please."

I cocked a brow, looking down at the register. "So you have a death wish?"

Wells tilted his head, removing his baseball cap and running his fingers through his messy hair. "What?"

I gestured to the order screen. "That's a lot of caffeine."

His grin turned playful. "Aww, you care."

I gave a dry, humorless laugh. "I didn't say that. I'll happily serve you more if it means you get out of here quicker."

"Ah, that's the Rose I've come to know." Wells tapped his card to pay, his tone dripping with amusement. "It's funny. Everyone in this town thinks you're nice. You're a great actress."

I glared at him as I brewed his coffee. "You don't know the first damn thing about me." The nerve of him, acting like he had some insight into my life. He'd seen me cry on a plane for all of three seconds, and now he thought he could read me like an open book. The joke is on him because the walls I've put up are ten feet thick.

"You might be surprised. People talk 'round here."

I slid the small cup of espresso toward him, my hands gripped the edge of the counter.

"Thanks, Sunshine." Wells didn't move, just watched me as he picked up the cup.

I watched him take his seat at the nearest table, his massive frame blocking half my view. My patience was already wearing thin, and the last thing I needed was Wells Calloway adding to the noise in my head. I pulled my book back out and started reading, hoping the words on the page could shield me from the weight of his gaze.

But I could feel the steady burning of his eyes on me. It was like he was trying to read the very thoughts I was trying to hide. My breath hitched, and I refocused on the book, trying to block out the intrusive presence in my line of sight. The man had an uncanny way of making you feel like he was everywhere, even when you tried to pretend he wasn't.

I finally lost myself in the book enough that I forgot Wells was even still there, taking up too much space.

"Why are you still here?" I asked through gritted teeth, my patience fraying.

"Am I not allowed to sit and drink my coffee?" Wells placed his phone down on the table, his grin still there, like he had all the time in the world to get under my skin.

"No, because you're ruining my peace," I countered, never looking up from the pages.

Wells didn't respond, just kept scrolling on his phone like he hadn't heard a word I'd said.

"You don't have any social media." He stated plainly, trying to steer the conversation.

I could feel his eyes shift to me, but I ignored him.

"Are you really going to ignore me?"

I *really* was.

He pushed his chair back with a squeak, stood up and walked toward the counter. I let out a quiet sigh of relief, thinking he was finally going to leave me in peace. But then he leaned on the counter, his hands resting there as his gaze turned serious.

"For whatever it's worth," he said, his voice quieter now, "I wish I never said a word to you on the plane. I didn't know what you were going through."

I looked over my book at him, eyes narrowing. "You still don't."

He didn't move, didn't even flinch. Instead, he leaned in a little closer, like he had something important to say.

"Oh, but I do," Wells said, a glimmer of something—understanding? Sympathy?—in his voice.

I shook my head, the messy bun on top of my head shaking with it. "You're a liar."

Wells lifted a shoulder, nonchalant, like I wasn't shoving every wall I had up between us. "I know that you were basically engaged and he decided he didn't want to move here with you."

Hearing those words sliced through me like a fresh wound. It was too much. Still too raw.

He didn't stop. "I know you didn't really have a job when you lived out in Seattle. I also know that your favorite color is blue."

I froze, my breath catching in my throat. My eyes shot up at him. "How did you—?"

Wells smirked, the smug jerk. "Wren can't keep a secret to save her life; you know that."

I pushed the awful emotions threatening to resurface back down deep where they belonged. Swallowing hard against the lump in my throat, I forced myself to speak, my voice cold. "So what? You think you know me?"

Wells didn't flinch. There was a flash of something across his face, but it disappeared too quickly for me to place.

"Hell no," he said, his tone firm. "I do have a proposition for you, but I need you to let me talk and not bite my head off. You can say no when I'm done."

I didn't respond, I just stared at him, my gaze hard. I wasn't ready for whatever he was about to offer, but I wasn't going to give him the satisfaction of knowing that.

I remained silent, waiting.

"Let me start out with the fact that it's mutually beneficial," Wells said, his voice calm and measured.

I didn't even hesitate. "Are you looking for a friends-with-benefits situation? Because I am *not* that type of girl."

He shot me a look, the corner of his mouth twitching into a smirk. "What did I say about letting me talk?"

I narrowed my eyes, but didn't respond.

"Anyways," he continued, "I know you're in need of a place to live and work. I have a spare bedroom you can live in for free, but I need help around the farm. I also need help at the Sunday farmer's markets. If you could run the flower stand, I'll take care of the produce. You can keep all the money you make."

I couldn't help it. I literally laughed out loud. "I have a place to live and a job. I'd rather chew on broken glass than be around you."

Wells leaned back, his gaze never wavering. "You mean the same room that Blythe and Charlie are going to be turning into the baby's room?"

That hit me like a punch to the gut. I froze, every bit of blood in my body draining away. I hadn't even considered that they would need that room for Silas. Not for a second had I thought about what that would mean for me—what it would mean for the space I had come to call my own.

The world shifted beneath me as I felt that crushing pang of what could've been. The family. The husband. The life I thought I was building. I had imagined it all—vacations, children, that stupid white picket fence. Everything I thought I'd have within the next few years had slipped through my fingers a month ago, leaving nothing but an empty, aching void.

I could feel my chest tightening, that familiar sting creeping back into my eyes, but I fought it down.

"You should leave now," I said, my voice sharp, the words like daggers. I stood from behind the counter, hands clenched into fists at my sides. The cold fury in my eyes matched the heat bubbling under my skin.

Wells turned on his heel, his boots scraping against the floor as he started to walk away. "Can't say I didn't offer you an option," he called over his shoulder, his voice just a bit too casual, like he didn't have a care in the world.

I didn't watch him leave. Instead, I kept my eyes fixed on the counter, my fists still clenched at my sides, fighting the urge to throw something, anything, to shatter the tension in the room. His words hung in the air like a weight, the sting of them leaving an almost physical bruise on my chest.

CHAPTER 16

CHAMPAGNE PROBLEMS

Rose

BLYTHE NEVER BROUGHT UP THE CONVERSATION SHE HAD undoubtedly overheard between Wells and I at the coffee shop earlier this week. It was one of the things I appreciated most about her—she knew when to give me space.

A soft knock on my bedroom door pulled me from my thoughts.

"Come in," I called, barely shifting from my well-worn spot in bed.

The door cracked open, and Blythe's head peeked through. "Can I come in?" Before I could answer, her eyes flicked to the TV. "Oh. Bethany goes home."

I gasped. "You said you wouldn't watch without me."

She slid onto the bed beside me, stealing a handful of popcorn from my bowl. "It was on in the waiting room this morning. Not my fault. Total accident."

"Uh-huh," I muttered, but I let it slide. "What's up?"

She took a deep breath.

I groaned. "Oh no. That's the serious talk inhale."

Blythe kept her gaze locked on the screen. "We need to talk."

"About…?"

She twisted her hands in her lap. "This room."

I felt the shift in my stomach before she even said the words.

"We need to start moving Wren's things in here," she continued carefully. "She needs the bigger room. And we have to get the nursery set up."

Even though I'd known this conversation was inevitable, hearing it out loud hit me harder than I expected.

"I know," I said, swallowing against the lump in my throat. "Wells told me." I reached for her hand, giving it a squeeze. "I'll find a place. I've got enough saved to rent an apartment."

Her eyes softened, misty with unshed tears. "For what it's worth, I think it's a good idea."

I let my head fall to the side with a groan. "Blythe, no. You know I hate his guts."

She lifted a shoulder in a lazy shrug. "I didn't mean to overhear, but neither of you are exactly quiet." Another handful of popcorn. Another pause. "He's a good guy. Probably wouldn't even make you do much. Chivalry and all that shit."

Despite myself, I let out a small laugh. As much as Wells irritated the hell out of me, she wasn't entirely wrong. He seemed like a shirt-off-his-back kind of guy.

Blythe nudged me. "What do you even have against him?"

I scoffed. "I asked him to leave me alone, and he persisted."

She raised an eyebrow. "So let me get this straight. You're mad because someone actually gave a damn about you?"

I opened my mouth, then snapped it shut. Damn her and her logic.

I groaned, dragging my hands down my face. "When you say it like that, you make me sound ridiculous."

Blythe shrugged, her expression smug as she tossed another piece of popcorn into her mouth. "I'm just saying. You're over here sulking when you've got a solid option staring you in the face. Wells isn't the worst thing to ever happen to you."

"He's annoying," I muttered.

"He's a *man*," she corrected. "They're all annoying."

I snorted, despite myself. "Fair point."

Blythe squeezed my hand. "Look, I know this isn't what you wanted. I know you had a different plan for your life, and it sucks that it fell apart the way it did. But you're still standing, Rose. And maybe—just *maybe*—this could be a fresh start."

I exhaled slowly, staring at the ceiling. A fresh start. That's what everyone kept saying. Like it was so easy. Like I could just shed my past like an old coat and slip into a new one.

But the truth was, I had nowhere else to go. And as much as I hated to admit it, Wells' offer was the best one on the table.

"I hate you for being right," I mumbled.

Blythe grinned. "I know. But you'll thank me when you're selling out that flower stand every Sunday."

I rolled onto my side, groaning. "I need copious amounts of wine before I agree to anything."

Blythe just laughed, "Take your time. But not too much, because I have a baby to prepare for, and you need a new address."

"Thanks for always being there for me. I love you, Bee." My voice was barely above a whisper, thick with emotion.

Blythe squeezed my hand. "I love you, too." She paused, giving me a knowing look. "And I'm not kicking you out. I just… I want you to start putting some roots down."

I swallowed hard, nodding. As much as I hated to admit it, she was right. I'd been floating—untethered, afraid to land. Maybe it was time to figure out where I actually belonged.

Blythe gave my hand one last squeeze before standing. "I'll let you think about it." She offered me a small smile before heading toward the door.

I nodded but didn't say anything, watching as she slipped out, leaving me alone with the weight of my own thoughts. The soft click of the door shutting felt heavier than it should have, like a chapter of my life was quietly closing behind me.

I pulled my knees to my chest and stared at the blank wall across the room. The same four walls I'd woken up to for the past few weeks were temporary and borrowed.

I traced an invisible line on the comforter, my mind wandering through the maze of choices that had led me here. If I had stayed in Seattle, would Thad had wanted me enough? Would I be engaged by now? Would we be planning for a future instead of me scrambling to find a new place to land?

A bitter laugh escaped me. That life didn't exist. It never had.

And now, I had a choice to make.

I could take the safe route: find an apartment, keep my head down, pretend I was fine. Or, I could take Wells up on his ridiculous offer.

I groaned, rubbing my hands over my face. Living with him? Working with him? The man had been a thorn in my side since the moment he sat next to me on that plane.

But as much as I hated to admit it, part of me wondered... if I wasn't so afraid of getting hurt again, would I already have said yes?

It was all laid out for me on a silver platter. A place to live. No rent. More money than I made at Coastal Cup.

Logically, it made sense. It was the smart choice. The practical choice.

So why did the idea of saying yes make my chest feel tight?

I stared at the wall, my mind waging war with itself. Accepting Wells' offer meant more than just a roof over my head. It meant stepping into a life I hadn't planned for. A life that, no matter how much I wanted to ignore it, would be tangled up with him.

I sighed, flopping back onto the bed and staring at the ceiling. Maybe it wasn't about the offer itself. Maybe it was about what saying yes would mean.

Surrendering. Admitting I needed help. And worst of all, letting Wells be the one to give it to me.

I slithered out of bed and made my way downstairs.

"I'm going out for a walk." I called out, not sure of who was there.

The door clicked behind me and the cooler evening air brushed against my face. I rolled my neck and started down the path towards the main road.

"Auntie Rose, where are you going?" I heard Wren call before running towards me.

I turned towards her and threw a fake smile on my face, "I'm going for a little walk."

"Can I come with you?" her eyes were big.

My heart softened. "Of course you can. Just go tell your parents so they're not looking for you."

"Dad!" Wren screeched. "I'm going on a walk with Auntie."

"Kay!" Charlie called back.

Wren gripped my hand and we walked down the gravel path together, her small fingers wrapped tightly around mine. The rhythmic crunch of our steps filled the quiet space between us, the cool evening air carrying the scent of rain-soaked earth and salt from the nearby marsh.

"Where are we walking to?" Wren asked, swinging our hands back and forth.

"Nowhere in particular," I admitted. "Just needed some fresh air."

She hummed thoughtfully, her gaze drifting up to the sky. "Mom says when she needs fresh air, it's because she has too many thoughts in her head."

I huffed a small laugh. "Your mom is a very smart woman."

Wren nodded sagely, then looked up at me. "What are you thinking about?"

I hesitated, staring at the darkening horizon. How could I explain everything running through my mind without making her worry? The weight of my next decision, the fear of change, the unresolved tension between me and Wells—none of it was something a little girl should carry.

"Grown-up stuff," I finally said.

Wren wrinkled her nose. "That sounds boring."

I smiled. "It is."

We walked in silence for a few more moments before she spoke again. "Are you sad?"

The question hit me like a gut punch.

I swallowed hard and forced another smile. "I'll be okay."

She squeezed my hand, her little face serious. "You always take care of me, so I'll take care of you."

My throat tightened, emotions threatening to break through the surface. "That's not your job, kiddo," I whispered.

But as we walked down that quiet road together, hand in hand, I realized something—maybe I didn't have to do everything alone.

As soon as we stepped back into the house, I spotted Blythe folding clothes on the couch. I didn't hesitate.

"I need Wells' phone number."

Her hands stilled, and she slowly lifted her gaze, amusement flickering in her eyes. "Oh?"

I exhaled sharply. "Please don't make this a thing."

A smirk tugged at the corner of her lips. "Too late."

"Blythe."

She held up her hands in mock surrender, but the teasing glint remained. "Alright, alright. I'll send it." She tapped away on her phone, and a second later, mine buzzed in my pocket.

I stared at the screen, my thumb hovering over his number.

Blythe tilted her head. "So, are you gonna call him?"

I swallowed hard. "I don't know."

But we both knew I wouldn't have asked if I wasn't already considering it.

CHAPTER 17

THINKING 'BOUT YOU

Wells

It's been nine days since I walked into the Coastal Cup and asked Rose to move in with me, to help out on the farm. Looking back, I probably should've heeded Charlie's warning and left well enough alone. He's always telling me I stick my neck out for people, and it always comes back to bite me.

"Granger, come on!" I called, watching as my black lab darted through the field—his favorite pastime. He came bounding toward me, tongue lolling, just as I stepped onto the back porch.

I leaned against the railing, eyes fixed on the fields stretching wide beneath the evening sky. The sun dipped low, spilling gold across the fruit trees, and for a moment, everything was quiet.

My phone buzzed in my pocket. I pulled it out, eyeing an unfamiliar number on the screen. Probably spam. With a sigh, I pressed decline and shoved it back where it came from.

Lowering myself into the old rocking chair—my father's chair—I let the familiar creak of the wood settle around me. My thoughts drifted to Rose. To the mess she'd found herself in. When my life got turned upside down, at least I had a roof over my head and work to keep me going. She had nothing but bad news and no warning.

The phone buzzed again. Same number. I exhaled sharply and hit decline. Whatever it was, it could wait. I wasn't in the mood for small talk—especially not from someone trying to sell me an extended warranty on my truck.

Granger flopped down beside me with a satisfied huff, his head resting on my boot. The evening air was thick with the scent of earth and ripe fruit, the kind of smell that settled deep in your chest and made you feel like you belonged to the land. I rocked back and forth, my gaze fixed on the horizon, where the last streaks of sunlight melted into the trees.

Then, my phone buzzed again.

I let out a slow breath, gripping the worn arm of the chair. Whoever it was, they were persistent. A nagging feeling crawled up my spine, the kind you get when something isn't quite right.

This time, I answered.

"Take your extended warranty and shove it up your ass."

Silence, then a hesitant breath.

"Wells?"

The voice was soft, uncertain. But I knew it. My stomach tightened.

"Sunshine?"

"Yeah, it's me." Rose's voice was quiet—softer than I'd ever heard it before. A stark contrast to every conversation we had up until now.

"I was just thinkin' about you," I admitted.

"You were?" She sounded surprised, like that was the last thing she expected me to say.

"Yeah." I kept my tone light. "Was about to head inside and have some orange Skittles."

"That's disgusting. Forget I called."

"Don't be so sensitive about the color of my candy, Rose." I paused, something clicking in my head. "Wait, I didn't give you my number."

"You didn't," she admitted. "Blythe did."

"Ah."

A beat of silence stretched between us before she spoke again, her voice edged with hesitation. "I've been thinking about your proposition."

"My *very* generous offer," I corrected.

"Can you just let me finish?"

I smirked. "Now you know how it feels."

"I'm trying to swallow my pride here, alright?"

There was a beat of silence, like she was weighing every word.

"I'm taking you up on your offer."

I sat up straighter, the chair creaking beneath me. My stomach knotted. When I made the offer, I never actually thought she'd accept.

"Is that so?"

"Yes." Her voice was steady, but I caught the hint of uncertainty tucked beneath it. "Although you should know… I have a black thumb. Anything green I touch dies."

A slow smile tugged at the corner of my mouth. "Good news for you, these plants are damn near impossible to kill. Believe it or not, things that grow outside are a lot tougher than the fragile little plants you kept in that apartment of yours."

"Is that your way of calling me fragile?"

"Maybe."

"You're an asshole, Calloway."

"You'll grow to like me."

"Not so sure about that," she shot back, sounding more like the Rose I met on the plane—sharp, quick-witted.

I wasn't sure how to move on from here. "You like dogs, right?"

"Yeah. More than people."

I let out a soft chuckle. "Me too."

Silence stretched between us, long enough that I glanced at my phone to make sure she hadn't hung up.

"When are you thinking about moving in?" I finally asked.

"I'll pack this weekend and move in next weekend. The girl I was filling in for at the Coastal Cup comes back Friday."

My mind raced. I had a hell of a lot of cleaning up to do before then.

"Yeah, that works."

"Alright," she said, and I could hear the uncertainty in her voice. "Guess I'll see you next weekend then."

"Guess so."

More silence. I could practically hear her second-guessing this whole thing.

"You having doubts already, Sunshine?"

"No," she said quickly, then sighed. "Maybe. It's just… a lot."

"Yeah," I admitted. "It is."

I heard her shift, the sound of fabric rustling like she was lying back on a couch or bed. "Are you sure about this?"

I frowned. "Wouldn't have offered if I wasn't."

Another pause, then a soft exhale. "Okay."

That one word held more weight than I expected.

"Get some rest, Rose," I said, keeping my voice even. "You'll need it before moving onto a farm."

She let out a quiet laugh. "God help me."

The call ended, leaving me sitting there in the dark, Granger snoring softly at my feet.

I stared out at the fields, my mind still catching up to what just happened.

Rose Solace was actually moving in.

CHAPTER 18

I KNOW IT WON'T WORK

Rose

MOVING INTO WELLS CALLOWAY'S HOUSE MIGHT BE THE stupidest thing I've ever done. Considering my track record, that's saying something.

I stare at the half-packed suitcases on my bed, hands on my hips, willing them to pack themselves. If I hesitate long enough, maybe the universe will intervene—send a sign, a sudden change of plans, anything to get me out of this ridiculous arrangement. But nothing happens, so I shove another dress inside and zip it shut.

The reality is, I don't have a better option. Not yet.

The Coastal Cup gig was temporary, and the savings I have won't stretch far. I'll do this for a while—play house on the farm, save up, and then get the hell out before Wells realizes what a mistake he's made.

The morning of the move has come way too fast. Between shifts at the Coastal Cup, helping with inventory at Sea Reads, and packing, the week disappeared in a blur.

Charlie's truck is once again packed to the brim, every inch crammed with my too-many clothes and just-enough belongings.

"You ready to head over?" Blythe called from the front porch.

I shake my head. "I think I've changed my mind." I turn toward the truck bed, fully prepared to start unloading, but Charlie steps in front of me, arms crossed.

Blythe makes her way over, her expression warm but unwavering. "It's going to be so much better than you think," she says. "You'll learn new things. You won't kill plants—"

"This feels like a college drop-off," I interrupt, exhaling sharply. "You two are giving me a pep talk like my parents did."

Blythe just smiled, wrapping me in a hug.

"Are you sure you can't come?" I ask, even though I already know the answer.

"You know I can't. I have the book signing at Sea Reads. I need to head over there now." She squeezed me tighter. "Text me tonight when you're settled, okay?"

I nod, resting my head against her shoulder. "Love you."

"Love you too, Rose." Then, lowering her voice just for me, she adds, "This is going to be good for you. You might even be surprised. Wells isn't the bad guy you make him out to be."

I scoff. "We'll see about that."

"Ready to hit the road?" Charlie called from the driver's seat.

With one last squeeze, I pull away from Blythe and climb into the truck. As we drive away, I watch the house fade from view, my stomach twisting with nerves.

The drive is quiet, except for the hum of the radio and the buzz of my own restless energy. Charlie and I sit in silence until he finally turns the volume down and glances my way.

"I promise he's a good guy, Rose," he says, his voice steady. "When Wren's mom skipped town, Wells was the first one at my door. He helped me for weeks—watched Wren so I could work, made sure we had what we needed. When I didn't think we'd make ends meet, he offered us money. His heart is bigger than it should be. Every time he puts his neck out for someone, he always gets burned."

I swallow hard, staring out the window as the somewhat familiar backroads blur past.

Maybe Wells Calloway isn't the villain I've made him out to be. But that doesn't mean this is a good idea.

When we pull up, Wells is already waiting on the porch, leaning against the railing with that lazy confidence he always carries. A dog is at his feet, ears perked up, tail wagging.

Charlie threw the truck into park and hopped out like he's coming home from a long trip. "Calloway," he greeted with a nod.

Wells stepped down from the porch, his usual slow, confident stride in place. "Charles."

There's a pause before Charlie grinned and pulled Wells into one of those back-slapping bro hugs.

"You finally talked her into it, huh?" Wells asked, nodding toward me.

Charlie smirked. "She's still convinced this is the worst decision of her life."

"I'm standing right here!" I threw my hands up.

"Didn't think you'd actually show," he called over to me.

"Neither did I," I mutter, stretching my stiff limbs.

Wells' gaze slid to mine. "Give it a few weeks. You'll never wanna leave."

I roll my eyes. "Let's just get this over with."

The guys start unloading the truck, hauling my overstuffed suitcases toward the house. I should be helping, but instead, I linger outside, gravitating toward the only living being here that doesn't immediately test my patience—the dog.

The black lab trots over, sniffing at my shoes before pressing his whole weight against my legs, like he's decided we're best friends. I crouch down, scratching behind his ears. "At least *you* seem happy to have me here."

"That's Granger." Wells said in passing as he carried one of my suitcases inside.

Granger let out a satisfied huff and flopped onto the grass, rolling onto his back for belly rubs. I oblige, because honestly? This is better than standing around, making awkward conversation with Wells while he drags my possessions inside.

The sun is warm on my skin, the quiet stretch of land around me open and endless. It should be peaceful. But instead, my chest feels tight, like I'm standing at the edge of something I can't quite name.

A door creaks open behind me.

"You plan on helping?"

I glance over my shoulder to find Wells leaning against the porch railing, arms crossed, smirking.

I pat Granger's belly one last time and rise to my feet. "Pretty sure you and Charlie have it handled."

Wells shakes his head, but there's something almost amused in his expression. "Come on, Sunshine. Let's get you settled."

With a sigh, I follow him inside, already counting down the days until I can leave.

The house is way nicer than I had expected. Not that I had any preconceived notions or anything like that, but Wells struck me as the type of guy whose house wasn't the neatest. Man, was he going to regret having me here. My parents always joked that I was a cyclone, making a mess in every room I went into. Which, judging by my college dorm, they weren't wrong.

The inside of the farmhouse is the perfect blend of modern simplicity and rustic charm. The walls are painted in a soft, pale gray that catches the natural light filtering through the large windows, giving the space an open and airy feel. The ceilings are high, with exposed wooden beams that add just the right amount of warmth against the cool-toned walls.

The kitchen is sleek but inviting—white shaker-style cabinets line the walls, their crisp finish contrasting against the rich, dark oak floors. Butcher block countertops stretch across the counters, their smooth, honeyed wood grain showing years of careful maintenance. A farmhouse sink sits beneath a window that overlooks the vast pastures, and open shelving displays neatly stacked dishes and glass jars filled with dry goods.

In the living area, a stone fireplace is the focal point, its gray and white tones blending seamlessly with the rest of the house. A worn dark leather couch faces it. The dark oak floors ground the space, their deep, weathered hues adding contrast to the light walls and cabinets.

The entire house carries the scent of fresh wood and coffee, a mix of earthy and comforting.

With this level of attention to detail, it was clear this was the work of a woman's touch—not Wells' doing. I could see why Wren enjoyed it here—it was undeniably homey.

This place was almost cozier than Blythe and Charlie's…not that I would *ever* tell them that.

Charlie spoke up after we returned to the kitchen from our little tour of the first floor. "I'm gonna head out." He looked at me. "You good?"

I nodded slowly, my eyes falling. No matter how nice this place was, it wasn't my home—it would never *be* my home—and that stung.

Not to mention I was going to have to live with my sworn mortal enemy. Maybe that was a bit of an overstatement.

Charlie left and the tension in the room was palpable.

"So…" Wells shoved his hands in his front pockets. "I can show you to your room." It was a statement but it came out more like a question.

My eyes didn't meet his. "That'd be great."

Wells started up the stairs and I followed closely behind while Granger wove in between us to get to the top first.

"Your room's across the hall from mine," Wells said as he pushed open the door to a guest room.

It's simple—plain furniture, fresh sheets, a window overlooking the pastures. It doesn't feel like mine. Because it isn't.

I set my bag on the bed, glancing toward the hall.

Across from his. Yeah, this won't work.

I'll stay long enough to get on my feet, save what I can, and then move back home where I belong. Where things make sense.

Because whatever this is—whatever *he* is—none of it makes sense at all.

CHAPTER 19

RIGHT WHERE YOU LEFT ME

Wells

I WATCHED AS ROSE TOOK IN HER ROOM, HER GAZE SWEEPING over the space. I wondered if she silently judged the overly floral comforter on the bed—she didn't strike me as the type who'd appreciate pink roses and ruffled edges. It was the only one I could find in the closet where my mom stashed the extra linens.

A flicker of sadness crossed her face. This wasn't what she wanted. I didn't know the full story, but Wren had mentioned an ex-boyfriend who was supposed to move here with her. I could only imagine how badly that had screwed up her plans—and how much it had messed her up. Was that why she cried on the plane? Had it happened that day?

What a dick.

"The bathroom's right there." I nodded toward the door beside mine. "It's all yours. I won't go in."

Her eyes met mine briefly. "Thanks."

"There are towels in the linen closet. Take whatever you need."

"I appreciate it."

"Want me to put 'em on your bed?" I gestured toward her suitcases.

Rose rolled her eyes. "Your accent is going to get old really fast."

"Ain't much we can do about that, eh, Sunshine?"

"Stop calling me that," she muttered through gritted teeth, dropping to her knees to unzip a suitcase.

I smirked. "Dinner will be ready soon." Then I pulled the door shut behind me and headed downstairs.

In the kitchen, I grabbed a cutting board and laid out the steaks. Then it hit me.

Shit. Does she even eat meat?

I pulled out my phone and fired off a text.

Wells: Do you like steak?

Rose: Yes.

Good. One less thing to worry about.

I resumed my prep, sliding the baked potatoes into the oven before stepping outside to fire up the grill. The scent of charcoal and salt-kissed air mixed as I laid the steaks over the flames, the sizzle breaking the quiet. I tossed on a handful of fresh vegetables from today's haul, the colors vibrant against the heat.

As the steaks seared, I leaned against the porch railing, watching the last light fade over the fields. The quiet hum of crickets filled the air, blending with the distant sound of waves rolling onto the shore. Wippowa had a way of settling into a person—slow and steady, just like the tide.

I flipped the steaks, the smoky aroma curling up around me. Inside, I heard faint movement—Rose unpacking, probably trying to make sense of this place, this situation.

A timer chimed from the kitchen. I pulled the potatoes from the oven, their crisped skins giving under the press of my thumb. I grabbed plates and cups out of the cabinet and set the table. I stepped back and looked at the table, it was weird seeing two place settings. Something I knew not to get used to because I don't think Rose will last long.

A good meal wouldn't fix everything, but it was something. A small peace offering.

I made my way back upstairs and paused at her door. The movement had stopped and all I could hear were sniffles. Rose was crying.

I exhaled slowly, my hand hovering over her door. Knocking felt like an intrusion but ignoring it didn't sit right either.

She hadn't asked to be here. Hadn't wanted to start over in a strange place with someone I didn't really know. Whatever happened before she landed in Wippowa had cracked something deep, and now she was trying to hold the pieces together.

I left her be and texted her to let her know there was food when she was ready.

Back in the kitchen, I wrapped up her plate and set it aside in case she decided to come down. I sank into my chair, my own plate waiting where it belonged, the table looking as it always had.

Just me.

The quiet stretched around me, familiar and steady. I ate, savoring the stillness, knowing it wouldn't last.

The rhythmic scrape of my fork against the plate was the only sound in the house. I took my time, letting the quiet settle around me like an old habit.

By the time I finished eating, the house felt even emptier. I rinsed my plate and placed in the dishwasher—another routine, another piece of normalcy. But when I glanced at the wrapped plate on the counter, a nagging thought tugged at me.

Would she come down?

I doubted it.

Still, I left the kitchen light on as I made my way upstairs. Her door was still shut, and the house had gone silent again. I hesitated for a second, then shook my head and kept walking.

She didn't need me prying.

Back in my room, I stretched out on the bed, staring at the ceiling. Wippowa nights were slow, the kind that made you sit with your thoughts whether you wanted to or not.

And right now, mine kept circling back to the combative woman down the hall.

I showered and settled onto the couch with a new book, letting the dim light and quiet wrap around me. For the first time all day, peace. I lost track of time until I heard the familiar click of a door.

Glancing toward the stairs, I caught sight of Rose easing the bedroom door shut behind her. I turned back to my book, feigning disinterest.

She moved carefully down the stairs, light on her feet, as if trying not to make a sound. Granger stirred from his spot beside me, stretching before padding after her into the kitchen.

"Oh, hey, buddy," she murmured, her voice carrying a soft sadness. I heard the jingle of his collar. "Did your dad spit in my food?"

I smothered a laugh.

"Probably." She answered her own question.

The rustle of aluminum foil reached me as she unwrapped the plate. A beat of silence. Then—

"Mmm."

Good sign.

I listened as she fumbled around the kitchen, stubbornly refusing to turn on a light.

"Where are the stupid knives in this place?"

I rolled my eyes. She really was something else. Sighing, I dog-eared my page and pushed off the couch.

The moment I flicked on the light, Rose gasped, clutching her chest as she stumbled back.

"Holy shit!" she hissed. "Are you crazy?"

Leaning against the doorframe, I met her wide eyes. "Probably."

She straightened, exhaling sharply.

"Knives are in the first drawer on the left," I said, nodding toward the island before turning back toward the couch.

Behind me, I heard the drawer slide open, the clink of metal as she grabbed what she needed. Then the soft hum of the microwave. When she finally sat at the kitchen table, I hesitated, unsure if I should join her.

Silence stretched between us, punctuated only by the occasional scrape of her fork against the plate.

"You didn't tell me dinner was ready," she muttered through the wall between us, an edge still clinging to her voice.

"Check your phone."

A pause. Then, a quiet, "Oh."

I shrugged, eyes on my book. "Didn't know if you'd be eating or not."

Another pause. Then, softer—"Thank you."

I needed help on this farm. If giving Rose space was the way to get it, I'd take that trade.

I let the quiet settle again, flipping a page without really reading it. In the kitchen, Rose ate in slow bites, her fork barely scraping against the plate now. Granger had curled up at her feet, his tail thumping lazily against the floor every so often.

I quietly leaned so I could see around the wall and glanced at her, just for a second. Her shoulders weren't as tense as before. That was something.

The wind rattled against the windowpanes, the old house creaking in response. The storm was still rolling in, thick clouds swallowing the moonlight.

"Does it always sound like the house is about to fall apart?" she asked, her voice quieter now.

"Only when it storms."

Rose huffed. "That's comforting."

I smirked, eyes flicking back to my book. "Takes a lot more than wind to bring this place down."

She didn't respond, just took another bite. I could tell she was winding down, the exhaustion catching up to her.

Rose had a long day ahead of her tomorrow and I don't think she was the least bit prepared.

CHAPTER 20

COWBOY LIKE ME

Rose

SWALLOWED THE LAST BITE OF FOOD, SITTING IN SILENCE AS
I let the flavors settle. I had to give it to Wells—he knew how
to cook. My own kitchen skills never developed past the basics.
I was a master of cereal assembly and takeout orders. My parents
used to joke that the only thing I could make was a reservation and
that still holds true.

Scraping my plate into the trash, I rinsed it before tucking it
into the dishwasher. Then, with a deep inhale, I made my way into
the living room. Wells was still on the couch, nose buried in a book.
I tried to make out the title, but the cover was just out of sight.

"Thanks again for dinner." My voice was quiet, reluctant.

"Not a problem. I like cooking." He set the book down, meeting my gaze. "You don't have to hide in your room, y'know. You can
use the house however you'd like."

"I know," I snapped. "We're not friends."

His expression didn't change. "I'm painfully aware." He leaned
back against the couch. "Think of this like a dorm. Just two people
working together who happen to live across the hall."

I bit the inside of my cheek. I didn't want Wells as a friend.
He'd seen me at my lowest, and the embarrassment still sat heavy

in my chest. It was easier to keep my walls up than to try to make peace. Just looking at him reminded me of the worst day of my life.

"Fine," I muttered. "And there will be no funny business."

His brows lifted. "Definitely no funny business." He raised his hands in mock surrender. "Look, I don't know you, but I'm not a bad guy. I just need help on this damn farm. It's too much for one person."

My eyes narrowed. "What time should I set my alarm?"

A smirk tugged at the corner of his mouth. "5:15."

I gasped at him. "I didn't know that when I agreed to this."

"You live on a farm now, Sunshine. We're up before the sun."

I spun on my heel. "This was a horrible idea," I muttered, stalking toward the stairs.

Behind me, Wells let out a low, smug laugh.

Up in my room, I shut the door. I stripped out of my shorts and tank top, swapping them for pajamas before clicking on the television for background noise. Anything to drown out my thoughts.

After Wells showed me to my room earlier, I lost it.

This wasn't the life I wanted. I should've been settling into a beautiful new apartment with Thad, not living in some random guy's spare bedroom. I should've been waking up next to someone who loved me, not feeling like I'd been cast aside. I wanted to feel adored—not be told I was hard to love. But those words stuck to me like a stain I couldn't scrub away.

I shook the thought off and rummaged through my bag, laying out clothes for the morning. Workout shorts and a tank top—good enough. Blythe swore I wouldn't have to do much work.

I set my alarm for 5:15 and groaned. It was already close to eleven, which meant I'd be lucky to get six hours of sleep.

Crawling into bed, I rolled onto my side and stared out the window. The pastures stretched endlessly, bathed in the soft glow of the moon. It was beautiful.

This wasn't my bed.

This wasn't my room.

I wasn't even in a house I felt comfortable in. I was a stranger, stuck in the dumbest arrangement I'd ever agreed to.

How the hell was I supposed to live and work with Wells when I hated him for witnessing me at rock bottom? I knew Blythe was right—I had to get over it. But I just couldn't. Not yet.

I tossed and turned for hours, my mind restless. The last time I glanced at the clock, it was close to three.

When the alarm blared, I groaned, slapping it off and rolling over.

Just another half hour…

A loud knock rattled my door fifteen minutes later.

"Sunshine, you up in there?"

Wells' voice, first thing in the morning, made me want to stab my eardrums with an icepick.

"No," I grumbled, tossing the covers over my head.

"Wrong answer." I could hear the grin in his voice when he answered.

"No one should be awake at this hour."

"If you're not dressed and downstairs in ten minutes, I'm sending Granger in to get you moving."

I threw the covers off my head with a groan. "Ugh!"

From the other side of the door, Wells chuckled. "See you soon."

I waited until I heard the creak of the stairs before sitting up. The coast was clear.

Dragging myself out of bed, I changed into my first-day-on-the-job outfit, washed up, and headed downstairs twenty minutes later.

The house was quiet. Too quiet.

I checked the living room. Empty. Peered into the office. No sign of him. Even the kitchen was deserted—until my eyes landed on a fresh cup of coffee sitting on the counter with a note.

Morning, Sunshine.
- W

I picked up the cup and took a sip, the warmth spreading through my body like the first real sign of life. Maybe I hated him slightly less now.

Movement outside caught my eye. Through the window over the sink, I spotted Wells out in the yard, tossing a ball for Granger. The sun was still tucked behind the horizon, but a soft, silver light stretched over the fields.

I sighed. No more stalling. Time to get out there.

Sliding on my flip-flops, I stepped outside, the morning air cool against my skin.

Wells turned as I approached, his eyes scanning me from head to toe. His brows shot up. "What in the hell are you wearing?"

I glanced down at myself. "Clothes?"

He let out a slow exhale, shaking his head. "Yeah, that won't work."

I balled my fists defensively. "What do you mean, 'that won't work'?"

Wells crossed his arms, looking me over like I was some kind of lost cause. "Sunshine, you're wearin' flip-flops and somethin' that looks more suited for yoga than farm work."

I put my hands on my hips. "Well, forgive me for not having a closet full of cowboy couture."

He smirked. "Yeah, we're gonna have to fix that."

I narrowed my eyes. "Fix it how?"

"Trip to town," he said simply. "Boots, jeans, work shirts—the whole deal. Unless you'd rather step in goat shit with those flip-flops."

I glanced down at my feet and wiggled my toes. Not exactly ideal farm gear.

"Fine," I muttered. "But you're paying."

Wells snorted. "Nice try. You agreed to work here. That means dressing the part."

I huffed but didn't argue. There was no winning with him.

"I'll level with you—I'll buy your boots, but everything else is on you."

I rolled my eyes. *Generous.*

Wells tipped his head toward the truck. "Let's go."

I folded my arms. "It's six-thirty in the morning. Nothing is even open yet."

He smirked. "I know a guy who sells boots."

"I'm not wearing cowboy boots."

"Blythe has them." He countered.

"I don't care."

"Suit yourself. But don't come crying to me when you step in shit."

I opened my mouth to argue but thought better of it. With a sigh, I climbed into the passenger seat, while Granger leapt into the back, tail wagging like this was the best thing to ever happen to him.

As Wells started the truck, I glanced over. He looked perfectly at ease, one hand on the wheel, the early morning sun casting a light over his face.

This was going to be a long damn day.

As Wells pulled down the gravel path, I noticed him grab his phone and type out a quick text.

"To your boot guy?" I asked, raising an eyebrow.

He smirked but didn't look over. "Something like that."

Suspicious. But I let it go, watching as the darkened countryside blurred past the window.

The drive was quiet for a while, only the low hum of the radio and the occasional thump of Granger shifting in the backseat. The sun had barely started stretching across the sky, turning the horizon a soft peach. I stifled a yawn and folded my arms.

"This is cruel, you know," I muttered. "Forcing someone to function at this ungodly hour."

"Not everyone lives on city girl hours." Wells shot back.

I turned my head toward him. "For your information, my hours were perfectly fine before I moved here."

He didn't flinch, just kept his eyes on the road. "Might do you some good. Early mornings build character."

I scoffed. "So does sleeping in."

Wells just chuckled, shaking his head like I was hopeless.

Ten minutes later, we pulled into a gravel lot beside a squat building with an old wooden sign that read Brett's Boots & Western Goods. A few rusted-out trucks were parked along the side, and a large German Shepherd lay sprawled across the front porch, tail flicking lazily.

"Of course you know a guy who sells boots," I mumbled, stepping out of the truck. The moment my flip-flops hit the gravel, I winced.

"Watch your step," Wells said with an amused drawl.

I shot him a glare as we walked up to the shop. The old wooden door creaked open, and inside, the air smelled like leather and sawdust. Rows of boots lined the walls, along with belts, hats, and other cowboy essentials I had zero intention of ever wearing.

Behind the counter stood a tall, broad-shouldered guy in his early forties, arms crossed over his chest. He had the same rugged look as Wells—minus the smugness.

"Well, well," the man drawled. "Wells Calloway in my store at seven in the morning. Must be important." His gaze flicked to me, amusement tugging at his lips. "And I assume this is the city girl you texted me about?"

I turned sharply to Wells. "You texted about me?"

Wells just grinned. "Brett, meet Rose. Rose, meet Brett. He's got the best boots in town."

Brett gave me a nod. "Pleasure."

"Likewise." I huffed, crossing my arms. "Let's just get this over with."

Brett chuckled, stepping out from behind the counter. "Alright, sweetheart, let's find you some boots before you break an ankle."

I muttered something under my breath about how dramatic cowboys were, but I followed him toward the endless rows of boots.

This was already shaping up to be *way* too much for this hour.

CHAPTER 21

BOOTS

Wells

WATCHING BRETT HELP ROSE WAS EXACTLY WHAT I NEEDED this morning—a solid dose of entertainment.

I hadn't slept well last night, tossed and turned for hours. Maybe it was having someone else in my house, or maybe it was just knowing she was down the hall, shaking up my usual routine. Either way, I was running on caffeine and the sheer joy of watching Rose try to pick out a pair of cowboy boots.

"These are all hideous," she announced, holding up a pair of red boots with intricate stitching like they personally offended her. "Are you absolutely sure I can't just wear my sneakers?"

Brett snorted. "Not if you wanna survive out here."

I bit back a laugh as she scowled at the rows of boots like they were some kind of personal betrayal.

"You're gonna need something with grip, city girl. Trust me, you don't want to be out on the farm in those fancy little shoes of yours." Brett responded to her scowl.

Rose huffed, crossing her arms. "Fine. But I'm not wearing anything with fringe."

Brett grabbed a pair off the shelf and held them up. "What about these?"

She eyed the boots warily. "Are those… pink?"

I lost it, laughing outright as her face twisted in pure horror. "Oh, this is too good."

Rose shot me a glare that could have set fire to the barn. "I don't like you."

I smirked. "Yeah? Well, you're gonna hate me even more when you realize you have to break them in."

Her groan was downright theatrical, and it just made my morning even better.

Brett, clearly enjoying this way too much, plopped a stack of boxes in front of Rose. "Alright, princess. Let's find your Cinderella moment."

She frowned at him before nudging a box with her toe. "Do any of these not look like something out of a country music video?"

Brett ignored her dramatics and flipped open the first lid. "Classic brown. Simple. Reliable."

Rose wrinkled her nose. "Boring."

I grinned, leaning against a nearby shelf. "You just said they were all too much. Now they're boring?"

She shot me a withering look. "I'm a woman of mystery, Mr. Orange."

"Mr. Orange?" Brett cocked a brow.

"Don't ask." I smirked.

Brett sighed and grabbed another box. "Alright. How about these?"

Rose stared at the pair in his hands. "Are those snakeskin?"

"Yep. Fashion meets function," Brett said, wiggling them.

Rose took a step back. "I'm not walking around with dead reptiles on my feet."

I chuckled. "You're in the South, Sunshine. You're lucky they're not still alive."

She huffed, brushing past Brett to grab a box herself. Lifting the lid, she let out a long, suffering sigh. "Why is there green embroidery? Who asked for this?"

Brett smirked. "People with taste."

She shoved the box back onto the shelf. "Next."

After vetoing everything with fringe, rhinestones, or what she dramatically deemed "unnecessary boot flair," she slumped onto a nearby bench. "This is hopeless."

I shook my head, reaching down to grab one of the last boxes in the stack. "Try these."

Rose eyed me warily, as if I was setting her up. But when I pulled out a simple, well-worn pair of brown boots with just enough scuff to give them character, she hesitated.

She ran a hand over the leather, her brows furrowing. "These aren't the worst things I've ever seen."

I smirked. "We're getting somewhere."

Brett clapped his hands together. "Let's see if they fit."

Rose took them, muttering under her breath as she attempted to slide them on with her bare feet. "These stupid freakin' things won't go on."

"You just need the right socks," Brett piped up.

"I have socks in my purse." Rose dug in her bag and pulled out her socks.

"Oh, honey, those won't work."

Rose frowned, glancing down at her feet. "These will be just fine."

I snorted. "Yeah, if you plan on getting blisters the size of quarters."

She lifted her foot slightly, revealing the thin no-show socks. "These work fine with my sneakers."

Brett let out a low whistle. "Not with boots, they won't. Unless you want to shred your heels in the first five minutes."

Rose groaned, already looking like she regretted every life choice that brought her here. "Great. Now I have to buy socks, too?"

I grinned. "Heavy socks. Thick ones. Preferably wool if you don't want to be crying later."

She let out an exaggerated sigh. "Of course I do. Because nothing says 'fun new adventure' like suffocating my feet."

Brett handed her a pack of boot socks. "Welcome to country living, city girl."

Rose snatched them from his hands, grumbling under her breath. Something about this being the worst idea.

I smirked. "What was that?"

"Nothing." She slipped the heavy socks on and then stomped her feet into the boots.

I grinned. "Welcome to the world of actual footwear."

She shot me a glare. "These are horrible."

I leaned in slightly, just to get under her skin. "Yeah? Well, you're gonna hate me even more when you realize you still have to break them in."

Her groan echoed through the store, and I had a feeling this was only the beginning of my entertainment.

Brett gave her an approving nod. "Not bad. How do they feel?"

"Too tight."

"Probably the socks." I countered.

"Then I need mine."

"I would highly recommend you don't wear yours." Brett added.

"You both are making this impossible!" Rose threw her hands up.

"We're just lookin' out for you," I tried to mitigate the situation. I could tell she was pushed way out of her comfort zone.

"I promise ya they'll stretch out." Brett chimed in.

"Fine. I'll take these stupid boots." Rose poked my chest. "And you're paying for the ugly ass socks, too."

"Figured I was."

Watching Rose slip on her first pair of boots brought a warmth to my chest I hadn't expected. This city girl was about to embrace the cowboy life, and I could already see the transformation unfolding.

It made me think back to my own first pair of boots. I was just six years old when my dad took me to the same store. It's been nearly thirty years since then, and a lot's changed. Brett Jr. now runs the place, having taken over from his father, but walking through those doors still feels the same.

I can still remember the excitement buzzing through me as we walked into the store, the smell of leather thick in the air. Dad's boots were well-worn, a testament to years of hard work put in the fields. I tried to stand as tall as him, my small hand gripping the edge of his jacket. We'd been out in the fields that morning, and I knew this shopping trip was a big deal—a rite of passage.

He led me straight to the boot section, and I remember feeling so small next to the towering shelves filled with rows of leather. The boots were massive on me back then, but the moment I slid my feet into the first pair, something clicked. They felt like they were made just for me. Dad's eyes lit up, a rare smile tugging at the corners of his lips. "You'll grow into them," he'd said, his voice gruff but warm.

It wasn't just about the boots. It was about him teaching me, passing down the weight of what it meant to be a Calloway. That day, the boots weren't just a pair of shoes—they were a symbol of who I was becoming. A cowboy, just like my dad.

CHAPTER 22

GIRL IN A COUNTRY SONG

Rose

GRABBED A FEW ILL-FITTING JEANS AND LONG-SLEEVE SHIRTS from Brett's store before we headed home. The complete opposite of the elegant gowns and designer heels I used to wear to galas with Thad. Now, standing in front of my bathroom mirror, I barely recognized myself. I looked like I'd walked straight out of a country song.

I sighed, taking in the full effect—an oversized flannel layered over a tank top, jeans that did absolutely nothing for my butt, thick socks, and clunky boots that pinched my toes. I even braided my hair. I groaned at my reflection. "What happened to you?"

Shaking my head, I made my way downstairs. Wells had mentioned he'd be outside, so I stepped onto the porch, immediately squinting against the sun. I'd left my sunglasses inside, a rookie mistake. Shielding my eyes with my hand, I scanned the property until I spotted him.

By the goats.

No way. Not now. This was too soon.

Wells straightened as I approached, giving a baby goat a final pat on the head before stepping out of the pen. His signature grin stretched wide. "Oh hey, Sunshine." His gaze flicked down, taking in my new outfit. Amusement twinkled in his eyes. "Look at you—a proper coastal cowgirl."

"Does that make you a coastal cowboy?" I shot back.

He smirked. "I prefer saltwater cowboy, actually."

I rolled my eyes. "Of course you do."

Wells held out a bottle of milk. "Here. Go feed Bronco."

I blinked at him. "And how am I supposed to know which one Bronco is?"

He nodded toward the corner of the pen, where a little goat was aggressively head-butting a fence post.

I raised a brow. "That one?"

"Yep."

Cautiously, I stepped closer, hands outstretched as if that would stop him from ramming into me. "Hi, little guy..."

Bronco cocked his head at me, suspiciously.

"I'm Rose," I tried, holding up the bottle. "I brought some breakfast for you."

Squatting down, I glanced over at Wells. "Do I just... hold it out?"

"Yep."

I extended the bottle, and Bronco latched on immediately. My eyes widened. "He's drinking it!" I whisper-yelled.

"Don't scare him, or he'll head-butt you."

I snapped my gaze up to Wells. "You're not kidding, are you?"

He shook his head, lips twitching. "If you wanna find out..."

I shot him a glare.

I turned back to Bronco, who was guzzling down his breakfast like he hadn't eaten in weeks. His little tail flicked happily, but I stayed on high alert, ready to dodge if he decided to take me out.

"He's kind of cute," I admitted.

Wells chuckled. "Don't let that fool you. He's a menace."

As if to prove him right, Bronco yanked his head back suddenly, nearly knocking the bottle out of my hands. I yelped, scrambling to keep my grip.

Wells grinned. "Told ya."

I shot him a look. "Are you enjoying this?"

"Immensely."

Shaking my head, I refocused on Bronco. "Alright, buddy, slow down." But he had no interest in taking it easy. The second the bottle ran dry, he released it with an offended huff and immediately head-butted my knee.

"Ow!" I stumbled back as Wells burst into laughter.

"Tough love," he said, clearly entertained.

"You could've warned me!" I scowled, rubbing my knee.

"I did." He stepped closer, his hands settling on his hips. "But you're a city girl. Gotta learn these things firsthand."

I narrowed my eyes. "Oh, is that how it is?"

"Yep."

Bronco, apparently deciding I was no longer interesting, trotted off to rejoin his herd. I brushed dust off my jeans, sighing. "Well, that was an experience."

Wells smirked. "Ready for your next lesson?"

I crossed my arms. "Dare I ask?"

He reached for another bottle from a nearby crate. "You're feeding Storm next."

I glanced over at the goat in question—a bigger one, standing in the shade, staring at me like he was already planning my demise.

I exhaled. "This feels personal."

Wells laughed, handing me the bottle. "Oh, sweetheart. It's just getting started."

I eyed the next bottle in Wells' hand, then flicked a glance at Storm, who was still sizing me up like I owed him money.

"I don't think he likes me," I murmured.

Wells smirked. "He doesn't know you yet. Go on, introduce yourself."

With a sigh, I cautiously approached, bottle at the ready. "Hey there, Storm. Be nice to me, okay?"

Storm took one slow step forward, then another, his eyes locked on the bottle. I held it out, bracing for impact. But instead of a full-speed head-butt, he simply latched on and started drinking.

My shoulders sagged in relief. "Oh, thank goodness."

"See? You're a natural."

I turned to Wells, suspicious. "Was this some kind of test?"

He just grinned. "Maybe."

I rolled my eyes, but a smile tugged at my lips. As Storm finished his bottle, I gave him a tentative pat on the head, half-expecting him to retaliate. But he just flicked his ears and wandered off.

"Well," I said, dusting my hands off. "That was… oddly rewarding."

Wells leaned against the fence, arms crossed. "Always is."

I shot him a look. "Don't get cocky."

His grin widened. "Too late."

I shook my head, turning back toward the house. "Next time, I'm wearing knee pads."

Wells' laughter followed me all the way to the porch.

"Are we done for the day? Blythe swore I wouldn't have to do manual labor, and I've already done more outdoorsy things than I ever planned on."

Wells swiped his arm across his forehead, checking his watch. "I love her dearly, but Blythe was wrong." His lips quirked. "You hungry?"

I hesitated, glancing over my shoulder. "Depends. Are we talking actual food, or is this another one of your cowboy initiation tests?"

He chuckled, pushing off the fence. "Actual food. I was thinking sandwiches."

I considered it for a second, then shrugged. "Alright. But if you try to serve me goat milk or something, I'm out."

Wells grinned. "Noted."

We ate in comfortable silence at the table on the porch—he tapped out messages on his phone while I was immersed myself in a book. The occasional rustle of wind through the trees and the distant bleating of goats made for an oddly peaceful setting.

After a while, Wells leaned back in his chair. "Ready to head out to the fields?"

"No." I didn't look up. "I just hit a plot twist."

I caught the smirk tugging at his lips. "It's like I'm dealing with Wren. Five more minutes."

I didn't answer, eyes glued to the page.

"Your five minutes are up," Wells announced, standing. He gathered our plates, rinsed them, and loaded them straight into the dishwasher without a second thought.

I raised a brow. "You're neat."

"Or maybe you're just messy."

I scoffed. "I prefer 'selectively organized.'"

Wells shook his head, drying his hands. "C'mon. Don't forget your sunglasses this time. Unless you wanna wear a hat."

"Hell no." I shot up from my chair. "Let me grab my sunglasses."

I sprinted upstairs, snatched them off my chest of drawers, and paused just long enough to glance at my bed longingly. All I wanted was a nap. But instead, I sighed and trudged back downstairs, where Wells was waiting by the door.

We stepped outside into the late afternoon sun, the heat clinging to my skin as we crossed the yard toward a fenced-off section of land. Rows of vegetables stretched out in front of us, a mix of vibrant greens, deep reds, and pale yellows.

"You have vegetables," I said, adjusting my sunglasses.

Wells nudged me lightly with his elbow. "That's what a farm is, Sunshine."

I rolled my eyes. "I figured you were all about the livestock—what little you do have."

"Can't have one without the other." He reached down, plucked a ripe tomato from the vine, and tossed it my way. I caught it—barely.

"So, what's the plan here?" I asked, eyeing the rows warily.

"You're gonna help me pick vegetables for dinner."

I made a face. "Manual labor. Again."

He shot me a knowing smirk. "You'll survive."

I sighed dramatically. "Fine. But if I get dirt under my nails, I'm adding this to my growing list of grievances against you."

Wells smirked, handing me a woven basket. "Now, start with the tomatoes. Just gently twist them off the vine."

I crouched down and reached for a tomato, hesitating. "What if I break the whole plant?"

"Then we'll know farming isn't your calling."

I shot him a look before carefully twisting the tomato free. It popped off easily, and I held it up like I'd just won a prize. "Look at that. Natural-born farmer."

Wells snorted. "One tomato doesn't make you a farmer. Let's see if you can handle the squash."

"Is that a euphemism, Calloway?"

He ignored my question and led me over to a row of bright yellow squash nestled under thick green leaves. I crouched again, pushing the leaves aside. "Which ones do I pick?"

"The firm ones. Give 'em a little squeeze."

I did, then wrinkled my nose. "This feels inappropriate."

Wells let out a bark of laughter. "Just pick the damn squash, Rose."

Rolling my eyes, I plucked a few, adding them to the basket. The sun beat down on my back, sweat gathering at my neckline, but strangely enough, I didn't hate this. There was something satisfying about pulling vegetables straight from the earth, knowing they'd end up on our plates later.

"Alright, what's next?" I asked, shifting the basket to my hip.

Wells assessed the rows. "Let's grab some peppers."

I followed him to another section, eyeing the bright red and green peppers hanging from their stems. "You sure you trust me with these?"

He gave me a lazy grin. "You're doin' alright so far."

Something about his approval made my stomach flip, but I ignored it, focusing on plucking a pepper and dropping it into the basket of vegetables. After a few more, I wiped the sweat from my forehead. "Okay, I've officially reached my limit of farm work for the day."

Wells glanced at the full basket. "Not bad for a city girl."

"Not bad?" I scoffed. "I'd say I excelled."

He smirked. "We'll see how you do with dinner."

I raised a brow. "Oh no. You're cooking. I just harvested the ingredients. That was my contribution."

"Mm," he mused, picking up the basket. "We'll see."

I had a feeling I'd just walked into another one of Wells Calloway's little challenges.

CHAPTER 23

RAIN IS A GOOD THING

Wells

"I think I deserve tomorrow off," Rose announced, settling into the rocking chair on the front porch, her so-called emotional support water bottle resting against her chest.

I leaned against the railing, arms crossed. "Is that so?"

She didn't look at me, just kept her gaze fixed on the sprawling land. "Yes."

She still made it clear she didn't like me, but I was starting to think her walls weren't as impenetrable as she wanted everyone to believe. Today had been a long one, and I had to admit, she put in the work. She was still a city girl, but when a garden snake slithered through the zucchini bed, she didn't run screaming for the hills—just screamed like a banshee.

"That's not happening," I shot back. "I brought everything in. The vegetables just need to be washed before you prep them."

She finally looked up, thick lashes framing her unimpressed expression. "I told you—I'm not cooking."

I smirked. "How 'bout a compromise? I'll handle the protein, but you do everything else."

"No thanks." Rose shot back.

"I thought that was a fair offer."

She shrugged. "Not really."

"Then I guess we're not eating tonight." As if on cue, my stomach growled.

Pushing off the railing, I headed toward the door. "I'm gonna shower. I'd suggest you do the same—you smell like goats and sweat."

Rose let out a dramatic sigh. "Wow. What a gentleman. I can't believe women aren't lined up at your door, desperate for your compliments."

I just shrugged, kicking off my boots as I stepped inside. Upstairs, I grabbed clean clothes and headed toward the bathroom, but before I could close the door, I heard her footsteps on the stairs—boots still on.

Then came the yelp.

"Babe, I need help!"

Instinct kicked in. I spun around and rushed into her room. She was sprawled out on the bed, hands covering her face.

"What's wrong?"

"The boots!"

I leaned against the doorframe, arms crossed. "What about them?"

She peeked at me through her fingers, full-blown panic in her eyes. "Wells, get these claustrophobic things off me!"

I grinned. "Did you just call me 'babe'?"

She shot upright, glaring daggers. "Get. Them. Off."

"What's the magic word, Rose?"

"I'll kill you!"

I shook my head. "Nope, not it."

Her nostrils flared. "Wells-whatever-your-middle-name-is Calloway, get these freakin' things off my feet. Cut them off, I don't care!"

"I'm not cutting three-hundred-dollar boots, Sunshine."

"Please get these boots off me!"

"Since you asked so nicely." I crossed the room and knelt in front of her. With a nod toward her boots, I asked, "May I?"

"Hurry! I think my feet are bleeding."

"Probably." I gripped the top of the boot with one hand and braced the heel with the other. "Pull your foot."

She tried, but the thing wouldn't budge.

"Try wiggling it." I instructed.

"It hurts!" she whined, full panic setting in.

I let go and met her wide-eyed stare. "Rose."

"What?"

"Take a deep breath."

She did.

"You're panicking. That's not doing a thing. I'm gonna pull, okay?"

She gave a jerky nod.

"One. Two. Three."

The boot popped off, and Rose sagged in relief.

"One more," I said, repeating the process with the other foot.

She fell back against the bed, exhaling. "Thank you." There was a pause. "Why didn't my feet hurt all day?"

"You were busy. Didn't notice." My gaze dropped to the blood-stain seeping through her sock. I knew she wouldn't ask, so I didn't offer. "First-aid kit's under the sink."

"You're not going to help me?"

I glanced over my shoulder. "Do you want help?"

Her shoulders tensed. "No."

"Then why'd you ask?"

She chewed her bottom lip. "Thanks," she muttered.

I hesitated at the door, waiting to see if she'd say anything else. When she didn't, I shook my head and went back to my room.

The shower was quick—just enough to wash off the sweat and dirt from the day. By the time I stepped out, towel slung around my waist, I heard movement in the hallway.

Curiosity got the better of me. I cracked the door open.

Rose stood outside her room, one sock still on, her injured foot hovering above the floor. She was staring down at it like it had personally betrayed her.

"Need a lift?" I asked.

She jolted, eyes snapping up to mine. Her gaze flicked over my bare chest, and I swore I saw her swallow hard before she recovered. "I've got it."

"You look like a baby deer trying to find its legs."

She shot me a glare, then turned and hobbled toward the bathroom.

"Put some damn clothes on next time," she called over her shoulder.

I smirked. "I'm still in my room."

"Still indecent," she muttered before shutting the door.

I chuckled, shaking my head as I closed mine.

After changing, I headed downstairs. From the slow, uneven sounds of Rose moving around, I already knew dinner was on me—not that I'd expected otherwise.

I seasoned the chicken, washed and prepped the vegetables, and had just started cooking when I heard the soft, hesitant hobble of footsteps on the stairs.

Poking my head around the corner, I caught Rose's gaze. "You sure you don't need help? I can have you on a couch in ten seconds, and you won't have to lift a finger."

She lifted her chin, still managing attitude despite the obvious discomfort. "You don't strike me as the type to eat dinner in your living room."

"And you don't strike me as someone in a position to be mouthy right now."

Her lips pressed into a thin line as she carefully placed her right foot down on the step—only to wince.

I sighed. "Rose, just swallow your damn pride. You can stop pretending to be a callous human being for three seconds."

Something flickered in her eyes, her defenses faltering just slightly.

"Fine," she muttered. Then, after a deep, pained breath, she added, "But we're still not friends."

I smirked. "Who said anything about being friends? I'm just being a gentleman."

She exhaled sharply, like simply agreeing to this was more painful than her foot.

I set the tongs down on the counter and went up the stairs to her.

I slid one arm behind her back and the other under her knees, scooping her up before she could protest.

Her body was tense under my touch. She smelled like lavender and bad decisions. I carried her over to the couch and set her down gently, adjusting a pillow behind her.

"There. Now you can stop limping around like a wounded stray."

She crossed her arms, eyeing me with suspicion. "You enjoy bossing people around, don't you?"

I smirked. "Only when they're this damn stubborn."

She opened her mouth, probably to throw another jab, but I raised a hand.

She grumbled something under her breath, but when I walked away, I still heard the telltale sound of her shifting, getting comfortable.

Back in the kitchen, I finished up dinner, plating everything and bringing her a plate before settling into the chair across from her.

She eyed the food. "You really didn't have to do this."

"Yeah, well. If you were making dinner, it'd be tomorrow night before we ate."

She exhaled a laugh—short, but real.

I dug into my food, watching as she took her first cautious bite. Her lips parted slightly in surprise.

"This is… good."

I smirked. "You sound surprised."

"I am."

"Well, don't get used to it. Tomorrow, you're cooking."

She snorted. "Not happening."

I leaned back, stretching out my legs.

She shook her head, focusing on her food. But there was something softer in her expression now. Like, maybe, she was starting to realize I wasn't the enemy.

We weren't friends.

But I'd take a meal without a fight as progress.

Rose and I ate mostly in silence, the soft patter of rain against the window filling the quiet.

"You know what's funny?" she murmured, breaking the stillness.

I glanced up, brow raised. "What's that?"

"If Thad saw a picture of me before I showered, he wouldn't even recognize me."

"Who's Thad?" I asked, watching her carefully.

She took a slow, measured breath. "My ex."

"The guy I said looked like a douchebag when I saw his picture on your phone?"

I swore I caught the ghost of a smile as she absentmindedly stroked Granger's fur. "Yeah. Basically your antithesis."

"What'd he do?"

Her eyes flicked to mine, guarded but not unkind.

"He didn't want to move last minute," she admitted. "The car was packed, but none of his stuff was in it."

I nodded, letting that settle before clarifying, "I meant—what did he do for work?"

Her eyes widened slightly. "Oh." She stretched her neck like she was shaking something off. "Investment banker."

I huffed. "Yeah, you weren't wrong. Definitely the opposite of me."

A beat of silence passed before she shifted gears. "I like storms," she said, almost to herself.

I smirked. "Wait until you get caught in an afternoon one."

She wrinkled her nose. "Do we even work outside when it rains?"

I nodded. "In moderation."

She sighed dramatically, sinking deeper into the couch. "Of course we do."

I smirked, taking another bite of my food. "You signed up for this."

"I did not sign up for this. I signed up for a fresh start. I just didn't realize it involved blisters, snakes, and manual labor."

"You still got time to quit." I offered.

Rose scoffed, shaking her head. "Not a chance. I'm not giving you the satisfaction."

I chuckled, standing to clear my plate. "Suit yourself."

As I rinsed my dish, I heard her shifting behind me.

"You really think I would've gone back?" she asked, her voice quieter now.

I glanced over my shoulder. She wasn't looking at me, just absently tracing the rim of her glass with her finger.

"No," I answered honestly. "I think you wanted out long before your car was packed."

She let out a slow breath, finally meeting my gaze.

"Yeah," she admitted. "I think you're right."

For once, I didn't have a smartass response.

Instead, I grabbed a dish towel, tossed it over my shoulder, and nodded toward her plate. "You done?"

She blinked like I'd pulled her from a thought, then nodded. "Yeah."

I took it from her, brushing past as I carried it to the sink.

When I turned back, she was still watching me, something unreadable in her expression.

I leaned against the counter. "What?"

Her lips parted like she might say something, but then she just shook her head. "Nothing."

I dried my hands on the dish towel and turned to find Rose eyeing the stairs like they were her mortal enemy.

I smirked. "Want help?"

She shot me a look. "I've got it."

"Uh-huh." I crossed my arms. "Because that worked out so well earlier."

She straightened, gripping the railing like it was the only thing keeping her pride intact. "I can make it up a flight of stairs, Wells."

I raised a brow. "You couldn't make it down."

She exhaled sharply, rolling her eyes.

I watched as she took the first step, her movements careful, deliberate. She winced but kept going.

"You know," I drawled, leaning against the counter, "I'd make a great knight in shining armor if you'd just let me."

She scoffed, gripping the railing tighter. "You? A knight? More like an outlaw who got kicked out of the kingdom."

I grinned. "Even outlaws can be charming."

She shook her head, finally reaching the top of the stairs. "Good night."

"Night, Sunshine."

She disappeared down the hall, and I found myself still smirking as I turned off the kitchen lights.

Damn if she wasn't the most stubborn woman I'd ever met.

And damn if I didn't like it.

CHAPTER 24

NIGHT CHANGES

Rose

I REGRETTED MY DECISION THE SECOND I REACHED THE TOP of the stairs.

Every step had been a battle between my pride and the throbbing ache in my feet, and now that I was finally in my room, the pain pulsed in time with my heartbeat.

I sank onto the bed with a wince, stretching my legs out and letting my head fall back against the pillow.

"Totally fine," I muttered to myself. "Not suffering at all."

I stayed like that for a while, eyes closed, breathing through the pain. Eventually, I turned onto my side, reaching blindly toward the nightstand.

And came up empty.

My water bottle. I'd left it downstairs.

I groaned, debating whether dehydration was worse than making the trip back down. Just as I was convincing myself I could survive until morning, there was a knock at the door.

I blinked, pushing up onto my elbows.

"Yeah?"

"Can I come in?" Wells asked from the other side of the door.

"Sure."

The door creaked open, and Wells leaned against the frame, my water bottle dangling from his fingers.

I stared at him, very grateful. "Are you psychic?"

He smirked. "Nah. Just figured you'd want it."

I rolled my eyes, but my traitorous heart did a little flip at the fact that he thought of me at all.

He stepped inside, crossing the room in a few easy strides, and placed the bottle on my nightstand. "Now you don't have to hobble back down."

"Thanks," I mumbled, reaching for it. The cool metal felt like heaven against my palm.

He hesitated for a beat, like he had something else to say.

"What?" I asked.

"You can sleep in tomorrow," he said simply.

I frowned. "What?"

"I'm not a monster, Rose. We'll work in the flower fields, so you can wear those ridiculous flip-flops and give your feet a break."

I blinked up at him, caught off guard by the unexpected kindness.

"Oh."

His lips quirked, like he was trying not to smile. "Don't get all emotional on me."

I scoffed. "Please. I just didn't think you were capable of human decency."

He chuckled, already backing toward the door. "Don't get used to it."

I watched as he disappeared into the hallway, leaving me alone with my thoughts.

Maybe Wells wasn't so bad.

Maybe, just maybe, he was the kind of guy who paid attention.

And that was somehow even more dangerous than the rest.

I took a long sip from my water bottle, the cool liquid soothing against my dry throat. Wells had thought of me before I even had the chance to complain. That was dangerous.

I wasn't used to people paying attention like that.

Not in a way that wasn't transactional.

Not in a way that didn't feel like an obligation.

I shook the thought away, setting my water bottle down before easing onto my back. My feet throbbed, but at least tomorrow wouldn't involve stuffing them back into those godforsaken boots.

Flower fields.

I didn't even know what that meant.

Do we just wander through them? Pick flowers like some kind of romance movie montage? It had to be easier than the fresh hell he had me doing today.

I yawned, the exhaustion of the day finally hitting me. The rain outside had picked up, steady and rhythmic against the roof, lulling me into something close to comfort.

Maybe this place wasn't as awful as I kept telling myself.

Maybe Wells Calloway wasn't either.

That was the last thought I had before sleep took me under.

I woke up slowly, warmth pressing into my sheets, the faintest hint of honeysuckle in the air. It was the kind of morning I would have killed for back in the city—quiet, unrushed, without the blaring sounds of car horns or sirens.

I stretched, only to groan when my feet protested the movement.

I turned onto my side, checking my phone. Wells hadn't come banging on my door at dawn, so I supposed he was serious about letting me sleep in.

I was debating whether I could get away with staying in bed a little longer when there was a light knock at the door.

"Come in." I called, my voice still thick with sleep.

The door cracked open, and Wells peered in, brows raised. "You're awake. Thought I might have to come in here and roll you out of bed."

"I'd like to see you try."

He grinned but didn't take the bait. Instead, he nodded toward the hallway. "Breakfast is ready. Figured you might want to eat before we head outside."

I blinked. "You made breakfast?"

"Don't look so surprised," he said, smirking. "I'm full of hidden talents."

I snorted. "Right. Like your charm and impeccable manners."

"Exactly." He winked. "Now get your ass downstairs before I change my mind and make you put the boots back on."

I grumbled under my breath but swung my legs over the edge of the bed, wincing as my feet hit the floor.

Wells was already halfway down the hall, but I swore I saw him pause—like he was listening, making sure I wasn't in too much pain.

Maybe I was imagining it.

Regardless, I grabbed my water bottle and hobbled downstairs, following the smell of coffee and something warm and buttery. My stomach rumbled.

When I reached the kitchen, Wells was at the stove, flipping something in a cast iron skillet. The sight was almost unsettling—big, broad cowboy manning a stove like he did it every day.

He glanced over his shoulder, eyes scanning me like he was assessing whether I was about to collapse. I straightened, trying to look less like someone who needed help.

"Thought you might've changed your mind about letting me sleep in," I said, lowering myself into a chair at the kitchen table in front of a steaming cup of fresh-brewed coffee.

Wells smirked. "Figured if I let you sleep, you might complain less today."

I rolled my eyes and a smile played on my lips. "Doubtful."

He chuckled, turning back to the stove. A few seconds later, he slid a plate in front of me—scrambled eggs, crispy bacon, and what looked like a homemade biscuit.

I eyed it suspiciously. "You made this?"

"Nah," he deadpanned. "The breakfast fairy stopped by."

I bit back a smile and picked up my fork. The first bite of biscuit was warm and buttery, practically melting in my mouth. I hated to admit it, but it was good. Like, *really* good.

Wells sat across from me with his own plate, taking a bite of bacon. "How's it feel to be boot-free today?"

I exhaled dramatically. "Like I've been released from a medieval torture device."

"You're welcome."

I scoffed. "For what?"

"Giving your feet a break," he said like it was obvious.

I took a sip of coffee, leveling him with a look. "You're acting like you gave me the day off."

He smirked. "Not a day off. Just an easier day."

I should've known there was a catch. "What exactly are we doing in the flower fields?"

"Planting, pruning, maybe harvesting, depending on what's ready. It's easier than yesterday. Less running from garden snakes." Wells paused, "Maybe."

I stabbed a piece of egg with my fork. "I didn't run."

Wells tilted his head. "You screamed like someone was trying to murder you."

"That was a natural reaction."

"Uh-huh." He took another bite of bacon. "Hope you've got a decent sunscreen. You're gonna fry out there. The sun is hot today."

I scowled. "I have sunscreen, Wells. I wasn't raised in a cave."

"Could've fooled me."

I huffed, stuffing a bite of eggs into my mouth instead of responding. I wasn't minding the banter.

The worst part?

I was starting to not mind Wells, either.

After breakfast, I took my time getting ready, partly because my feet still ached and partly because I was mentally preparing for whatever "easier day" Wells had planned.

Flower fields sounded nice in theory, but knowing him, there would be some kind of catch.

I slipped into shorts and a tank top, the light fabric a welcome relief after yesterday's disaster of an outfit. No boots, no jeans—just my perfectly worn in flip-flops. If Wells had a problem with it, he could take it up with the fact that I was technically injured.

By the time I stepped outside, the sun was already high, draping the land in a golden glow. Wells stood beside some kind of four-wheeled contraption, arms crossed, watching me like he was waiting for a complaint.

I refused to give him the satisfaction.

"Flower fields, huh?" I said as I approached. "Sounds like something out of a romance novel."

"Don't go getting any ideas," he drawled, swinging onto the seat with effortless ease. Then, he extended a hand.

I hesitated only a second before taking it, ignoring the way my stomach flipped at the small gesture. Settling into the seat behind him, I adjusted my shorts and scoffed.

Wells smirked, turning the key. The engine rumbled to life beneath us. "Ready?"

The vibration of the machine buzzed up my spine as I slipped my sunglasses over my eyes. "And what, exactly, is this death trap?"

"It's a four-wheeler," he said, motioning toward the grips on either side of me. "You can hold on there… or you could hold on to me."

I snorted. "I'd rather walk than hold onto you."

He didn't say another word before we took off down the dirt road, winding past pastures and barns until we reached a stretch of land that looked straight out of a painting.

Rows of flowers stretched out before us, wild and bright—sunflowers, daisies, roses, lavender, zinnias, and blooms I didn't even have names for. The air smelled sweet, the breeze carrying the soft scent of earth and petals.

For a second, I just stared.

This wasn't what I expected.

It was beautiful.

Wells glanced at me, catching my expression. "Better than wrangling goats?"

I swallowed, tearing my gaze away. "I'll let you know in a few hours."

He chuckled and swung off the four-wheeler, grabbing a pair of gardening shears from the small storage compartment. "Come on, city girl. Let's see if you can handle a day in the flower fields."

I sighed dramatically but climbed off after him, my flip-flops smacking against the packed dirt.

Maybe today wouldn't be so bad.

CHAPTER 25

FLOWERS IN YOUR HAIR

Rose

WELLS LED ME DOWN A NARROW PATH BETWEEN THE ROWS of flowers, the scent of lavender and wild blooms thick in the warm air. The colors were almost overwhelming—sunbursts of yellow, deep purples, fiery reds. If I hadn't known better, I would've thought I'd stepped into some kind of enchanted garden.

He stopped in front of a row of sunflowers, taller than both of us, and handed me the shears. "Alright, first lesson—you don't just go hacking at 'em like you're in a horror movie. There's a method."

I playfully rolled my eyes. "And here I thought I could just start swinging."

Wells ignored my sarcasm, crouching beside one of the smaller flowers. "You always want to cut at an angle, right above a healthy set of leaves. Keeps the plant strong and encourages more blooms." He demonstrated, slicing cleanly through the stem.

I mimicked his stance, eyeing a bright zinnia. "Like this?" I clipped the stem, and the flower flopped over like a tragic love story.

He snorted. "Close. Maybe don't kill it in the process."

I scowled before trying again, this time paying closer attention. When I successfully snipped a bloom without looking like a botanical assassin, I stood a little taller. "Not bad for a city girl, right?"

Wells glanced at me, an unreadable expression flickering across his face before he straightened. "Not bad," he admitted. "But let's see if you can last more than an hour before you start complaining."

I narrowed my eyes. "I don't complain."

He let out a full laugh at that. "Sure, Sunshine. Whatever you say."

I huffed but followed him as he moved to another section of the field. The work was surprisingly peaceful—the rhythmic snipping, the soft rustle of petals in the breeze, the occasional hum of a bee drifting by. This was the first time in a long time that my head felt clear.

As we worked, the minutes stretched into an easy rhythm. The sun beat down gently, and the only sounds were the steady clip of shears and the soft rustle of leaves in the wind. Wells moved with practiced ease, trimming and pruning flowers, while I fumbled with every snip, trying not to make a mess of things. I kept my head down, concentrating hard, but every now and then, I caught myself glancing at him.

Finally, he spoke, breaking the silence. "What's your favorite flower?"

I paused, my shears hovering over a sunflower. The question caught me off guard. I hadn't really thought about it before. "I don't know," I said after a beat, my voice unsteady. It wasn't the answer I'd expected to give, but it felt true.

Wells raised an eyebrow, his expression curious. "You don't know?"

I shook my head slowly, as if it were a minor confession. "I guess I never thought about it." I looked at the rows of flowers around us. "No one's ever gotten me flowers before."

His face softened, and I could tell he was trying to process my words. There was a moment of quiet between us, and the sound of the shears snipping filled the air again. He wiped a hand across his forehead before glancing at me, an unreadable expression on his face.

"Never?" he asked, his voice low.

I nodded, shrugging a little, but I could feel my chest tighten as

I said it. "I mean, I've gotten flowers at a party, like in a vase or something, but no one's ever thought to give them to me for no reason. I've never gotten 'just because' flowers." I dropped my gaze, feeling suddenly vulnerable.

For a moment, Wells didn't speak. He just stared at the row of flowers in front of him, his lips pressed together as if he was mulling something over.

"Huh," he said after a moment, his voice quieter than usual. He stepped over to the next row, cutting through a few stems with ease, but his eyes flicked back to me. "I'd say sunflowers would suit you."

I raised an eyebrow, glancing at the bright yellow blooms swaying in the breeze. "Sunflowers?" I laughed softly, though the sound felt a little uncertain.

He gave me a sidelong glance and then offered a half-smile. "Sunflowers are bold, unapologetic. They stand tall and proud."

I wasn't sure what to say to that, so I just shrugged and returned to my task, feeling my cheeks warm slightly. "I never thought of it that way."

Wells's expression softened, and I could see a flash of something in his eyes—something that wasn't teasing or dismissive. It was genuine. He watched me for a second longer, then nodded.

I smirked, still feeling the awkwardness of the moment. "We'll see if you can find one I like."

He chuckled, but there was something else in the sound—a hint of sincerity, maybe even a quiet challenge. "Oh, I'll find something, Rose. You might be a little harder to figure out than most, but I'm stubborn. I'll find something you like."

I looked at him, considering his words. I couldn't remember the last time someone had really tried to figure me out.

As I bent down again to snip another flower, the thought lingered. Maybe flowers weren't the only things that could surprise me today.

We worked in silence for a while, the sun relentlessly beating down on my scalp. "I think my head's burning," I muttered, shading my face with a hand.

Wells paused, grabbing my head gently and inspecting the top. "Yep. Sure are," he said, letting go and raising an eyebrow. "Where's that sunscreen you mentioned?"

"I put it on earlier," I replied defensively.

"That was hours ago," he replied, his gaze drifting to my shoulders, now a bright shade of red. "Your scalp's burnt, and your shoulders are fried. You need to go inside and re-apply."

I sighed dramatically, rolling my eyes. "Yes, sir."

"We could always head back to the house," he suggested, a playful smirk tugging at his lips.

"You mean the place with the air conditioning?" I clarified.

"That very place."

I pulled off my sunglasses and met his eyes. "I wouldn't be mad. My water's running low anyway."

"Let's load up these flowers and head back," he said, his voice smooth as he began packing the freshly cut blooms into the carrier.

I couldn't help but notice Wells wasn't wearing his usual long-sleeve flannel today. Instead, he sported a simple white t-shirt that made his tattoos pop against his sun-kissed skin.

"Stop staring and start helping," he teased, catching me in the act.

I shook my head, forcing my attention back to the task at hand. "What are we going to do with these flowers anyways?"

Wells smiled, his eyes lingering on me for a beat before he turned his attention back to securing the last of the flowers in the carrier. "Most of these are going to the nursing home down the street," he said, his voice soft but purposeful.

"That's kind of you," I replied, impressed by the gesture.

He swung a leg over the four-wheeler, facing me with that familiar, easy confidence. "Get on," he said, his tone inviting yet firm.

I climbed onto the back of the four-wheeler, wrapping my hands around the grips as he gunned the engine, kicking up a trail of dust behind us. The breeze on the ride back was a welcome break from the heat, and I couldn't help but feel a little giddy—like the fresh air was clearing out more than just the humidity. There was something about the air here that felt different. It carried the familiar salt of the nearby ocean, but with a hint of something else—something unmistakably country, grounding and free all at once.

We made it back to the house, and Wells didn't waste any time. He hopped off and walked around to the back of the truck, lifting the carrier with the flowers and gently placing it in the bed. He dusted his hands off and turned to me with a grin.

"You're in the clear for the day," he said, a teasing edge to his voice. "No need to worry about reapplying that sunscreen. We're not going anywhere for a while."

I raised an eyebrow, watching him as he wiped the sweat from his brow. "I'll happily take the break."

He gave me a nod, "You want a late lunch?"

I stretched, feeling the weight of the sun's burn fading, and nodded. "Lunch sounds great. Something light."

"Gotcha," he said with a wink. "We'll head out in a bit, but it won't take long. The folks at the nursing home will appreciate these flowers."

I followed him inside, the cool air of the house a welcome relief from the heat. As we walked through the door, Wells looked over at me.

"We could grab something before we head over to the nursing home. There's a diner down the road."

I raised an eyebrow, feigning surprise. "There's other life out here?"

Wells laughed, his grin widening. "More than you think. It's a small town, but it's got its charm."

He smirked, heading toward the kitchen. "We've got good food too."

"That's debatable."

He cocked an eyebrow, turning to face me with a playful glint in his eye. "Is that so?"

I nodded, crossing my arms. "You've not truly lived until you've had a plate of spaghetti and meatballs from Il Pomodoro. It was this adorable little restaurant near my old apartment."

He leaned against the counter, a thoughtful expression on his face. "Maybe if I make it back out there one day, I'll give it a shot."

I grinned, my thoughts drifting to the cozy little spot I missed so much. "That restaurant alone is worth the trip."

He chuckled, the sound warm. "I'll keep that in mind." Wells paused, his gaze meeting mine. "Do you want to get washed up and then we can head out?"

I nodded, "Yeah, I won't be long."

I made my way up the stairs, each step deliberate as I moved through the quiet house. I splashed cold water on my face, letting the chill clear away the remnants of the afternoon heat. After dabbing my skin dry, I reached for my mascara, swiping it over my lashes with a practiced hand.

I slipped into a light sundress, the soft fabric perfect for the warm day. My favorite sandals followed, the ones that wouldn't tear up my heels like the boots had. I grabbed my purse, checking for my phone before heading back downstairs to start the next adventure.

CHAPTER 26

WHATEVER SHE'S GOT

Wells

I WAS LEANING AGAINST THE KITCHEN COUNTER WHEN I HEARD the soft creak of the stairs. It was a familiar sound, one I'd gotten used to over the last couple of days. But this time, when Rose came down, it was different.

She appeared in a sundress, the kind of dress that fluttered around her legs with every step. The bright yellow fabric made her look like a ray of sunshine, and for the first time since I'd met her, that frosty exterior seemed to have softened just a bit. Her usual guarded demeanor had melted, if only for a moment.

"Ready to go?" she asked, her voice light and easy, though there was still that edge of hesitation in her eyes. I could tell she wasn't quite sure about this whole small-town thing, but it was nice to see her letting go of the tension she usually carried.

"You look nice," I said, straightening up as she walked toward the door. She didn't reply right away, but I saw the faintest pink blush color her cheeks. *Good.* I was getting through to her, even if it was just a little bit.

We climbed into the truck together, the engine rumbling to life. The drive wasn't long, but it was quiet and comfortable. The road was lined with old trees and houses with peeling paint, giving the town a rustic charm that I always appreciated. It was the kind of place where time seemed to slow down.

After a quick stop for lunch at the diner, where Rose had insisted I order something more "exciting" than a burger, we were ready to head out to the nursing home.

By the time we reached the nursing home, the familiar faces on the porch were already waiting, settled into their chairs and soaking in the warmth of the afternoon. As soon as they spotted the flowers, their expressions brightened, and a quiet sense of joy filled the air.

I stepped forward, plucking a bouquet from the box and handing it to an elderly woman who had always been kind to me.

"Wells, always a pleasure," she said, her voice soft but laced with affection.

"Figured you could use a little sunshine today," I replied with a smile. It wasn't much, but I liked doing this for them. Over the years, they'd given me something invaluable—company when I needed it most and conversation when silence felt too heavy.

Rose lingered near the stairs, letting me take the lead. She didn't stay unnoticed for long. One of the residents, a sharp-eyed woman with years of wisdom behind her gaze, curled a finger in Rose's direction, beckoning her closer. Rose hesitated for just a beat before stepping forward.

"You're new around here, aren't you?" the woman asked, her voice carrying the weight of someone who had seen a lifetime of stories unfold.

Rose offered a small smile. "Just visiting for a bit."

The woman's lips curved in a knowing grin. "You won't want to leave. People here have a way of making you feel like you belong."

Across the porch, Rose met my gaze, something unreadable flickering behind her eyes. Then, slowly, a soft smile tugged at her lips. And in that moment, I saw it—the way she was starting to see this place the way I did.

I shifted the weight of the flower box in my arms. "Come on," I said. "Let's head inside and spread a little more sunshine."

Inside, the scent of lavender and clean linens filled the halls, mingling with the warmth of home-cooked meals drifting from the dining room. The hum of quiet conversation and the occasional burst of laughter created a kind of gentle comfort that settled deep in my chest.

I spotted Mrs. Lillian in her usual chair by the window, her silver hair pinned back neatly, a book resting in her lap. She looked up as I approached, her eyes lighting up the way they always did when I visited.

"Well, if it isn't my favorite cowboy," she teased, setting her book aside. "Come to sweep an old woman off her feet?"

I chuckled, kneeling beside her and handing her a bouquet of soft pink peonies. "Thought I'd try my luck."

She took the flowers with a delighted smile, bringing them to her nose and inhaling deeply. "Lord have mercy, Wells Calloway, you sure know how to make a lady feel special."

"Only the best for you, ma'am," I said, adjusting the blanket draped over her legs. "How've you been?"

"Oh, the usual. Beating everyone at cards," she said with a playful glint in her eye.

I grinned, leaning in. "I bet you still got a few up your sleeve."

Mrs. Lillian patted my hand, her grip soft but steady. "You always were a good boy, Wells. The kind that gives people something to look forward to."

Across the room, Rose stood quietly, watching the exchange. I didn't notice her at first, but when I glanced up, I caught the expression on her face—eyes warm, lips parted just slightly, like she'd just stumbled upon something unexpectedly beautiful.

Her gaze lingered on me, then on Mrs. Lillian, and I saw it clear as day. The way this moment touched something deep inside her, the way it shifted something in her chest.

Maybe she was starting to see Wippowa differently.

She gave me a soft, knowing smile, and for once, she didn't look like she was just passing through.

I stood, lifting the flower box with one arm, and nodded toward her. "You gonna help me play flower delivery, or you just here for the show?"

Rose smirked, stepping closer. "Depends. You always this charming with the ladies?"

Mrs. Lillian let out a delighted chuckle. "Oh honey, you have no idea."

Rose laughed, and I felt something settle inside me.

As Rose stepped closer, I handed off another bouquet, but my attention was pulled away by a chuckle from the corner of the room.

"Well, well," Mr. Grady drawled, straightening in his chair as his cane rested against his knee. "Ain't often we get such a vision of beauty walkin' through these doors."

Rose blinked, then let out a small laugh. "Are you talking about me?" She pointed to herself.

Mr. James, sitting beside him, adjusted his suspenders with a dramatic sigh. "Darlin', if I were fifty years younger—hell, even thirty—I'd be fighting off the rest of these old fools for a chance to take you out dancing."

"Oh, hush now," Mrs. Lillian teased. "You'd have to remember how to dance first."

The men chuckled, but Mr. Grady wasn't backing down. "I remember just fine. And I'd be happy to refresh my skills if this lovely lady here would grant me the honor." He held out a shaky hand, his grin full of mischief.

Rose played along, placing her fingers lightly over his. "I have a feeling you'll put me to shame."

Mr. James shook his head, looking to me. "Boy, you better hold onto this one. She's got charm and a good sense of humor—rare qualities these days."

Rose glanced at me, her cheeks slightly pink, but her smile was wide and genuine.

I smirked, shaking my head. "Y'all are gonna scare her off."

"Oh, nonsense," Mrs. Lillian said with a wave of her hand. "If she was scared, she wouldn't be smiling like that."

And she was. A real, unguarded smile that made something deep in my chest tighten.

Rose turned back to Mr. Grady. "You know, I think you just made my whole day."

"Well, sweetheart," he said, patting her hand, "you just made mine."

She squeezed his hand gently before stepping back toward me. "I like them," she murmured, her voice soft but sure.

I caught her gaze, and for the first time, I knew—she wasn't just saying it to be polite.

I nudged the flower box toward her. "Then let's go make some more people's day, yeah?"

She grinned, linking her arm through mine just for a second before reaching for a bouquet.

At the far end of the room, an older couple sat side by side on a floral loveseat, their hands intertwined as if they'd been holding on for decades and had no intention of letting go.

"Now there's my favorite lovebirds," I said, grabbing a bouquet and walking over. "How are we today, Mr. and Mrs. Turner?"

Mrs. Turner, a petite woman with soft white curls, beamed up at me. "Oh, we're just peachy, sweetheart. But I have to say, these afternoons are much more exciting when you visit."

Mr. Turner gave a slow nod, a twinkle of humor in his eyes. "She went and fixed her hair when she saw your truck pull up."

"Oh, hush, Harold," Mrs. Turner swatted his arm, but her cheeks flushed pink. "You're embarrassing me."

Rose chuckled as she stepped beside me, her gaze drifting to their still-clasped hands. "How long have you been married?"

Mr. Turner straightened with pride. "Sixty-three years and counting."

Rose's eyes widened. "Sixty-three? That's incredible. What's your secret?"

Mrs. Turner smiled warmly. "Oh, darling, there's no secret. Just choose someone you like as much as you love. Makes all the hard days a little easier."

Mr. Turner leaned forward, his voice dropping to a playful whisper. "And make sure they let you have the last bite of dessert every once in a while."

Mrs. Turner gasped. "Harold Turner, you rascal! I let you have the last bite all the time."

He winked. "That's why I married you, honey."

Rose let out a soft laugh, and I could tell she was completely charmed.

I handed Mrs. Turner the bouquet, but she surprised me by taking Rose's hand instead. "Now, sweetheart, you hold onto this one." She tilted her head toward me. "Good men are hard to come by."

Rose opened her mouth as if to respond, then shut it again, her fingers tightening just slightly in Mrs. Turner's grasp before she pulled back with a small, hesitant smile. "Isn't that the truth."

Mrs. Turner's sharp eyes studied her for a beat before she pursed her lips. "Those are the words of a woman with a broken heart." She turned to me, arching a brow. "Now, what exactly did you do to this sweet girl?"

I held up my hands. "Don't look at me. She was already mad when she got here."

Rose shot me a flat look before turning back to Mrs. Turner. "Not him—though he does talk too much."

Mrs. Turner gave her husband a shove, clearing a space beside her. "Darlin', you sit down right now and spill the whole story."

Rose plopped onto the seat with a dramatic sigh, then waved me off. "You can go now. The ladies have important things to discuss."

Mrs. Turner practically lit up at that. I knew for a fact it had been too long since she had a proper gossip session—her words, not mine.

I took the hint and made my way across the room, handing out the rest of the flowers before carrying the empty box back to the car. By the time I returned, Rose and Mrs. Turner were deep in conversation, their voices hushed but animated.

Mrs. Turner suddenly gasped, her hand flying to her mouth. "He did not!"

Rose nodded slowly, her expression darkening. "Oh, he did. Left me standing there on the sidewalk."

Mrs. Turner's expression hardened in an instant. "What a jackass."

Rose let out a dry chuckle. "Yeah. I'm just figuring it out as I go."

Mrs. Turner patted Rose's knee, her expression softening. "Well, honey, you're in good company. We've all had to find our way at some point."

And for the first time since we arrived, Rose looked like she truly believed that.

"Whatever you do, Wells, you treat this girl right. She's had a rough go of it." Mrs. Turner turned towards me.

"Doing my best, ma'am."

She pinched Rose's cheeks. "She's such a delight." She needs to stay; don't do anything stupid."

Rose stood up and I nudged her elbow. "Looks like you've got a fan club."

She scoffed. "You're the one they treat like a hometown celebrity."

I smirked. "What can I say? I'm charming."

She rolled her eyes. "Yeah, yeah. Keep telling yourself that."

We finished up with the residents and headed back to the truck. Rose climbed in next to me, the quiet hum of the engine filling the space between us.

"It's sweet that you do this." She spoke up.

I shrugged, my gaze softening as I glanced over at her. "It's the least I can do. They've always been good to me."

"They seem like wonderful people."

"You know," I said, after a long pause, "You're not as tough as you think you are."

CHAPTER 27

HIGH HORSE

Rose

'VE SURVIVED AN ENTIRE WEEK ON THE CALLOWAY FARM. *Barely*.

The last seven days have been...interesting to say the least.

I've been chased by an aggressive rooster that I'm convinced was possessed.

I nearly fell into a water trough trying to carry a bucket twice my size.

I learned goats have zero respect for personal space.

I discovered that the farm life requires waking up at an ungodly hour.

And now, apparently, I'm learning to ride a horse—on a Friday night.

Normal people went to happy hour. Some went for a nice dinner. But no. Here I was, standing in front of a thousand-pound animal with eyes that screamed, 'I know you have no idea what you're doing.'

"This is Bandit," Wells said, patting the horse's side like they were old war buddies. "He's real gentle. Perfect for beginners."

I narrowed my eyes at the horse. "Are we sure about that?"

Bandit blinked at me. I swear he was judging me.

Wells grinned. "You'll be fine. Just put your foot in the stirrup and swing your leg over."

It sounded simple. It was *not* simple.

For starters, the stirrup was much higher than anticipated. I attempted to lift my foot, but I might as well have been trying to scale a mountain.

"This is a lot," I muttered. "Maybe I should start with a pony. Or, like… a horse simulator."

Wells sighed, coming up behind me. "Here, I'll give you a boost."

Before I could protest, his hands were on my waist, and suddenly, I was airborne. Which was all fine and dandy, *except* he launched me with way too much enthusiasm.

I cleared the saddle like an Olympic gymnast.

For a glorious second, I was flying. Weightless. Free.

And then I wasn't.

I landed on the other side of the horse in a very ungraceful heap, smacking the ground with an *oof*.

Silence.

Then—Wells. Wheezing.

"Oh—" he bent over, hands on his knees. "Oh, hell—" A full-body laugh shook him. "I didn't—" He gasped for air. "I didn't mean to throw you *over* the damn thing."

I groaned, staring up at the darkening sky. "So this is how I die. On a farm. Launched like a rag doll."

Bandit turned his head to look at me, utterly unbothered.

Wells finally got himself under control and leaned over me, grinning way too wide. "You good, Sunshine?"

"I think my soul left my body for a second, but yeah." I lifted a hand. "Give me a moment to gather my pride."

He shook his head, laughing, before offering me a hand up. "Alright, alright. Let's try this again. With less enthusiasm."

Round two went slightly better. Mostly because I demanded no launching this time. Wells helped me into the saddle—at a normal human speed—and after some tense moments of gripping the reins like my life depended on it, I was officially on a horse.

"See?" Wells smirked. "Not so bad."

I exhaled slowly. "Not so bad."

Bandit shifted slightly, and I immediately yelped and grabbed Wells' arm. "Nope. Nope. Too high. I changed my mind."

He laughed, steadying me. "Relax. He's just adjusting. You got this."

I gave him a suspicious look. "Are you sure? Because I feel like this is how people end up on YouTube compilations."

He just grinned. "Guess we'll find out."

I let out a long breath. I was officially on a horse.

Now what?

I glanced down at Wells, who was standing way too confidently beside me, arms crossed like he was admiring his work. "Alright. What now?"

"Now, you take the reins and give him a little nudge with your heels."

I blinked at him. "A nudge?"

"Yeah, just a little tap so he knows to move." Wells clarified poorly.

I looked at Bandit. Bandit looked at me. We had an understanding—he knew I had no business being up here, and I knew he could end me in one wrong step.

"Okay," I muttered, gripping the reins like they were my last lifeline. I took a deep breath and—

Nothing.

Bandit didn't move.

I tried again, this time tapping my heels against his side a little firmer.

Still nothing.

I shot Wells a look. "I think he's broken."

Wells pressed his lips together, fighting a smile. "He's not broken. You just have to be a little more assertive."

Assertive. Right.

I gave it one last go, pressing my heels in with as much confidence as I could muster.

And *that* was apparently the magic touch.

Because Bandit took off.

Not fast, but definitely faster than I had anticipated. I let out a startled shriek and immediately grabbed onto the saddle horn for dear life. "Nope! I hate this! Get me down now!"

Wells was laughing. *Laughing.*

"You're fine!" He called after me, casually walking beside the horse like this was all a big joke. "Just sit up straight and relax!"

Relax? Was he insane? I was on a moving beast with a mind of its own.

"Easy for you to say when you're not about to meet your demise via farm animal!" I shouted, clinging tighter as Bandit kept his steady trot.

"You're not gonna die," Wells said, still way too amused. "Just pull back on the reins a little to slow him down."

Oh. Right. I had reins.

I yanked them like I was stopping a runaway train.

Bandit skidded to a halt so fast I nearly flew forward.

I let out a strangled noise, regaining my balance while my heart tried to climb out of my throat. "This is it. This is how I go. Tell my family I love them."

Wells leaned against the fence, shaking his head as he tried—and failed—to hide his laughter. "You're so dramatic."

I shot him a glare. "Dramatic? I have never been on a horse before in my life, and you just threw me into the equestrian deep end!"

He smirked. "And yet, you're still on the horse. Look at you."

I exhaled, shaking my head as my pulse finally started to settle. "I hate you."

"No, you don't."

I groaned, rubbing a hand down my face. "Fine. I mildly dislike you."

He chuckled. "Come on, city girl. One more lap, and then we'll call it a night."

I looked at Bandit. He looked at me.

"Alright," I muttered, shifting in the saddle. "But if I die, I'm haunting this farm."

Wells just grinned. "Wouldn't expect anything less."

I had survived one lap.

Barely.

And now, apparently, I was doing another.

Wells was still standing by the fence, looking all too pleased with himself, like this was the best entertainment he'd had in years.

I shot him a glare. "I swear, if I make it out of this alive, I'm making you do something equally terrifying. Like, I don't know… yoga."

He smirked. "You think horse riding is terrifying?"

I motioned dramatically to myself. "I am atop a moving animal with no seatbelt. If I was meant to be this high up, I'd have wings."

Wells just chuckled. "You're doing fine. Loosen up a little. You're stiff as a board."

"My life might've gone to shit, but I still value my existence," I snapped, still gripping the reins like I was bracing for impact.

Bandit, completely unaffected by my panic, let out a lazy huff, like this lady is exhausting, and took another step forward.

I yelped and immediately tensed again.

Wells pinched the bridge of his nose, laughing under his breath. "Okay, let's try this—just hold the reins steady, sit up straight, and—"

At that exact moment, Bandit decided to scratch his side.

By violently shaking his entire body.

I screamed. I flailed. I grabbed onto anything within reach, which turned out to be Wells' shirt, because in my blind panic, I had somehow yanked him forward over the fence.

Next thing I knew, he was halfway over the rail, clutching at my leg to stop himself from face-planting into the dirt.

"Wells!" I shrieked.

"Rose!" he shot back, one hand gripping the saddle, the other fisting the front of my jeans. "If you pull me further over this fence, I'm making Bandit gallop just to watch you suffer."

"Don't you dare!"

Bandit, the only reasonable one here, finally stopped shaking, standing perfectly still like nothing had happened.

I stared at him. He stared at me.

Then he lost it.

Full-on, head-thrown-back, wheezing laughter.

"You—" He gasped, wiping his eyes as he let go of my jeans and climbed back down. "You screamed like someone was trying to murder you."

I scowled. "I thought someone was trying to murder me. I didn't know horses had a built-in earthquake function!"

He grinned up at me, shaking his head. "You are the worst cowgirl I have ever met."

I exhaled, loosening my grip on the reins, my heartbeat finally returning to normal. "You know what? I accept that title. Crown me and let me go inside."

But Wells just folded his arms and smirked. "One more lap."

I groaned. "You're a tyrant."

"And yet, you keep listening to me."

I muttered something under my breath that I was pretty sure counted as a threat, but I did it anyway—one more lap, much to Wells' amusement.

And, okay. Maybe—just maybe—it wasn't as horrifying this time.

But I'd die on this horse before I admitted that to him.

Wells walked up to Bandit's side, looking up at me with that same cocky smirk that had been plastered on his face all evening.

"Alright, Sunshine. Time to dismount."

I stared down at him, then at the ground, which suddenly seemed way farther away than when I first got up here. "You say that like it's easy."

"It is easy," he said, reaching up. "Just swing your leg over and slide down."

I snorted. "Slide down? Like I won't dislocate a knee?"

He rolled his eyes and held out his hands. "Come on, I got you."

I hesitated. "Don't let me fall."

Wells sighed, like I was personally testing his patience. "Trust me."

I exhaled and, very carefully, swung my leg over. The second my foot left the stirrup, gravity betrayed me, and I half-slid, half-plummeted straight toward Wells.

He barely caught me.

For a second, we just stood there, my hands gripping his shoulders, his arms wrapped around my waist, his chest shaking with silent laughter.

"You're supposed to help me down, not let me free-fall," I muttered.

"I did help you," he said, grinning. "You're in one piece, aren't you?"

I scowled. "Debatable."

He finally let me go, stepping back with that damn smirk still in place. "Not bad for your first ride."

I huffed, brushing off my jeans. "Yeah, yeah. Next time, we'll see how you like being completely out of your element."

His laughter chased me all the way back to the house. "Does this make us friends yet?"

I glanced over my shoulder with a deadpan look. "I almost just died, cowboy. Absolutely not."

CHAPTER 28

SLOW BURN

Rose

LAST NIGHT, AFTER MY DISASTROUS EXPERIENCE ON BANDIT, Wells surprised me by agreeing to do yoga with me this morning. It caught me off guard—especially since, in all our time together, Thad had always dismissed it as a waste of time, insisting I do it alone.

I was already rolling out my mat when I heard the screen door creak open behind me.

I turned and immediately had to stifle a laugh.

Wells stood on the porch, arms crossed, looking absolutely unimpressed with life. I scanned his body and he was in jeans and a t-shirt.

I blinked at him. "Is this…" I motioned towards his body. "Is this your yoga attire?"

He shrugged. "Didn't know there was a dress code."

I let out a slow, dramatic sigh, shaking my head. "Wells, buddy. Pal. You cannot do yoga in denim."

"Why not?"

"Because you have to bend," I said, motioning wildly to his legs. "You're gonna cut off your circulation and pass out before we even get to downward dog."

His brows lifted. "I don't even know what the hell that means, but it sounds inappropriate."

I snorted. "Just—go put on something comfortable."

With another sigh—one that made it very clear he regretted ever agreeing to this—he turned and headed back inside.

I stayed outside, stretching idly as the sky slowly shifted from deep blue to soft orange, the early morning light casting a warm glow over the fields.

Then, from above, I heard a window creak open.

I looked up just in time to see a pair of basketball shorts dangling out of it.

"This work?" Wells called, holding them up for approval like he was asking me to inspect a fine wine.

I laughed, shaking my head. "Yeah, those are acceptable."

"Good," he said, disappearing back inside.

A minute later, the screen door opened again, and this time, Wells was dressed in the shorts and a plain t-shirt, barefoot, looking a lot less like a cowboy and a lot more like someone about to get his ass handed to him by basic stretching.

He stopped in front of me, arms crossed. "Alright, let's get this over with."

I grinned, unfolding my mat. "Oh, we're just getting started, Calloway."

Wells eyed my mat like it was some sort of alien artifact, his lips tugging into an uncertain grin. "I'm pretty sure the only stretch I do is when I reach for a cold beer."

I laughed, setting my feet wide apart and demonstrating a simple stretch. "I'll take that as a challenge."

He tilted his head, sizing me up. "Alright, but don't expect me to start chanting or anything."

"Noted." I smirked, then guided him through the first few moves.

He was stiff at first, like a tree trying to bend without breaking. I showed him how to stretch properly, keeping it simple, but he still looked like he was suffering with every breath.

After a couple of minutes, I paused, trying not to laugh at his awkward stance. "Okay, so you're supposed to be relaxed. You look like you're trying to wrestle a bear."

He shot me a side-eye. "I'm pretty sure the bear would win, sweetheart."

I stifled a grin. "You might be right. Let's try a forward fold—don't worry, this one's easy."

I bent down, touching my fingers to the mat, then looked up to see Wells trying to do the same. He got halfway down before his face twisted in confusion, his hand barely touching his knees.

"This isn't yoga, this is a test of my dignity."

I burst out laughing. "You're doing great! Just breathe and let it go."

He inhaled deeply, then exhaled with a groan. "I think I just pulled something."

"That's called progress," I teased, straightening up. "You've just unlocked your first yoga injury."

Wells rolled his eyes, but I could tell he was loosening up a bit, his shoulders less tense. "I'm going to tell everyone I was tortured in the name of Zen."

"Fine by me," I grinned. "Go ahead and tell people you're a yoga guru. But hey, don't forget the shorts. You're clearly a natural in the athleisure department."

Wells raised an eyebrow but couldn't suppress the smirk creeping up his face. "I'll take the shorts win for today."

"Good, because that's as close as you're getting to a win." I stretched my arms above me, trying to hide my smile. "Next time, you might even surprise me and show up in proper yoga pants."

Wells raised both brows, looking horrified. "You really think I'm gonna trade in my jeans for stretchy pants?"

"C'mon, don't knock it 'til you've tried it."

"I'm good with my denim, thanks," he shot back, wiping sweat from his forehead. "I'll leave the spandex to you."

I laughed. "You're more predictable than a weather forecast."

He shrugged, his smile never fading. "That's why you keep coming back for more, isn't it?"

I smirked. "I just enjoy torturing you."

I would never tell Wells, but doing yoga with me this morning has helped heal a part of my heart he didn't break.

We rolled up our mats and headed back inside.

"You want breakfast?" Wells called from the sink.

I yawned, stretching my arms above my head. "I'm not hungry." I patted my stomach. "I'm still full from last night."

I couldn't help but smile thinking about the dinner Wells cooked up. He went from 'there's nothing to eat' to *Michelin-star* level in what felt like no time. The man could work some serious magic in the kitchen.

"What time is Wren coming over?"

Wells pulled his phone out of his pocket, scanning the screen. "Charlie texted me a little while ago. They're on the road, so I'd say about thirty minutes or so."

"Cool. What's the plan for your W Squared Day?"

Wells grinned. "Wren mentioned wanting to head to the nursing home. Her and Mrs. Turner are like this," he said, crossing his fingers with a wide grin.

"That sounds fun."

"You're welcome to join us, if you want."

I shook my head, leaning against the kitchen counter. "Nah, I've got a date."

Wells raised an eyebrow. "With who?"

I shot him a playful look. "Jealous much? My book." I smiled as I tapped my fingers on the counter. "Since you were kind enough to let me off the hook for work today, I'm going to find a quiet spot and dive into it."

Wells looked at me, eyes widening. "A date with your book?"

I smirked. "Yep. No interruptions, no yoga, just me and my next chapter."

He shook his head, chuckling. "I can't compete with that."

I winked. "No one can."

Wren and Charlie pulled up to the house about thirty minutes later, the sound of their car tires crunching on the gravel driveway drawing my attention. As I opened the door, I caught sight of Wren's grinning face through the windshield, her little blonde curls bouncing with each movement. She was practically bouncing out of her seat by the time the car stopped.

I stepped outside, grinning at her enthusiasm.

"Uncle Wells!" Wren squealed as she dashed over to him, her arms flung wide. Wells caught her up in one smooth motion, lifting her off her feet with ease.

"Hey there, kiddo. How's my favorite girl?" he asked, his voice warm with affection as he kissed the top of her head.

"I'm awesome!" Wren giggled, her arms squeezing his neck as she hung there.

The kid outstretched her arms and I grabbed her. "Hi, Wrenny."

"Hi, Auntie Rose." She looked between the two of us. "It's *so* cool that my favorite people live in the same house."

"I guess we're chopped liver?" Charlie piped up as I put Wren down.

"You and mom aren't cool like Uncle Wells and Aunt Rose."

Charlie put his hands up. "Fair enough. I'm gonna head out. I'll see y'all later."

"Bye, dad!"

Wren turned her attention back to us. "What are we doing today?"

"I was thinking maybe you could help us pick some flowers for the farmer's market tomorrow and then we could go see Mrs. Turner."

"She's still alive?"

"Wren!" Wells and I scolded her at the same time.

She shrugged. "What? She's old."

I bit back a smile. The kid had a fair enough point there.

Wren grinned at me, her face lighting up. "Are you hanging out with us today?"

I raised my hands in mock surrender. "Ah, well, my name doesn't start with a W, so I think I'm out."

Wren's little face scrunched in thought for a second before she shrugged. "You can be the honorary W. You just have to come hang out with us!"

I laughed, the warmth of her insistence almost impossible to resist. "You're hard to say no to, Wren."

"Please, please, please!" She tugged on my arm, her excitement contagious.

I glanced at Wells, who was watching us with a knowing look, and sighed. "Fine. You win."

Wren's face lit up like a Christmas tree. "Yay! You won't regret it!"

We all headed to the back of the house, and Wells grabbed a couple of baskets from the shed. Wren and I followed him into the fields where the sunflowers, lavender, and wild daisies grew in abundance. It was the perfect morning for flower picking, the air warm and sweet with the scent of fresh blooms.

Wells set out gathering a few large stems of lavender, showing Wren how to carefully clip them at the base. I crouched down beside them, filling my own basket with colorful daisies, the sun above warming my back.

"It's peaceful out here," I said, glancing over at Wells as he tied a bundle of flowers together with twine.

Wells nodded, a soft smile on his face. "It's one of my favorite things about this place. It always feels like you're a world away from everything else."

Wren, her little hands full of wildflowers, looked up at us both. "Uncle Wells, do you think we can make a big bouquet for Mrs. Turner? She loves flowers, and I'm really good at arranging them."

"That sounds like a great idea," Wells replied, grinning at her. "Let's make sure we get the prettiest ones, then."

I couldn't help but smile at how easily Wells fell into his role as Uncle Wells. His bond with Wren was something special, a quiet but strong presence, the kind of connection that needed no words to be understood.

Wren handed me a particularly bright sunflower and tilted her head. "Here, Auntie Rose. You can hold this one."

I took it with a nod. "Thanks, Wren. This is pretty."

After we picked flowers for a little while longer, we headed back to the house to get ready to head to the nursing home. Wren was practically bouncing with excitement as she talked about all the residents she hoped to see.

At the nursing home, we made our way through the front door, where Mrs. Turner was sitting on the porch, chatting with a couple of the other residents. As soon as Wren spotted her, she rushed over, and Mrs. Turner's face lit up in a smile as bright as the sun.

"Well, if it isn't my favorite little flower girl," Mrs. Turner said, reaching out to hug Wren. "Did you bring me more of your sunshine today?"

Wren giggled, holding out the bouquet of flowers. "These are for you, Mrs. Turner! I picked them just for you!"

Mrs. Turner's eyes twinkled with delight as she took the flowers. "Well, aren't you just the sweetest thing?"

Wren leaned down, speaking in a conspiratorial whisper. "You know, Mrs. Turner, we're going to the farmer's market tomorrow. You can come if you want! There'll be flowers, and cookies, and a lot of fun!"

Mrs. Turner chuckled softly. "I may be too old for all that running around, but I'll be there in spirit, my dear."

I watched the interaction from a distance, feeling that quiet warmth inside that comes from watching something so simple, yet so pure. Wells had wandered off and I was content to stay back, giving Wren and Mrs. Turner their time together.

"Why don't the three of us head inside?" Mrs. Turner offered.

Wren and I exchanged a glance and followed her inside. For now, I was happy to watch the quiet moments unfold, knowing that these were the kinds of memories that made life truly rich.

CHAPTER 29

ROCK AND A HARD PLACE

Wells

LEANED AGAINST THE BRICK WALL OF THE NURSING HOME, watching the residents move about, each caught up in their own routines. It was one of those quiet afternoons when time seemed to slow, and your thoughts drifted like leaves on a stream, whether you wanted them to or not. I should've been inside with Wren and Mrs. Turner, but I found myself wandering off to the side, craving a moment of solitude.

I wasn't used to this. Not used to having time to just think. To be still. But then there was Rose. Somehow, when she was around, everything felt different, more tangible, like she had a way of making the world seem more… real.

A soft voice pulled me from my thoughts.

"Wells, how's it going?"

It was Marie, the head nurse, with her clipboard in hand. She had that warm smile of hers, the kind that made you feel like you could tell her anything, and she'd listen with the patience of someone who genuinely cared.

"Hey, Marie," I said, straightening up from the wall. "It's going well. How about you?"

She returned my smile, voice light and easy. "Doing pretty well." Then she glanced out the window. "Who's the blonde?"

At the mention of Rose, my throat tightened. I quickly cleared it, unsure of how much I wanted to say, or maybe how much I could say. "That's Rose. She's helping out on the farm."

Marie raised an eyebrow. "So, not a girlfriend?"

I shook my head, a little too quickly. "No, not a girlfriend."

Marie's gaze flicked back to Rose, then back to me. "It's nice you got some help. But she doesn't exactly seem like she's the farm type."

"She's getting the hang of it," I replied, a little defensively.

The silence between us stretched, a quiet hum that felt like it held more than the words we were exchanging. I'd been doing a lot of thinking over the last couple of days, and Rose had somehow opened my eyes to things I hadn't realized. Maybe it was time to let someone in. Maybe it was time for more than just me and Granger around the house.

"That's cool," Marie said, breaking the silence, but her voice carried that awkward undertone of someone unsure of how to fill the gap.

Marie was smart and kind, but right now, I wasn't sure if I was really thinking about her or something else entirely. With my mind spinning, I decided to take a leap.

"What are you doing next Friday?"

Marie raised an eyebrow, clearly surprised by the question. "Next Friday?" she repeated, her voice thoughtful. "I haven't really made any plans yet. Why, what's up?"

I leaned against the wall again, trying to play it cool, even though the idea of asking her out had my stomach tied in knots. "Well, I was thinking maybe we could grab dinner. You know, something casual. Get away from all this for a bit."

Her expression softened, and I saw a flicker of surprise in her eyes, but it quickly turned into a smile. "Dinner, huh? You're not really my type, Wells," she teased, "but I'll take that as a compliment."

I couldn't help but laugh, the tension in my chest easing just a little. "Yeah, I've been called a lot of things, but I'll take 'not your type' as a challenge."

Marie chuckled, her gaze flicking over to the window again. "You're bold, I'll give you that." She thought for a moment, then shrugged. "Alright, Friday works. But if you start talking about farm animals, I'm out."

"Deal," I said with a grin, feeling like I had just taken a small victory lap.

Before she could turn away, I added, "But just so you know, I'm not the kind of guy who asks around a lot. This... it's new for me."

Marie's smile softened, and for a moment, it felt like I was talking to someone who understood more than I'd given her credit for. "Well, I'm all for new things."

As she walked away, I couldn't help but feel a surge of something I hadn't felt in a while. *Hope*. Maybe I had been wrong all along. Maybe opening myself up, even just a little, was exactly what I needed.

I turned back toward the nursing home, hoping the brief moment of boldness hadn't left me looking like a fool. My footsteps felt heavier now as I made my way inside, like the weight of my thoughts was suddenly too much to carry.

When I pushed the door open, I spotted Rose and Wren sitting with Mrs. Turner in the cozy corner, the three of them deep in conversation.

I leaned against the doorway, watching as Wren tugged on Rose's hand, giggling as she whispered something that made Rose roll her eyes but smile. Mrs. Turner sat back in her chair, looking mighty pleased with herself like she was watching her favorite soap opera play out in real time.

"You three scheming over there?" I asked, pushing off the doorframe and walking into the room.

Wren grinned up at me. "Auntie Rose needs to come with us every W Squared Day."

Rose arched a brow. "I told you, my name doesn't start with a W."

Wren waved her off. "You're an honorary W, remember?"

Mrs. Turner chuckled, patting Rose's hand. "She's got you there, dear."

I smirked. "She does have a point."

Rose sighed, "I don't want to intrude on your time together. We can have Auntie and Wrenny days."

Wren pouted in response. "I want you to spend more days with you before baby brother gets here."

I watched as the corner of Rose's mouth twitched. "Did you ask your uncle how he feels about that?"

Wren glanced at me.

"I don't mind. Your aunt is more than welcome to hang with us."

Rose piped up. "Fine. But only if we only start calling it W Squared Plus Day."

"Now that's a mouthful." I added.

Wren cheered like she'd just won the lottery, pulling Rose into a tight hug. "Best news ever!"

Mrs. Turner winked at me. "She's a keeper."

I cleared my throat, ignoring the way my ears burned at the implication. "Y'all ready to head out?"

Wren practically bounced out of her chair, still clinging to Rose. "Yep! Let's go!"

With a soft smile, Rose let Wren lead her toward the door, and I followed behind, shaking my head.

Damn. I had no idea what I was getting myself into.

There was something about the way Rose let her guard down around Wren that gave me a glimpse into who she was before she came here. A version of her untouched by whatever had made her so wary. She's been to Wippowa a handful of times, but our paths never crossed—until now. And the woman in front of me? She was different.

With Wren, she was light. Playful. Free in a way I hadn't seen before.

But back at the farm? She was cautious, like she was waiting for the other shoe to drop. The difference was striking, and I wasn't sure which version of her was closer to the truth. Maybe both. Maybe neither.

A few bricks in her wall had crumbled, but not enough for me to see inside.

We piled into the truck, Wren chattering away in the backseat while Rose stretched out in the passenger seat, her head tilted back against the headrest.

"That was a solid day," she mused, glancing over at me.

I nodded, shifting gears as we pulled onto the main road. "You didn't expect to enjoy yourself, did you?"

She smirked. "I expected chaos. Turns out, it was nice."

Wren popped her head between the seats. "That's 'cause W Squared Days are the best."

"W Squared Plus," Rose corrected, poking Wren's knee playfully.

Wren giggled. "Right, right. We're making history."

By the time we got back to the farm, the late afternoon sun was hanging low, stretching warmth across the fields. I expected Rose to escape inside with her book the second we stepped out of the truck, but she lingered, following Wren toward the back porch.

I grabbed a couple of sweet teas from the fridge and brought them outside, handing one to Rose as she sunk into the porch swing. Wren had sprawled out on the steps, flipping through one of her turtle books.

Rose took a sip of her tea and sighed. "I could get used to this."

I leaned against the railing. "Sitting around doing nothing?"

She side-eyed me. "Existing in peace. *Big* difference."

I huffed a quiet laugh, watching the way the sunlight wove through her blonde hair, turning it gold. Right now, she looked like she didn't have a single worry, like she'd never been more at ease in her life. The weight she usually carried—whatever it was, wherever it came from—seemed to have disappeared, at least for now.

And damn if that wasn't something to see.

Wren looked up from her book. "Auntie Rose, can I paint your nails?"

Rose grinned. "Do you even have nail polish with you?"

Wren scrambled up and ran inside, yelling about her options.

I smirked. "You're really letting her get you with the nail polish?"

Rose shrugged, setting her tea down. "The kid's persuasive."

I watched her for a second, how easily she had started to settle in here, even if she didn't realize it yet. There was something about seeing her like this—comfortable, unguarded—that made my chest feel too tight.

Maybe Wren was onto something. Maybe W Squared Plus wasn't such a bad idea after all.

CHAPTER 30

SUPERMARKET FLOWERS

Rose

THE DAY HAD FINALLY ARRIVED—MY FIRST FARMER'S MARKET. I had successfully dodged last weekend's market thanks to the rain, but this time, luck wasn't on my side. There was no excuse, no last-minute reprieve. I was in for the full Wippowa Sunday experience.

After Wren went home last night, Wells and I spent the evening loading up the truck, making sure everything was packed and ready to go. He'd handle the produce, and I was officially on flower booth duty. Not that I had any clue what I was doing, but he reassured me we'd be set up side by side in case I needed anything.

My alarm went off while the world was still wrapped in darkness. The market started at eight, and with an hour-long drive ahead of us, we needed to be on the road by 6:15 to have enough time to set up.

When I asked about the dress code, Wells—so helpfully—told me to wear whatever I was most comfortable in. Which was a non-answer if I'd ever heard one. So, with no one to impress and zero interest in looking like I belonged, I pulled on my favorite sundress and a pair of well-worn sandals. Practical? Probably not. But I was leaning into my strengths, and fashion was one of them.

I grabbed my phone and opened the door, still groggy from sleep, ready to head to the bathroom. But as I stepped forward, something on the ground caught my eye.

A single sunflower.

I froze. My breath hitched in my throat as I stared at the bright yellow petals, soft and full, resting right outside my door like it had been waiting for me. My heart clenched, warmth unfurling in my chest. I didn't think Wells would actually do it.

It had taken over three decades, but someone had finally given me flowers.

Swallowing hard, I bent down and picked it up, my fingers brushing against a small piece of folded paper underneath. My pulse quickened as I smoothed it open, my eyes scanning the familiar scrawl.

Roses seemed like the obvious choice.
- **W**

A shaky breath left my lips.

The simplicity of it, the quiet thoughtfulness—it undid me. Tears pricked at the corners of my eyes, the kind that came when you weren't sad, just overwhelmed in the best possible way.

It wasn't just a flower. It was proof that someone had paid attention. That someone had thought of me, just because.

I set the flower and note gently on my dresser before heading to the bathroom, the quiet weight of the moment still lingering in my chest. By the time I made my way downstairs, the first soft streaks of sunlight were filtering through the windows, casting a light golden hue over the kitchen.

A to-go cup sat waiting on the counter, steam curling from the lid.

I wrapped my hands around it, taking a slow sip as my thoughts drifted. My past. Every twist and turn that had led me here. The emotional damage Thad had left behind had made me swear off relationships entirely. I had no desire to open myself up to that kind of hurt again. So, I was going to take full advantage of this arrangement—live here rent-free until I could comfortably move out. I had savings, sure, but this gig was buying me time until I found something more stable.

Through the window, I spotted Wells outside with Granger. The easy way he moved, the way he spoke to his dog like he was an old friend—it was something to see. He had a deep, unwavering love for that dog, and it was obvious in every small interaction.

I took another sip, watching them until they finally headed inside.

"Ready to head out?" Wells asked, running a hand through his hair as he stepped into the kitchen.

I tapped my phone screen to check the time. "Yep. I'll take the rest of this to go."

His eyes flicked to my phone, then narrowed. "Sunshine, is that your background?"

I tilted my head. "What?"

"Is your phone wallpaper really just… black?"

"Sure is."

He crossed his arms, amused. "Finally removed that douchebag, huh?"

The corner of my mouth twitched. "It was time."

"Good. Now give me your phone."

I hesitated. "For what?"

"I'm changing your background."

I rolled my eyes. "Just leave it. I'll change it eventually."

"But I have just the photo." Wells swiped through his phone, then a text popped up from him.

"Hand it over," he said, holding out his hand expectantly.

With a sigh, I gave in, passing him my phone. A moment later, he handed it back. "Much better."

I tapped the screen, and there it was—a photo Wren had insisted we take to commemorate W Squared Plus Day yesterday. The three of us, side by side, grinning like idiots.

Something in my chest softened.

I glanced up at him, a genuine smile tugging at my lips. "Thanks."

He placed his cowboy hat on his head with an easy confidence, tipping it slightly as he glanced at me. "Let's hit the road."

I grabbed my coffee and followed him out the door, the crisp morning air wrapping around us as we stepped onto the porch. The sky was still painted in soft shades of dawn, the world just beginning to stir.

Wells moved ahead, unlocking the truck and loading in the last of the crates. I slid into the passenger seat, tucking my dress beneath me as I got settled.

As Wells climbed in and started the engine, he shot me a sideways glance. "You ready for this?"

I exhaled slowly, gripping my coffee cup a little tighter. "Not even a little."

He chuckled, shifting the truck into gear. "You'll do fine."

With that, we pulled onto the road, heading toward the farmer's market and whatever the day had in store.

The drive was quiet at first, the kind of easy silence that came with too-early mornings and half-awake minds. Wells had one hand on the wheel, the other resting on the open window, his fingers drumming lightly against the side of the truck.

"You ever been to this market before?" he asked after a while.

I shook my head, stretching my legs out in front of me. "Nope. This is a first."

He smirked. "Gotta say, you don't strike me as the farmer's market type."

I scoffed, feigning offense. "What's that supposed to mean?"

"Just that you seem more like a boutique coffee shop, shopping-on-your-phone kind of girl."

I gasped dramatically. "Wow. You know, I could've been raised on a farm for all you know."

Wells shot me a knowing look. "Were you?"

"...No."

He chuckled. "That's what I thought."

The rest of the ride was filled with easy conversation, the

occasional tease, and moments of comfortable silence as the sun climbed higher in the sky.

When we finally arrived, the market was already buzzing with vendors setting up their booths, stacking fresh produce into neat displays and arranging handmade goods with care. The scent of baked goods filled the air, mixing with the earthy sweetness of ripe fruit and saltwater.

Wells backed the truck into our designated spot, hopping out before I could so much as unbuckle my seatbelt. "Alright, city girl," he said, pulling down the tailgate. "Time to get to work."

I groaned, dragging myself out of the truck. "Why did I agree to this again?"

"Because deep down, you love manual labor." He tossed me a wink before handing me a crate of flowers.

I rolled my eyes but took the crate anyway, following him to our booths. True to his word, our setups were side by side—mine bursting with colorful blooms, his stacked with farm-fresh fruits and vegetables.

I stood back, surveying my work. The flowers were arranged in pretty little bundles, each wrapped in brown paper and tied with twine. It actually looked… cute. Like something out of one of those small-town romance movies.

Wells glanced over, nodding in approval. "Not bad."

I smirked. "You almost sound impressed."

He leaned on the edge of his stand, arms crossed. "Don't push it."

As the morning market officially opened, a steady stream of people wandered through, stopping at booths, chatting with vendors, and carrying baskets filled with fresh produce and homemade treats. I wasn't sure what to expect when Wells dragged me into this, but to my surprise, I was having fun.

It started slow—just a few passersby glancing at the flower stand. But then, a woman stopped and picked up a bouquet, her eyes lit up.

"These are beautiful," she said, bringing the bundle closer to her face to inhale the soft scent of lavender and wildflowers.

"Thank you," I said, standing a little straighter. "We grow them right on the farm."

"You and your husband have a great little thing going." She complimented.

I was so stunned I couldn't speak. Of course Wells heard it and shot me a cheeky grin.

That one sale turned into another. And another. People were drawn to the flowers, and for the first time in what felt like forever, I found myself genuinely enjoying a conversation with strangers.

A mother and her little girl stopped by, the child's fingers grazing over the petals as she stared at them in wonder.

"You like flowers?" I asked with a smile.

The girl nodded shyly. "Pink ones."

I crouched down, picking out a bundle with soft pink roses and daisies. "This one has your name all over it."

Her face lit up as she turned to her mom.

"We'll take it," the woman said, smiling warmly as she handed me cash.

"That's my gift to you." I pushed the money back.

"That's very kind of you. Thank you."

By midday, my hands were covered in bits of twine and petals, and I had sold more than half of the bouquets I brought. A sense of pride swelled in my chest—something I hadn't felt in a long time.

I glanced over at Wells, who was handling the produce stand with ease, chatting with customers like he'd been doing this his whole life—which, knowing him, he probably had. He caught me watching and shot me a knowing grin.

"Told you you'd be a natural," he said.

I rolled my eyes, but I couldn't fight the smile tugging at my lips.

As the afternoon wore on, the steady trickle of customers turned into a full-blown rush. One by one, bouquets disappeared from the stand, exchanged for cash and grateful smiles. People stopped to admire the setup, complimenting the arrangements, asking about the farm.

And then, just like that—I was sold out.

I blinked down at the empty table, the last bouquet in the hands of an elderly man who grinned as he shuffled away.

Holy crap.

I sold out.

I wiped my hands on my dress, barely able to believe it. "Wells," I called over, still staring at the bare table like more flowers would magically appear.

He turned, a crate of tomatoes in his hands, and when he saw my booth, he froze. Then his brows lifted.

"Well, I'll be damned," he said, setting the crate down and walking over. "You sold out?"

I nodded slowly, still processing. "Does this usually happen?"

Wells let out a low chuckle, shaking his head. "Nope. Normally, I have to haul half of 'em back home." He leaned against my empty table, eyes twinkling. "Guess people liked what you were selling."

A surprising swell of pride spread through my chest. It wasn't just that the flowers were pretty—it was the way I had connected with people, the way they trusted me when I talked about them, the way their faces lit up when they found the perfect bouquet. The hours of studying up on flowers had paid off.

"I can't believe it," I murmured, running a hand through my hair.

"Well, believe it, Sunshine." Wells nudged my shoulder with his. "Looks like you've got yourself a new title—Flower Saleswoman Extraordinaire."

I snorted, shaking my head.

But the truth was, I felt something I hadn't in a long time.

Capable. Confident. Happy.

CHAPTER 31

I AM NOT WHO I WAS

Rose

EVER SINCE THE FARMERS MARKET ON SUNDAY, I'VE BEEN ON cloud nine. I didn't think it was possible to feel so light and free, especially after how weighed down I'd been by all the emotional baggage I've been carrying. But those bouquets, the way people's faces lit up when they bought them, the compliments, and even the simple act of arranging the flowers—I'd never thought I'd find something that could make me feel *this* good.

It wasn't just about the flowers themselves, it was about the connection. Something about handling them, choosing the right combinations, knowing how each bloom interacted with the others—it made me feel like I had a purpose. Like I could create something beautiful, something that mattered. Each stem I cut, each arrangement I made, was like putting a piece of myself into something more lasting, something people would take home and cherish. And, unexpectedly, it felt like I was doing more than just working—like I was healing.

But the truth was, I was only healing in small increments. The deeper stuff—the things that had made me who I was before all this—those wounds were still there, buried under layers of distractions, a crumbling sense of trust. My past, the way it had shaped me, wasn't something I could simply push aside and forget. It clung to me like a shadow, no matter how bright the sunlight was in front of me.

Wells had been nothing but supportive, though I wasn't sure if he fully understood the emotional weight I'd carried before all of this. Still, he encouraged me to embrace this new passion. He wasn't the type to throw around praise easily, but every time he complimented me on my work, I couldn't help but feel a little more confident. I couldn't shake the feeling that maybe I was still playing pretend—like at any moment, the mask I'd carefully put on would slip and he would see the real me, the one who still wasn't sure she could trust herself enough to move forward.

So, every morning since then, I've been helping feed the animals, picking produce, pruning plants, and picking flowers to arrange into perfect bunches, making sure each stem had a place. With each day, I was becoming more comfortable with my hands in the dirt.

The rhythm of it, the act of carefully bending and trimming the flowers, felt like it slowed the world down for a moment. It was a type of peace I hadn't expected to find. It felt so simple, yet so fulfilling.

But every time I felt that rush of peace, a voice—small but insistent—would remind me that this was temporary. That at some point, I'd have to face the fact that I couldn't outrun the past forever. The emotional damage Thad had caused—it wasn't something I could just bottle up and ignore. I couldn't pretend it didn't affect me. I still wasn't sure how to fully process it all, and honestly, I wasn't sure if I ever would.

I'd been talking to Wells about ideas, brainstorming how we could expand, how I could do more. I'd been thinking about it for days, and the idea of offering dried arrangements had been gnawing at me for a while.

"Wells," I said one morning, adjusting the bouquet in my hands. The warm morning sun filtered through the trees, casting golden rays over the petals. "What if we offered dried arrangements too? You know, for people who want something they can take home and keep longer?"

Wells paused, looking at me over the top of the crate of tomatoes he was sorting. "Dried arrangements?" he repeated, his brows knitting in thought. "How would that work?"

I set down the bouquet I'd been arranging and stepped closer to the worktable, starting to carefully arrange a few dried lavender sprigs with some preserved eucalyptus I had gathered. "Well, I've been reading up on it. People love them for their homes, especially for gifts. We could offer them at the farmers market. We could do a whole line of different dried flowers. Think about it—people from out of town would be able to buy something they can take home and last longer than the fresh stuff. Calloway Farms could be part of their home forever."

Wells didn't answer right away. Instead, he looked at me, his eyes scanning the bouquet I was holding, and then he gave a small nod. "You think people would buy that?" he asked, his voice thoughtful, but not dismissive. There was something in his tone that made me feel like he was considering it more seriously than he probably had at first.

I didn't hesitate. "I know they would. I mean, you already have a solid customer base with the fresh flowers. People come back every week for that. If we offered dried flowers too, we could really expand. There's no reason it couldn't work."

Wells was silent for a moment. I could see him thinking it over. Then, finally, he shrugged, as if deciding the idea wasn't as crazy as he'd originally thought.

I didn't let his uncertainty deter me. "Think about it. There are people who come here for the market, who drive for hours just to get a taste of the local scene. We could give them something they can't get anywhere else. Something that lasts. And we could even sell them online. If we can make a name for your farm here, why not take it further?"

Wells chewed on that, his gaze drifting down to the crate of tomatoes, then back to me. "You've got a point," he said slowly, like the idea was settling in. "People do like the unique stuff. And if anyone can pull it off, it's you."

His approval felt like a small victory. I smiled, feeling the warmth of his encouragement spread through me. "I'll start working on a few designs and see what I can come up with. I've been thinking of starting with small bouquets—something people can buy as a gift or take home. I already have a few ideas."

Wells gave me a nod, his expression softening. "Do it. I know you'll make it work. You've got a good eye for this stuff."

A sudden sense of relief washed over me. I'd been holding onto this idea for a while, unsure if it would be enough or if Wells would think it was too much, but now it felt like the first real step toward making something of my own. For the first time in a long time, I was ready to take a leap of faith.

But beneath all that excitement, there was still a quiet tug at my chest. The truth that I couldn't ignore—the past was always lurking, waiting to sneak its way in. But maybe I was learning how to carve out something good for myself. Maybe I was learning how to take control, to build something that wasn't defined by the mess Thad left behind.

I'd just have to keep walking, one step at a time. And for the first time in ages, I felt like I could.

The sun sat high overhead, casting a golden glow over the fields as Wells and I worked side by side, plucking ripe vegetables from the vines and tossing them into crates. The dirt was warm beneath my feet, the scent of fresh earth filling the air, and for the first time in what felt like forever, I didn't mind getting my hands dirty.

It had been a few weeks since I started working on the farm, and against all odds, I hadn't run screaming back to the city. In fact, I was thriving. Who would've thought?

Wells glanced over at me as I inspected a particularly plump tomato. "You planning to pick that or just admire it all day?"

I held it up dramatically. "You know, there's an art to selecting the perfect tomato."

He snorted. "Yeah, it's called grab the red ones and move on."

I rolled my eyes, dropping the tomato into the crate. "You have no appreciation for the finer things in life."

"Says the girl who thought basil was just a fancy garnish."

I gasped in mock offense. "First of all, I know what basil is. Second of all, I just didn't realize people grew it in actual dirt. I thought it came from those little plastic containers at the grocery store."

Wells let out a full belly laugh, shaking his head. "City girl through and through."

"I am adapting, thank you very much," I shot back, swiping a stray strand of hair from my face. "I wake up early, I work with flowers, I haven't worn heels in weeks—"

"And yet, you still complain every morning about getting up before sunrise."

"Because it's unnatural!" I huffed. "Humans were not meant to be functional before coffee."

Wells smirked, tossing a cucumber into the crate. "You seemed pretty functional at the farmers market last weekend. I don't think I've ever seen anyone sell out of flowers that fast."

I preened a little, unable to hide my pride. "That's because I have a natural gift."

He gave me a pointed look. "You spent the first twenty minutes of the market verifying the names of half the flowers."

I waved him off. "Details."

Wells chuckled, shaking his head. "Look, all I'm saying is, you clearly have a knack for this. And if you really want to go all in with the dried arrangements, I think you should."

I hesitated, staring down at the tomato in my hand. Hearing Wells say it out loud made it feel real.

"So many things could go wrong," I murmured, starting to second-guess myself.

Wells nudged me lightly with his shoulder. "But how many things could go right?"

I looked up at him, my heart doing a weird little flip at the sincerity in his gaze.

I exhaled slowly, letting the thought settle.

"You really think I can do this?" I asked softly.

Wells smirked. "Rose, you convinced half the town to buy

overpriced bundles of flowers last weekend just by smiling at them. Yeah, I think you can do this."

I let out a laugh, the warmth of his words sinking in. Maybe he was right. Maybe this could be something.

"Alright," I said, squaring my shoulders. "Let's do it."

Wells grinned. "That's what I like to hear."

He reached for another tomato, but before he could grab it, I snatched it up and tossed it at him. He caught it effortlessly, raising a brow.

"Really?" he said.

I shrugged innocently. "Just making sure you're paying attention."

Wells shook his head, but there was laughter in his eyes. "You're gonna be trouble, aren't you?"

"Oh, Wells," I teased, flashing him a grin. "I've always been trouble."

And just like that, the weight in my chest felt a little lighter.

We worked in silence for a while before Wells spoke up again. "What would you call it?"

"Call what?"

"Your business." He lowered himself onto the grass, tugging off his cowboy hat. Running a hand through his tousled brown hair, he held the hat out to me. "Here. Put this on."

"Oh, absolutely not. That thing reeks."

He shot me a look. "Your scalp's burning because you're too damn stubborn to wear a hat. Take it, Sunshine."

"I can smell it from here."

"And you claim you're not a city girl anymore."

"Is it so wrong to care about personal hygiene?" I tossed back.

His laugh was low and amused before he plopped the hat onto my head. "Deal with it."

I wrinkled my nose. "This smells like sweat, dirt, and questionable life choices."

Wells smirked, stretching his legs out in the grass. "You forgot hard work and Southern charm."

"Oh no, those definitely weren't in the scent profile." I adjusted the hat, which was entirely too big for my head. "I think it just slipped over my ears. I might be trapped."

He let out a lazy chuckle. "Guess you're part cowgirl now."

"Fantastic. Do I get a lifetime supply of dust and denim?"

Wells leaned back on his elbows, watching me with an amused glint in his eye. "Yep, you also get a healthy fear of snakes and a tan all-year 'round."

I shuddered. "Snakes are a dealbreaker."

He grinned. "That's what you think. Wait 'til one slithers into your boot one morning."

I smacked his arm. "Why would you say that? Why would you put that energy into the universe?"

He shrugged, completely unbothered. "Just preparing you for the full cowboy experience."

I groaned and flopped back in the grass, tipping the hat forward to shield my face. "I hate it here."

"Nah," Wells drawled, swiping the hat back and plopping it onto his own head. "You love it."

And the worst part? He wasn't wrong.

He let a beat pass before speaking again. "You never answered my question. What are you gonna call your dried flower business?"

I huffed. "I didn't think it was my business." My voice came out muffled under the hat, but I didn't move.

The strangest thing? The hat smelled... familiar. Yeah, it reeked of sweat, but beneath that, it smelled like Wells—sandalwood and bad decisions. And for some inexplicable reason, that was comforting.

"You keep talking like you're just passing through," Wells said, his voice softer now. "Like this isn't something you're actually gonna do."

I peeked out from under the hat, finding him watching me, his dark brows slightly furrowed. Not teasing. Not pushing. Just... noticing.

"I don't know," I admitted. "I guess it doesn't feel real."

"Well, it is." He leaned back on his elbows, gazing up at the sky. "And you're gonna be damn good at it."

Something in my chest tightened. People had encouraged me before, sure. But Wells wasn't just throwing out empty words. He actually believed it. In me.

I turned my head to look at him. "Why do you care?"

He smirked, but it wasn't his usual cocky grin. It was softer. "Just do."

I swallowed, suddenly feeling warmer than the Georgia sun should've allowed.

"Now," he continued, breaking the moment before it got too serious. "What are we naming this empire of yours? 'Sunshine & Stems'? 'Petals & Poor Life Choices'?"

I snorted. "Absolutely not."

"Well, that's just rude. I worked hard on those."

I shook my head, but I was smiling. Maybe Wells Calloway was a good guy and maybe I was starting to trust him.

CHAPTER 32

SPIN YOU AROUND

Wells

I WON'T LIE—THERE WAS SOMETHING DOWNRIGHT DISTRACTING about Rose wearing my cowboy hat. The way she kept it on for the rest of the day did something to me. Couldn't say if it was the hat, the boots, or just the way she carried herself, but damn if she wasn't starting to look like a proper coastal cowgirl.

And that was dangerous.

Because the more she looked the part, the harder it was to remember she wasn't staying. She made that abundantly clear. As soon as she was able to, she was good as gone.

I caught myself watching her more than I should've—tucking stray petals into a basket, brushing dirt off her jeans, tipping the brim of my hat like she'd been born knowing how. And the worst part? She didn't even realize she was doing it.

"Quit staring, Calloway." She smirked without looking up. "You're making me nervous."

I leaned against the fence post, crossing my arms. "I wasn't staring. I was admiring."

She huffed out a laugh. "Big difference."

"Sure is," I said easily. "One's rude. The other's just good manners."

She shook her head, fighting a smile. "You are impossible."

"And yet," I said, pushing off the post and stepping closer, "you're still here."

That wiped the smirk right off her face. Not in a bad way. Just in a way that made me wonder if she was feeling the same slow pull I was.

She glanced away, fiddling with the brim of my hat like she suddenly wasn't sure if she should be wearing it. "I should probably give this back."

"Keep it," I said before I could think better of it. "I have more inside."

Her gaze snapped to mine. "Seriously?"

I shrugged. "Looks better on you."

She studied me, like she was trying to figure out if I was messing with her. I wasn't.

And when she gave a small nod and settled the hat back on her head, something in my chest tightened.

I was in trouble.

Big, damn trouble.

Because watching Rose in my hat, fiddling with the brim like she was still deciding if she had the right to wear it, made me want to do something stupid. Like grab her hand. Or maybe her waist. Maybe even—hell, I don't know. But something.

Instead, I did what any self-respecting cowboy would do—I shoved my hands in my pockets and looked at the ground like an idiot.

"Alright," she said, clearing her throat. "I should probably get back to work."

"Right. Work." I nodded like I had a single thought left in my head that wasn't about how good she looked standing there in the golden afternoon light.

She turned, heading toward the barn, and I was about to force myself to do something productive when she paused and threw a glance over her shoulder.

"You coming, or are you just gonna stand there looking pretty?"

I blinked. "Did you just call me pretty?"

She smirked. "Nope."

"You definitely did."

"I absolutely did not."

"Rose, I heard it with my own two ears."

She kept walking, tossing a hand up in the air. "You heard what you wanted to hear, Calloway."

I grinned, shaking my head as I followed her.

Yeah.

I was in big, damn trouble.

And I didn't even mind.

I followed her into the barn, doing my best not to stare at the way her jeans hugged her just right. Failing, but trying.

Rose stopped near the workbench, hands on her hips as she eyed the bundles of dried flowers laid out in neat rows. "You should feel honored, you know."

I leaned against the doorway, crossing my arms. "Oh yeah? And why's that?"

She turned, arching a brow. "Because I don't wear just anybody's hat."

That got a laugh out of me. "Sunshine, I'm the only cowboy you know."

"Exactly," she said, smirking as she reached for a pair of shears.

I dragged a hand down my face, grinning despite myself. She was impossible. Absolutely impossible.

"So," I said, stepping closer, "do I get a say in what you name this operation of yours? Seeing as I'm now the official supplier of headwear?"

She rolled her eyes but didn't tell me no.

Progress.

"I was thinking something simple," she said, running her fingers over the dried petals. "Maybe just 'Solace.'"

Something about the way she said it made my chest go tight. Like she hadn't even realized what she'd done.

"Solace," I repeated, quieter now. "That your way of telling me you're starting to feel at home here?"

She hesitated, like she hadn't meant to give that much away. Then, finally, she sighed. "It's my last name."

Damn if that didn't do something to me.

I picked up a bundle of dried lavender, twirling it between my fingers. "I like it."

She looked up at me, something softer in her expression now. "Yeah?"

I nodded, and for a second, neither of us said anything. Just stood there in the late afternoon light, the smell of flowers and hay thick in the air, something unspoken settling between us.

Then, because I was clearly a glutton for punishment, I reached over and tucked the lavender behind her ear.

"There," I murmured. "Now you really look the part."

She swallowed, eyes flicking to mine, and for the first time all day, she didn't have some smartass remark locked and loaded.

I should've stepped back. Should've let her go back to work.

But I didn't.

Because right then, standing in the middle of my family's barn, wearing my hat and my damn lavender, Rose Solace had never looked more like she belonged.

And that thought?

It scared me more than anything.

I leaned up against the workbench, watching Rose work. The way she moved—focused, determined, like she'd been doing this her whole life—had my thoughts drifting somewhere unexpected.

To my mom.

She would've loved Rose.

Mom always said I needed a woman who'd keep me on my toes. Someone who wouldn't put up with my nonsense, who'd call it like it is. And Rose? Well, she did that without even trying.

But it wasn't just that.

The way she was throwing herself into this, turning something small into something real, something that was hers—that would've made my mom happier than anything.

"You're staring again," Rose murmured, not looking up.

I smirked. "Admiring, remember?"

She huffed, cutting a piece of twine. "You're thinking about something. Your face is doing that thing."

I frowned. "What thing?"

She waved a hand toward me. "The broody cowboy thing."

I scoffed. "I do not brood."

Rose finally looked up, tilting her head like she was examining a piece of art. "Hmm. No, you definitely do."

I shook my head, biting back a grin. "You are impossible."

"So I've been told."

She turned back to her work, but I wasn't ready to let the moment go.

"My mom would've liked you," I said, voice quieter now.

Rose's hands stilled. Slowly, she glanced back at me, curiosity flickering in her eyes. "Yeah?"

I nodded, clearing my throat. "She liked women who didn't take my crap."

That made her smile. A small one, but real. "She sounds like she was smart."

"She was." I hesitated, running my thumb along the edge of the workbench. "She also liked people who went after what they wanted."

Rose studied me for a beat before softly saying, "Sounds like you miss her."

I swallowed, nodding once. "Every day."

She didn't say anything right away, just reached for another bundle of flowers. But her movements were slower now, more thoughtful.

"Well," she said after a moment, "I like her already."

Something in my chest tightened.

I cleared my throat, pushing off the workbench before I did something stupid—like reach for her hand. "I should check on the horses."

Rose didn't try to stop me, but as I walked away, I swore I heard her whisper, "She'd be proud of you, Wells."

And damn it if that didn't almost bring me to my knees.

I had to push these feelings aside because I have a date tomorrow.

CHAPTER 33

WISHFUL DRINKING

Rose

AFTER A LONG DAY OUTSIDE, DINNER CAME TOGETHER without much thought. It had started happening more and more—Wells and I moving around the kitchen like a well-oiled machine. I chopped vegetables while he manned the stove. I grabbed plates while he pulled a casserole from the oven. It was unspoken and effortless every single night.

"Feels like we should be keeping track," I said, nudging his hip with mine as I passed him a spatula.

"Of what?"

"How many meals we've made together." I clarified.

He smirked, flipping a piece of chicken in the pan. "You thinking we should start a tally on the fridge?"

"Maybe." I shrugged. "Or maybe it just means we're dangerously close to being domestic."

That made him laugh, a low, easy sound that warmed something in my chest. "Careful, Sunshine," he teased. "You'll give a man ideas."

I rolled my eyes and set the table, pretending my stomach hadn't just done a little flip.

After dinner, we lingered outside, watching the sky turn into soft shades of pink and purple, our plates empty but our conversation easy. We talked about the horses, about what I was planning for the upcoming market—about everything and nothing.

It was simple, and it was the best part of my day.

When it was time, we went our separate ways—no rush, just a quiet end to the evening. I changed into my pajamas and brushed my teeth, crawling into bed with a book. But the day's exhaustion hit me all at once, and before I knew it, I was lying there with my eyes closed, letting the quiet of the house lull me toward sleep.

Just as I was about to drift off, there was a knock at the door.

I blinked, startled. "Hmm?"

The door creaked open, and Wells stepped inside. He was barefoot, wearing a faded gray T-shirt and gray sweats that hung just a little too low on his hips, and suddenly, I couldn't think straight.

"You okay?" I asked, sitting up a little, trying to act normal.

He shifted from foot to foot like he wasn't entirely sure about what he was doing. "Actually, I need your help with something."

That made me sit up fully. Wells wasn't the kind of guy who asked for help—ever.

"Yeah, what's up?"

He scratched the back of his head, his usual confident demeanor gone, replaced by something almost... hesitant. "I need to pick out a nice outfit."

I raised an eyebrow. "A nice outfit? For what?"

"I've got a date tomorrow." He said it with a casual shrug, but I caught the flicker of uncertainty in his eyes.

My heart skipped. "A date?"

"Yeah." He seemed almost embarrassed now, rubbing his neck awkwardly. "With Marie from the nursing home."

I blinked. "Marie? The one who's like... pushing ninety?"

Wells chuckled, but it was a little forced. "Not that Marie. The head nurse. Early-thirties, real sharp. I got her to agree to dinner."

"I didn't know you were interested in her."

"Yep. She's a tough one to impress, but I've got my ways." His grin returned, but there was something almost shy about it.

I took a second to process. I hadn't expected Wells to be

interested in someone like Marie—not that I had any reason to be jealous, right? I was just his roommate.

"So you need my help?" I asked, trying to sound casual.

"Yeah, I want to look nice for her. But I don't know if I've got the right stuff." He stuffed his hands in his pockets and gave me that sheepish look of his. "You think you could help me out?"

I shrugged. "Of course. What kind of date is it?"

"Just dinner. Nothing too fancy. But you know, I want to make sure I look decent. Don't want to show up looking like I rolled out of the barn."

I smiled at the image of Wells trying to get all dressed up, but I could tell he was genuinely invested in making a good impression on Marie. There was something about the way he spoke about her—respectful but a little nervous—that made me realize this wasn't just a casual date for him.

I rolled myself out of bed. "Alright, let's see what we've got."

We walked down the hall to his room, and when I stepped inside, it felt strangely intimate. His room was warm, decorated in deep, earthy tones with soft lighting that made everything feel cozy and inviting. There was a guitar propped against the dresser, a few framed pictures of his family, and a bookshelf filled with well-worn paperbacks.

I noticed a photo of Wells and his mom on the nightstand, a snapshot of them laughing. It hit me, then, how much of his life was still tied to this place, to his roots.

"You play?" I nodded towards the guitar on a stand.

"Sometimes."

Wells opened his closet, revealing a variety of shirts, jeans, and jackets, along with a few boots lined up neatly at the bottom. It was exactly what I'd expected—nothing too flashy, just solid, dependable pieces.

I grabbed a navy blazer from the rack, holding it up for inspection. "How about this? It's sharp but not too fancy."

He eyed the blazer and then glanced back at me. "You think it'll be too much?"

I smiled, tapping the fabric. "It'll be perfect. Marie's not going to expect you to show up in a tux, but you'll want to look like you've put some thought into it."

He nodded, looking a little less sure than before but trusting me nonetheless. "If you say so."

I grabbed a crisp white button-down shirt next, holding it up to his chest. "This one's got that clean, fresh vibe that always works."

I could feel him watching me as I worked, though I kept my focus on the clothes. There was something a little too personal about helping him pick out an outfit. Maybe it was the way he trusted me to make the right call, or maybe it was the realization that Wells was someone I cared about more than I was ready to admit.

I stepped back, holding up a pair of dark jeans. "These will match the blazer without making you look too dressed up."

"Good choice," he said, nodding in approval. "Looks like I'm in good hands."

I forced a smile, though my chest felt tight. "Just make sure you show up looking good. Don't make me regret helping you."

"Trust me," Wells said, his voice low and sincere. "I won't."

"Marie will think you're the most charming man in the room, no matter what you wear."

Wells raised an eyebrow, his lips twitching like he was trying not to smile. "You think so?"

I grinned. "I know so."

He nodded, seeming to appreciate the effort. "I trust you."

Something about that made my heart stutter.

Wells stepped closer, peering over my shoulder at the outfit I'd picked out. "I never thought I'd need help picking out clothes. Guess I was wrong."

I looked up at him, really looked at him, and realized just how comfortable we were together. How natural it felt. My chest tightened, but I forced the feeling down.

"You're set," I said, handing him the clothes.

He grinned and tossed the clothes onto the bed. "Thanks, Sunshine. I guess I owe you one."

"Just make sure Marie knows how lucky she is." I shrugged, heading toward the door.

Wells didn't say anything, just watched me leave, his gaze lingering for a moment longer than it should have. I felt the weight of it as I stepped out of his room, the door clicking shut behind me.

I couldn't figure out why my heart felt so heavy.

Maybe it was the fact that he was going on a date tomorrow—something I should've been completely fine with.

Maybe it was the way his space felt like it belonged to someone who wasn't planning on leaving anytime soon.

Or maybe it was something else entirely.

But whatever it was, I couldn't shake the feeling that this was all changing. That Wells was becoming someone I cared about in a way I wasn't prepared for. I fought it tooth and nail, but it happened.

I walked back to my room, my footsteps sounding louder than usual in the quiet hallway. The door clicked shut behind me, and I leaned against it, taking a deep breath. Wells had trusted me to help him, to pick out something that would make him look good for a date. It was a simple thing, but it made my heart do something strange.

I sat on the edge of my bed, trying to shake off the lingering feeling that had settled in my chest. I should've been happy for him. Marie was a good person—smart, sharp, with a dry sense of humor that Wells seemed to respect. She had been kind to me, but for some reason, the thought of him going out with her left me feeling... off.

I stretched my legs out on the bed, staring at the ceiling. Was I jealous? That felt ridiculous. Wells and I were barely friends, right? I was here for a fresh start, and so was he. A date with Marie didn't mean anything in the grand scheme of things.

But why did it sting?

I rolled over, burying my face in the pillow for a moment, trying to force myself to relax. It didn't help. The fact that Wells was putting so much thought into his date with Marie made me realize how much he cared. It was the same care I'd seen when he talked about the farm, or when he'd gone out of his way to help me. But Marie was different. She was older than me, more experienced, and—let's face it—better suited for someone like him.

The thought didn't sit right, no matter how hard I tried to push it down. It wasn't like I had any claim on him. He was free to date whoever he wanted. So why did the thought of him with Marie bother me so much?

I let out a frustrated sigh and reached for my phone on the nightstand, scrolling through a few messages to distract myself. But the nagging feeling wouldn't go away. I'd helped him pick out an outfit, something simple, but it had made me realize how well I knew him. It wasn't just about the clothes. It was the little things—the way he'd trusted me to make that choice for him, the way he smiled when he said thank you. It was all those little moments that had started to add up over the past couple of weeks.

I groaned, burying my face in my hands. "You're overthinking this," I muttered to myself.

I grabbed the blanket, pulling it over my head like a shield. But even under the covers, I couldn't shake the feeling that something was changing. Maybe it wasn't just Wells who was evolving here. Maybe it was me, too.

Maybe I was starting to care more than I was ready to admit.

CHAPTER 34

SLOW DANCING IN A BURNING ROOM

Wells

THE SUN HAD DIPPED BELOW THE HORIZON, LEAVING A GOLDEN haze over the land as I went inside and got changed. I glanced at the time—just after seven. It felt like a normal Friday night, but tonight was anything but.

I looked at myself in the mirror—I looked like a more polished version of myself thanks to Rose. Was I nervous? Hell, yes. And I wasn't sure if it was because of Marie or because of something else. There was something about the quiet moments I'd shared with Rose this week that had been gnawing at me. Nothing had been overt— just little things. The way she looked at me when I helped her with the horses or when we spent hours fixing things around the property.

That damn cowboy hat.

But this wasn't about Rose. This was about Marie.

Don't say the wrong name tonight.

I exhaled sharply and went downstairs, taking a quick glance at the living room. Rose was curled up on the couch, eyes glued to a book. She was wrapped in my mom's worn-out throw blanket that had clearly seen better days. For a moment, I almost backed out. But no, I had to do this.

"Hey, Sunshine," I said, my voice deep and calm as I entered the living room.

She looked up from her book, startled for a moment, then blinked. "Hey," she said quietly, her gaze flicking over me, then quickly down to the pages of her book.

Something was off. I could feel it in the air.

"Everything okay?" I asked, leaning against the doorframe.

She nodded, but her eyes seemed distant. "Just a quiet evening."

I could see through that. She was a terrible liar, and I could tell there was more to it. But I didn't push it.

I had a date, after all.

"Alright," I said, trying to keep it light. "Well, I'm heading out. I'll be back later." I ran a hand through my hair, adjusting my shirt in the hallway mirror.

Rose's gaze flicked up again, and this time, she met my eyes. She opened her mouth as if she was about to say something, then closed it. There was that strange shift again.

"Uh, you look nice," she said after a beat, her voice quieter than usual. "Really... handsome."

The words hit me in a strange way, leaving me feeling both satisfied and oddly self-conscious. "Thanks." I couldn't help but smile at her, though I felt a heat creep up the back of my neck. I wasn't sure if it was from her words or the weight of everything else that had been hanging between us lately.

She gave a little nod, her fingers curling around the edge of the blanket. There was a moment of silence, and then she offered me a soft smile that didn't quite reach her eyes.

I hesitated before turning to leave. "I'll be back later."

"Have fun," she said, though her voice had an odd edge to it.

The door closed behind me, and I let out a breath I'd been holding.

I drove over to the nursing home to pick Marie up—where she insisted I pick her up. The usual sense of calm from the drive turning into a low hum of nervousness in my chest. It wasn't anything big, but there was an unfamiliar tension now that I wasn't sure how to shake.

I made it to the nursing home in record time, and when I walked inside, I was greeted by the usual soft murmur of conversations, the faint smell of antiseptic mixed with the comforting scent of something homey in the kitchen. Marie wasn't hard to find—she was sitting at the nurse's station, flipping through some paperwork with a pen tucked behind her ear.

"Marie," I said, leaning against the doorframe.

She looked up, startled at first, then smiled. "Wells."

I took her in, and I'll admit, she looked great. It wasn't anything over the top—just a soft green blouse that made her dark eyes pop and a pair of black pants that fit her perfectly. Her hair was up in a loose bun, though a few strands had slipped free, framing her face in a way that made her look effortlessly chic.

"Ready to go?" I asked, offering her my arm.

She stood, adjusting her blouse and grabbing her small purse from the counter. "I've been ready for hours," she said with a grin.

We left the nursing home together, stepping into the cool evening air. As we drove toward the restaurant, the conversation flowed easily. Marie was funny, smart, and didn't shy away from teasing me about how nervous I seemed. I did my best to shrug it off, but there was a part of me that wasn't quite as present as I should've been.

We arrived at the restaurant, a cozy little spot on the water with candles flickering on the tables and soft jazz music filling the air. It was quiet and intimate. The kind of place where you could actually hear each other talk without shouting over background noise.

"I love this place," Marie said as we walked through the door. "It's so peaceful."

"Yeah, I thought you might like it," I said, pulling out her chair for her.

The conversation during dinner was light, filled with small talk and a few jokes, but the more I got to know Marie, the more I realized she was exactly the kind of woman I had imagined: confident, steady, with a sense of purpose that was hard to ignore. She'd worked at the nursing home for almost a decade, and it was clear she cared about the people there like family.

I found myself genuinely enjoying the evening, even if there was a strange part of my mind that kept drifting back to the farm, to *Rose*. What she'd said earlier. The way her voice had sounded.

I pushed it aside. Tonight wasn't about her.

Marie and I made small talk about her work and the island, and I had to admit, I appreciated the ease with which we were able to carry on. But it wasn't just her. There was something about the whole night that left me unsettled in a way I hadn't expected. It was like I couldn't stop comparing everything to the comfort I felt with Rose.

And that wasn't fair to Marie.

After dinner, we strolled outside, the night cool against my skin.

"I had a good time," Marie said, glancing up at me with a smile. "Thanks for inviting me out, Wells."

"Of course," I said, smiling back. But the smile didn't quite feel right. "I'm glad you came."

The words hung in the air as we stood there for a moment, a soft silence stretching between us.

Marie looked up at me with a knowing glint in her eye. "You okay, Wells?"

I blinked, caught off guard by the question. "Yeah, I'm fine. Just… you know, thinking."

"Thinking about what?" she asked, her brow furrowing in concern.

I hesitated. I wasn't about to unload everything on her, but the truth was, I wasn't sure where my head was at. "Just… a lot on my mind."

She nodded, her lips curling into a small, understanding smile. "It's alright, Wells. I get it."

We shared one last look before I drove her to her house. The whole night had been a strange mix of enjoyment and distraction, and by the time I got back to my truck, I felt more lost than when I had left.

The drive home was quiet, and when I stepped inside the house, I half expected to hear Rose's voice calling out, but the place was still. The weight of the night sat heavily on my shoulders.

CHAPTER 35

THAT'S HILARIOUS

Rose

KNEW I HAD NO RIGHT TO FEEL ANYTHING ABOUT WELLS going on a date. None at all.

But as I laid in bed, staring at the ceiling, my chest felt tight, my stomach unsettled in a way I couldn't quite name. It wasn't jealousy. It couldn't be. Wells wasn't mine. I had no claim on him, no reason to feel this strange hollowness in my ribs.

Still, the thought of him sitting across from someone else, making her laugh, making Marie feel special, twisted something deep inside me.

I turned onto my side and squeezed my eyes shut.

Get over yourself, Rose.

Wells had been nothing but kind to me, and I should be happy for him. If anything, this just proved what I already knew—he was a good guy. The kind of guy who deserved to be out with someone warm and smart and beautiful.

But as I lay here, trying to shove the feeling down, my phone vibrated against the nightstand. The sound cut through the quiet, sharp and sudden.

I reached for it, not thinking much until I saw the name on the screen.

Thad.

My breath caught. My body tensed, muscles locking up like I'd been braced for an impact I couldn't see coming.

The buzzing stopped.

Then started again.

I should've let it go to voicemail. I *wanted* to let it go to voicemail.

Instead, I swiped my thumb across the screen and brought the phone to my ear.

I said nothing.

For a moment, there was only breathing on the other end. A hesitation. And then—

"Rose."

His voice was careful. Measured. Like he knew I had every right to hang up.

I should have.

But I didn't.

"Thad," I finally said, my own voice barely above a whisper.

He let out a slow breath, like he was relieved I'd answered. "I wasn't sure you'd pick up."

"Neither was I."

A beat of silence.

"I think we should talk." He spoke up.

I sat up, pressing my palm against my forehead, trying to push away the pounding that had started there. "There's nothing left to say."

"Come on," he said, his voice dipping into that familiar mix of exasperation and charm, the same tone he'd used a hundred times before when he was trying to wear me down. "You don't believe that."

"I do."

"You don't."

I clenched my jaw and swung my legs over the edge of the bed, staring at the wooden floor. "I'm not doing this."

"Rose, listen to me," he said, suddenly more urgent. "You need to come back home."

My stomach dropped. A cold kind of nausea curled in my gut. "Home?" I repeated, my voice sharp.

"Yes. You've had your fun, but it's time to stop running."

I let out a bitter laugh. "That's what you think this is? *Fun?*"

"I think you made a mistake."

My throat tightened. I felt the walls of the room closing in, my vision tunneling in the way it always did when I talked to him for too long. "No, Thad. The mistake was staying there as long as I did."

He sighed, deep and heavy. "Rose, don't be overly dramatic."

I squeezed my eyes shut, gripping the phone so hard my fingers ached. "Is that why you called? To gaslight me into thinking I imagined everything?"

"I called because I care about you," he said, too smooth, too easy. "Because you're out there pretending this is some kind of fresh start when we both know it's not. You don't belong there. You belong with me."

A cold chill ran through me.

"I'm your only option, Rose."

The words landed like a punch to the gut.

For a second, I could barely breathe.

I could hear it in his voice—the certainty. The unshakable belief that he still had some kind of claim over me, that he could just say the right things and I'd fold.

I used to.

I used to let him win. Let him convince me. Let him pull me back into the orbit of his world until I forgot what it felt like to be anything other than his.

But not this time.

I inhaled sharply and pressed my lips together, forcing my voice to stay steady. "Go to hell, Thad."

Then I hung up.

My hands were shaking. My heart slammed against my ribs, too fast, too loud. I dropped the phone onto the bed and curled my fingers into my palms, digging my nails into my skin just to ground myself.

The room suddenly felt too small, like there wasn't enough air. I needed to move. Needed to breathe.

I stood up and walked to the window, pressing my forehead against the cool glass. Outside, the land stretched wide and open under the moonlight, the fields bathed in soft silver. It was nothing like the city. Nothing like the life I'd left behind.

I chose this. I chose to be here.

So why did one phone call have the power to make me feel so small?

I squeezed my eyes shut, my breath coming uneven.

He still had a hold on me. Maybe not in the same way he used to, but enough that a single conversation could shatter my sense of peace.

And that realization? It made me angry.

Angry at him. Angry at myself. Angry at the version of me that still let his words sink their claws in.

I wasn't that girl anymore.

I took a deep breath and stepped away from the window, rubbing the lingering tension from my arms. Sitting in this room, trapped with my thoughts, wasn't going to help. I needed air. Space. A moment to clear my head before I suffocated under the weight of it all.

I pulled a sweatshirt over my head and slipped into my boots and padded quietly down the stairs, the old floorboards creaking beneath my feet. The house was still and empty, the kind of quiet that felt too big, too loud in my ears.

Granger was curled up on the couch, his big brown eyes flicking open as I approached. His tail thumped lazily against the cushions, and I couldn't help but smile, sinking down beside him.

"Hey, buddy." My voice was softer than I meant it to be, but he didn't seem to mind. I ran a hand over his warm fur, scratching the spot on his belly I knew he loved. His tail wagged a little harder.

"I'm heading out to the flowers," I murmured, more for myself than him. I placed a kiss on the top of his head. "I'll be back soon."

I glanced at the clock on the wall. **10:42 PM.** Wells would probably be home soon. The thought made my stomach twist.

I exhaled sharply and pushed off the couch, making my way

into the kitchen. My fingers closed around a bottle of wine on the counter—no glass necessary. It was that kind of night.

On the way out, I snagged the four-wheeler key from its hook by the door. I hesitated for half a second, then shook my head. It'll be fine. *Probably.* I had ridden on this thin a few times.

The cool night air wrapped around me as I stepped into the garage, the familiar scent of engine oil and old leather filling my lungs. Wells' four-wheeler sat exactly where he always kept it, sturdy and waiting. I didn't know if I should be driving this thing alone.

But right now, I didn't care.

I needed to find my peace.

And I knew exactly where to look.

The four-wheeler rumbled to life beneath me, the low hum filling the quiet night. I tightened my grip on the handlebars and eased it out of the garage, the cool air brushing against my flushed skin. The night stretched out before me, dark and endless, broken only by the occasional flicker of fireflies dancing in the fields.

The farm was quiet at this hour, the world stripped down to the simple sounds of crickets chirping and the soft rustle of the wind through the trees. I pressed the throttle harder, the four-wheeler kicking up a small trail of dust as I made my way down the worn dirt path.

The farther I went, the lighter my chest felt. The house, the conversation with Thad, the strange weight of knowing Wells was out on a date—it all faded into the background. Here, surrounded by nothing but open land and sky, I could just be.

When I reached the flower field, I slowed to a stop and killed the engine. The sudden silence rang in my ears, thick and heavy. The flowers stretched out in front of me, their soft petals glowing under the moonlight, a sea of delicate color swaying gently in the night breeze.

I swung my leg over the four-wheeler and stepped into the field, letting my fingers graze the tops of the blossoms. The scent of lavender and wildflowers filled the air, warm and familiar. It smelled like peace. Like something untouched by the chaos of the real world.

With a sigh, I dropped down in the middle of the flowers, feeling the earth cool and firm beneath me. The sky above was endless, littered with stars that felt almost too bright, too sharp against the inky blackness.

I reached for the bottle of wine, twisting off the cap with ease.

"To making bad decisions," I muttered, raising it slightly before taking a long, slow sip. The red wine burned warm as it slid down my throat, and I let my head fall back against the soft grass.

Everything felt quieter here.

Easier.

And for just a little while, I let myself pretend I wasn't coming apart at the seams.

I took another sip of wine. Then another. The warmth spread through my chest, but it wasn't enough to drown out the ache clawing at my ribs.

Lying there in the middle of the flowers, I let my fingers drift over the petals, tracing the delicate edges. Everything felt too quiet, too still. Like the night was holding its breath, waiting for me to shatter.

My mind wouldn't stop spinning.

Thad's voice echoed in my head, smooth and careful, just like always.

"Come back home. We should talk. I'm your only option."

God, what a load of shit.

I pressed the heel of my hand against my chest, trying to push away the weight settling there. The worst part? Some small, stupid part of me still wanted to believe him.

I squeezed my eyes shut, but that only made it worse. Because then I wasn't just hearing his voice—I was seeing it all. Every moment that led me here, lying in a field with a bottle of wine and a heart stitched together with frayed thread.

The late nights waiting for him to come home. The empty apologies. The way he made me feel small, like I was something to be tolerated instead of cherished.

And then—Wells.

His steady hands. The way he looked at me like I was someone. Like I mattered.

A tear slipped down my temple, disappearing into my hairline. Then another. I curled my fingers into the earth, gripping it like it could hold me together. But the dam was breaking, and I was powerless to stop it.

I let out a shaky breath. Then, before I could think twice, I opened my mouth and screamed into the night.

"Why me?"

My voice cracked on the last word, splintering into the darkness like glass shattering on concrete. The sound felt too big for my body, too raw. It ripped straight from the deepest part of me, the part I kept locked up, buried beneath every forced smile and quiet nod.

The wind carried my voice away, but the pain still sat heavy in my chest.

I sucked in a sharp breath, my shoulders shaking.

No one answered.

Of course, no one answered.

I was alone.

Just like always.

I squeezed my eyes shut and let the tears come. For Thad. For Wells. For myself.

For everything I lost.

For everything I didn't know how to want.

CHAPTER 36

WASTING ALL THESE TEARS

Wells

"Rose?" I called out, my voice cutting through the thick silence.

Nothing.

The house felt hollow, too quiet. Like something was missing.

I found Granger sprawled on the couch, his tail thumping lazily against the cushions as I ran a hand over his head. "Where's Sunshine, buddy?"

He wagged his tail in response.

A strange feeling tugged at my chest as I made my way upstairs. Rose's door was open. Not just cracked—wide open.

I hesitated for half a second before stepping closer, my pulse hammering in my ears. I knew I shouldn't look, but hell, I was already here.

Inside, the room was still. The bed untouched. But what caught my attention was the dresser.

The sunflowers.

The ones I had left outside her door, thinking she'd probably toss them without a second thought. But there they were, laid out neatly beside the notes I'd been leaving her every morning with her coffee.

She kept them. She kept *all* of them.

My chest tightened. Rose didn't seem like the sentimental type. If anything, she acted like half the things I did annoyed her. But she hadn't thrown these away.

Did that mean something?

I dragged a hand down my face, pushing the thought aside as I stepped back into the hall. The bathroom door was open. The whole upstairs was empty.

She wasn't here.

Where the hell did she go?

"Why me?"

The cry echoed in the distance, raw and broken, slicing through the night air. My stomach dropped.

Rose.

I shrugged off my blazer and bolted down the stairs, my boots pounding against the hardwood. I reached for the four-wheeler key.

Gone.

Shit.

I didn't have to think twice. I knew exactly where she was.

The flower field.

These boots weren't made for running, but I didn't give a damn. I took off in a dead sprint, my lungs burning, my heart slamming against my ribs with every step.

The flower field came into view just as my legs started to burn, but I didn't slow down. Not when I saw the four-wheeler parked haphazardly at the edge of the field. Not when I caught sight of her, sprawled out in the grass, nearly swallowed by the wildflowers.

My chest tightened.

She was crying. No—sobbing. Her body shook with it, shoulders curled in like she was trying to hold herself together, but it wasn't working. The nearly empty bottle of wine rested beside her, its dark silhouette barely visible against the petals.

I didn't think. I just moved.

"Rose."

She didn't react.

I lowered myself onto my knees beside her, brushing away a few fallen stems to get a better look at her face. The moonlight caught the streaks of tears on her cheeks, her breath coming in sharp, uneven gasps.

"Sunshine," I tried again, softer this time.

Her eyes flickered open, unfocused at first, then locking onto me. Her lips parted slightly, but no words came out.

I exhaled, relieved she was at least aware of me. I reached for the bottle, slipping it from her loose grip and setting it aside.

"What the hell are you doing out here?" I asked, keeping my voice low, steady. "You scared the shit outta me."

She sniffled and dragged a hand over her face, as if she could wipe away the evidence of whatever had just wrecked her. But there was no hiding it.

"I needed to get out," she mumbled.

"And drink yourself into oblivion in the middle of a field?" I shook my head, running a hand through my hair. "Damn it, Rose."

"Why do you care?" she shot back, her voice cracking.

That hit me straight in the chest.

"Because it's you," I said simply.

She let out a choked, bitter laugh, turning her face toward the sky. "That's not a reason."

"The hell it isn't."

Silence stretched between us, the wind rustling through the flowers, carrying the scent of lavender and something heartbreakingly familiar.

Her fingers twitched, brushing against a petal beside her. "I don't know what's wrong with me," she whispered.

I didn't know what broke inside her tonight, but I sure as hell knew she didn't deserve to feel like this.

"Nothing's wrong with you."

She let out a shaky breath. "Then why do I feel like I'm falling apart?"

I hesitated for only a second before lying down beside her. Close, but not touching. Just enough to let her know she wasn't alone.

We stared up at the sky, the stars stretching infinitely above us.

"Maybe you're not falling apart," I murmured. "Maybe you're just breaking free."

Rose let out another shaky breath, her fingers twisting into the grass like she was trying to anchor herself. But she was unraveling right in front of me, and I couldn't just sit there and watch.

Without thinking, I reached for her.

She stiffened as I slipped an arm beneath her shoulders, pulling her against me. But the second her body pressed into mine, she melted, her face burying into my chest like she belonged there.

A fresh sob wracked through her, muffled against my shirt.

"Hey, hey," I murmured, tightening my hold. "I've got you, Sunshine."

She didn't say anything. Just clenched her fists into the fabric of my shirt like I was the only thing keeping her from shattering completely.

I rested my chin on top of her head, breathing her in. The scent of flowers and wine clung to her, but beneath that was something softer—something Rose.

She shook against me, her breath still uneven, and I rubbed slow circles against her back, letting her get it all out.

Minutes passed. Maybe longer.

Finally, her breathing evened out, though she still didn't move away.

"I don't—" She swallowed hard. "I don't know why I'm like this."

I exhaled, resting my cheek against her hair. "Because you've been holding it in too damn long."

She let out a quiet laugh—more breath than sound. "Feels like I could cry forever."

"You won't," I said. "Not forever."

She tilted her face up, her cheek still resting against my chest, eyes red-rimmed but searching.

"Why'd you come find me?" she whispered.

I gave her a look like she had to be kidding. "Because you're you, Sunshine."

Something flickered in her expression, something fragile and unsure.

I pulled her in a little closer. "And I'll always come find you."

She didn't answer, but I felt the subtle shift in her body as she relaxed even more into my arms. The weight of her head against my chest, the way her fingers gradually loosened their grip on my shirt—it all told me the same thing: I was exactly where I was supposed to be.

CHAPTER 37

DRUNK ME

Rose

RESTED MY HEAD ON WELLS' CHEST AND IT WAS ODDLY comforting. The steady rise and fall of his breath beneath me felt solid, grounding. He was sturdy, dependable, reliable. Everything I hadn't realized I'd been craving.

We lay there for what felt like an eternity, the quiet of the night wrapping around us. I felt safe yet exposed all at once. There was so much I still hadn't said, so much that had been building up inside me for far too long.

Wells didn't push me to talk. He just let the silence linger between us, the weight of his presence saying everything I needed to hear without a word. But eventually, it all came tumbling out, like I couldn't hold it in any longer.

"I never told you what happened with Thad," I whispered, breaking the silence between us.

Wells shifted slightly, making sure he was paying full attention. I could feel his fingers gently brushing through my hair, waiting for me to continue.

"He…" I swallowed hard, remembering the way Thad's words had felt like a punch to my gut. "We were together for a long time. We were building a future, or so I thought. He got me a promise ring, told me we were going to move and start a life together. I really thought I had it all figured out, you know?" I let out a breath, trying to steady myself. "But the morning of the move, everything was packed. My stuff was in the car, and then he… he told me he wasn't coming with me."

Wells didn't say anything right away. He just let the weight of my words hang in the air between us, his hand gently massaging the back of my neck as if to remind me he was here, that I wasn't alone.

"He told me while standing on the sidewalk, Wells," I continued, my voice shaking. "Like it was no big deal. He just… left me there. With all my stuff packed in the car. He wasn't coming with me."

I wiped my eyes quickly, my throat tightening with the sting of it all. "But it wasn't just that day. It was everything before that. The more I think about it, the more I realize I never really knew him at all. He was so good at pretending, at making me feel like everything was perfect, but when it came down to it, it wasn't."

Wells' voice was calm but firm when he spoke. "You don't need him, Rose. You're better off without someone who can just walk away like that."

I nodded, the pain still fresh in my chest. "I know. But it's not just that. It's everything he said to me." I took another deep breath, feeling the tears well up again. "He told me I was hard to love. That I bounced from one idea to another, never sticking with anything. That I was too much for him. And for the longest time, I believed him."

Wells' grip on me tightened, and I could feel the warmth of his breath against my skin. "You're not hard to love, Rose," he said quietly. "You're passionate and you have a lot of ideas. That doesn't make you too much. You're exactly who you're supposed to be."

I closed my eyes, trying to hold it together, but it was too much. The weight of those words—*too much*—had haunted me for so long. It was why I had hesitated to share my dream with anyone, why I had kept my idea of the dried flowers to myself for so long. I was afraid that I'd be too much for anyone to handle. That it wouldn't be enough. That I wasn't enough.

"Thad made me feel like I was a project," I whispered, my voice cracking. "Like I was something he had to fix. He said I was always moving on to the next thing, that I'd never be able to stick with anything. And it broke me, Wells. Because I thought maybe he was right. I thought I was just some mess of ideas that couldn't figure it out."

Wells was silent for a long moment, but when he spoke again, it was with such conviction that I almost believed him. "He didn't understand you, Rose. And I do. I see what you're doing. You're figuring it out. You're building something that's uniquely yours, and you've got the heart and the strength to see it through."

I shook my head, pulling away just slightly, though I didn't want to. "But I was afraid, Wells. I was afraid to even tell you about the flowers. Afraid you'd think it was silly for wanting to make something out of it."

"You're not silly," he said simply, his voice soft but steady. "You're brave for taking a chance on something you care about. You're real. And that's what matters."

I exhaled slowly, feeling the weight in my chest begin to lift, just a little. It was hard to believe what he was saying, but somehow, with the way he was looking at me, I wanted to believe it.

I swallowed hard, wiping my eyes again. "I just—sometimes I don't know who I am without all of this. Without him. Without the things he made me feel."

"Then you get to figure that out," Wells said, pulling me back into his chest, his arms wrapping around me as if to protect me from the world outside. "But you don't have to do it alone."

I rested my head against his chest again, listening to the steady beat of his heart beneath me, and for the first time in what felt like forever, I felt like maybe I was starting to believe it. That I wasn't too much. That I could be exactly who I was meant to be and maybe that was enough.

"I don't have to be afraid anymore, do I?" I whispered. The words more for myself than for him.

"No, you don't," he said softly. "You don't have to be afraid of anything."

I let his words settle deep inside me, and for the first time in a long while, I allowed myself to believe them. I wasn't broken. I wasn't too much. I was *enough*.

I held onto Wells, letting his warmth and comfort fill the spaces I had left hollow. The scent of him—earthy and familiar—was like a steadying force against the storm of thoughts racing through my mind. For a moment, I allowed myself to stop thinking, to just exist in the silence between us, with only the quiet hum of the night outside and the soft rise and fall of his chest beneath my ear.

But the relief didn't last long. It couldn't. Because, as much as I wanted to let go of the past, as much as I wanted to believe that I was enough, the weight of everything still lingered like a shadow I couldn't shake off.

Thad's words echoed in my head, his voice sharp and condescending. You're hard to love. I had tried so hard to prove him wrong, to show him that I was worth it, but now I knew better. He wasn't the problem. I was. Or so I had believed for so long.

I pulled back slightly, enough to look at Wells, though I didn't want to leave the comfort of his arms. "You really don't think I'm crazy?" I asked, the insecurity creeping back into my voice.

Wells's eyes softened, and he tilted his head to meet my gaze, his hands gently cupping my face. "You're real, Rose. You feel everything deeply, and you're passionate about the things you love. That's beautiful."

My chest tightened, and I had to swallow against the lump in my throat. "I don't know if I can believe that yet," I whispered. "But I want to. I want to believe that I'm not just this mess of ideas and dreams that never come true. I want to believe that what I'm doing—what I'm starting with the flowers—is enough."

Wells smiled, that soft, reassuring smile that seemed to ease the turmoil inside me, even if just a little. "What you're doing is already enough. It's a part of who you are, Rose. You're figuring it out, one step at a time. That's all any of us can do."

I closed my eyes and let out a shaky breath, trying to calm my racing heart. "But what if I fail?" I asked, the fear creeping back into my chest. "What if I'm not cut out for it? What if it all falls apart?"

"Then you try again," he said, his voice steady. "And if it still doesn't work out, then you pivot. You don't give up. And you don't let anyone—especially not Thad—tell you that you're not worthy of chasing your dreams."

His words felt like a balm to my soul, soothing the scars I had hidden away. I couldn't help but lean into him again, my forehead resting against his chest as I closed my eyes, trying to steady my breathing.

"You really mean that, don't you?" I asked, my voice barely more than a whisper.

"I do," he said simply, his fingers running through my hair. "I see you, Rose. All of you. And I don't need you to be anything other than who you are. You don't have to prove anything to me."

I let his words sink into my skin, and for the first time in a long time, I felt like maybe I was enough. That the pieces of myself that I had been so afraid to share were worth something. That I wasn't too much, or too broken, or too anything. I was just me.

"I'm sorry for holding all of that inside for so long," I said softly, pulling away just enough to look up at him. "I should have trusted you. I should have let you in sooner."

"You don't have to apologize," Wells said, brushing a strand of hair from my face. "We all carry our baggage, Rose. But we don't have to carry it alone. *You* don't have to carry it alone. You have so many people who love you—who would be willing to help you carry that baggage."

I nodded, feeling the weight of his words settle into my chest. I had spent so long trying to do everything on my own, trying to prove that I didn't need anyone. But in this moment, with Wells holding me, I realized that I wasn't supposed to do it all alone.

"I don't want to carry everything by myself," I admitted, my voice trembling slightly.

"You won't have to," Wells promised softly. "I'm here for you."

I closed my eyes again, letting the warmth of his words wrap around me like a blanket. I didn't know what the future held or if the dried flowers would turn into something bigger than I could imagine. But for the first time in a long time, I felt like I was on the right path. I was moving forward, and I wasn't doing it alone.

We stayed like that for a while, the world outside fading away as I let myself rest in the comfort of Wells' presence. I knew there would be hard days ahead but I felt ready to face them. With Wells by my side, maybe I could finally stop running from who I was. Maybe I could stop hiding from the pieces of myself that I had kept buried.

When I finally lifted my head to look at him, I found him watching me, his gaze soft and full of understanding. I smiled faintly, feeling the first stirrings of hope in my chest.

"How was your date?" I asked, afraid of the answer.

"It was fine. She was lovely."

I swallowed my pride and rolled onto my back and looked up at the stars. "That's great." I poked his side, trying to hide any emotion. "Going out again soon?"

"Maybe." Wells deadpanned.

I tried to swallow the lump in my throat, my eyes searching for the stars above as I tried to push down the strange mix of emotions swirling inside me.

"Probably not."

I froze, sitting up sharply. "Why not?"

Wells sat up with me, his expression thoughtful. He shrugged, a flicker of uncertainty in his eyes. "I'm not sure if she's my type."

"Oh," I said quietly, the word barely more than a breath. I paused for a moment, processing. "I'm sure the right woman is out there for you," I added.

Wells met my gaze, his eyes soft, and for a brief moment, I saw something flicker there—something that felt too personal, too raw for him to share out loud. But before I could try to decipher it, he cleared his throat and leaned back, stretching his legs out in front of him.

"Yeah, I'm sure," he said, his tone steady but distant.

I nodded, though I wasn't entirely sure if I believed him or if he believed it. The silence between us grew heavier. I couldn't shake the feeling that something unsaid lingered in the air, between us, like the unspoken things that always hang in the spaces where two people get too close.

I tried to focus on the stars, to pull my mind away from the sudden discomfort, but it was hard. There was a strange ache inside me, something I wasn't ready to admit even to myself.

"So," I said, breaking the silence before it swallowed us whole, "what do you think makes someone your type?"

Wells let out a slow breath, as if he was still considering how to answer the question. "Someone who doesn't make me feel like I have to change who I am."

I felt a tightness in my chest at his words, though I wasn't sure why. Maybe it was the way they resonated with me, how I felt like I'd been trying to change for so long, trying to fit into expectations I never really signed up for.

"That makes sense," I said softly, glancing over at him. "I get that."

He looked over at me, and this time there was no mistaking the look in his eyes—a mixture of curiosity and something else I couldn't quite place. "What about you, Rose? What's your type?"

I felt my heart race at the question. It wasn't something I'd expected to be asked, and suddenly, I felt exposed. What did I even want? What kind of person did I think I could trust, after everything?

"I don't know," I admitted, my voice a little quieter. "I think I've been so busy trying to figure out what I need to do with my life that I haven't really thought about who I need in it."

Wells nodded slowly, like he understood what I was getting at, even though I wasn't entirely sure myself. "It's hard to figure that out when you're just trying to keep your head above water," he said quietly. "But I think when you do, you'll know."

I wasn't sure what to say to that. I wanted to believe him, but the more I thought about it, the more I realized I didn't have all the answers. I didn't even have half of them.

The air around us felt warmer now, the weight of the unspoken things settling between us like a shared understanding. It was the kind of quiet that felt comforting in a way I hadn't expected, especially after hearing about his date. But as we sat there, side by side, under the stars, something shifted.

I turned to look at Wells again, his profile etched against the dim light of the moon. "Do you think you'll find her? The right woman?"

He didn't answer right away. He just stared ahead, his jaw tight, his fingers drumming absentmindedly on the ground.

"I think I'm not lookin' for someone to complete me. I think I just want someone who can be there. Who's with me, you know?" He finally said, his voice a little gruff.

I nodded. I couldn't explain why, but his words hit something deep inside me. I didn't know if it was the vulnerability in his voice, or the realization that maybe I'd been looking for the wrong things too.

The words lingered between us as we sat there in silence, both of us lost in our own thoughts.

Finally, I broke the quiet, unable to resist any longer. "I'm glad you're here, Wells."

He turned to look at me, his gaze steady and warm, and I could have sworn I saw something flicker there—something I wasn't quite ready to name.

"Me too," he said, his voice low and sincere.

And for a brief, fleeting moment, the ache in my chest lessened. Not because everything was perfect, but because I realized that I didn't need to have it all figured out right now. Maybe I just needed to keep moving forward, one step at a time. With Wells by my side, I could.

The night stretched on, the air cooling around us, but the warmth between us, unspoken and steady, lingered.

"Ready to head inside?" Wells asked, his voice breaking the comfortable silence.

"Yeah," I replied.

We both stood up and made our way toward the four-wheeler. Wells climbed into the driver's seat and looked over at me.

"What, you don't want me to drive?" I teased.

"Hell no," he shot back with a grin. "Hop on, Sunshine."

I followed his command, this time doing something I hadn't

done before. Instead of grabbing the handles like I had been for weeks, I placed my hands around his torso. His muscles tensed under my touch, and I instantly regretted it. I pulled my hands back, a little embarrassed by the unintended closeness.

"You didn't have to move them," Wells said, his voice warm but surprised.

I hesitated, feeling a flush creep up my neck. "Sorry, I didn't mean to make things weird."

He shot me a reassuring smile, his eyes softening. "You didn't, Rose. Just wasn't expecting it, that's all." With that, he revved the engine, and we took off into the night, the wind whipping around us, but somehow it felt a little different now—more intimate, in a way I couldn't quite explain.

CHAPTER 38

WILDFLOWERS

Wells

I WAS SHOCKED WHEN ROSE OPENED UP ABOUT HER PAST LAST night. Granted, she'd had the majority of the bottle of wine by the time I had gotten to her, but still, the fact that she trusted me enough to share something so personal meant more than I could put into words.

It wasn't like Rose to let her guard down so easily, and that only made me wonder what she saw in me—why she felt safe enough to talk about something that clearly still lingered in her heart. I had a million questions running through my mind, but I didn't want to press her too hard, not when she'd been so vulnerable.

I leaned against the porch rail, looking out over the land, trying to calm the storm inside me. I didn't know if it was the late hour or the warmth of the wine, but I felt a connection to her that I hadn't expected. Something deeper, more real, than I'd been prepared for.

The whole evening replayed in my mind—the way she'd laughed on the way back to the house on the four-wheeler, how her face softened when she spoke of him, and then how quickly that softness faded when she caught herself. It was a glimpse into a part of her she had kept hidden from the world.

I tried to quiet my mind and get some sleep, but it never came.

I tossed and turned for hours, staring at the ceiling until my alarm finally cut through the silence—another Sunday, another farmer's market. With a tired sigh, I got up, got dressed, and loaded the truck.

Rose hadn't come downstairs yet, and the house was still, no signs of movement. I took it as my chance to make her a coffee. It had become a quiet ritual, one I never acknowledged out loud but couldn't seem to stop myself from doing.

Stepping outside with Granger, I watched as the first light stretched across the horizon, golden rays spilling over the land. I grabbed Rose her daily sunflower from the truck. The air was crisp, carrying the scent of fresh earth and morning dew. As I turned back toward the house, the soft creak of the screen door caught my ear.

Rose stood against the porch column, coffee in hand, her gaze on me. The steam curled around her face, her expression unreadable in the soft morning light.

I met her eyes, unsure if she'd say something or just sip her coffee in the quiet way she did when she had too much on her mind. The breeze tugged at the hem of her t-shirt, her hair loose and wild from sleep. She looked soft, untouched by the weight of the day ahead, and damn if that didn't do something to me.

I cleared my throat, shifting the sunflower in my hand before stepping up onto the porch.

"Morning," I said, my voice lower than I expected.

Her lips curved slightly over the rim of her mug. "Morning."

I held the sunflower out to her. She glanced down at it, her fingers brushing mine as she took it, her touch light but lingering. "You know," she said, twirling the stem between her fingers, "you never actually told me why you do this."

I shrugged, leaning against the railing. "Just seems like a good way to start the day."

She studied me for a moment, like she was deciding whether to push for more or just let it be. Then she smiled—small, but real. "Well, I like it."

Something in my chest eased.

Granger let out a low huff and curled up near my feet, the

picture of contentment. The morning stretched between us, unhurried and comfortable in a way I hadn't expected.

Rose exhaled, her shoulders relaxing as she looked out over the land. "I'll be ready to go in ten minutes. I just need to get changed."

"We have time, no need to rush."

She nodded, but lingered a second longer, her fingers still absently twirling the sunflower. I could tell she wasn't quite ready to step away from the quiet of the morning, and truth be told, neither was I.

Her gaze drifted toward the horizon again, the early light catching in her blonde hair. "I didn't expect to like it here as much as I do," she admitted. "I thought it'd just be a stop along the way, a place to figure things out before moving on."

Something in my chest tightened at that. "And now?"

She glanced at me, a small smile playing at her lips. "Now I'm not so sure."

I wanted to ask what that meant—if she was thinking of staying, if she was still planning to leave. But instead, I just nodded, letting her words settle between us. Pushing for answers wouldn't change whatever was already unfolding.

Rose let out a breath, as if shaking off whatever thoughts had crept in. "Alright, ten minutes," she said, stepping past me toward the door.

I watched her go, her sunflower tucked loosely in her grip.

Granger huffed again, stretching out on the porch like he had all the time in the world. I gave his head a scratch before pushing off the railing, running a hand over my stubbled jaw.

I had a feeling today was going to be different. Maybe not in some big, obvious way, but in the little things—the ones that mattered.

And for once, I wasn't in a hurry to figure out why.

The drive to the farmer's market was quiet, but not in a way that felt awkward. It was the kind of silence that came with early mornings, where the world was just starting to wake up, and words didn't feel necessary yet. Rose had her coffee cupped in both hands, staring out the window as the sun climbed higher over the tree line.

I glanced over at her when I could, catching the way she absentmindedly tapped her fingers against the ceramic mug, deep in thought.

"You good?" I asked eventually, my voice breaking through the quiet.

She blinked, as if just remembering I was there, then turned to me with a small smile. "Yeah. Just thinking."

I nodded, leaving it at that. Rose wasn't the type to be pushed when she wasn't ready, and I wasn't the type to force a conversation just to fill the space.

By the time we pulled up to the farmer's market, vendors were already setting up, the air rich with the scent of fresh bread, roasted coffee, and salt from the nearby water. People wandered through the rows of tents, some carrying baskets, others clutching warm pastries wrapped in paper.

I parked the truck in our usual spot, cutting the engine before stretching out my sore shoulder. "Looks like it's gonna be a busy one," I said, nodding toward the crowd already lining up.

Rose followed my gaze and let out a slow breath. "Yeah, it does." She reached for the door handle but hesitated, looking back at me. "Thanks for driving. And, y'know… for the sunflower." She lifted her mug, "And for the coffee."

I smiled and nodded, not really trusting myself to say much more.

We got to work unloading. I carried the heavier crates while she focused on setting up her flower stand, her movements quick and practiced. I watched as she fluffed up bouquets, adjusting stems and tying ribbons with careful hands. There was something about the way she worked—focused, almost lost in the process—that made me pause longer than I should.

Longer than I had time for.

Once she was fully in setup mode, I pulled out the surprise I'd been waiting to give her. The banner was crisp, the fabric smooth under my fingers as I unfolded it. The logo—a delicate sunflower intertwined with the words *Solace Blooms*—stood bold against the white background. It was simple, clean, and exactly what she deserved.

Hooking it onto the front of her stand, I stepped back just as she turned around.

She froze, her eyes widening. "Wells…"

I shoved my hands into my pockets. "Figured you needed something official."

She stepped closer, her fingers skimming over the fabric. The way she looked at it—like it was something more than just a sign—sent a strange warmth through my chest.

"You did this for me?" Her voice was quiet, almost disbelieving.

I shrugged, suddenly feeling self-conscious. "Thought it was time to make this thing real."

For a second, she just stood there. And then, without warning, she stepped forward and wrapped her arms around me.

The hug caught me off guard. Rose wasn't the kind of person to do things just for the sake of it, which meant this wasn't just a casual thanks. It meant something.

Her warmth pressed against me, her hair brushing my jaw as I hesitated for half a second before resting my hand on her back. She smelled like lavender and something sweet—maybe honey. It was a little thing, but it settled something inside me I hadn't even realized was restless.

When she pulled away, she looked up at me, her eyes softer than I'd ever seen them. "This means a lot, Wells. More than you know."

I swallowed, nodded. "Glad you like it."

She turned back to her stand, exhaling and swallowing hard before diving into setting up her dried flowers. I watched as she carefully arranged the bundles, tying them off with twine, her movements methodical. There was something almost reverent in the way she handled them, like each one held a story.

The market came alive around us, people filtering in with that easy Sunday pace, stopping to browse the stalls. And then, just like last week, Rose's stand drew attention fast.

I watched as she greeted customers, her face lighting up as she talked about her arrangements. People leaned in, nodding along, charmed by her warmth. Some asked for recommendations, others picked up bouquets like they were carrying home something sacred.

It didn't take long before she had a full-on line. I caught glimpses of her between customers, the way she tucked loose strands of hair behind her ear, the way she smiled as she handed off each bouquet like it was meant for that person.

By midday, she was sold out—again.

She walked over to my stand, breathless, her cheeks flushed from the rush. "That was insane."

"Told you," I said, smirking as I wiped my hands on a rag. "You're the main event here."

She shook her head, laughing. "I don't know about that, but..." She glanced at her empty crates, then back at me. "I think I'm starting to believe you."

I leaned against a table, watching as she traced a finger over the *Solace Blooms* banner, that thoughtful look back in her eyes.

And for the first time in a long time, I found myself wondering if she was starting to see what I'd seen in her all along.

"Auntie Rose! Uncle Wells!" Wren's excited voice rang out as she sprinted toward us, her little feet barely touching the ground. Blythe followed behind, a knowing smile on her lips.

"Wrenny!" Rose and I said in unison.

Wren came to an abrupt stop in front of us, her curls bouncing as she tilted her head. "Wait, where are your flowers?"

I crouched down so we were eye level. "Your aunt sold out. Isn't that so cool?"

Wren's face lit up like a sparkler on the Fourth of July. She spun toward Rose, throwing her arms around her waist in a fierce hug. "I'm so proud of you!"

Rose let out a soft laugh, wrapping her arms around Wren in

return. "Thank you," she said, her voice quieter now, touched by the moment.

Blythe stepped forward, her eyes warm as she pulled Rose into a quick hug of her own. "I'm so proud of you for doing this."

A faint blush crept onto Rose's cheeks. "Thank you," she murmured again, tucking a loose strand of hair behind her ear.

Then Blythe turned toward me, her expression shifting into something far more mischievous. "You."

I raised an eyebrow and pointed to myself. "Me?"

"Yes, you." She turned back to Rose. "Can you watch the produce stand while I steal Wells for a second?"

Rose glanced between us, clearly amused. "Of course."

Blythe didn't wait for a response from me. "Follow me."

I barely had time to shoot Rose a questioning look before Blythe was dragging me away. As soon as we were out of earshot, she playfully punched my shoulder. "You are smitten, Wells Calloway."

I scoffed, rubbing the spot where she hit me. "I am not."

Blythe crossed her arms, giving me the kind of look that only family could master. "Oh, you so are."

I let out a dry laugh, shaking my head. "You're seeing things."

Blythe just arched a perfectly skeptical brow. "Oh, am I? Because from where I'm standing, you're looking at Rose like she hung the damn moon."

I glanced back toward the stand, where Rose was laughing at something Wren had said, her shoulders loose, her face soft in a way I didn't see often.

I looked away just as fast. "She's a good person, that's all."

"Mmm-hmm." Blythe smirked, arms still crossed. "And that banner? The logo? The way you practically beam every time she so much as breathes in your direction?"

I sighed, pinching the bridge of my nose. "I just want her to succeed, Blythe. She's been through a lot. The least I can do is help."

Blythe studied me for a long moment, her gaze softer now. "You don't just want to help her. You care about her. Maybe more than you're willing to admit."

I didn't answer. I didn't know how to.

She let out a small sigh, shaking her head. "Look, I'm not here to push you, Wells. But I do know you. And I've never seen you act like this with anyone before."

I stuffed my hands into my pockets. "It's not like that."

"Sure," she said, clearly not believing me. "But if—or should I say when—you realize it is like that, don't be a dumbass about it. She's my best friend and she's been through a lot."

"I know."

Blythe's eyes went wide. "She told you?"

I nodded slowly. "Last night."

"I can't believe she told you. She keeps shit bottled up."

"I am painfully aware."

"I'm shocked she told you. She barely told me and I've known her for years. That means something, whether you realize it or not."

Before I could come up with a retort, Wren's voice rang out again. "Mom! Uncle Wells! Auntie Rose's famous now!"

Blythe and I turned just in time to see Rose standing behind her stand, a small group of customers still lingering even though she had nothing left to sell.

Rose shrugged, looking a little bashful as she explained something to an older woman who nodded enthusiastically.

I felt that familiar warmth settle in my chest again, but I ignored it.

Blythe, however, didn't. She elbowed me. "Uh-huh. Not like that, my ass."

I sighed and started walking back. "Let's go before you get any more ideas."

But as I approached Rose, who looked up at me with bright eyes and a soft smile, I had to wonder if Blythe saw something I wasn't ready to acknowledge.

CHAPTER 39

HELL OF A VIEW

Rose

FOR THE PAST THREE WEEKS, I'VE BEEN SELLING OUT OF flowers halfway through the market. It was a great problem to have, but it left me scrambling at the end of every day, wishing I had brought more. This time, I was determined to be ready.

The dried flowers had been such a hit that I knew I needed to double the amount I brought for this week's market. After spending the day helping Wells on the farm, I'd been devoting my evenings to putting together new dried flower arrangements. Lavender was my latest experiment—I had started drying it and putting it into little sachets that people could buy for their drinks, syrups, or baked goods. It sounded like a good idea, but the last thing I needed was for it to be a flop.

I just hoped I wasn't getting ahead of myself. With every arrangement I made, I couldn't help but feel excited. The idea of offering something unique—something personal—made me proud. It felt like the perfect way to bring a little extra magic to the market.

The sun had set, casting a deep orange glow across the sky, and Wells and I had just finished another full day of farm work. The evening air was crisp but still carried a warmth from the last rays of daylight, which made the whole farm feel like it was settling into a quiet rhythm. Wells was checking on the chickens, moving through his tasks with the ease of someone who'd done this a thousand times before. Meanwhile, I was struggling to keep up with the farm's most persistent residents—goats.

I was standing by the pen, rope in hand, attempting to coax Mr. Nibbles—the most stubborn goat of the bunch—back into the fence. It was harder than I expected, especially after a day of working non-stop. Every time I thought I had him settled, he darted off again, munching on whatever plant he could find.

"Hey!" I shouted, pulling the rope tighter as he tried to escape once more. "Stop eating the fence!" But the goat wasn't interested in my commands. Instead, he darted past me with a victorious bleat and started nibbling on the hem of my shirt.

"Not the shirt!" I growled, swatting at him as I tried to pull away. Of course, this only made him more determined, like he was trying to "help" me with the chore.

Wells glanced over at me, clearly stifling a grin. "Need some help?" he called out, his voice full of amusement.

"Need a miracle," I huffed, my frustration mounting as I struggled to free my shirt from Mr. Nibbles' eager chewing.

Wells strolled over, taking his time and looking completely unbothered. He stood there with his hands on his hips, like he had all the time in the world. "I've got a way with goats," he said with that signature, cocky smile. "You just have to be patient."

I threw my hands up in exasperation. "Oh, I'm being patient alright," I muttered under my breath, finally tugging hard enough on the rope to get Mr. Nibbles' attention and lead him back to the pen. It felt like hours of back-and-forth, but eventually, I managed to get him inside and slammed the gate shut behind him.

"That was… an experience," I said, wiping my hands on my shirt as I tried to catch my breath.

Wells chuckled, shaking his head. "You're getting the hang of it."

I rolled my eyes, brushing some of the dirt from my clothes. "I think I'll stick to flowers from now on. At least they don't bite."

He grinned, offering me a hand to help me up. "You sure? I think you make a pretty good farmer."

"Farmer?" I stared at him, taking in the sight of myself—covered in dirt and goat slobber. "Wells, I'm the worst farmer ever. I feel gross."

"Nothing a shower can't fix," he said with a wink, his voice warm and teasing.

I glanced down at myself, suddenly aware of how grimy I was. "Right, well… I'm going to call it a night. You've got everything else, right?"

Wells gave me a thumbs-up, still chuckling as I headed toward the house.

The thought of a hot shower was too tempting to resist. I inhaled the cool evening air, letting it fill my lungs as I walked toward the house. The last few hours of farm work had left me covered in dirt and hay, and a moment of peace was exactly what I needed.

I quickly stripped off my muddy clothes and headed into the shower. The water pummeling my skin washed away the day. The warmth of the bathroom felt like a luxury and the sound of the water rushing from the shower was soothing. I closed my eyes for a moment, letting the steam settle around me as I tried to relax.

But, as always, things couldn't stay peaceful for long.

Just as I stepped into the shower, I heard a tap-tap-tap on the bathroom door.

I froze and the door opened.

My heart skipped a beat. I waited, hoping it was just my imagination.

With my heart racing, I cautiously pushed the shower curtain open a crack, peering around the corner.

And there—standing in the middle of my bathroom—was freakin' Mr. Nibbles, chewing on the edge of the shower rug like it was the most delicious thing he'd ever tasted.

I stared at him, too stunned to react at first.

Then, my brain caught up with reality and I wrapped a towel around my body.

"Wells!" I yelled, clutching the towel tighter around my body and scrambling to cover myself. "Wells!"

His voice filtered through the hall, muffled by the walls. "What's up?"

I felt the panic rise in my chest. "There's a goat in the bathroom!"

I heard Wells' footsteps approaching the door, slow and deliberate. A moment later, the door creaked open, and I saw his head peek around the corner. His eyes widened at the sight of Mr. Nibbles, who was casually munching away at the shower mat like he was at a five-star restaurant.

"What the hell?" Wells said, his voice full of disbelief as he took in the scene. He stepped into the bathroom, raising an eyebrow as Mr. Nibbles continued his snack without a care in the world.

"I didn't invite him in!" I hissed, my face burning with embarrassment. "I was just trying to take a shower, and—" I motioned towards the goat.

Mr. Nibbles didn't even glance up, too busy enjoying his meal to be bothered by the chaos he'd caused.

Wells, on the other hand, couldn't contain his laughter. He shook his head, clearly finding the whole situation way too funny. "Guess he thought the bathroom was the new hangout."

"Get him out!" I pleaded, desperate to end the awkwardness of the moment.

Wells grinned, enjoying every second of my discomfort. "Alright, alright. I'll get him out of here."

He crouched down, calmly grabbing Mr. Nibbles by the horns and guiding him toward the door. "Come on, buddy," he murmured, leading the goat out of the bathroom. "No more naked ladies for you."

As Wells and Mr. Nibbles disappeared from view, I stood there frozen in place, still clutching the towel to my chest like it was the only thing keeping me sane.

Once the door shut behind them, I leaned against the sink, trying to steady my breath.

I couldn't help it. I let out a small, incredulous laugh. How is this my life?

A few moments later, I heard Wells' voice from the other side of the door. "Just wait until you see what happens when I try to fix the fence again."

I groaned. But I knew. The farm was only going to get more interesting from here.

After a moment of collecting myself, I finally emerged from the bathroom.

I slipped into a comfortable pair of leggings and a soft sweater, the warmth of the fabric a welcome comfort against the coolness of the evening. After brushing my hair out, I headed downstairs, hoping to find some peace and maybe a cup of tea to wind down.

The familiar smell of dinner wafted from the kitchen, and I smiled at the thought of Wells handling the evening meal. As I reached the bottom of the stairs, I caught a glimpse of him in the kitchen, standing by the counter with his back to me. He seemed focused on whatever he was cooking, but I couldn't help but notice the way his shirt hugged his shoulders as he moved, the familiar ease with which he worked in his element.

I hesitated for just a second before stepping into the kitchen, trying to shake off the last vestiges of embarrassment from the goat fiasco.

"Well, look who's finally clean." Wells said, his voice playful and teasing as he glanced over his shoulder. His eyes ran over me with a smile that was half-amusement, half-admiration. "I was starting to wonder if you were planning on living in that towel forever."

I rolled my eyes, walking over to the kitchen counter where he had set a plate of food. "Ha-ha, very funny," I said, trying to sound unbothered. But I couldn't help but laugh. "If I had known what this farm life would be like, I might've opted to swallow my pride and head back to Seattle."

Wells chuckled and turned back to the stove, flipping something in the pan with practiced ease. "You'll get the hang of it," he said with that easy confidence. "Maybe next time, you won't have to wrestle a goat into submission just to get a little peace."

"Don't remind me," I muttered, taking a seat at the table and tucked my legs underneath me. "I swear, I'll never look at goats the same way again."

Wells grinned, his voice a mix of amusement and something warmer. "You looked pretty cute with your hair all wild and covered in goat slobber. You should consider it your new look."

"Don't even joke," I said, poking at my food with a mock glare.

He gave me a sidelong glance, clearly enjoying every second of my discomfort. "I'm just saying, you make it work."

I rolled my eyes again but couldn't suppress the smile tugging at the corners of my mouth. As much as I tried to act annoyed, there was something about Wells' teasing that made the whole situation less ridiculous.

"Thanks for the food, by the way," I said, trying to shift the focus away from the subject of goats and showers. "I'm starving."

"You're welcome," Wells replied easily, sliding into the chair opposite me. "Figured you'd worked up an appetite wrangling livestock all day."

"Livestock?" I snorted. "I was wrestling with one goat and I'm pretty sure he was winning most of the time."

"Well, maybe you just need a few more lessons in goat-wrangling," Wells said with a cheeky grin. "Or, we could just let you stick to the flowers. You know, where they don't bite."

I couldn't help but laugh at his teasing tone. "I think that's the smartest idea I've heard all day."

Wells smirked, raising his water glass in a mock toast. "To flowers and no goats," he said, his eyes twinkling with mischief.

I clinked my glass against his, smiling despite myself. "To flowers and no goats," I agreed, knowing this was only the beginning of many more farm-related adventures.

CHAPTER 40

CHASING AFTER YOU

Wells

THE SOFT GLOW OF CANDLELIGHT FLICKERED ACROSS THE small farmhouse table, casting long shadows on the walls. The air smelled of fresh herbs and roasted vegetables from dinner, the only sound being the occasional clink of silverware against plates. It had been a long day—hell, a long week—and I couldn't help but notice how tired Rose looked.

She sat across from me, eyes still heavy with exhaustion, pushing food around on her plate. I knew she was hardly eating. She'd been like that for days now—constantly busy, always working on something, always putting everyone else before herself. It had been a lot—too much—and I could see the weariness in her. But Rose didn't exactly wear her exhaustion like a badge; she kept pushing through, determined as ever.

I'd been watching her for a while now, stealing glances as she tried to carry on, but even she couldn't hide how tired she was. The energy that had been there when she first came to the farm had started to wane, and while I admired her work ethic, it was clear she needed a break.

I set my fork down and leaned forward, studying her. "You've been working nonstop, Rose."

She didn't meet my gaze. "I'm fine," she replied, the words lacking their usual conviction. She smiled, but it was weak, not her usual bright grin. "It's just a lot right now."

I didn't believe her for a second, but I didn't push. Rose was the kind of person who would rather suffer in silence than admit when she needed help. And while I respected that, I wasn't about to sit back and watch her run herself into the ground.

"You've been pushing yourself hard," I said, trying to keep my tone light. "And I think it's time we celebrate."

She blinked, clearly taken aback. "Celebrate? What for? The fact that I've barely slept in a week?"

"No," I said, chuckling. "Celebrate the launch of Solace Blooms. You've worked so damn hard to get here, and it's time to enjoy the fruits of your labor."

She looked skeptical, her brow furrowing as she glanced at me. "I don't know. Maybe I'll just relax for the night, catch up on some sleep."

I smiled softly. "I think sleep can wait."

She laughed lightly, though it was more out of politeness than amusement. "Well, sleep's kind of the only thing I want right now."

"You'll sleep plenty tomorrow," I assured her, leaning back in my chair. "Tomorrow, you sleep in. I'll handle everything on the farm. I promise you, it'll all get taken care of."

She raised an eyebrow, still unconvinced. "And what's your plan, then? What do you want me to do?"

I leaned forward again, my voice turning playful. "You can do whatever you want tomorrow. Take the truck if you'd like. But in the evening, we're going out. Just like you would back in Seattle. You're going to enjoy yourself for once, and no more farm work for the day. Deal?"

Her eyes widened in surprise. "Wait—what? You're planning a night out for me?"

"Of course," I said with a grin. "You've been working too hard. Tomorrow, you get to enjoy yourself. No excuses."

She hesitated, looking down at her plate before glancing back up at me. "I don't know, Wells. I'm not sure I'm in the mood to go out right now. I'm honestly too tired for anything too exciting."

"Then something low-key," I suggested. "We'll just grab a drink, maybe catch a bite to eat, and talk. You deserve a break."

Her lips quirked upward, a teasing glint in her eyes. "Are you asking me out on a date?"

I froze for a second, caught off guard by her comment. Then I shook my head, laughing softly. "Not a date. Just two people who happen to be friends, enjoying a drink together. You've been working your ass off, Sunshine. You deserve to unwind a little. Just one night. That's all I'm asking."

She raised both eyebrows, clearly amused. "Uh-huh. Sure. You're not trying to woo me with a nice dinner and drinks?"

I chuckled. "Rose, I'm not trying to woo you. I'm trying to get you to stop working for five minutes and let yourself have a little fun. So, what's it going to be?"

She leaned back in her chair, tapping her fingers on the edge of the table. I could see the wheels turning in her head, weighing the idea. She still looked hesitant, but I could see the exhaustion in her eyes begin to soften, like maybe the idea of taking a break didn't sound so bad after all.

"I guess I did like going out with friends in Seattle," she said after a beat, her tone more thoughtful now. "Grabbing a drink, chatting, just doing something that wasn't related to work. I miss that."

"I know," I said quietly, understanding the sentiment all too well. Rose had given up a lot to come here—leaving behind a life that, despite everything, she'd seemed to enjoy. I didn't want her to feel like she'd left it all behind without getting something out of this new chapter, too.

"Well," I said, breaking the silence, "that's exactly what we're doing tomorrow night. We'll go out, get a drink, have some fun. No farm work, no Solace Blooms—just a little downtime for you. Think of it as a way to unwind."

She studied me for a moment, as if deciding whether or not

she could trust me to follow through with my plan. Finally, her shoulders sagged in resignation, and she gave a small nod.

"Fine," she said, though there was a reluctant smile on her lips now. "I'll go. But only because I'm too tired to argue."

I grinned, feeling a surge of triumph. "That's what I like to hear."

She rolled her eyes, shaking her head. "You're relentless, you know that?"

"That's part of my charm," I said, my grin widening.

She laughed, the sound light and genuine. For the first time all evening, she looked like herself again—like she was letting go of some of the weight that had been on her shoulders. And that, in itself, felt like a small victory.

I stood up, walking over to her side of the table. I offered my hand, pulling her to her feet. "Come on. Let's get you some rest. Tomorrow's going to be a good day."

She took my hand, allowing me to lead her toward the stairs, but not before giving me a teasing look. "You really think you can handle everything on the farm tomorrow?"

"Absolutely," I said, my confidence unwavering. "I did it for years."

She smirked. "I'm going to sleep. Don't wake me unless there's some sort of natural disaster." Rose paused. "On second thought, just let me sleep."

"I can do that. Good night, Sunshine."

She gave me a playful shove as we reached the stairs. "Good night."

I was just glad to see her smiling again. Maybe it was because of my plan or maybe it was because, for once, she was letting herself have a little fun. Either way, I'd take it.

Tomorrow night, we were going to celebrate more than just Solace Blooms. We were going to celebrate Rose.

Since all the things to do were in downtown Wippowa, I texted Charlie to see if we could crash at their house so we didn't have to drive back after having some drinks.

Wells: Can Rose and I crash with y'all tomorrow?

Charlie: Sure can. What's going on?

Wells: Rose needs a break so we're going out for dinner and drinks. Even gave her the day off.

Charlie: Are you going on a date, Calloway?

Wells: Why does everyone think that? No, I'm just trying to be nice.

Charlie: Sounds like a date.

Charlie: Which, I wouldn't be mad about. Y'all are cute.

Wells: You've officially turned into a softie.

By pure luck, my favorite restaurant had a reservation for two available at seven o'clock tomorrow night. The food was amazing, and the drinks were top-notch, so I knew Rose would love it. I quickly grabbed the reservation and shut my phone with a satisfied smile.

I rinsed off the plates and wiped down the counters, the rhythmic sound of the sponge against the surface soothing in a way I hadn't expected. The day had been long, but there was a quiet satisfaction in knowing Rose had finally given herself the space to relax for the first time in days. She had worked herself ragged on the farm, and I was determined to make tomorrow night something special for her.

Once the kitchen was clean and the last dish was in the dishwasher, I headed upstairs. The house was unusually quiet, the kind of silence that made everything feel more intimate, more personal.

I stretched as I reached the top of the stairs, my body aching from the day's work but my mind still buzzing.

I changed into a pair of comfortable sweats and collapsed onto the bed, my eyes closing for a brief moment. But my thoughts immediately turned back to Rose. I couldn't shake the image of her—the way she had looked when she finally let herself unwind, her face softening as she sank into the chair, too tired to do anything but enjoy the quiet. It was clear that the weight of the farm was heavy on her shoulders, and I couldn't help but admire how hard she worked to keep everything running smoothly.

Tomorrow night needed to be perfect. I didn't just want to take her out; I wanted to give her something she could truly enjoy— something to remind her that she deserved to take a break, that she was allowed to have fun without thinking about work for once.

I ran a hand over my face, exhaling slowly.

Tomorrow would be about her, about giving her a night where she could just let go.

And hopefully, I'd make it one she wouldn't forget.

CHAPTER 41

SLOW DANCE IN A PARKING LOT

Rose

MY MIND LINGERED ON THE CONVERSATION AND THE strange warmth that had settled inside me. I loved how Wells seemed to just know what I needed without me saying a word. A night out, a little fun—who would've thought it would be so easy to let go?

I closed the door behind me and changed into my comfy clothes. The bed looked too inviting, and I couldn't resist. I crawled under the covers, the softness of the sheets making it feel like I was sinking into a cloud. I grabbed the book I'd been reading and settled in, the quiet of the room wrapping around me like a cocoon.

It didn't take long before the words blurred together, the fatigue of the past few weeks catching up with me. Slowly, my eyelids grew heavier, and the book slipped from my hands.

I woke up with a start, blinking at the soft light pouring in through the window. My eyes darted to the clock on the nightstand. It was almost eleven.

A groan escaped me, and I buried my face into the pillow. I'd definitely overdone it. I never slept this late, especially with so much to do. The guilt crept in quickly, but I couldn't deny how good the rest had felt. I needed it. I *deserved* it.

I sat up, glancing out the window, and the sight that met my eyes made me smile. Wells was out in the garden, his sleeves rolled up as he tended to the vegetables, moving with that calm precision I had come to associate with him.

I let out a long breath, standing up and stretching as I pulled myself out of bed. The room still felt warm and cozy, but I knew I had to get moving. A quick shower would help wake me up.

A few minutes later, I stepped into my jeans and a simple T-shirt before heading downstairs. I paused by the door, catching one last glimpse of Wells in the garden, then walked outside, my footsteps soft against the porch.

"Oh hey, Sunshine." Wells greeted me with a smile. He dropped a zucchini into the basket.

"Hi." My voice felt a little groggy from sleep, but I was definitely starting to feel more awake.

"Did you get some good sleep?" He asked, turning to face me with that easygoing smile I'd come to love. He adjusted his hat so he could see me.

"Yeah, I feel a lot better. I'm ready to go out tonight. I wanted to see if you were in the mood for lunch?" I added, crossing my arms over my chest.

"What are you making?" His grin widened, and I could tell he was already imagining something delicious.

"Grilled cheese is about the extent of what I can do on my own." I shrugged, laughing at how simple it sounded. But honestly, I wasn't trying to impress him with anything fancy.

"That sounds great." He said, the approval in his voice making me feel better about the idea of such a simple lunch.

"I'll come get you when it's ready." I turned on my heel and went back inside.

"Don't burn the house down." Wells joked.

"I won't!" I called over my shoulder.

I smiled to myself as I gathered the bread and cheese for the grilled cheese sandwiches. It was such a simple, small thing, but I couldn't shake the feeling it was just another sign of how much I was starting to care about Wells. As I rummaged through the kitchen drawers in search of a spatula, I came across one I hadn't opened before. My hand froze when I saw it—tucked neatly inside was the sour Skittles bag I'd sassily given Wells during our flight a few months ago. My heart skipped.

I couldn't help but stare at the bag, a mix of surprise and warmth spreading through me. I hadn't expected to see it here, tucked away in his kitchen. The bag looked slightly crumpled, evidence of it having been carried around and perhaps enjoyed more than once. I thought back to that flight—how heavy my world had felt then. Yet now, seeing that bag, it somehow felt like a little piece of our connection, still lingering.

I picked it up, my fingers grazing the faded label, then shook my head, chuckling softly to myself. "Of course," I muttered under my breath. It was such a Wells thing to keep something like this, even though I had been awful to him on that flight and for a while after.

I turned the bag over in my hands for a moment before carefully setting it back in the drawer. It felt like the kind of small, unexpected gesture that meant more than I could articulate. I quickly snapped myself out of my thoughts, reminding myself that I still had grilled cheese to make. But a smile lingered on my face as I turned back to the stove, a quiet warmth settling in my chest.

Once I set the plates on the counter, I headed outside to let Wells know lunch was ready. As I stepped through the door, he was already making his way in, wiping his hands on a rag.

"Lunch ready?" he asked, his voice easy and familiar.

I met his gaze with a small smile. "It is."

This all felt very domestic.

We sat down at the table, the scent of buttery, toasted bread filling the air as I slid a plate in front of Wells. He picked up his sandwich without hesitation, taking a big bite. I watched, waiting for his reaction, but he chewed thoughtfully, nodding to himself like he was genuinely impressed.

He swallowed, then leaned back in his chair. "That," he said, pointing at the sandwich, "might just be the best grilled cheese I've ever had."

I snorted, picking up my own. "You're such a liar."

He shook his head, completely serious. "Nope. Perfectly crispy, the right amount of cheese... I don't know, Rose, you might've just found your true calling."

I rolled my eyes but couldn't help the small laugh that escaped. "Well, if all else fails, at least I know I can survive on grilled cheese."

He took another bite, grinning at me. "Hey, if you ever want to open a grilled cheese food truck, I'd be your first customer."

I smirked, shaking my head as I took a bite. "Good to know I've got at least one guaranteed sale."

Wells' usual relaxed posture made it hard not to smile.

"You know, I've been thinking," he said between bites. "You didn't get to do much today. How about after dinner tonight, we go out somewhere else? You said you enjoyed hanging out with friends back in Seattle. I'm thinking we could do something like that."

I raised a brow. "Are you sure this isn't a date?"

He gave me a half-smirk, his eyes twinkling with mischief. "Just asking you to hang out. Not everything has to be a date, you know."

I rolled my eyes playfully, trying not to laugh. "Oh sure, because asking me out for drinks and a good time isn't a date."

"Consider it a night of fun and freedom," he said with a shrug.

I couldn't help but feel a little more at ease hearing him say that. I wasn't the only one noticing how hard I'd been working lately. "Okay, okay," I said with a nod. "I'll go along with it. But only because you're buying the drinks."

He chuckled, and I felt a little flutter in my chest at how easy it was to be around him. How simple it was, even with all the chaos of the farm and the busy days.

"Deal," Wells said, finishing his sandwich and standing up. "I'm going to go finish up outside and then we can start getting ready for tonight." He placed his plate in the dishwasher and paused at the door. "Thanks again for lunch."

After cleaning up from lunch, I grabbed my book from my room and curled up on the couch, letting the quiet afternoon settle around me. The sound of the wind outside, the faint creaks of the old house, and the comforting weight of the book in my hands made it easy to lose track of time.

I was deep in my story when the door opened, and Wells stepped inside, smelling like sun and fresh air. He ran a hand through his hair, shaking off the last bit of the afternoon chill.

"Hey, Sunshine."

I glanced up, tucking my bookmark between the pages. "Hi."

He leaned against the doorway, his easy grin in place. "I'm gonna shower and start getting ready. We've got about three hours until our reservation."

I blinked. "You made us reservations?"

His lips twitched. "You've been to Wippowa before—you know how packed downtown gets on a Friday."

"Fair enough."

He tilted his head. "How long will it take you to get ready?"

I set my book on the coffee table and stretched. "Well, that depends… You still haven't told me where we're going." A small smile played on my lips.

His grin widened like he was enjoying having the upper hand. "Guess you'll just have to trust me."

Wells shot me a wink before disappearing down the hall, leaving me with a mix of curiosity and anticipation. I sat there for a moment, staring at the space where he'd just been, before shaking my head and heading upstairs to get ready.

Even though I didn't know where we were going, I figured a Friday night in downtown Wippowa called for something a little nicer than my usual jeans and T-shirt. I settled on a soft sweater and a pair of fitted jeans, something comfortable but still put together. I took my time fixing my hair, letting it fall in loose waves, and swiped on a little mascara and lip gloss before stepping back to check my reflection.

Not bad.

Just as I was slipping on my heels, I heard Wells' footsteps in the hallway. A second later, there was a light knock on my door.

"You decent?"

I smirked. "That depends."

The door cracked open, and Wells peeked in, his eyes sweeping over me before he leaned against the frame. "Look at you," he said, his voice warm with approval.

I raised an eyebrow. "Good or bad?"

His lips quirked up. "Definitely good."

I tried not to let that go to my head. "And you clean up pretty well yourself," I said, eyeing his dark jeans and button-up shirt. It was a small shift from his usual T-shirts and flannels, but damn, did it make a difference. "Didn't need help this time, I see."

"Sure didn't." He chuckled. "Ready to go?"

I grabbed my jacket and nodded. "Lead the way."

As we stepped outside, the cool night air wrapped around us, carrying the distant hum of weekend life in town. Wells opened the truck door for me, and I climbed in, settling into the worn leather seat. The one I've become very used to sitting in.

"Still not telling me where we're going?" I asked as he slid into the driver's seat.

He shot me a sideways glance, the corner of his mouth lifting. "Nope."

I sighed dramatically, but truthfully, I didn't mind. For once, it was nice to sit back and let someone else take the reins.

And something told me that whatever Wells had planned, it was going to be a night worth remembering.

Wells turned the key in the ignition, and the truck rumbled to life. The familiar scent of leather and something distinctly him filled the cabin, making it feel impossibly cozy. As he pulled onto the road, he reached for the radio dial, glancing at me with a playful smirk.

"So, you wanna listen to some country music?"

I groaned, already knowing where this was going. "Do I have a choice?"

He chuckled, flicking through the stations until a twangy guitar filled the truck. "Not really."

I shot him a look. "You realize I didn't grow up on this stuff, right?"

"Oh, I know." His smirk deepened and a dimple popped in his right cheek. "That's why I'm doing my part to fix that."

Shaking my head, I leaned back against the seat, crossing my arms. "I can appreciate a good song, but if it's all about trucks, beer, and heartbreak, I'm out."

Wells tapped the steering wheel in time with the beat, looking entirely too pleased with himself. "Alright, how about this—one song. If you hate it, I'll switch to whatever you want."

I narrowed my eyes. "Any song?"

"Any song."

I exhaled dramatically. "Fine. But it better be a good one."

He nodded like he took the challenge seriously, adjusting the volume just as the first verse started. The melody was smooth, the lyrics less about trucks and more about slow dancing in a parking lot, love that felt like home.

I glanced at him out of the corner of my eye. "Okay… this isn't terrible."

Wells grinned. "See? Told you."

I rolled my eyes, but I didn't fight it. There was something about the way he sat behind the wheel, so at ease in his world, that made me want to enjoy it too.

The road stretched ahead, leading us into downtown Wippowa, and as the song played on, I found myself tapping my fingers lightly against my knee, letting the music settle in. Maybe country music wasn't the worst thing in the world.

CHAPTER 42

WHAT MY WORLD SPINS AROUND

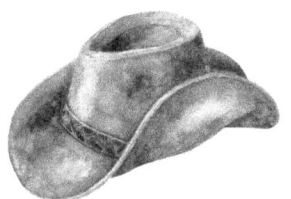

Wells

I WAS NERVOUS. MORE NERVOUS THAN I HAD BEEN ON MY FIRST date with Marie—not that this was a date.

At least, that's what I kept telling myself.

"Alright, you get to pick the song now." I handed Rose the aux cord.

She took the cord and plugged her phone in, scrolling through her playlist as the truck rumbled down the quiet roads of Wippowa. Rose settled on a song I had heard on the radio and in the grocery stores, but I sure couldn't tell you what it was.

"Is this okay?" Rose looked over at me, eyes unsure.

"Whatever you'd like to listen to."

The melodies danced in the air between us and I drummed my fingers on the steering wheel.

It wasn't a date.

We both knew that. I had made sure to say it outright, to set the expectation, to keep things light. But as I pulled into a parking spot just a few blocks from the restaurant, my hands tightened on the wheel, and my pulse picked up like I was some kid taking his high school crush out for the first time.

I just wanted tonight to be… good. No, scratch that—I wanted it to be perfect.

Rose had been running herself into the ground between the farm, her business, and adjusting to life here. I saw it every day. The exhaustion in her eyes, the way she threw herself into work like it was the only thing keeping her upright. But she was more than that. She deserved more than that.

And if I could be the person to remind her that life in Wippowa wasn't just about work and responsibility, that it could be fun, too— well, I wanted to be that person.

I glanced at her as she unbuckled her seatbelt, her fingers brushing over her jeans. She looked good. More than good. But it wasn't just that, there was something about her tonight, something lighter in her expression, like maybe she was finally letting herself breathe.

"Ready?" I asked, clearing my throat.

She nodded, reaching for the door handle. "I hope you know I'll be judging this restaurant hard. Since you're keeping it a secret."

I huffed a laugh, stepping out of the truck. "Good thing I know it'll live up to the hype, then."

She shot me a teasing look over the roof of the truck before we started down the sidewalk. The streets were alive with people heading in and out of shops and restaurants, the warm glow of string lights making downtown Wippowa feel like something out of a movie.

I slid my hands into my pockets as we walked. My nerves still buzzed under my skin, but I shoved them down, keeping my focus on her.

The cool evening air mingled with the warm glow of the restaurant's neon sign. "Here we are." I announced, trying to sound more confident than I felt. The building was nice—nothing too fancy, just a cozy, casual spot with exposed brick, mismatched wooden tables, and string lights that draped the windows like a soft, warm invitation. I could see that Rose thought so too; her eyes lit up as she took in the sight.

"This is cute. Blythe and I have walked by this place a few times."

Inside, we were seated in a snug booth that creaked pleasantly under the weight of memories from previous dinners. The atmosphere was relaxed—no pretentiousness, just a place that felt like a well-kept secret in downtown Wippowa. I watched as Rose settled into her seat, her expression a mix of wonder and ease, and I felt that familiar nervous excitement flutter in my chest, even though I kept reminding myself, "*It's not a date. It's just a fun night out.*"

Our waiter, a cheerful guy with a quick smile and a quirky sense of humor, handed us menus. I noticed Rose scanning the pages with a curious sparkle in her eyes, as if each dish held a promise of something delightful. I couldn't help but feel proud that I'd chosen this place—one I'd come to love over countless family visits.

Before we even ordered, the conversation took a playful turn. I leaned over and said, "So, what are you in the mood for? Something light or something that'll make you forget all about the farm for a while?"

Rose's laugh was soft but genuine. "Honestly? I'd love to forget about being responsible tonight."

I leaned back, intrigued. "What's your go-to drink?" Up until now, the only thing I'd ever seen her drink was wine—the night her ex called her.

"Ideally? Bourbon, neat."

My brow lifted. "You're serious?"

She tucked a loose strand of hair behind her ear, her lips quirking in amusement. "Yeah. I know, it's probably not what you're used to hearing from a lady as proper as myself, but I love it." She paused, her gaze flickering somewhere distant. "The night I turned twenty-one, my dad poured us two glasses, and we sat outside talking about life. It was one of those nights you never forget, you know?"

There was something wistful in her voice, a quiet longing that settled between us. This was the first time she had ever mentioned her parents.

I nodded, understanding more than I cared to admit. Some memories—good or bad—become part of you, etched so deeply that you carry them forever.

"What about you?" she asked, pulling herself back to the present. "What are you ordering?"

I smirked. "Would you believe me if I said the same thing?"

Her lips parted slightly. "Really?"

"Is it that surprising that a southern boy likes his bourbon?"

She tilted her head, studying me. "I suppose not."

Her eyes dropped to the menu, and I watched as she traced her fingers over the options.

"What's good here?" she asked.

"Everything," I said without hesitation. "This place was a favorite of mine growing up. My parents and I used to come here all the time."

She glanced up, something unreadable in her expression. For a moment, it felt like we were sharing more than just a meal—it felt like we were sharing pieces of ourselves, little glimpses into the past that shaped us.

As soon as the waiter walked up, Rose set her menu down with a confident smile. "I'll have a bourbon, neat."

The guy barely blinked before nodding. "And for you, sir?"

I smirked. "Same."

The waiter took our drink menus and left and Rose shot me a look across the table. "He didn't even hesitate. You think he judged me?"

"Nah," I said, leaning back. "But if you'd ordered it with a little pink umbrella, then maybe."

She snorted. "You'd be surprised how many bartenders do that automatically when a woman orders bourbon. As if I'm about to say, 'Oh, sorry, I actually meant a daiquiri with a sugar rim and a cherry on top.'"

"Now I kind of want to see you order that just to mess with people."

She rolled her eyes but laughed. "Maybe next time."

Next time.

The drinks arrived, and Rose took her glass with both hands, giving it a little appreciative nod before taking a sip.

She barely got the glass back down before her nose scrunched. "Okay, wow. That's stronger than I remember."

I bit back a laugh. "You were trying to act all tough, weren't you?"

"No," she said, setting the glass down like it personally offended her. "I just wasn't prepared for it to punch me in the throat."

I took a sip of mine, enjoying the burn. "Don't worry, Sunshine. If you need me to get you a daiquiri with a sugar rim and a cherry on top, I got you."

She narrowed her eyes, but there was a smile tugging at her lips. "I don't like you."

I smirked. "You definitely do."

The waiter returned to take our order, and I went with the steak, while Rose ordered the shrimp and grits.

"Classic," I said after the waiter walked away.

"I'm in the South. I figured I had to, right?"

"You won't regret it. I promise." I confirmed.

She swirled her glass in her hand, studying me. "You seem more relaxed."

"Yeah, well," I took another sip, "it turns out bourbon is a pretty good cure for nerves."

Rose leaned forward, resting her elbows on the table. "Wait, were you nervous?"

I hesitated for half a second too long.

Her grin was immediate. "Wells Calloway. You were nervous about dinner."

I shook my head, but my smirk gave me away. "I was not nervous."

She tilted her head, eyes gleaming with amusement. "Mm-hmm. Sure."

There was a beat of silence between us.

Rose rested her elbow on the table, leaning in slightly. "Okay, tell me something embarrassing about yourself."

I nearly choked on my drink. "That's the first thing you ask me?"

"Well, I figure since we're having fun tonight, we should set the mood with some humility. And I already know you fell off a horse as a kid, so that one doesn't count."

I groaned. "Charlie told you that, didn't he?"

"He sure did."

I dragged a hand down my face. "When I was ten, I tried to impress a girl at the county fair by winning her a stuffed bear at the ring toss."

Rose's lips twitched and her eyes lit up. "And?"

"And I got so frustrated missing every single shot that I flung the last ring in pure rage and accidentally smacked the guy running the game in the face."

She burst out laughing, nearly knocking over her drink. "You assaulted the ring toss guy?"

"It was an accident! But I panicked and ran, which probably made me look guilty."

Rose shook her head, wiping at her eyes. "That poor man. I hope he got hazard pay."

"I wouldn't be surprised if they put up a picture of me behind the counter with a 'Do Not Serve' sign."

Her laughter softened into a grin, and she took another sip of bourbon. "Okay, that was a good one. I'll give you that."

I leaned forward, resting my arms on the table. "Your turn. Most embarrassing moment."

She hummed, tapping a finger against her glass. "Alright, when I was in high school, I had the biggest crush on this guy in my math class. One day, I worked up the nerve to talk to him. I was going for casual and charming, but when I walked over, I tripped on absolutely nothing, face-planted in front of him, and—this is the worst part—he thought I passed out and called the nurse."

I let out a sharp laugh. "No way."

"Oh, it gets better. The nurse insisted on calling my parents, and when my dad showed up, instead of being concerned, he asked if I was just that clumsy."

I was laughing so hard I had to set my drink down. "Damn. That's tough."

She sighed dramatically. "Yeah. Safe to say, I never shot my chance again. I even tried to get my parents to transfer me to a different high school."

I tried to compose myself. "I guess that didn't pan out."

"Not at all."

Our food arrived, saving her from further interrogation, and I watched as she took her first bite of shrimp and grits. Her eyes widened, and she chewed slowly before swallowing.

"Well?" I asked.

She dabbed at her lips with her napkin, then set it down with exaggerated care. "I'll allow you to keep your Wippowa citizenship."

I smirked. "Told you."

She rolled her eyes, but there was a warmth to her expression, a lightness in her posture that hadn't been there earlier.

And just like that, the nerves I'd been carrying all night faded away. Because this? This was exactly what I'd hoped for.

Rose took another bite, nodding approvingly. "Okay, fine. I'll even admit it's better than what I had back in Seattle."

I feigned shock. "You mean to tell me that a small-town Southern kitchen might actually know a thing or two about shrimp and grits?"

"Alright, don't get cocky," she said, pointing her fork at me. "It's a close call."

I chuckled and took a bite of my steak, savoring the rich, smoky flavor. The tension I had been holding onto fully unraveled as we ate, slipping into an easy rhythm of teasing and conversation.

"So," I said, wiping my mouth with my napkin, "if high school you was that unlucky, what's the most embarrassing thing adult you has done?"

Rose groaned, setting her fork down. "Oh, you're evil."

"You brought up the math class fiasco. Now I have to know."

She sighed, pretending to think. "Alright. A couple years ago, I was in a client meeting—big presentation, lots of important people, very serious business. And about ten minutes in, I started gesturing with my pen. Didn't think much of it—until I flung it right at the CEO's forehead."

I choked on my drink. "No."

"Oh, yes. Full-on 'thunk' sound and everything. I swear the entire room sucked in a breath at the same time."

"Please tell me you played it off."

"I wish. My brilliant response was, 'Oh my god, I have terrible aim.'"

I burst out laughing. "That's amazing."

She shook her head, laughing along with me. "I think he was too stunned to fire me on the spot. Either that, or he respected my honesty."

"Well," I leaned back in my chair, smirking, "remind me never to let you hold sharp objects near my face."

"No promises." She grinned, sipping her drink.

The night stretched on with more stories, more laughter, the warmth of it settling into my chest. I hadn't expected it to feel this easy—this natural—but sitting there, watching Rose smile across the table, I realized I didn't want the night to end just yet.

As the waiter cleared our plates, I glanced at her. "So, how do you feel about one more stop before we call it a night?"

She raised an eyebrow. "That depends. Are we talking a bar, a crime spree, or a spontaneous road trip?"

I grinned. "Guess you'll just have to trust me."

CHAPTER 43

BUTTERFLIES

Rose

"Trust you? Please. I already live in your house and sleep across the hall from you. I think we're well past the trust phase, Wellsy boy."

Wells grimaced like I'd just insulted his entire family. "Never call me that again. That was gross."

I smirked. "Noted."

I hadn't been sure what to expect from tonight. We were both out of our element, stepping into something that wasn't friendship but definitely wasn't anything more. And yet, it had been... nice. Easier than I thought. I'd gotten to see a new side of Wells, learned things about him I never would have guessed. And, without realizing it, I'd let down some of the walls I'd been holding up so tightly.

Wells handed his card to the waiter before I could even think about reaching for mine. I narrowed my eyes at him, but he just shot me a look that said, *Don't even try it.*

As we stepped outside, the night air wrapped around us, warm but crisp enough to remind me it wasn't summer anymore. The streets of downtown Wippowa were alive, a mix of locals and tourists weaving in and out of shops and restaurants, laughter and music spilling onto the sidewalks.

Wells walked beside me, his hands tucked into his pockets, his gait easy and relaxed. I, on the other hand, was still suspicious.

"Where are we going now?" I asked as we turned down a side street.

"A bar."

I arched a brow.

He shot me a knowing smirk. "Oh, Sunshine, you're in for a great time."

I didn't have much time to question him before we stopped in front of a brick building with a faded wooden sign hanging above the door. *Buck and Barrel.*

Inside, the scent of old whiskey and fried food hit me first, followed by the unmistakable sound of someone butchering a country song on a karaoke mic. The place had all the hallmarks of a proper dive bar—dim lighting, mismatched furniture, and a handful of regulars parked at the bar like they owned the place. A neon beer sign flickered against the back wall, casting a soft blue hue over a pool table where a few guys were mid-game.

I let out a small laugh. "Wow. Fancy."

Wells grinned. "Told you."

I barely had time to take in the full scene before a man on stage hit an impressively terrible high note, earning a mix of cheers and groans from the crowd. A woman near the bar waved her beer in the air, encouraging him to keep going, while an older man in a cowboy hat shook his head with the weight of someone who had heard far too many bad renditions of 'Neon Moon' in his lifetime.

I turned to Wells, arms crossed. "Karaoke? Really?"

"Oh yeah." He looked far too pleased with himself. "Wippowa tradition."

I raised a skeptical brow. "So you're saying *you* get up there and sing?"

He pressed a hand to his chest in mock offense. "What, you don't think I've got the chops?"

"I know you don't."

He laughed, nudging me toward the bar. "Let's get you a drink before you start talking crazy."

We wove our way through the small crowd, and Wells slid onto an open barstool, motioning for me to take the one beside him. The bartender, a woman with a messy blonde ponytail and a t-shirt that read *Drink 'til He's Cute*, leaned on the counter and gave Wells a knowing grin.

"Well, well, if it isn't Calloway." She tossed a bar rag over her shoulder. "Didn't think I'd see you in here on a Friday night."

Wells smirked. "What can I say? I'm full of surprises."

Her eyes flicked to me, curiosity sparking. "And who's this?"

"This is Rose," Wells said, then added with a teasing drawl, "She's new to Wippowa. Thought I'd show her the finer things in life."

I snorted. "So you brought me *here?*"

The bartender let out a loud laugh and stuck out her hand. "I like you already. I'm Katie."

I shook her hand, already feeling more at ease. "Nice to meet you."

"What can I get y'all?"

I glanced at Wells. "Round of bourbon?"

His brows lifted. "Look at you, already knowing the Wippowa way."

Katie smirked, reaching for a bottle behind her. "I like a girl who drinks whiskey. You might just survive here after all." She poured our drinks and set them in front of us before nodding toward the stage. "You getting up there, Calloway?"

Wells groaned. "Absolutely not."

I smirked over the rim of my glass. "I knew you didn't have the chops."

He leaned in, eyes narrowing. "You're talking real big for someone who's never heard me sing."

Katie grinned and wiped down the counter. "You should go up, Rose. Show him how it's done."

I let out a light laugh, shaking my head. "Not a chance."

Wells took a slow sip of his drink. "What's the matter? Big city girl scared of a little Wippowa crowd?"

I narrowed my eyes at him. "Oh, you wish that was the case."

He shrugged. "Only one way to prove me wrong."

I stared at him, then flicked my gaze to the karaoke stage, where the current singer had just finished to a mix of cheers and playful boos. My stomach flipped, but maybe this wasn't such a bad idea.

I downed my drink, stood, and smirked. "Fine. You're on."

Wells leaned back in his chair, arms crossed, looking entirely too pleased with himself. "This is gonna be *real* good."

I strode toward the karaoke sign-up sheet, ignoring the warmth creeping up my neck. The last time I sang in public was probably in my car with the windows rolled up, but I wasn't about to let Wells think I was too chicken to follow through. The alcohol would kick in soon and my confidence would grow.

Flipping through the song choices, I searched for something that wouldn't completely embarrass me. Nothing too slow, nothing that required vocal gymnastics, and definitely nothing that screamed I take myself too seriously. Then I found it—Dolly Parton. Classic. Fun. And if all else failed, everyone would be too busy singing along to notice if I was terrible.

I scribbled my name on the list and turned back toward the bar. Wells was still watching me, an easy smirk pulling at his lips.

"You look mighty confident over there, Sunshine," he teased as I reclaimed my seat.

I lifted my glass—empty, but it was the principle. "Fake it 'til you make it."

Katie walked by and let out a whistle. "She's singing? This I gotta see."

I rolled my eyes, but before I could respond, the guy running karaoke called "Rose Solace".

"Oh, hell," I muttered under my breath.

Wells chuckled. "No backing out now."

Squaring my shoulders, I walked up to the small stage. The room wasn't huge, but it felt bigger when everyone turned their attention my way. I adjusted the microphone stand, took a deep breath, and waited as the opening notes filled the room.

And then, I sang.

The first few words wobbled, but by the time I hit the chorus, the whole bar was clapping and singing along. Someone in the back whooped. A few people started swaying, drinks raised in encouragement. I caught Wells watching me with a mix of amusement and something else I couldn't quite place.

By the time the song ended, my heart was pounding, but I was grinning. The bar erupted into cheers, and I let out a breath, feeling lighter than I had in weeks.

I hopped off the stage and made my way back to the bar. Wells was shaking his head, a lopsided smile spread across his face.

"Well?" I asked, grabbing my now-full glass and holding it out.

He clinked his against mine. "I stand corrected. You've got guts."

I took a sip, savoring the burn of bourbon. "Don't forget it."

He leaned in slightly, his voice low and teasing. "Oh, I won't."

I had to admit it—the butterflies in my stomach were in full flight. Maybe it was the bourbon, or maybe it was the way Wells was looking at me, but either way, I was in trouble.

Big trouble.

Wells leaned in closer, his elbow resting on the worn wooden bar, his gaze steady on mine. The dim lighting softened the sharp lines of his face, but it did nothing to dull the intensity in his eyes.

"You're thinking real hard over there," he murmured, his lips twitching.

I huffed out a small laugh, willing my pulse to settle. "Just enjoying the moment."

He tipped his glass toward me before taking a sip. "Glad to hear it. Night's not over yet, though."

Before I could ask what he meant, it was too late. He was already standing, already making his way toward the sign-up sheet.

I watched in horror—and a little bit of amusement—as Wells scribbled something down on the sign-up sheet. He turned back to me with a smirk, all too pleased with himself.

He walked back, hands in his pockets, looking downright smug.

"Tell me you didn't just sign me up," I called over the music. "One time was enough."

"I didn't just sign you up."

I narrowed my eyes. "Wells."

He shrugged. "I signed *us* up."

My jaw dropped. "No. Absolutely not."

"Oh, come on, Sunshine." He nudged my knee with his, eyes glinting with challenge. "Where's that 'forget about responsibility' energy you had at dinner?"

I let out a groan, dragging my hands down my face. "You're the worst."

"The worst would've been signing you up solo again."

"What are we even singing?" I asked, bracing myself for the answer.

A slow grin spread across his face. "A classic."

Before I could press him for details, the karaoke host called our names. "Rose and Wells, y'all are up!"

I closed my eyes, exhaled sharply, and shook my head. "You're really making me do this?"

He stood and held out a hand. "No one's making you do anything."

His tone was teasing, but there was something else there, something softer.

Maybe it was the bourbon, or maybe it was the way he was looking at me, but I found myself slipping my hand into his without another word.

Wells led me toward the small stage, his grip warm and steady around my fingers. My stomach twisted with nerves, but I wasn't about to back down—not when he looked so damn pleased with himself.

I had done it once, I could do it again.

The bar was loud, buzzing with chatter and off-key singing, but as we stepped up to the microphones, everything else faded into background noise. I turned to Wells, eyes narrowing. "So, what's this 'classic' we're singing?"

The opening notes filled the air, and I instantly recognized it.

"Islands in the Stream?" I asked, half laughing, half horrified.

He waggled his brows. "Told you it was a classic."

I groaned. "Wells."

But there wasn't time to argue because the lyrics were up, and he was already singing the first line. And, someone help me, he wasn't bad.

His voice had that deep, easy southern drawl, the kind that made you want to lean in and listen. He sang the first verse, shooting me a look that was half teasing, half expectant.

I brought the mic to my lips. The moment I started singing, the crowd cheered, and I couldn't help but grin.

Wells stepped closer as we hit the chorus, our voices blending surprisingly well. His eyes never left mine, and suddenly, I wasn't thinking about the crowd or the song or how ridiculous this was.

It was just us, standing way too close under the neon lights, singing about love like we meant every word.

As we hit the last notes of the song, the bar erupted into cheers and applause. I let out a breathless laugh, cheeks warm from both the alcohol and the unexpected rush of adrenaline. Wells grinned down at me, looking way too pleased with himself.

"Not bad," he teased, handing his mic back to the emcee.

I shook my head, still catching my breath. "I'm never doing it again."

He chuckled, placing a hand on the small of my back as we stepped down from the tiny stage. "You say that now, but I'm pretty sure you just became a dive bar legend."

I swatted at his arm. "Please. They're just cheering because they're drunk."

The truth was, I hadn't had this much fun in… well, I couldn't remember the last time. Something about this night—about Wells—had a way of making everything feel lighter.

We made our way back to the bar, where two glasses of water

were already waiting for us. Wells clinked his glass against mine before taking a sip.

"To Wippowa's newest karaoke queen," he said with a wink.

I smiled wide. "To never doing that again."

He just laughed, shaking his head as he took another sip of his water. But his gaze lingered, something unreadable flickering behind his eyes.

I ignored the way it made my pulse pick up.

This *wasn't* a date.

So why did it feel like one? And why didn't I mind?

CHAPTER 44

HEAD OVER BOOTS

Wells

I'M IN BIG TROUBLE. I'M IN HEAD OVER BOOTS FOR THIS GIRL.

CHAPTER 45

COWBOY TAKE ME AWAY

Rose

A S WE STEPPED OUT OF THE BAR AND ONTO THE SIDEWALK, the crisp night air wrapped around me, making me instantly regret not bringing a jacket. Wells walked beside me, his hands shoved into his pockets, looking entirely unaffected by the cold.

"We've got one more stop," he said, nodding down the street.

I glanced at him. "You sure you're not just dragging this out because you don't want the night to end?"

He smirked. "Maybe."

We made our way to the surprisingly long line.

A cool Wippowa breeze rolled through, and I shivered before I could stop myself.

Wells caught it instantly. "You cold?"

"Nope," I lied, my teeth practically chattering as another gust of wind cut through me.

His eyes narrowed, unconvinced. "Rose..."

"I'm fine," I insisted, but my body betrayed me with another full-body shiver.

He let out a soft chuckle before reaching for me without hesitation. Before I could react, he pulled me against his chest, his arms wrapping around me like it was the most natural thing in the world.

I froze.

Everything in me told me to step back, to put space between us before I let this moment sink in too deep. But then I felt the warmth of his body against mine, the steady rhythm of his heartbeat beneath my cheek, and just like that, every worry I'd been carrying—the stress, the exhaustion, the confusion—all melted away.

I shouldn't have let this happen.

But for a few stolen seconds, I did.

"You're terrible at lying," he murmured, his chin lightly grazing the top of my head.

I swallowed, resisting the urge to close my eyes and sink further into him. "And you're good at calling me out."

He chuckled, the sound vibrating through his chest, and *dammit*, why did that make my knees feel weak?

Before I could embarrass myself any further, the line started moving, and we were ushered toward the entrance. A security guard checked our IDs, and just like that, we were inside.

I blinked, taking in my surroundings.

A mechanical bull sat in the center of the room, surrounded by a padded floor and a crowd of people cheering as a guy barely clung to the saddle before getting thrown off with a dramatic flop. The whole place smelled like beer, leather, and cheap cologne, and country music blared from the speakers.

I turned to Wells, brow raised. "Seriously?"

He grinned. "Oh, Sunshine, just you wait."

Before I could stop him, he made a beeline for the sign-up sheet.

I folded my arms, watching as he scribbled his name down like this was the best idea he'd had all night.

When he turned back, there was a mischievous glint in his eye. "Hope you're ready to be impressed."

I couldn't help but smirk. "By what? Watching you get thrown off in one second?"

"You doubt me?"

"Absolutely."

He smirked, shaking his head. "You'll see."

And, oh, I did.

A few minutes later, Wells climbed onto the bull like he was born for it. The second it started moving, he settled into the rhythm with ease, gripping the handle with one hand while the other stayed raised in the air.

I expected him to last a few seconds at most, but he didn't just stay on—he rode that damn thing like it was second nature. Muscles flexing, hat tilted just right, a cocky smirk on his lips like he knew exactly what he was doing to me.

And the worst part?

He was right.

Because I was absolutely, one hundred percent hot and bothered.

I crossed my arms, pressing my lips together as I watched him ride like some damn rodeo champion. It wasn't fair. It shouldn't have been this attractive. But my brain had officially shut down, and all I could focus on was the way his body moved with the bull, the way his muscles flexed under his shirt, the pure confidence rolling off him like heat.

I swallowed hard.

Oh, I was in trouble.

Big trouble.

The crowd whooped and hollered as he held on longer than anyone before him. And when the bull finally jerked hard enough to send him flying onto the padded floor, he rolled onto his back, laughing, completely unfazed.

I should've been smug. I should've thrown some sarcastic remark his way.

Instead, I was too busy trying to remember how to breathe.

Wells pushed himself up and sauntered toward me, that stupid, cocky grin still in place.

"Well?" he asked, a little out of breath. He tilted his head. "Still think I was gonna last three seconds?"

I forced a smirk, ignoring the way my stomach was currently a war zone of butterflies. "I mean, you did okay. I've seen better."

His eyes flickered with amusement. "Oh yeah? Who?"

I shrugged, taking a sip of my drink. "I don't know. Someone."

He stepped closer, just enough to invade my space, and dammit, I let him.

"Sounds like you're just afraid to admit you were impressed." His voice was smooth, teasing, laced with something I wasn't prepared to face head-on.

I scoffed. "I think you're just looking for an ego boost."

He leaned in slightly, his breath warm against my ear. "And I think you liked watching me ride."

I nearly choked on air.

He pulled back, his smirk widening at my flustered expression before he grabbed his beer and took a long, slow sip.

Oh. He was playing dirty.

I cleared my throat, desperate to regain control. "Are you done showing off? Or should I expect you to lasso something next?"

He laughed, the sound deep and full. "I think I've done enough damage for one night."

Lies.

The damage had been done the second he pulled me into his arms outside. The bull riding? That was just overkill.

And as much as I wanted to play it cool, to brush it off like this was just another fun night out, I knew the truth.

I was falling for Wells Calloway and had absolutely no idea how to stop it.

Wells finished his beer and shot me a look that said he knew exactly what he was doing to me. That smug, easy confidence made me want to either smack him or kiss him. Maybe both.

I needed to get out of my head. Fast.

"Alright, cowboy," I said, tilting my chin up. "Since you're so damn good at it, let's see if you can handle a real challenge."

His brows lifted. "Oh? And what's that?"

I turned toward the bull, then back to him with a slow, deliberate smirk. "Me."

His eyes darkened just enough to send a shiver down my spine, but I ignored it. Instead, I marched up to the attendant, handed over my cash, and climbed onto the bull before I could second-guess myself.

Wells leaned against the railing, arms crossed, watching with barely concealed amusement. "You sure about this, Sunshine?"

I shot him a glare. "Just shut up and watch."

The attendant started the bull at an easy pace, and I did my best to hold on, squeezing my thighs tight and gripping the handle like my life depended on it. Which, honestly, it kind of did.

Wells whistled. "Looking good up there."

I gritted my teeth. "Not helping."

The bull jerked suddenly, and my body pitched forward. I barely caught myself, gripping harder, but it was no use. A few more bucks, and I lost my balance completely, tumbling off with a not-so-graceful yelp.

I landed with a soft thud on the padded floor, blinking up at the ceiling while Wells' laughter echoed around me.

"Ow," I groaned, pushing myself up.

He was already there, offering a hand, which I begrudgingly took.

He grinned. "So, does this mean I win?"

I narrowed my eyes but couldn't bite back the smile. "No one was competing."

He stepped closer, voice dipping. "Felt like a competition."

I swallowed hard, every nerve ending in my body suddenly hyperaware of how close he was.

"I'm buying the next round," I blurted, desperate to shift the energy between us.

He chuckled, shaking his head. "Alright, Sunshine. Lead the way."

As we made our way back to the bar, I told myself this was all just fun. No stakes. No meaning.

But the way my pulse pounded and my skin tingled where he had brushed against me?

I wasn't fooling anyone.

CHAPTER 46

YOU PROOF

Wells

THERE WAS SOMETHING IN THE AIR THAT SHIFTED BETWEEN Rose and me. Maybe it was the bourbon, or maybe it was just her—carefree, unburdened, lighter than I'd ever seen her before. She was always beautiful, but tonight? Tonight, her ocean eyes were bright, her laugh unrestrained, and her lipstick was long gone, leaving nothing but that natural, effortless pink of her lips.

I wanted nothing more than to pull her against me and kiss them.

I scrubbed a hand down my face and pulled my phone from my pocket, shooting a text to Charlie.

> Me: Any chance you can come get us?

It took less than a minute before he responded.

> Charlie: You're drunk?

> Me: Buzzed.

> Charlie: Rose?

Me: Also buzzed.

Charlie: So what you're telling me is I get to
be the responsible one for the first time ever?

Me: Yes?

Charlie: Hell yeah. Be there in five.

I glanced over at Rose, who was twirling the last bit of her drink with her straw, a lazy, satisfied smile on her face.

"Charlie's on his way," I told her.

She nodded, then pointed at me. "You're a gentleman, Wells Calloway." Her words were slightly slurred.

I huffed a laugh. "That bourbon's making you soft, Sunshine."

Before she could respond, Charlie walked in, his ballcap low over his face, looking downright smug. "Well, well, well," he drawled. "If it isn't the responsible adult calling for backup." He clapped me on the shoulder.

I rolled my eyes. "You gonna make fun of me all night?"

"Sure am," he said cheerfully, leading the way out.

Charlie was already smirking when we stepped outside.

"Look at you two," he said, shaking his head as we walked toward the truck. "Can't handle a little bourbon."

Rose snorted. "Hey, I handled it just fine."

Charlie gave her a skeptical once-over, then turned to me. "And what about you, Calloway? Still standing?"

"Just drive the damn car," I muttered, climbing into the passenger seat while Rose slid into the back.

Charlie started the engine and let out a long, exaggerated sigh. "You know, I gotta say," he looked at Rose in the rearview. "I never thought I'd see the day Wells Calloway called me for a ride home. It's a proud moment, really. Like watching your kid take his first steps."

I shot him a glare. "You're enjoying this way too much."

"Of course, I am," he said, pulling onto the road. "And let's not forget that I'm doing you a favor. I could've made you two walk home. It would've been real romantic, though. Stumbling down Main Street under the stars—"

"Charlie," I warned.

"Relax, lover boy, we're almost there," he said, turning onto the driveway. "But you gotta admit, you two do make a cute drunk couple."

"Not a couple," I muttered.

Rose hummed behind me. "Nope, definitely not a couple. Barely friends."

Barely friends?

Charlie grinned as he threw the truck into park. "Right. Keep tellin' yourselves that."

Blythe was curled up on the couch when we stumbled through the front door. She barely spared us a glance before pressing pause on whatever show she was watching and shaking her head.

"Oh," she mused, standing up and disappearing into the kitchen. "Look who rolled in."

Charlie flopped onto the couch, stretching his arms behind his head. "They had a real cute night."

Rose groaned. "I hate that you were involved in any of this."

"You're welcome," Charlie shot back.

Blythe returned with two bottles of water and a couple of Tylenol, handing them to us with a knowing look. "Because you guys look like you'll need it."

Rose accepted hers with a sheepish smile and wrapped her arms drunkenly around Blythe. "You're an angel. You're the bestest friend I could've ever asked for. I love your face more than anything in this world."

Blythe laughed, shaking her head. "Love you too." She carefully peeled Rose's noodle-like arms off her shoulders. "You need to chug that water and go to sleep, because morning is going to be a nightmare for you. Dare I remind you of the night I got my fake promotion?"

Rose flopped onto the couch, curling into the corner like it was the most comfortable place in the world. "I'll sleep here."

Charlie leaned against the armrest, ever the problem-solver. "Rose, you can take the bed with Blythe. Wellsy and I can crash on the couch."

Rose cracked one eye open.

"I would rather walk home barefoot than sleep next to you again. Four years of college was more than enough. It's a miracle we're still friends."

Charlie clutched his chest like I'd mortally wounded him. "I was a fantastic roommate."

"You snore like a malfunctioning snorkel," I added.

Rose snorted. Blythe giggled. I pointed at them. "There's my validation."

Blythe grinned. "The nursery has an air mattress. And there's always the couch."

Before another word could be said, a soft snore slipped from Rose's mouth.

Blythe smirked at me. "The air mattress is for you, Wells."

I hesitated. "I can wake her up, get her to—"

Blythe cut me off with a knowing look. "I wouldn't. She gets mean." She tossed me another blanket, amusement written all over her face. "Also, she doesn't share blankets."

"I'm not sleeping in there with her."

Blythe's smirk deepened. "Sure you aren't."

Charlie bumped her shoulder. "Man's got it bad." Then he turned to me with a lazy salute. "Good night, Wells."

"Night, guys. Thanks for letting us crash."

As they disappeared upstairs, I looked from the stairs back to Rose. She was out cold, limbs tangled up in the couch cushions.

I sighed. Without thinking twice, I scooped her up. She barely stirred—just a sleepy little murmur before she instinctively curled into my chest, her fingers briefly gripping my shirt.

Damn.

Pushing the nursery door open with my hip, I carried her inside and set her down gently on the air mattress, pulling a blanket over her.

"You should stay," she mumbled.

"I'm fine on the couch."

One of her eyes cracked open. "Just stay. It's fine."

The mattress definitely looked better than the couch and arguing with a half-asleep Rose didn't seem like the best plan.

I debated for half a second before laying down, rolling onto my side to face away from her.

Tonight had been... something.

Rose let out another soft snore, and I huffed out a quiet laugh. She was completely dead to the world.

A few minutes passed, nothing but the rustling of blankets and the soft rhythm of her breathing. Just as I started drifting off, she shifted.

Not much. Just enough.

Her back barely brushed against mine.

I went completely still, my body locked up like I'd been caught doing something I shouldn't. The warmth of her was enough to send every nerve in my body into overdrive.

I held my breath. I should move. Put space between us. Do literally anything other than lay here, feeling things I wasn't supposed to feel.

"This was fun," she mumbled sleepily.

I swallowed hard. "Yeah. It was."

She sighed, her voice soft, already slipping back into sleep. "We should do it again."

I turned my head slightly, even though she probably couldn't see me. "Go out drinking and watch you make bad decisions?"

A sleepy little laugh. "Shut up."

I smiled, staring up at the ceiling.

As much as I knew I shouldn't... I kind of wanted that something to happen again.

Rose didn't say anything else after that, just let out a slow, content breath.

I, on the other hand, was wide awake.

Maybe it was the exhaustion. Maybe it was the slight buzz still lingering in my system. Or maybe it was the way Rose had looked tonight—like she was finally letting herself enjoy Wippowa instead of just surviving it.

That did something to me.

CHAPTER 47

RUMOR

Rose

THE MORNING SUNLIGHT STREAMED THROUGH THE WINDOWS, forcing my eyes open with a sluggish blink. My head throbbed faintly as I took in my surroundings.

The crib. The rocking chair. The pastel-colored wallpaper.

I was in the baby's nursery.

How in the world?

I frowned, pushing myself up onto my elbows. The last thing I remembered was crashing on the couch downstairs.

A shift beside me made me freeze. Slowly, I turned my head. Wells was sprawled out next to me, dead asleep.

I inhaled sharply and yanked the blanket up, glancing down at myself. Fully clothed. Nothing out of place.

I sat up carefully, my head still fuzzy from last night. Wells didn't stir. He was flat on his stomach, one arm slung over the edge of the air mattress, his face turned toward me. His hair was a mess, and his breathing was slow and even.

I had no business noticing how good he looked first thing in the morning.

I rubbed my temples, trying to piece together how I got here.

The last thing I clearly remembered was curling up on the couch. Blythe handing me water. Charlie making some smart-ass comment.

And now, somehow, I was upstairs.

A thought struck me. *Please tell me he didn't carry me up here.*

Wells shifted again, sighing in his sleep, and before I could think better of it, I nudged him.

Nothing.

I poked his shoulder harder. "Hey. Wells."

A groggy grunt. Then, very slowly, he blinked one eye open, squinting at me.

"Morning, Sunshine," he rasped. His voice was deep and sleep-rough, and I ignored the way it sent a shiver down my spine.

"How did I get up here?" I asked, cutting straight to the point.

He rolled onto his back, scrubbing a hand over his face. "You fell asleep. I carried you up."

I groaned, flopping back against the pillow. "Please tell me you're joking."

"Nope." He stretched, his T-shirt riding up just enough to be distracting. "You were out cold. It was either that or let you sleep on the couch."

I covered my face with my hands. "That's so embarrassing."

"Why?" He sounded genuinely amused.

"Because I'm a grown adult. I don't need to be carried to bed. My dad used to do that for me when I was a kid."

Wells chuckled. "Trust me, it wasn't a big deal. Do you not remember the boot debacle? You couldn't get downstairs."

I peeked at him between my fingers. He was smirking.

I groaned again. "I hate everything."

"No, you don't." He nudged my foot with his. "You're hungover."

"No shit." I joked. "How are you feeling?"

"Like I held my liquor better than you." Wells stood, stretching again before offering me a hand. I hesitated for a second before taking it, letting him pull me to my feet.

My stomach did an annoying little flip at the warmth of his touch.

Wells opened the door and Wren stood there, leaning against the railing, smiling.

"Are you guys dating?" She piped up, a wide grin across her face.

"No." Wells and I said in unison—a little too defensively on both of us.

"Sure." Wren turned on her heel and went back into her room.

Wells shook his head with a chuckle. "She's a menace."

"She sure is." I sighed, still feeling the heat creeping up my neck. I stepped past him and made my way downstairs, pretending I didn't feel his eyes on me the whole way down.

The smell of coffee hit me as I reached the kitchen, and there was Blythe, leaning against the counter, sipping from her mug.

She raised an eyebrow as she looked me up and down. "Well, don't you two look—" she waved a hand vaguely, "—disheveled."

I scowled. "Nothing happened."

"I didn't say anything happened."

"You implied."

She sipped her coffee, eyes twinkling. "I would never."

Charlie walked in behind her, grabbing a piece of toast off a plate. "Yeah, yeah, nothing happened. But did you see Wells' hair? That's bedhead if I've ever seen it."

I groaned, covering my face. "I hate this house."

"You love this house," Blythe corrected. "I got your car for you."

"Thank you." Wells sounded more than appreciative.

"Now, do you want coffee before or after you shower?" Blythe looked between both of us.

"After." I tugged on the hem of my shirt. "Do you mind if I borrow some clothes? I was thinking about walking to the Coastal Cup."

Blythe perked up. "Trish is working today, right?"

"Yeah. I haven't seen her in a while, and I figured I'd stop in."

Wells, who had been quietly pouring himself coffee, looked over at me. "Want company?"

I hesitated, then shook my head. "I think I'd rather go solo, if that's alright."

He nodded easily. "Go do your thing."

There was something unreadable in his expression, but before I could overanalyze it, Blythe was already grabbing my arm and dragging me toward the stairs.

"Come on," she said. "I've got the perfect outfit for you."

Charlie called after us. "Make sure it's something that screams I totally didn't sleep in the nursery with Wells."

"Shut up, Charlie! You're the older brother I never wanted." I yelled, making Blythe laugh as she pulled me into her room.

Blythe yanked open her closet doors and started flipping through hangers with the kind of enthusiasm that made me a little nervous.

I crossed my arms. "Please don't dress me like a Barbie. I just want to be comfy."

She gasped, "Rose, I would never—" Then she pulled out a soft, oversized sweatshirt and a pair of leggings. "This okay?"

I exhaled. "Perfect. Thank you."

Blythe tossed them onto the bed and perched on the edge, watching me with a smirk. "So, nothing happened?"

I groaned, pressing the heels of my hands into my eyes. "Why do you keep asking me that?"

She shrugged. "Because you both look guilty as hell."

I dropped my hands. "Nothing happened."

She grinned. "I'll let it go. For now." Blythe paused. "Did you have fun last night?"

I nodded. "It was a good time. Reminded me of our wild nights out at that gross little beach-themed bar in Seattle."

Blythe's eyes went wide. "The Riviera."

Both of us shuddered.

"I'm going to go shower." I grabbed the clothes off the bed. "Thanks again for letting us stay here."

By the time I was dressed and walking downstairs, I felt like a new person. Or, at the very least, like someone who wasn't still partially dead from last night.

Wells was sitting at the kitchen table, sipping his coffee while scrolling on his phone. He looked up when I walked in.

"You look better," he said.

I huffed. "Gee, thanks." I slipped a pair of Blythe's sneakers on my feet.

Charlie leaned against the counter, grinning. "You sure you don't want Wells to escort you? You know, in case you get lost?"

I shot him a look. "It's a ten-minute walk."

"Exactly," he said. "Things could happen."

I ignored him and turned to Wells. "I'll be back soon."

Wells nodded, his expression unreadable. "See you later."

I turned toward the door, but as I stepped outside, I couldn't shake the feeling of his eyes following me.

The crisp morning air did little to clear the haze in my head as I walked toward the Coastal Cup. Each step I took, the events of last night trickled back in slow, mortifying fragments.

Karaoke. The bull. The way I had been openly ogling Wells like he was some kind of godsent cowboy from my deepest, most repressed fantasies.

And then—oh no. "*You should stay.*"

I cringed so hard I nearly tripped over a crack in the sidewalk.

I told him to stay. Not just that—I insisted on it. And he did. Which meant he was there, next to me, all night while I slept off my bad decisions.

Groaning, I picked up my pace, as if walking faster would help me outrun the embarrassment burning in my chest.

By the time I reached the Coastal Cup, the familiar scent of roasted coffee beans and freshly baked pastries wrapped around me like a warm hug.

Trish was behind the counter, adjusting the pastry display, but as soon as she saw me, her face lit up.

"Oh! If it isn't my favorite former co-worker." Trish came around the coffee bar and gave me a hug. "How have you been?"

I hugged her back, grateful for the distraction. "Oh, you know. Just out here making questionable life choices."

Trish pulled back, eyeing me with an amused smirk. "Now that sounds like a story I need to hear."

I groaned, sliding onto a stool at the counter. "I'd rather just drink an unreasonable amount of coffee and pretend last night didn't happen."

She snorted, already reaching for a mug. "So, that kind of night, huh?"

I dropped my head onto the counter with a dramatic thud. "It was a mess."

Trish set the coffee in front of me and leaned her elbows on the counter. "Was it the good kind of mess?"

I hesitated. My immediate answer should've been no, because what kind of disaster ends with waking up next to Wells Calloway?

But when I thought about it—the way he looked at me, the way he carried me upstairs like it was nothing, the way he just stayed—the answer wasn't as simple as I wanted it to be.

I took a sip of coffee and shrugged. "I don't know yet."

Trish grinned like she had me all figured out. "Then it definitely was."

We chatted about Solace Blooms for a while, catching up on the shop and the latest gossip, before she finally cracked.

"So... there's a bit of a rumor floating around Wippowa."

I lifted a brow. "Oh?"

She leaned in, voice teasing. "You and Wells. People have been noticing you two at the farmer's market. And I even had a customer come in this morning saying they saw *the* Wells Calloway looking downright smitten last night with a pretty blonde at a bar."

I nearly choked on my coffee. "We're just friends. Absolutely platonic. Nothing romantic."

Trish didn't look convinced. "Mhm. That's what they all say right before it stops being platonic. This is a proper love story in the making."

"It is not a love story." I didn't make eye contact; instead I focused on the coffee in front of me.

She hummed like she wasn't convinced at all. "So you wouldn't mind if I told this very excited townsperson that there's absolutely no shot of you and Wells ever being a thing?"

"Tell them exactly that."

Trish grinned. "Cool. I'll just be sure to also mention how flustered you got the second I brought him up."

I pointed at her. "Don't you dare."

"You love me."

I huffed, taking a long sip of coffee. "Yeah, I do."

Trish just smirked, entirely too smug.

I rolled my eyes, deciding to let her have her fun. For now. But deep down, I knew this conversation wasn't over—especially since the rest of Wippowa had started talking. I know how fast rumors fly in this town.

Trish's grin only widened as she leaned in closer, clearly enjoying my discomfort. "I'm just saying, Rose," she teased, "the way you were blushing when I mentioned Wells, I'd say you're not fooling anyone."

I narrowed my eyes at her, resisting the urge to throw a balled-up napkin at her face. "I'm not blushing."

"Oh, you absolutely are," she shot back, eyes sparkling with mischief. "And it's adorable. Don't worry, I'll keep your little secret safe… for now."

I groaned and dropped my head into my hands, trying to hide the fact that my face was, indeed, on fire. "I knew we shouldn't have gone out last night."

Trish chuckled, her voice softening just a bit. "For what it's worth, I've known Wells since we were kids. I've seen how he acts around you at the markets, and let me tell you, he's never looked at anyone the way he looks at you."

Her words hung in the air for a moment, and I could feel my heart rate pick up. I opened my mouth to say something but before I could, the bell above the door chimed.

Trish stood up straight, slipping into her barista persona like a switch had been flipped. She shot me one last look as she made her way to the counter, still grinning like a cat who'd just eaten the canary. "But hey, if you change your mind about Wells, I'll be your biggest fan."

I watched her walk away, shaking my head, both amused and

anxious. Wippowa had officially gone full small-town gossip mill, and here I was, right in the middle of it.

As Trish started taking orders, I could already feel the weight of the town's collective eyes on me. Every passing customer felt like they were waiting for the next chapter of this unfolding drama. And, knowing me, I'd end up giving them exactly what they wanted.

I took another sip of my coffee, the bitter taste grounding me as I tried to ignore the fluttering in my stomach. drained the last of my coffee and gave Trish a quick wave.

"See you soon," I called, hoping my voice sounded casual.

She gave me a knowing smile, her eyes sparkling with too much curiosity. "Take care, Rose. And remember, I'm rooting for you."

I stepped out of the Coastal Cup, the late morning sun shining down and making everything feel a little too alive.

As I walked back to Blythe and Charlie's house, I couldn't help but replay everything that had happened last night. It wasn't just the drunken chaos—it was Wells. The way he'd been there, looking after me without hesitation, pulling me into his warmth like it was the most natural thing in the world. I hadn't imagined that, right?

I shook my head, trying to shake off the warmth in my chest, the heat still lingering from his touch.

By the time I got back to the house, the nerves in my stomach had settled enough to at least appear somewhat composed. Blythe was sitting in the living room, scrolling through her phone. Her head snapped up when she saw me enter.

"Hey, look who's back." She tossed her phone aside and stood up. "How was coffee?"

"Good. Trish was… Trish." I gave her a small smile as I walked further inside. "I should've known she'd be all over it."

Blythe arched an eyebrow. "All over what?"

I let out a sigh, sitting on the couch. I glanced around the corner to be sure Wells wasn't in earshot. "All over me and Wells. The whole town's got a front-row seat to whatever mess I've gotten myself into."

Her grin was teasing but warm. "Ah, small-town life. Can't hide from it. You'll get used to it."

I buried my face in my hands. "I hope not."

She laughed, sitting down next to me. "So, what now?"

"What now?" I repeated, glancing at her with a rueful smile. "I guess I'm going to try to pretend like I didn't just get caught in a giant rumor mill."

"Good luck with that," Blythe chuckled. "But seriously, if you're planning to avoid Wells or whatever, don't bother. I've seen how he looks at you. And you definitely don't look like someone trying to avoid someone else."

I could feel the heat rise in my cheeks again, but I forced a nonchalant shrug. "We're just friends, Blythe. Nothing more. Trust me, nothing happened last night."

She leaned in, raising an eyebrow. "I know."

I sighed and threw myself back on the couch. "I'm doomed."

Blythe reached over and patted my arm. "You're fine. Just don't let the whole town make you feel like a walking soap opera."

As much as I wanted to take Blythe's advice, I knew it wasn't going to be that simple.

I nodded slowly, still processing everything that had happened in the last twenty-four hours. My mind was still tangled in the mess of last night and everything that came with it.

The sound of the door opening broke my thoughts, and I looked up to find Wells standing in the doorway, looking slightly disheveled but somehow still effortlessly handsome. He raised an eyebrow when he saw me.

"Ready to head home?" he asked, his voice low and casual, as if last night hadn't happened at all. It was both comforting and a little unnerving.

Home.

I blinked, caught off guard by his sudden presence. "I guess so." I pushed myself off the couch, trying to ignore the nervous flutter that had settled in my stomach.

As I grabbed my purse, I couldn't help but feel the weight of Wells's presence in the room. It was easy to pretend everything was fine when I wasn't around him, but when I was, it felt like everything was magnified. The little things, like the way he stood so close to me, the way he always seemed to know what I was thinking, the way his touch lingered in my mind long after it was gone.

"Rose," Blythe's voice cut through my thoughts, and I looked up to find her watching me carefully. "You okay?"

"Yep." I gave her a tight smile. "I'll see you guys soon."

With one last knowing look with Blythe, we went outside.

Wells opened the passenger door for me, his gaze softening as he looked at me. "Let's get you home."

I slid into the truck, the warm leather of the seat feeling like a small comfort as Wells climbed in. The drive back to the farm was quiet, the only sound the hum of the engine and the occasional crackle of the radio. I couldn't help but steal glances at Wells as he focused on the road ahead.

"You sure you're okay?" he asked after a few moments, his voice low.

I swallowed hard and nodded, though I wasn't entirely sure. "Yeah. Just a little hungover."

"At least you showered. I couldn't borrow any of Charlie's clothes. I feel gross."

The corner of my mouth perked up. "You sweat buckets all day outside and step in goat shit and a night out is what makes you feel gross?"

Wells poked my thigh. "You can be quiet."

I laughed, despite myself, and we fell into a comfortable silence, the tension from earlier easing as the miles between us and downtown Wippowa grew.

After a while, I sighed. "Sorry for asking you to stay in the nursery last night."

He glanced over at me, his eyebrows raised, but said nothing, letting me continue.

"I'm embarrassed," I admitted, my gaze dropping to my hands in my lap. "I mean, it wasn't like anything happened, but... still."

Wells looked over at me, his eyes gentle but with a hint of amusement. "I carried you up after you passed out on the couch.

You asked me to stay. I told you I would take the couch and you insisted. Nothing to be embarrassed about."

The quiet between us was suddenly comfortable, like we were in sync, even if I didn't fully understand what that meant.

Then, before I could say anything else, Wells spoke again, this time with a seriousness that made me pause.

"You know," he started, his voice low, "I'm glad we're friends."

I felt a wave of relief flood through me. "Me too."

The words felt right, but heavier than they should have.

CHAPTER 48

COWBOYS CRY TOO

Wells

THE MOMENT WE GOT BACK TO THE FARM, EVERYTHING FELL right back into place—morning chores, slow afternoons in the flower field, quiet evenings on the porch. It should've felt the same. Hell, it looked the same. But Rose was different this week.

She wasn't distant, but something about her felt off. Like she was here, going through the motions, but part of her was somewhere else. I caught it in the way she moved, the way she smiled—quick and practiced, like she didn't want me looking too close.

At first, I tried to ignore it. I told myself I was reading too much into things. But the more I paid attention, the more obvious it became.

Like now, she was standing by the stove, stirring her coffee, even though she hadn't taken a sip. Her grip on the spoon was too tight, her shoulders too tense.

I leaned against the counter next to her, arms crossed. "You okay?"

She looked up, eyes meeting mine for half a second before darting away. "Yeah," she said, too quick. "Just got a lot on my mind."

I nodded, not pushing, even though I wanted to.

I watched her for another second, waiting to see if she'd add anything. She didn't. Just went back to stirring that damn coffee like it held all the answers she wasn't giving me.

I pushed off the counter, grabbing my hat from the hook by the door. "I'm gonna go check on the horses."

She nodded, but she didn't look up.

Outside, the late afternoon sun cast long shadows across the yard. The air was cool, thick with the scent of cut grass and hay, but I couldn't shake the tight feeling in my chest. Something was wrong.

The horses were grazing lazily by the fence, their tails flicking at flies. I ran a hand over Boone's neck, the familiar weight of routine grounding me, even if my mind was still back in that kitchen.

Rose and I had settled into something steady here. Comfortable. But now, it felt like she was pulling away, little by little. And the worst part? I had no damn idea why.

I could ask again. Push her to talk. But Rose had walls, and the more you pushed, the higher they got.

So instead, I stood there in the quiet, staring out over the fields, hoping like hell she'd let me in before I had to break the damn door down myself.

I waited until after dinner to ask her. She was quieter than usual, still caught up in whatever had been on her mind all week, but I wanted to shake her out of it. Bring her back to me.

"You up for a bonfire tonight?" I asked, watching her reaction carefully.

She blinked, as if pulling herself out of her thoughts. "First one of the season?"

I nodded.

For a second, I thought she might say no. I could see it in the way she hesitated, lips parting like she was about to make up an excuse. But then she nodded. "That sounds nice."

It wasn't the excitement I was hoping for, but at least she wasn't shutting me out completely.

Rose had offered to clean up after dinner, so I left her to it, stepping out into the cool night air to get the fire going.

The familiar scent of burning wood filled my lungs as the flames took hold, crackling and spitting embers into the dark sky. I watched the fire build, feeding it piece by piece, the heat warming my face even as something colder settled in my chest.

Once the flames roared to life, steady and strong, I dusted off my hands and headed back inside. Rose was still at the sink, her back to me, lost in thought as she wiped down the counter with slow, methodical strokes.

"It's ready," I said, my voice softer than I meant it to be.

She paused, her shoulders tensing for half a second before she turned to face me. "I'll be right out."

I stepped back outside, the night air wrapping around me as I settled into my usual spot by the fire. The flames cast flickering shadows across the ground, their warmth doing little to thaw the unease sitting heavy in my chest.

A moment later, the door creaked open, and Rose slipped outside. She hesitated—just for a second—before lowering herself onto the bench beside me.

Neither of us spoke.

The fire crackled between us, orange embers drifting up into the night like tiny ghosts. The air smelled like burning wood and fall. It should've been peaceful.

But peace felt impossible when Rose sat beside me, stiff and quiet, her eyes locked on the flames like they held some kind of answer.

I'd been watching her all day, trying to figure out what was going on inside that head of hers. She wasn't acting like herself—not the woman who challenged me, teased me, softened against me when no one else was looking. She was somewhere else, lost in her thoughts, and it was driving me crazy. As we sat here with nothing but firelight and silence between us, I was getting tired of pretending everything was fine.

She let out a breath, taking a sip of her wine. "You ever notice how easy it is for you?"

I glanced over. "What do you mean?"

She shook her head like she was frustrated, but not at me—at something bigger, something she couldn't put into words. "You have a bad day, and you just… let it out. You don't hold it in. You get mad, you yell. You don't swallow it down and pretend everything's okay." She turned to me, her eyes darker in the firelight. "It must be nice."

Something inside me twisted.

"You think it's easy?" My voice was low, but there was an edge to it.

She exhaled sharply, rubbing at her temple. "I don't know, Wells. I just—sometimes I look at you, and I think, 'I wish I could do that. I wish I could just let it out.'"

She didn't get it.

She didn't understand what it cost me—what it had always cost me—to feel things this deeply.

"You think it's so easy being me?" My fists clenched at my sides, my whole body going rigid. "Do you know why I kept this place, Rose?" I let the words hang between us for a beat, daring her to guess.

She didn't.

"My mother's dying wish was for me to keep it running," I said, my voice rough. "She asked me to promise her, right before she—" My jaw locked. I shook my head, forcing myself to keep going. "Being here makes me want to crawl out of my damn skin. Every flower reminds me of her. Every damn sunrise over the fields feels like a punch to the ribs because she's not here to see it." I let out a shaky breath, my chest heaving. "I don't sleep because living in this house hurts."

Her face softened. "Wells, I didn't think—"

"I don't want to talk about it anymore, alright?" My voice came out sharper than I meant it to.

Rose stiffened beside me, her expression unreadable. She had every reason to walk away. To leave me to drown in the mess of my own making.

But she didn't.

She stayed, watching me unravel, watching as my anger gave way to something raw, something I couldn't control. I took a sip of my beer.

My breath hitched, and I turned away, pressing the heel of my palm against my eyes. My whole body was buzzing, like the weight of all these years was finally pressing down on me.

"I tried so hard to save her," I whispered, barely recognizing my own voice. "We tried everything. Every doctor, every treatment, every desperate last-chance prayer." My throat closed up, but I forced the words out anyway. "But nothing worked."

The fire crackled between us, but I barely heard it over the roaring in my ears.

"I'm trying to save this place to keep my parents' legacy alive," I choked out. "But it's killing me, Rose. And I don't know how to stop it."

I sucked in a breath that didn't seem to go deep enough.

I didn't want to cry.

But cowboys cry too.

And when Rose reached out—her fingers wrapping around my wrist, grounding me, holding me together—I didn't pull away.

Her grip was steady and warm. Like she knew I needed something to hold onto but wouldn't force me to take more than I was ready for. Years of grief pressing down on me, stealing the breath from my lungs.

For so long, I had carried this weight alone. It lived in the quiet spaces, in the late nights staring at the ceiling, in the ghosts that filled this farm no matter how hard I tried to outrun them. I had convinced myself that breaking wasn't an option. That as long as I kept moving, kept working, kept pushing, I could outrun the pain.

But I couldn't.

And now, sitting by this fire with Rose beside me, my walls crumbling at my feet, I had never felt more exhausted.

She didn't say anything at first. Didn't offer empty words or tell me it would get easier. She just held on, her fingers wrapped around my wrist like she was anchoring me in place.

"You don't have to do this alone," she said softly.

I let out a shaky breath, my head dropping forward as I clenched my jaw against the emotion rising in my chest.

"I don't know how else to do it," I admitted.

Rose shifted closer, her presence something solid in a world that had felt like it was slipping through my fingers for years. "Then let me help."

I looked at her then, really looked at her. There was no pity in her eyes, no hesitation—just understanding. And that's what finally cracked me wide open.

Because I wasn't used to being understood.

I sucked in another breath, feeling it shake all the way down to my ribs. My voice was hoarse when I spoke again, barely above a whisper. "I miss them so damn much, Rose."

Her face softened, and without thinking, I reached for her, pulling her against me like she was the only thing keeping me standing.

"I can't even imagine." Rose didn't try to pretend like she understood, which helped more than she knew.

Rose didn't pull away. She just let me hold her, the steady rhythm of her breathing grounding me as the storm inside me raged on. Her arms wrapped around my back, gentle but firm, offering a comfort I wasn't sure I deserved. I buried my face in her hair, the scent of her calming me, even as the weight of everything pressed down on me harder than ever.

"I don't know how to let go," I whispered against her, my voice cracking with every word. "I've been holding on for so long, I don't even know who I'd be if I stopped."

She ran her fingers along my back, slow and soothing, like she was trying to chase away the tremors rattling through me. "You don't have to let go all at once," she murmured. "You can let go of the reins a little at a time."

"I don't want to hurt you, Rose," I said, my voice hoarse as I pulled back slightly to look at her. "I don't know how to fix this without breaking everything."

She smiled, a soft, sad thing. "You're not breaking everything. You're just falling apart a little. And that's okay. Look at who I was when I got here."

I shook my head, my hand running through my hair as I looked down at the ground, the fire casting flickering shadows across the dirt. "I've been trying so damn hard to fix this place, to keep it to-gether. But every day it feels like it's slipping away."

Rose reached out, her hand lifting my chin so I had to meet her gaze. "You don't have to save everything, Wells. You can let go of the things that are holding you back. It's okay to put the pieces down for a while."

I wanted to believe her. God, I did. But all I'd ever known was holding on. My whole life, I'd been fighting to keep everything in place—to keep this place running, to keep the memories of my parents alive, to keep the farm from slipping through my fingers. If I let go, I was afraid I might lose it all.

"I don't know if I can do that," I confessed, the words tasting bitter on my tongue. "I'm scared of what will happen if I stop."

Rose didn't look away. Her gaze was steady, unwavering. "I'm not asking you to stop, Wells. I'm asking you to let me help. Let me hold some of that weight for you, just like you did for me."

And for the first time, I realized that I didn't have to carry everything on my own. That letting Rose in might be the thing that saved me, not the thing that broke me.

I drew in a shaky breath, the firelight dancing in my vision as I stared at the flames. "I'm scared," I admitted, the words barely more than a whisper. Saying it out loud felt like stripping myself bare, exposing the parts of me I'd kept locked away for so long.

Rose didn't say a word. She didn't need to. Instead, she pulled me back into her arms, her warmth folding around me like a shield against the weight of everything I'd been carrying. And in that moment, I understood something I hadn't before—I didn't have to have all the answers. I didn't have to know how to fix everything.

I just had to let go and trust that she wasn't going anywhere.

For the first time in a long time, I let myself believe that not everything was beyond repair. That even the pieces I thought were shattered beyond saving could still be put back together.

"Let's do this," Rose said at last, her voice steady in the quiet night. "You're taking tomorrow off."

I blinked, startled out of the moment. "A Wednesday?" I shook my head, a list of tasks ran through my head. "I can't."

"Oh, you sure can, Wells," she countered, crossing her arms. "I will manage all the morning tasks on my own."

I raised a brow, skepticism creeping in. "Even the goats?"

She pursed her lips. "I will handle almost all the tasks on my own."

A small laugh escaped before I could stop it. "I'll help you with your archnemesis. Don't worry."

"Mr. Nibbles has boundary issues."

"What can I say? He likes pretty girls."

Rose bit her bottom lip, eyes narrowing playfully. "Are you flirting with me?"

"No," I said, voice dripping with sarcasm. "I would never."

And just like that, for the first time in what felt like forever, the weight in my chest loosened—just a little.

Rose smirked, tilting her head as if she were deep in thought. "Well, if you were flirting with me… I wouldn't mind it."

My stomach did a somersault. I huffed out a laugh, shaking my head. "That so?"

She lifted a shoulder, all casual, but the glint in her eyes told me she knew exactly what she was doing. "I mean, it's not every day a rugged cowboy with excellent goat-handling skills flirts with a girl like me."

I winked at her. "I told you I wasn't flirting."

"Whatever you say, cowboy."

CHAPTER 49

SILENCE

Rose

SOMETHING SHIFTED IN THE AIR BETWEEN WELLS AND ME tonight. There was something undeniably attractive about the way he finally let me in—not just into his past, but into the parts of himself he usually kept locked away. My heart ached for him, but more than anything, I wanted to help him find peace in the quiet, the way the farm had done for me.

And after the slight flirting, I couldn't help but think we might be on the same page.

Over the last few months, Wells had helped me see that I hadn't been the problem in my relationship with Thad. That I wasn't hard to love.

After the bonfire, we had gone inside and parted ways, but I couldn't shake the feeling that something between us had shifted.

I carefully placed the sunflower Wells had left me this morning on the growing pile. I really needed to figure out what to do with them.

A soft knock at my door pulled me from my thoughts. It was already cracked open.

"Hey," Wells said quietly.

"You can come in." I caught a glimpse of myself in the

mirror—glasses on, hair in a messy bun, in my pajamas. Wells had never seen me like this.

He pushed the door open but didn't step forward.

"You good?" I asked.

His eyes lingered on mine. "Yeah… just wanted to thank you again for letting me get all that off my chest earlier."

I offered a genuine smile. "Nothing to thank me for. You let me sob into your chest when Thad called. It's only fair."

"You're doing better with that situation now?"

I nodded without hesitation. "Blocked his number. Deleted his contact. He's as good as gone."

"Cool."

A thick silence stretched between us. Charged. Heavy with something unspoken.

I tilted my head. "Anything else? Or are you just going to stand there like a statue?"

Wells swallowed hard, his jaw tightening. Then, under his breath, he muttered, "Fuck it."

Before I could respond, he closed the distance, his hand slipping to the back of my neck as he pulled me into him—his lips crashing into mine.

His lips were warm, firm, and completely consuming. A sharp inhale left my lips as Wells deepened the kiss, his hand splaying against my lower back, pulling me flush against him. Heat bloomed in my chest, spreading through my veins like wildfire.

I hadn't realized how much I wanted this until now.

A small sigh escaped me as I melted into him, my fingers gripping the front of his shirt, desperate to hold onto something solid. He tilted his head, deepening the kiss even further, and a slow, delicious warmth curled low in my stomach.

He kissed like he meant it.

Like he had been holding back for too long.

Like I was something he finally let himself want.

When we finally broke apart, my breath was ragged, my pulse

pounded in my ears. Wells rested his forehead against mine, his fingers still tangled in my hair.

"Oh," I whispered, struggling to steady my breath. "That was unexpected."

A slow grin tugged at the corner of his lips. "Yeah?"

I nodded, still dazed. "Yeah."

His thumb traced a slow, lazy circle at the base of my neck, sending a shiver down my spine. "Should I apologize?"

I bit my lip, pretending to consider it. "I'd be really disappointed if you did."

His low chuckle sent a thrill through me. "Good."

He kissed me again, slower this time, softer. Less of a desperate collision and more of an exploration, like he wanted to memorize me.

I wanted to memorize him, too.

This time, the kiss was unhurried, but it still stole the air from my lungs. Wells moved with purpose, like he was savoring every second, like he wanted me to know exactly what he felt without saying a word.

My fingers slid up, curling around the back of his neck as I pressed closer, feeling the steady rise and fall of his chest against mine. His hands—warm and calloused—held me like I was something he didn't want to let go of.

A quiet sound escaped me, something between a sigh and a soft hum of pleasure. That only encouraged him. He tilted his head, deepening the kiss, his fingers tightening slightly at my waist, like he was anchoring himself to me.

The rest of the world faded—my messy hair, my glasses, the pile of sunflowers, everything. All that mattered was this. The way he kissed me like I was the only thing on his mind and in his heart.

When we finally pulled apart, my lips felt swollen, my breath unsteady. Wells stayed close, his forehead brushing against mine. His hands settled at my waist, like he wasn't quite ready to let me go.

"That was…"

I murmured, a little breathless.

"A long time coming," he finished for me, his voice low and rough.

I swallowed hard, my heart still racing. "Yeah."

He exhaled a quiet laugh, his fingers tracing slow, absentminded circles against my hip. "You should probably tell me to leave before I make things more complicated."

I blinked up at him, still dizzy from his kiss. "Do you want me to tell you to leave?"

His jaw flexed, his grip on my waist tightening for a second before he forced himself to take a step back. "No."

Something warm curled low in my stomach.

I reached for his hand, threading my fingers through his before he could fully pull away. "Then don't."

Wells stared at me for a long moment, something unreadable flashing in his eyes. And then, just like that, his resolve cracked.

He pulled me back into him, his lips finding mine once more—this time with less hesitation, with more certainty.

I knew, without a doubt, that nothing between us would be the same after this.

This kiss wasn't careful. It was full of something wild, something unchecked, something that had been waiting too damn long to surface.

Wells backed me up slowly until my legs hit the edge of the bed. His hands, steady and warm, skimmed up my arms, over my shoulders, and into my hair, tugging my messy bun loose. My hair tumbled around my face, and he let out a low sound of approval, threading his fingers through it like he'd wanted to do that for a while.

I should have been self-conscious but Wells looked at me like none of that mattered. Like I was still the most captivating thing in the room.

My fingers found the hem of his shirt, fisting the fabric as he kissed me slow and deep, making me forget about everything outside this moment. The way he moved, the way he touched me—it was careful. It was careful in the way someone handled something they didn't want to break.

CHAPTER 50

SAVE A HORSE (RIDE A COWBOY) <u>SPICY!!!</u>

Rose

H E BROKE AWAY JUST ENOUGH TO DRAG HIS LIPS DOWN THE side of my neck, his breath warm against my skin. I tilted my head instinctively, my fingers tightening in his shirt.

"You have no idea how long I've wanted to do this," he murmured against my skin.

A shiver ran through me. "Please don't stop."

He pulled back just enough to meet my eyes, something heated and searching in his gaze. He lifted a hand, tracing the pad of his thumb over my bottom lip, his expression unreadable.

"You sure?" His voice was low, husky.

I didn't hesitate. "Yeah."

Something in him seemed to snap at that—like my answer was all he needed.

Before I could catch my breath, he kissed me again, harder this time, his hands skimming down my sides, over my hips, until he gripped the backs of my thighs and lifted me effortlessly. A surprised laugh bubbled out of me as I instinctively wrapped my legs around his waist.

Wells grinned, and damn it, that smile made my heart flip. "What's funny?"

I shook my head, breathless. "Nothing. Just didn't expect that."

His grip tightened on me as he slowly lowered us onto the bed, careful but deliberate. "There's a lot you probably don't expect from me."

A thrill ran through me at his words. I had a feeling he was about to prove that to me.

And I was more than ready to let him.

Wells settled over me, his weight grounding, his touch steady. His fingers traced along my jaw before sliding down my neck, over my shoulder, and finally stopping at my waist. His lips moved slow, deliberate, like he was memorizing the way I felt beneath him.

I arched into him, threading my fingers through his hair, letting myself sink into the moment. There was no hesitation anymore, no second-guessing. Just warmth, just want, just Wells.

His breath was heavy against my skin as he kissed his way down my neck, lingering just long enough to send a delicious shiver down my spine. My grip on his shirt tightened, and without thinking, I started to tug it upward.

He let out a quiet chuckle, his lips brushing against my collarbone. "Impatient, huh?"

I swallowed, my heart pounding. "Maybe."

Wells sat back just enough to pull his shirt over his head, tossing it somewhere behind him. My breath hitched at the sight of him—broad shoulders, tanned tattooed skin, muscles carved from years of hard work. He was strong, but not just in the way that showed.

In the way he carried himself.

In the way he carried everyone else.

He hovered over me again, his hands bracketing my waist, his eyes searching mine. "Tell me to stop, Rose."

I shook my head. "I won't."

His jaw clenched, and for a moment, I thought he might argue. But then, his mouth was on mine, stealing my breath, his hands sliding beneath the hem of my shirt, his touch setting fire to my skin.

I'd never felt like this before, like every nerve in my body was awake, like every piece of me had been waiting for this. For *him*.

"Wells," I murmured, not even sure what I wanted to say.

He pressed his forehead against mine, his breath warm and uneven. "Yeah?"

I opened my mouth, but the words tangled on my tongue. Instead, I let my hands speak for me—skimming over his shoulders, down his chest, holding onto him like I was afraid he'd slip away.

He exhaled sharply, like my touch unraveled something in him. "You're dangerous, you know that?"

A small smile played on my lips. "Me?"

His fingers ghosted over my ribs, making my breath hitch. "You're gonna ruin me."

I let my lips graze his in a teasing whisper of a kiss. "Good."

And then, there was no more hesitation.

No more space between us.

Only Wells, only warmth, only the quiet hum of something undeniable pulling us closer.

And I had no plans to stop it.

Wells kissed me like he was trying to brand the moment into his memory. His hands were warm and sure as they traced over me, fingers skimming beneath my shirt, mapping the curve of my waist, the dip of my spine.

I arched into him, craving the feeling of his skin against mine, of nothing between us but heat and breath and want.

His body pressed into mine, and my legs instinctively wrapped around his hips. When I arched to meet him, I felt exactly how hard he was under those sweatpants.

"Fuck," he groaned, grinding against me just enough to make my breath stutter. "You feel so damn good."

I gasped as he flipped us effortlessly, settling me on top of him. His hands roamed over my thighs, up my hips, his grip firm as he guided me against him, our bodies moving together in slow, intoxicating friction.

"You drive me crazy," he murmured, his voice thick with need.

I leaned down, kissing him deep, drinking in the way he groaned against my lips when I rolled my hips against him again. His hands slid under my shirt, pushing it up, and I let him pull it over my head, tossing it somewhere in the room.

His gaze darkened as he took me in, his thumb brushing over my hard nipples. "Perfect," he murmured, before flipping me onto my back again, his mouth trailing fire down my body. "Absolute perfection."

I gasped when he kissed the valley between my breasts, his tongue flicking out just enough to make me arch into him. His hands worked at the waistband of my pajama shorts, and with one lingering glance at me, he pulled them down, along with my underwear, leaving me bare beneath him.

Wells paused, his eyes raking over me, a muscle ticking in his jaw. "Goddamn, Rose."

Heat pooled low in my stomach at the way he looked at me, like he was barely holding himself back. I reached for him, tugging at the waistband of his sweats, wanting him just as bare as I was.

He let out a low, ragged breath as he kicked them off, and then there was nothing between us but heat and want and need.

He sprung to life and I knew I was in for a really fun ride.

He settled between my legs. A soft moan escaped my lips.

"Tell me you want this," he said, his voice rough, his restraint clear.

"I do," I breathed. "I want you, Wells."

"I need to grab a condom." He said into my neck.

"I'm on the pill and I'm clean."

Something snapped in him at that. His mouth crashed back to mine as he reached between us, lining himself up, and then—

Pure heat. Pure pleasure.

I gasped, my fingers digging into his back as he slowly sank into me, stretching me in a way that made my breath stutter. He groaned against my shoulder, his muscles tense as he gave me a moment to adjust.

"Fuck," he whispered. "You feel even better than I imagined."

"You've been imagining this?" My pulse sped up.

"Ever since I saw you on that damn plane."

A shiver ran through me at his words. "Move," I pleaded.

He started slow, each roll of his hips deep and deliberate, like he wanted me to feel every inch of him. My body responded instinctively, arching to meet him, desperate for more.

The room filled with the sounds of our breathing and moans.

"Faster," I begged.

Wells kissed me through it, his hands exploring every part of me, his pace quickening as I met him stroke for stroke. His name fell from my lips as heat built between us, coiling tighter, higher until I shattered.

Pleasure coursed through me, stealing my breath, making my entire body tremble. Wells groaned, his movements turning desperate as he chased his own release, and with one final thrust, he buried his face against my neck, his body shaking as he found his own pleasure.

For a moment, neither of us moved. We just lay there, tangled, breathing heavy, our hearts pounding in sync.

Wells finally lifted his head, brushing a damp strand of hair from my face, his thumb grazing my swollen lips.

He collapsed beside me, breathless, a lazy grin pulling at his lips as he pulled me against his chest.

"Well," he murmured, pressing a kiss to my forehead, his voice laced with satisfaction. "That escalated quickly."

A breathy laugh escaped me as I traced a lazy circle over his ribs. "Regrets?"

He rolled onto his side, tucking a strand of hair behind my ear as he studied me with a look so tender it made my chest tighten. "Fuck no. You?"

"Only one."

I watched as Wells' face fell. "I didn't ride a cowboy like that song said."

The corner of his mouth perked up. "If that's your only regret, I did something right."

"You did everything right." I confirmed.

We sat in silence for a few minutes, basking in the sexual glow.

"So you said you wanted to ride a cowboy…" Wells trailed off.

I looked up at him and he had a wide smile on his face. "I mean, if you wanted to, you could."

"Quick refractory period?" I joked.

"You have no idea." In a swift motion, Wells rolled me over and I was seated on top of him. His hands were holding my ass, squeezing with just the right amount of pressure.

I lowered my mouth to his ear, "I've never ridden a cowboy before."

Goosebumps popped up on his neck. "Allow me to be the first."

I positioned myself over him and he was already hard. I slowly sank down, stretching around him. I rolled my hips slowly, seeing how I could watch Wells unravel beneath me.

Wells moaned in response, his head fell back onto the pillow.

"I hope this is okay for you," I teased, speeding up my pace.

"This is the best sex I've ever had." He was in pure ecstasy.

Wells groaned as I picked up my pace. I wanted the satisfaction of making him come. I rocked my hips back and forth, making myself close in the process. Wells somehow sat up pressing his back against the headboard, all while still inside me. He left one hand on my ass, still squeezing while the other moved to my breast, filling his palm. He took my nipple in his mouth, licking in circles that ignited every nerve ending in my body.

I gripped the headboard to get some more leverage. I was able to shift on my knees to ride better. Between Wells hitting my sensitive spot and the grabbing and squeezing, we both came unwound. Our breaths were ragged and I collapsed on top of him, waves of pleasure rippling through me.

Both of us stayed in position, bodies sweaty, pressed up against each other, panting.

The quiet promise that nothing between us would be the same after tonight hung in the air.

CHAPTER 51

OUR SONG

Rose

THE MORNING SUN PEEKED THROUGH THE SLATS IN THE curtains, painting lazy golden streaks across the bed. I blinked against the soft light, the hazy warmth of sleep still wrapped around me.

And then I felt it.

The weight of an arm draped across my waist. The steady rise and fall of breath against the back of my neck.

Wells.

A slow, dreamy smile pulled at my lips as I shifted slightly beneath the covers. The movement stirred him, and his grip instinctively tightened, pulling me closer against his chest.

I exhaled a quiet laugh. "You awake?"

A low, sleepy groan rumbled from behind me. "Mm."

I turned my head just enough to glance at him over my shoulder. His eyes were still closed, but there was the faintest trace of a smirk at the corner of his lips.

"Is that a yes or a no?" I teased.

His voice was thick with sleep. "Dunno. What answer keeps you in my arms longer?"

My heart flipped. "Smooth."

Finally, he cracked one eye open, his gaze soft and lazy, his grip on me firm but gentle. "Morning."

Something about the way he said it made my chest feel too tight, like my heart was expanding too fast to keep up.

"Morning," I whispered back, rolling onto my back.

Wells studied me for a long moment, his expression unreadable. Then, before I could overthink it, he leaned in, pressing a slow, lingering kiss to my shoulder.

"Last night…" he started, voice rasping against my skin.

I swallowed hard, suddenly nervous. "What about it?"

He exhaled, brushing his nose along my jaw before pressing another soft kiss there, as if he was making sure I felt the words before he spoke them. "It wasn't just a night for me, Rose."

I turned fully in his arms, my pulse racing. "It wasn't for me either."

A slow, satisfied smile tugged at his lips, and before I could say anything else, he kissed me again.

His lips were slow and searching, like he was memorizing the way I tasted, the way I fit against him. I melted into it, my hands sliding up his chest, feeling the steady drum of his heartbeat beneath my palm.

Wells tilted his head, deepening the kiss, his fingers tracing lazy circles on my hip. "You're dangerous, Rose Solace," he murmured against my lips.

I smiled, still breathless. "Why's that?"

His hand skimmed up my side, slipping beneath the sheet. "Because I don't think I'll ever want to let you go."

A shiver danced down my spine at his words, at the quiet confession laced within them.

"Then don't," I whispered.

His expression darkened with something deeper, something almost reverent. "You mean that?"

Instead of answering, I kissed him again, pouring every bit of truth into it. Last night wasn't just heat and desperation—it was

something more. It was trust. It was letting go of the past and stepping into something new.

Wells groaned softly, his grip tightening as he pulled me flush
against him. I felt the shift in his body, the way his muscles tensed,
the way his breathing changed.

"Fuck, Rose," he muttered. "You're gonna ruin me."

I grinned, running my nails lightly down his chest, watching
the way his jaw clenched. "Good."

In a flash, he rolled us over, pinning me beneath him, his weight
pressing me into the mattress. His gaze flickered between my eyes
and my lips, like he was trying to decide if he wanted to speak or
kiss me senseless.

"Say it again," he murmured, his fingers threading through mine
as he pinned my hands above my head.

I arched beneath him, loving the feel of his body covering mine.
"Good," I repeated, breathy and teasing.

He let out a low curse before capturing my mouth in a kiss that
sent fire racing through my veins.

The sheets tangled around us as he pressed me deeper into the
mattress, his hands exploring, his lips trailing heat down my neck,
my collarbone.

Wells didn't rush this time. His hands moved over me like he
had all the time in the world, like he wanted to savor every inch of
my skin. His lips followed, pressing slow, open-mouthed kisses along
my throat, down the center of my chest.

I arched into his touch, my breath catching as he trailed lower,
his mouth teasing, his hands firm as he held me exactly where he
wanted me.

"Wells," I breathed, my fingers threading through his hair, tugging slightly, silently urging him on.

He hummed against my skin, the vibration sending a shiver
down my spine. "Patience, Sunshine," he murmured, his voice thick
with promise. "I plan on taking my time with you."

Heat pooled in my stomach, anticipation thrumming through
my veins. "You're torturing me," I whispered.

He smirked, glancing up at me with dark, hungry eyes. "No, darlin'. I'm worshipping you."

Wells finally let me escape the sheets—barely. Every time I tried to get up, he'd pull me back for one more kiss, one more lingering touch that made me forget what I was supposed to be doing. Eventually, I managed to slip out of bed, grabbing his discarded shirt from the floor and tugging it on.

He propped himself up on one elbow, watching me with a lazy, satisfied grin. "Where do you think you're going?"

I laughed, running a hand through my messy hair. "Taking care of the farm. That was the deal, remember? I told you I'd handle everything today."

Wells sat up, stretching, the sheets pooling dangerously low on his hips. "You don't have to do it alone. I can help."

I shot him a look. "You do this every day, Wells. You deserve a break. Let me take care of things."

He smirked, tilting his head. "That include me?"

My face burned, but I didn't look away. "Especially you."

Something shifted in his gaze, but before I could overthink it, he was swinging his legs over the side of the bed, standing and tugging on his sweats. "If you're insisting on running the farm this morning, at least let me make breakfast."

I considered arguing, but the thought of Wells in the kitchen, barefoot and shirtless, cooking for me—it was too good to turn down. "Fine. But nothing fancy."

He placed a hand over his heart. "I make no promises."

Rolling my eyes, I turned and headed downstairs, stepping out onto the dewy grass. The crisp morning air nipped at my bare legs, but I barely noticed. The goats were already at the gate, waiting for breakfast, their impatient bleats carrying across the farm.

"Alright, guys," I sighed, unlocking the latch. "I know you don't care about my personal life, but I am begging you—just this once, can you make things easy for me?"

The goats stared at me, unimpressed.

"I'm serious," I pleaded. "No chasing. No headbutting. No trying to escape. Just eat your breakfast like normal farm animals so I can go back inside and spend the morning with a very, *very* attractive cowboy."

A beat of silence. Then, as if on cue, one of them darted past me, heading straight for Wells's truck.

I groaned. "Of course."

I spun on my heel, ready to chase the little escape artist, but before I could take a step, another goat charged forward, knocking into the back of my legs and nearly sending me face-first into the dirt.

"Are you kidding me right now?" I shouted, arms flailing as I barely caught my balance.

The goats were not, in fact, kidding me. They were dead serious about their morning chaos.

One had climbed onto the hood of Wells's truck like it was his personal stage. Another had its head stuck in the feed bucket, thrashing around like a drunk partygoer in a lampshade. And the rest? They were staring at me like they knew exactly how much I wanted to go back inside and were personally offended by it.

"Guys, please," I begged, throwing my hands in the air. "Just one morning. One! That's all I ask!"

A deep laugh echoed from the porch, and I turned to see Wells leaning against the doorframe, arms crossed, watching the entire disaster unfold. He looked infuriatingly amused.

"Having fun?" he called.

I shot him a glare. "Don't you dare say anything unless you're coming down here to help."

He held up his hands in surrender, still grinning. "You told me to take a break, remember?"

I groaned. "I take it back. I take everything back. Come deal with your demon farm children."

But instead of coming down, Wells whistled—one sharp, commanding note.

And just like that, the goats froze.

I blinked.

Then, slowly, like this was some well-rehearsed trick, the goat on his truck jumped down. The one with the bucket over its head stopped thrashing, shaking it loose. The others trotted toward the feed bins like perfect little angels.

My mouth fell open. "What just happened?"

Wells shrugged, smirking. "They respect me."

"They fear you," I muttered, crossing my arms.

"Same thing." He sauntered down the steps and pressed a quick kiss to my forehead before swiping the empty feed bucket from my hands. "Go inside. Breakfast is waiting."

The smell of coffee and something buttery filled the kitchen as I stepped inside, my irritation with the goats already fading. I crossed my arms, leaning against the counter. "Oh, this smells heavenly. You're such a breakfast connoisseur." I winked.

He glanced over his shoulder, a smirk tugging at his lips. "Sweetheart, I've been making these since I was tall enough to see the stove. You think I survive out here on just charm and cowboy grit?"

I narrowed my eyes. "Honestly? Kinda."

He chuckled, turning back to his task.

Something warm curled in my chest, but I ignored it and slid onto one of the seats at the kitchen table. A plate was set in front of me a second later, stacked with golden French toast, crisp bacon, and scrambled eggs.

I blinked down at it. "Why does this look like something out of a food magazine?"

Wells sat beside me, grabbing his own plate. "Because I'm good at what I do."

I raised a brow. "You talking about breakfast or last night?"

He shot me a look, mouth twitching.

I laughed and took a bite. And holy hell—this French toast was perfect. Light, fluffy, with the slightest crisp on the edges. I let out a quiet moan, immediately regretting it when I saw the way Wells's eyes darkened.

"You can't make noises like that," he said, voice low, playful. "Not unless you're prepared to face the consequences."

I swallowed, trying—and failing—not to blush. "I was just appreciating the food."

"Mm-hmm." He took a slow sip of his coffee, watching me over the rim. "Remind me to make you breakfast more often."

"You already do." I rolled my eyes and focused on eating, though I was very aware of Wells watching me, his easy confidence making it impossible not to smile.

For a moment, the kitchen was quiet, the only sounds the soft clink of forks against plates and the occasional sip of coffee. It was comfortable, warm, like we'd been doing this for years instead of a few months.

And that was the part that scared me.

I glanced at Wells, at the way he looked so at ease, like waking up next to me and making me breakfast was the most natural thing in the world.

"Alright, cowboy. What's next on today's agenda? Or do I have to suffer through more farm animal betrayal before I can get you back in bed?"

He laughed, shaking his head. "Eat your damn breakfast, Sunshine."

CHAPTER 52

COUNTING CHICKENS

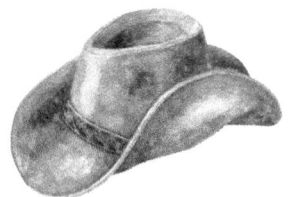

Wells

I SHOULD'VE KNOWN THINGS WERE GOING TOO SMOOTHLY. It had been a week since Rose and I stepped into the friends-with-benefits territory, and it had been nothing short of glorious.

The second I stepped outside, coffee in one hand and the other running lazily through my hair, I was greeted by chaos. Absolute, unhinged, poultry-based chaos.

The chickens, the ones that were usually well-behaved and went about their day like respectable farm animals had decided that today was the day they lost their damn minds.

Feathers were flying. Squawks filled the air like some kind of horror movie sound effect. And smack in the middle of it all?

Rose.

Standing on a feed bucket, arms flailing, eyes wide with terror.

"They know!" she shrieked the second she saw me. "They know what I did!"

I blinked. "What—"

"I ate eggs the eggs I gathered this morning! And now they know!"

I almost dropped my coffee. "Rose, they don't—"

"They're attacking me, Wells!" she yelled, pointing an accusing finger at the flock of enraged birds surrounding her makeshift perch. "They're coming for vengeance!"

I clapped a hand over my mouth, trying not to laugh. "Sweetheart, they're not attacking you."

"Then why is that one staring into my soul?" She jabbed a finger at Harriet, our meanest hen, who was, admittedly, giving her the world's most judgmental glare.

I sighed, setting my coffee down on the porch. "Alright, hold on. Let me—"

Before I could even take a step, the chickens lost what little collective sense they had left and launched themselves into a full-scale uprising.

One flapped up and smacked Rose in the arm with its wing. Another hopped onto her bucket like it was a goddamn boxing ring and squared up.

Rose screamed.

I lost it. Bent over, hands on my knees, laughing so hard I could barely breathe.

"This isn't funny, you traitor!" she yelled. "Do something!"

I wiped a tear from my eye, gasping. "Hang on, hang on—"

Then Harriet, deciding she was the main character, took flight.

And landed on Rose's head.

Her entire body went rigid. "Wells."

I sucked in a breath, biting my lip. "Yeah?"

"Get. It. Off."

"Okay." I stepped forward, trying to keep a straight face, but the second I reached for Harriet, she let out an ungodly squawk and flapped her wings—right into Rose's face.

Rose flailed, lost her balance, and toppled off the bucket into a pile of hay.

I stood frozen, hands half-raised, watching as she lay there in stunned silence. Chickens scattered. Feathers drifted in the air like we'd just survived a damn barnyard battle.

Then Rose sat up, her face red, hair a mess, a single rogue feather sticking out of her bun.

"I hate it here."

I finally lost it again, doubling over in laughter. "Oh my—"

"I'm breaking up with you."

That just made me laugh harder. "We're not even dating."

Rose groaned, flopping back into the hay. "Well, whatever it is that we are, we're done."

I smirked, crossing my arms. "So that's it? You're just gonna let the chickens win?"

"Yes." She threw a dramatic arm over her face. "Tell my family I loved them."

I huffed out a laugh, nudging her with the toe of my boot. "C'mon, get up."

"No. I live here now. The hay is my home. The chickens are my overlords."

I crouched down beside her, grinning. "You sure? 'Cause I was gonna make breakfast, but I guess I'll just eat alone…"

Rose peeked at me from under her arm. "What kind of breakfast?"

I pretended to think about it. "Bacon. Pancakes. Maybe some of those hashbrowns you like…"

She sat up so fast she nearly knocked me over. "Fine. But only because I don't want to waste food."

"Right." I helped her up, biting back a grin. "Not because you actually enjoy spending time with me or anything."

She dusted herself off, glaring. "Not after what just happened."

I chuckled, wrapping an arm around her shoulder as I steered her toward the house. "Hey, you're the one who picked a fight with a flock of chickens."

"I did not pick a fight," she grumbled. "I simply existed, and they took offense."

I shook my head, still grinning, as we stepped onto the porch. "Lucky for you, you're in the care of the best chicken-wrangler in the state of Georgia."

Rose scoffed. "Oh, please. You stood there and laughed while I was under attack."

I held the door open for her. "And I'd do it again."

She narrowed her eyes at me as she stepped inside. "You're lucky you're hot."

I barked out a laugh, following her in. "Damn right I am."

She headed straight for the fridge, still muttering under her breath about how "no one should ever have to endure that kind of trauma." I grabbed a pan and started heating it on the stove, already picturing how I was going to work my charm into making this moment a little less tragic for her.

I cracked a few eggs into the bowl and glanced over at her. "You know, I didn't think you'd be the type to get so worked up over a bunch of chickens."

She grabbed the butter and dramatically flung it onto the counter. "I wasn't worked up! But when you're trapped under a clucking chicken, it tends to shake you a little, okay?"

I snorted, turning my attention back to the sizzling bacon. "You should've seen how scared Harriet was after I pulled her off you."

She shot me a glare, not appreciating the irony. "No. You laughed while you yanked her off me and probably ruined her entire life by sending her into a panic."

I couldn't help it. "You screamed like she was a demon."

"Well, she was a demon!" Rose huffed, slamming the fridge door shut. "Who needs to be so aggressive about laying eggs?"

I flipped the bacon, then stirred the hashbrowns, trying to contain my amusement. "She's just doing her job, Sunshine."

Rose crossed her arms and sat at the counter, still grumbling. "I didn't realize I would be terrorized by animals living here. If I knew, I would have moved to a zoo."

I set the eggs to scramble, turning around with a smirk. "Come on, admit it. It was kinda fun."

She looked at me with complete deadpan. "Nothing about this was fun, Wells."

I couldn't hold back my laugh. "You sure? Because you've got that post-adrenaline glow happening."

"Shut up," she muttered, but the corner of her lips twitched upward.

I pulled the pancakes from the griddle, stacking them high. I placed the bacon and hashbrowns on a plate.

Rose rolled her eyes, taking a bite of pancakes. "Thank you."

I grabbed my own plate and sat down across from her, watching as she took a second bite, clearly enjoying it more than she'd admit. "You're welcome. Consider it a peace offering for surviving the chicken apocalypse."

CHAPTER 53

FROM THE GROUND UP

Rose

I LEANED AGAINST THE FENCE, WATCHING WELLS AS HE YANKED stubborn weeds from the ground with the kind of focus and determination I'd expect from someone who had grown up with dirt under their nails. Every muscle in his body flexed as he worked, his brow furrowed in concentration, and I couldn't help but stare.

"Here I was thinking Charlie had country in his bones, but you, Wells Calloway—you're the whole damn countryside."

Wells gave a shy grin.

His strong arms, the way he moved with ease, the confident swagger in his step when he walked across the field—it was like watching a man who belonged to the land itself. And as much as I hated to admit it, that pull in my stomach wasn't just because of how damn good he looked working the land. There was something about watching him get his hands dirty that made him even more irresistible.

I caught myself biting my lip, then quickly turned my gaze elsewhere, embarrassed that I was ogling him like some sort of love-struck teenager. But he wasn't making it easy. There was something about the way he handled the flowers and the plants as if they were the most important thing in the world, his fingers delicate as he placed each one carefully into the soil, that made me melt.

He caught me looking, and a smile tugged at the corners of his lips. "You know, you could help instead of just staring at me," he teased, wiping sweat off his brow with the back of his hand.

I straightened, brushing a stray strand of hair behind my ear. "I was just admiring your technique," I shot back.

He flashed me a wink sending a spark through me. "Not much technique, just skill."

"Are you always this modest?" I jokingly asked.

Wells didn't miss a beat. He pushed up his sleeves, clearly aware of the effect he was having on me. "Only when I'm around someone who doesn't appreciate the fine art of weed-pulling," he replied, as he tugged another weed free.

My gaze lingered on his arms for a moment longer than necessary. It was ridiculous how just the sight of him working in the garden made me hot under the collar. And just as I was trying to convince myself to stop thinking about him like that, Wells straightened up, wiping his brow with the back of his hand again, this time glancing at me with a much softer expression.

He walked over, closing the space between us, and in that moment, the world around us seemed to slow. He leaned down, his lips brushing gently against my forehead. The simple gesture sent a warmth rushing through me, my breath catching as I looked up at him, heart racing.

"If you don't start workin', the whole order pizza and watch a movie we had planned for this evening will go out the window." His voice low and sincere, his breath warm against my skin.

He ghosted his lips over mine and I wanted nothing more than to jump his bones.

Before I could say anything, his phone buzzed in his pocket, and he pulled away, glancing down at the screen.

"Hold on, I gotta take this," he said, offering a quick smile before stepping back.

He flipped the brim of his baseball cap backward and answered the phone, his posture shifting as he moved a little further away. I watched him as he spoke, the way he stood with his legs apart, hand resting on his hip in that confident, effortless way that drove me wild.

I couldn't help myself. The sight of him, standing there, phone pressed to his ear, every move exuding raw masculinity—it was like he was a magnet, pulling me closer and closer. And that damn hat. The way it sat cocked backward on his head made him look impossibly sexy. I crossed my arms in front of me, trying to ignore the way my heart rate was picking up.

Wells glanced over at me, catching my gaze as he spoke to whoever was on the other end of the line. His lips quirked up into an unsure smile.

I wasn't sure if it was the sweat glistening on his skin or the way the muscles in his arms flexed when he moved, but suddenly, I felt like I needed to breathe a little deeper.

He hung up a moment later and turned toward me.

"Something wrong?" he asked, his voice teasing, but I could tell he noticed the way I was watching him.

His smile flickered for a second, a hint of something unreadable passing through his eyes.

"You good?"

Wells gave a quick nod, his gaze dropping back to the weeds he was pulling up. "Yeah."

With that, he returned to his task, his focus back on the dirt.

I took the hint, stepping back into the quiet of the morning. Whatever had been said on the phone was clearly something he didn't want to share, and I wasn't about to push.

The rest of the morning passed in a strange, quiet rhythm. Wells and I worked side by side, but the easy banter we usually shared was missing. He was focused on the garden, ripping weeds from the soil with a quiet intensity that I hadn't seen before. It wasn't like him to be so closed off, and I couldn't help but feel a little off-kilter.

I tried to distract myself by pulling up the last of the weeds, but it wasn't long before my mind wandered back to him. Every movement he made seemed amplified in the silence between us.

But I couldn't ignore the fact that something felt different. He was distant, the space between us stretching farther than it should have. I caught him glancing at me a few times, his eyes soft but guarded. There was something he wasn't saying.

I didn't want to push, but the uncertainty was gnawing at me. I was used to Wells being straightforward, laughing off any awkwardness, always willing to tease or banter. But today, he was quiet. Almost too quiet.

I tried to fill the silence, making small talk about the upcoming farmer's market, about the flowers, anything to bridge the gap. But my words seemed to hang in the air, unanswered, as Wells worked, his focus never wavering.

By the time the sun started climbing higher in the sky, I was getting frustrated. Not with him, but with this invisible wall between us.

"Do you want me to finish up here?" I asked, hoping to break through the tension. "You've been at it for a while."

Wells straightened up, rubbing the back of his neck, his eyes meeting mine briefly. "Nah, I'm good. Just lost in thought." His voice was calm, but I could hear the subtle tightness beneath it.

I nodded, trying to keep the conversation going, but the words got stuck in my throat. I didn't know what to say or how to reach him. So, I focused on the flowers instead, even though my mind was racing.

I kept stealing glances at him, wondering what was going on in his head. He was always so open with me but today felt like I was trying to read a book with half the pages missing.

And that frustrated me more than I cared to admit.

Now I know how he felt when I moved here.

CHAPTER 54

SHE GOT THE BEST OF ME

Wells

THE LAST PERSON I EXPECTED TO HEAR FROM THIS MORNING was Marie. After that date last month, I'd ghosted her. I knew I'd handled it like an asshole. I should've just been upfront and told her I was in love with the chaotic city girl living under my roof. But, hell, I didn't think she'd take that too well.

So when Marie's name popped up on my phone earlier while Rose and I were working in the flower fields, I was caught off guard.

I stared at the screen for a second, my finger hovering over the answer button. I hadn't expected Marie to reach out, and I definitely hadn't expected an invitation to go out again. My gut twisted a little, guilt mixing with the surprise.

I could feel Rose beside me, focused on the flowers, her back turned as she carefully worked through the rows of plants. I knew I couldn't hide things from her, but how the hell was I supposed to explain this?

Marie's voice crackled through the phone when I finally answered. "Hey, Wells, it's been a while. I was thinking we could grab dinner sometime. Maybe catch up?"

I squeezed the phone a little tighter. I could almost feel the weight of Rose's presence without even looking at her, as if she were standing right behind me, hearing every word. My stomach flipped.

Before I could think, my mouth ran ahead of me. "Yeah, sure. That sounds good."

I immediately regretted it as soon as the words left my mouth. What the hell was I thinking? Rose was right there, and I had no business agreeing to another date with Marie. I didn't even want to. I just... panicked.

Marie laughed, clearly thrilled. "Great! How about Friday?"

I nodded, even though she couldn't see me. "Friday works."

I hung up before I could say anything else, feeling my heart race in my chest.

I turned to find Rose still focused on the flowers, her back to me. She hadn't heard the conversation, but the tension in the air between us felt thick, suffocating. I ran a hand through my hair, trying to shake off the panic that had started to settle in my chest.

I knew I needed to come clean. I couldn't keep pretending like everything was fine. But the words wouldn't come. Instead, I just stood there, watching her, feeling like a damn fool.

I stood frozen for a moment, staring at Rose's back, my heart pounding in my chest. I had just agreed to go on another date with Marie, and I had no idea how I was going to explain that to Rose. The last thing I wanted was to hurt her or make her feel like she wasn't enough.

But how the hell had I let it happen?

I took a few slow steps toward her, trying to gather my thoughts, but they were all jumbled. The silence between us was growing heavier with every passing second.

I let the awkwardness hang in the air, the weight of my mistake settling like a heavy stone between us. Rose didn't say a word as we finished up the chores for the day, her back turned to me as she worked silently beside me. My head was spinning, but I kept my mouth shut, hoping that the guilt would subside.

By the time we wrapped up the chores, the sun had started its descent, casting a warm, golden glow across the farm. Rose headed upstairs to shower, and I grabbed my phone to order pizza—one supreme with everything piled on for me, and a veggie one for her.

I made my way upstairs too, hoping the shower would somehow wash away the weight of guilt sitting heavy in my chest. I needed to figure out how to fix this, how to untangle the mess I'd created. The thought of going out with Marie again made my stomach twist. There was nothing wrong with her, but she wasn't Rose. She wasn't the woman who lit up my world, the one who made everything feel right. No one did that for me—except Rose.

As I stood under the hot water, letting it cascade over me, my mind raced. The steam wrapped around me like a veil, but it couldn't block out the tension that had been building in my chest all afternoon. The sooner I came clean, the better.

I finished up in the shower and quickly got dressed before heading downstairs. Rose was still in the bathroom when I made my way down to the living room. I flicked on the porch light for the delivery driver and flopped onto the couch, trying to shake off the uneasiness swirling inside me.

A moment later, Rose appeared, her hair damp and messy from the shower, and wearing one of my hoodies that she had "borrowed" last week. The sight of her hit me like a punch to the gut. She looked so effortlessly beautiful—her cheeks flushed from the warm water, her eyes soft with comfort.

"Hi, handsome," she said, plopping down beside me on the couch, her head finding its way to my shoulder. "Should we order dinner?"

I couldn't help but smile as I placed a soft kiss on her forehead and wrapped my arm around her, pulling her a little closer. "Already done."

Her face lit up, and her voice softened, teasing. "Gosh, I love you." Then, her eyes widened, and she scrambled to correct herself, her words stumbling over each other. "I mean—I love that you ordered pizza."

My heart skipped a beat, and I couldn't hide my grin. "My pleasure. I ordered you a vegetable one."

Rose snuggled closer to me, the warmth of her body easing some of the tension in mine. "You know me so well."

The doorbell rang just as I was about to say something, and I shot up from the couch to grab the pizza. I quickly paid the driver and brought the boxes back to the living room, the smell of warm pizza filling the air. Rose's eyes lit up when she saw the boxes, and she slid off the couch to help me set everything up on the coffee table.

I opened the vegetable pizza for her and the supreme one for me, both of us settling back into the couch with our plates in hand. I hit play on the movie, the soft hum of the opening credits filling the space between us.

Rose was curled up beside me, and for a while, we didn't say anything. We just ate, laughed, and shared quiet moments of contentment. I kept stealing glances at her, trying to enjoy the way her hair framed her face, how her lips curled into that relaxed smile when she found something funny. Every second felt precious, but also, like it was slipping through my fingers too fast.

The movie played, but my thoughts kept drifting back to Marie and that damn phone call. Every time I looked at Rose, I felt that same twist of guilt in my gut. But there was something else, too—something heavier. It wasn't just the guilt. It was the fear that I might lose what I had with Rose, that I might ruin something perfect.

I tried to focus on the movie, but every time I glanced at Rose, my heart softened. She was just so easy to love. She didn't have to try. She was real, and that's what I needed.

"Are you enjoying the movie?" Rose asked, her voice pulling me out of my thoughts. She was looking up at me, her expression soft and a little concerned.

"Yeah," I said, though I wasn't sure if I meant it. "It's good. Just thinking."

Her eyes searched mine, but before she could ask anything else, I dropped my gaze to my pizza. "Nothing important."

Rose leaned her head against my shoulder, her fingers lightly brushing mine. "You sure? You've been quiet today."

I swallowed hard. I wasn't sure what I was doing—whether I

was trying to pretend everything was fine, or whether I was hoping the guilt would just go away. "Just some stuff with the farm. You know how it is."

She nodded, though I could tell she wasn't fully convinced. I didn't blame her. I was barely convincing myself.

We sat in silence, the soft glow of the TV flickering across the room, and I couldn't shake the gnawing feeling that time was running out. The movie ended, the credits rolling, and Rose stifled a yawn. She shifted, climbed onto my lap, and gave me a mischievous look, waggling her eyebrows before leaning in to kiss me.

"Wanna head upstairs and do fun things?" she asked, her voice low and playful.

"Not tonight," I said flatly, my voice too sharp, too distant.

Rose tilted her head, her eyes narrowing slightly as she pressed a hand to my forehead.

"What are you doing?"

"Seeing if you're feeling okay," she said, her fingers gently tracing my skin. "You've never turned down my advances."

I let out a long, deep sigh. "I'm fine."

She gave me a skeptical look before trailing her lips down my neck, her breath warm against my skin. "Oh, you're grumpy," she teased. "I can help with that."

I shifted uncomfortably, not ready for that kind of closeness tonight. "Not now," I muttered.

Rose pulled away, frowning. "Is it because Granger is right there?" She pointed to the dog curled up at the foot of the couch.

I shook my head, but the guilt gnawed at me. "No."

She raised an eyebrow, a half-smile forming on her lips. "Man, a bug must've crawled up your ass..." she said, her voice dripping with mock concern.

I couldn't help but chuckle, even though I didn't feel like it. But the tension was still there, hanging between us like a cloud that I couldn't shake. I had to come clean about Marie, but the words felt too heavy, too difficult to say.

"Can we talk?" I finally managed to say, the words coming out slower than I intended.

"Are you hitting me with a 'can we talk,' Calloway?" Rose's voice held a playful edge, but I could see the hint of concern in her eyes.

I nodded, a lump forming in my throat.

She shifted, moving to her cushion on the couch, her expression unreadable. "Talk away."

She had no idea what I was about to say, and the weight of it made my chest tighten. I took a deep breath, knowing this conversation would change everything.

"I agreed to go out on another date with Marie."

CHAPTER 55

PIECE BY PIECE

Rose

"**Y**OU WHAT?" MY HEART POUNDED IN MY CHEST, THE WORDS barely leaving my lips. I stood up from the couch, my legs shaky.

"I'm sorry, Rose. I panicked."

"You *panicked?*" My voice cracked, disbelief flooding my system. I quickly pieced it together, the phone call earlier, his strange behavior. "Is that who you were talking to this morning? Before everything got weird between us?"

Wells' eyes dropped to the floor, and he nodded, unable to meet my gaze.

A sharp ache spread through my chest as tears welled in my eyes. I should've known. I should've kept my guard up, but I let him in. I let myself be vulnerable. The walls I'd built around my heart, the ones that had kept me safe, now felt like a cruel reminder.

"I know I'm not as smart as Marie," I choked, the words slipping out bitterly, "but damn it, I thought there was something real here. I *let you in*, Wells." My voice trembled, the tears falling freely. "I guess it was just an easy way for you to get laid."

Wells stood up, stepping toward me. "Sunshine, this isn't a joke to me. I care more about you than—"

I cut him off and poked him in his chest. "Don't ever call me that again." My breath hitched as I forced back a sob. "Whatever this was, it's over. Pretend like it never happened."

Without giving him a chance to speak, I turned and made my way to the stairs, my heart heavy with every step.

"Where are you going?" His voice called after me, desperate.

"Away from you."

"Rose, wait. Let me explain."

But I didn't stop. I sprinted up the stairs, slamming my bedroom door behind me. The tears fell in torrents now. How could I have been so stupid? I knew better than this. If you don't let people in, they can't hurt you. I should've remembered that.

There was a soft knock on the door. "Rose, please open the door. We need to talk."

I curled up on my bed, wrapping myself in the blankets, willing the pain to go away, but it wouldn't. It couldn't.

The knock came again, more insistent this time. "Rose, please. Let me explain."

I pressed my face into the pillow, my chest tight, my throat raw from holding back the sobs that kept coming, one after the other. The door remained closed, the room feeling smaller with every breath I took. I wanted to ignore him, to shut it all out, but my mind was spinning in circles, the words from earlier echoing in my head.

I care more about you than—

I cut him off. I didn't need to hear that right now. It didn't matter what he cared about; it didn't change what he'd done.

"Rose," Wells said softly, his voice muffled through the door, "please, I need to fix this. I know I messed up. I'm sorry."

I gripped the blankets tighter, my nails digging into the fabric as if holding on to something solid would make the pain stop. But nothing was solid anymore. Nothing felt real.

"Please," Wells' voice cracked, "please let me talk."

I wanted to yell at him. I wanted to tell him to leave me alone, that I couldn't do this right now. But instead, all I could manage was a whisper. "I don't want to hear it."

The silence that followed felt like it lasted forever. I could hear him pacing outside, his footsteps dragging, every movement an aching reminder of what had just shattered. I shut my eyes, trying to block out the reality of it all, but the sting of betrayal was too sharp to ignore.

After a while, the footsteps stopped. I heard his voice again, quieter this time, like he was talking to himself. "I never wanted to hurt you."

I could hear the regret in his words, but it didn't change anything. It didn't undo the way I felt.

I didn't move, didn't respond. There was nothing left to say.

Another knock, softer now. "Rose?"

Nothing. I couldn't speak. The house was so quiet that I could hear the sound of my own heart breaking, piece by piece.

And in the quiet, I realized something: I was angry at myself for letting him in.

I stayed in that silence for what felt like hours, my mind racing with everything I wanted to say, but I couldn't find the words.

Eventually, I heard his footsteps retreating down the stairs, slow and measured, as if he was finally giving up on me. My chest felt heavy, the weight of everything that had just unfolded pressing down on me. I reached for my phone with trembling hands, dialing Blythe's number.

"Hey, what's up?" Blythe's voice came through, calm and light, but I could feel the tension still sitting heavily in my bones.

"Wells is a jerk," I muttered, my words coming out like a bitter hiss.

"What happened?" she asked, her tone immediately sharp with concern.

"He's going out with Marie again," I said, the sting of it hitting me all over again.

"Remind me... Marie is..."

"The nurse he went out with a while ago."

"And Wells agreed to go out with her again?" she asked, disbelief coloring her voice.

"Yep."

"That's not like him. Want me to have Charlie pry it out of him?" she offered, clearly ready to step in.

"No," I sighed, running a hand through my damp hair. "I just needed to feel validated."

"Rose, you guys have such a complicated situation over there. Have you even talked about what you are?"

"No," I said quietly, feeling the weight of the question settle over me like a cold blanket.

"Then you can't really be mad at him for going out with her if you don't even know what you are."

I froze. Her words sliced through me, raw and honest. "We've had a lot of sex. I thought we were exclusive."

"But you never talked about it?" she pressed gently.

I shook my head, frustration and hurt bubbling up inside me. "No."

"Then you need to check your anger and admit what you want to yourself," Blythe said, her voice soft but firm.

I let out a shaky breath, feeling the weight of the situation settle deeper into my chest. She was right, but it didn't make the hurt any less.

Blythe changed the subject. "Are you two still coming over for dinner tomorrow?"

"Last I checked, we were."

"Great. Then let's pick this up when you get here tomorrow."

As I hung up, I stared at the phone in my hand, the silence around me pressing down on my chest. Blythe's words echoed in my mind: What do you want?

I sank back against the bed, staring at the ceiling, lost in thought. I hadn't considered it—what I really wanted. We'd been living in this gray area, a mix of intimacy and uncertainty, for so long that it felt like I'd forgotten how to ask myself the question.

Was I okay with this? With the not knowing, the not labeling, the never really talking about what we were doing? It felt like we were dancing around something bigger, something more, but I had no idea if Wells even felt the same way or if he was just in this for the fun of it.

I'd let him in, more than I had anyone else in a long time. I'd let him see me, raw and vulnerable, and I'd let him matter. But had I gotten too comfortable? Was this just the way it was going to be? One foot in, one foot out, with no real commitment or understanding?

The thought of Wells with someone else, especially Marie, hit a lot harder than I thought it would. I wasn't sure if it was jealousy or fear, but it felt like a punch to the gut.

I ran a hand through my hair, frustrated. I didn't even know how to talk to him about this. I wasn't sure I could, especially after the mess of today. But Blythe was right. I needed to figure out what I wanted from this situationship, as much as I hated that word.

I sighed and grabbed my phone, opening the messages between Wells and me. Scrolling through the random conversations, the jokes, the late-night memes. It all seemed so easy when it was just that. Fun, carefree, no strings attached. But I couldn't ignore the nagging feeling in the pit of my stomach anymore.

I needed to know where I stood with him. I needed to know if I was more than just a temporary distraction or if there was something real here.

And if he couldn't give me that answer, then maybe I needed to walk away. Because I wasn't sure I could keep giving pieces of myself without knowing if he wanted the whole damn thing.

CHAPTER 56

SAY SOMETHING

Rose

I HADN'T SLEPT AT ALL LAST NIGHT. MY MIND WOULDN'T settle, thoughts tangling and unraveling like waves against the shore—relentless, unyielding. The weight of the unknown pressed against my chest, making the walls of my small room feel too close, too confining.

All I wanted was to slip out of bed, past the stillness of the house, and lose myself in the wildflowers. The only place where the world softened, where I could breathe without feeling like I was drowning.

When my alarm went off, I pushed back the covers and made my way to the window. Wells was already outside, moving through the familiar rhythm of the farm. And judging by the order of things—the way the tools were put away, the quiet hum of a morning well spent—I knew he'd already finished the day's first round of work well ahead of schedule. Which means he didn't sleep well either.

I took a slow, steady breath, swallowing my pride as I prepared to go down and offer to help. It wasn't easy, but staying locked away in this room wasn't an option either. I slipped into my jeans and boots, shrugged on my jacket, and pulled open the door—only to stop short.

Sitting on the floor was a massive sunflower, a cup of coffee, and a note.

My pulse stuttered. Every rational part of me wanted to ignore it, to kick the flower aside and pretend I never saw it. But my stupid heart had other plans. It wouldn't let me turn away.

Being here, on this farm, in Wippowa, I had become something I never expected—a sentimental mess.

I crouched down, fingers hovering over the note before finally picking it up. The paper was thick, the edges slightly curled, as if whoever had written it hesitated before leaving it behind.

With a quiet breath, I unfolded it.

Good morning, Sunshine

No name. No unnecessary words. But I knew exactly who it was from.

Annoyance flared in my chest, sharp and immediate. After his admission last night, after the argument that still echoed in my head, he thought a flower and a cup of coffee would smooth things over?

I wanted to throw it all away. Wanted to stomp right past him, prove that a few quiet gestures wouldn't undo the damage. But instead, I picked up the coffee, cradling the warmth between my palms. And instead of ignoring him, I stepped outside.

The crisp morning air wrapped around me, carrying the scent of damp earth and something faintly sweet. Wells was by the barn, leaning against the fence, hat pulled low, arms crossed like he was waiting for me.

His eyes flicked to the coffee, then back to my face, unreadable.

"Didn't think you'd take it," he said. Not teasing this time. Just quiet. Just watching.

I took a slow sip of the coffee, letting the silence stretch before finally meeting his gaze. "I almost didn't."

His jaw tensed, like he had something to say but wasn't sure if it would make things better or worse. Probably because he knew me well enough to realize it could go either way.

"Rose—"

"I'm here to do my *job*," I cut in. "Not to talk about last night."

A muscle jumped in his jaw, but he just nodded, pushing off the fence. "Alright."

I wasn't sure if I was relieved or disappointed.

I followed him toward the barn, trying to convince myself that the coffee in my hands was just coffee. That last night still mattered, no matter how easy he made it feel to forget.

Because if I wasn't careful, Wells Calloway was going to make me forgive him.

And I wasn't ready for that.

The barn smelled like hay and cedar, warm and familiar despite the storm still brewing between us. Wells walked ahead, his boots scuffing against the dirt floor, the sound filling the quiet space between us. He grabbed a rope off the wall, looping it around his hand with an ease that told me he was thinking.

I leaned against the stall door, watching as he moved, the morning light filtering in through the slats, cutting across his broad shoulders. I hated that I noticed. Hated that, even after last night, some part of me still wanted to reach across the space between us.

"What do you need me to do?" I asked, my voice cool.

He glanced over, eyes sharp, assessing. "You haven't saddled a horse here before, have you?"

"No."

A hint of something flickered in his gaze—annoyance, amusement, maybe both. "Didn't think so."

I let out a slow breath. "You gonna teach me or just stand there feeling superior?"

That got a reaction. The corner of his mouth twitched, like he was fighting a smirk. "Thought you didn't want to talk."

"I don't." I folded my arms. "I want to work. You're the one who asked me a question."

He held my gaze a beat longer, then jerked his chin toward the tack room. "Saddle's in there. Bring it over."

I turned without another word, feeling his eyes on me as I moved.

The saddle was heavier than I expected, the leather worn but well cared for. I dragged it over, dropping it onto the wooden railing of the stall with a thud. Wells took it from there, moving with that quiet confidence that somehow made me want to strangle him and stare at him in equal measure.

"Pay attention," he said, securing the cinch strap. "You're doing it next time."

I rolled my eyes but watched as he worked, forcing myself to focus.

A long silence stretched between us, filled only by the sounds of the horses shifting in their stalls and the distant crow of a rooster. I wanted to keep it that way. I wanted to stay mad, to hold onto the sharp edges of last night's argument.

But Wells had a way of undoing things without even trying.

"You still mad?" His voice was low, rough like gravel.

I tightened my grip on the wooden stall and said, "Yes."

We finished up in the barn and made our way back to the house.

"Are we still going to Blythe and Charlie's this afternoon?" I asked, rinsing my hands under the cool stream of water in the kitchen sink.

Wells nodded. "Figured we'd leave in an hour or so."

I didn't respond, just turned and headed upstairs. A shower and fresh clothes—maybe that would help settle the restlessness stirring inside me.

When I caught my reflection in the mirror, I barely recognized the woman staring back. I wasn't the same person who had arrived on this farm, full of sharp edges and walls I swore I'd never let down.

I laced up my sneakers, timing everything perfectly so I wouldn't have to linger downstairs, wouldn't have to make small talk with Wells.

But when I stepped into the living room, he was already by the door, eyes on his phone, thumbs moving over the screen. From where I stood, I could see Charlie's name at the top of the text thread.

"Ready to go?" he asked, not looking up.

"Yeah." I shrugged into my jacket, and without another word, we stepped outside.

As always, Wells reached for the passenger door and pulled it open for me. The small, practiced gesture should've meant nothing.

But today, with the weight of last night still between us and the hour-long drive stretching ahead, it made me want to run.

Instead, I climbed in, bracing myself for the silence.

The truck rumbled to life, and Wells backed out of the driveway, one hand on the wheel, the other resting casually on the gearshift. The cab was quiet, except for the hum of the engine and the occasional chirp of his phone lighting up with another message.

I stared out the window, watching the fields blur past, arms folded tightly over my chest.

A few minutes passed before he finally spoke. "Do you want music, or are we sitting in silence the whole way?"

"Silence works for me."

He huffed out a soft laugh, like he expected that answer but was amused by it anyway. "Knew you'd say that."

I didn't respond.

A beat of quiet. Then, as if he couldn't help himself, he reached for the radio and spun the dial. The opening notes of an old country song filled the cab—one I knew, one I had accidentally admitted to liking weeks ago.

I cut him a sharp look. "Really?"

"What?" He smirked, drumming his fingers against the steering wheel.

"Nothing."

His grin deepened like he didn't believe me, and he started to hum along—low, lazy, intentionally off-key.

I exhaled sharply, pressing my fingers to my temple. "Please stop."

He whistled the next few bars instead, way too pleased with himself. He shot me a sidelong glance, all easy charm and mischief.

I tightened my jaw, refusing to give him the satisfaction of a reaction. Instead, I turned back to the window, pretending I wasn't hyper-aware of every move he made, every glance he stole in my direction.

For the next few miles, he kept the music playing but stayed quiet.

Because no amount of off-key singing or easy grins was going to make me forget last night.

When we finally turned onto Charlie and Blythe's long gravel driveway, my stomach tightened. Not because I didn't want to see them but because I knew the second we stepped out of this truck, we'd have to pretend everything was fine. That whatever was brewing between Wells and me wasn't lingering just beneath the surface.

Wells slowed the truck to a stop in front of the house, cutting the engine. For a second, he didn't move. Neither did I.

Then, just as I reached for the door handle, he leaned back in his seat, stretching out like he had all the time in the world. "You gonna keep avoiding me all afternoon, or do I get a truce while we're here?"

I shot him a look. "A truce?"

He shrugged, a slow, easy motion. "Figured Blythe and Charlie don't need to be caught in the crossfire."

I exhaled sharply. He wasn't wrong. The last thing I wanted was to ruin the afternoon.

"Fine," I muttered, pushing open the door. "A truce."

"Good." His voice carried a smirk, like he thought this was some kind of victory.

I ignored it, stepping out onto the gravel and adjusting my jacket. Before I could head up the porch steps, the front door swung open, and Blythe appeared, all warmth and excitement.

"Rose!" She beamed, arms already reaching for me.

The second she wrapped me in a hug, some of the tension in my chest loosened. Blythe had that effect—like stepping into sunlight after too many days of gray.

Charlie appeared behind her, giving Wells a knowing look before turning his attention to me. "Glad you made it."

I smiled, but before I could respond, Blythe was already tugging me inside, her voice bubbling over with excitement about dinner, some new project she'd started, and how we had *so much* to catch up on.

And for the first time since I stepped into Wells's truck, I let myself breathe.

Because here, in this house, I could pretend for a little while that nothing was complicated.

That Wells Calloway didn't still have his eyes on me as I walked through the door.

CHAPTER 57

THE MAN WHO CAN'T BE MOVED

Wells

I KNEW I'D MESSED UP. AND I HATED MYSELF FOR IT.

Watching Rose now—laughing easily with Blythe, moving through the room like she belonged here—it twisted something deep in my gut. She was at ease with Blythe in a way she hadn't been with me all day. And judging by the pointed looks Blythe kept shooting in my direction, Rose had told her exactly what happened.

Charlie stepped up beside me, arms crossed as he followed my line of sight. "What'd you do?"

I didn't take my eyes off Rose. "What do you mean?"

He let out a low chuckle. "Well, my wife is throwing daggers at you with her eyes, so I'm guessing you did something stupid."

I exhaled sharply. "I screwed up."

Charlie whistled under his breath. "How bad?"

I finally looked at him. "Probably the biggest mistake of my life."

His brows lifted. "Bigger than that one time in college when we—"

"Yes."

His lips pressed together in a low whistle. "Damn. That's bad. What happened?"

I dragged a hand over my jaw, eyes drifting back to Rose. She didn't look at me once. Not even in passing. "I agreed to go on another date with Marie."

Charlie's eyes went wide and he clapped a hand on my shoulder, shaking his head like he already knew this wasn't something I could joke my way out of. "You gonna fix it?"

I let out a slow breath, watching Rose as she leaned into Blythe's side, her head tilting back in laughter. It hit me like a punch to the ribs.

"I don't know if I can." The words tasted bitter. "I tried."

Charlie let out a low hum.

Rose was different here. Lighter. Freer. I used to think I had a hand in that—like maybe I'd helped her settle into this new version of herself. But now, looking at her, I wasn't so sure. Because that ease? That warmth? She still had it. Just not with me today and probably never again.

Blythe's gaze cut to me again, sharp as a blade. I didn't flinch. I deserved it.

Charlie sighed. "You want my advice?"

"Not really."

"Too bad." He leaned against the counter, arms crossed. "Fix it, Wells. If you think for one second that woman doesn't care about you, you're a bigger idiot than I thought."

His words landed like a weight on my chest. I let them settle, let the truth of them dig in.

Before I could say anything, Blythe called out from across the room, her voice too sweet to be anything but a warning. "Wells, can I talk to you for a second?"

Charlie smirked, patting me on the back as he stepped away. "Good luck, buddy. You're gonna need it."

I swallowed hard and turned toward Blythe, bracing myself for the storm I knew was coming.

Because if there was anyone who could make me answer for my mistakes, it was her.

And judging by the look on her face, she was about to let me have it.

Blythe didn't wait for me to respond. She just turned on her heel and walked toward the hallway, fully expecting me to follow.

Charlie muttered something under his breath, sounding way too entertained by my impending doom, but I ignored him. I knew better than to make Blythe ask twice.

I trailed behind her, feeling like a kid about to get sent to the principal's office. But when we reached one of the guest rooms, she just didn't pull me inside.

She grabbed Rose by the wrist as she passed, earning a sharp, "What the hell, Blythe?" before tugging her into the room too.

The door shut.

Rose spun around, eyes narrowing. "Seriously?"

Blythe crossed her arms, her expression firm. "You're in here until you both talk this out."

I ran a hand down my face. "Blythe—"

"Nope." She held up a hand. "I don't want to hear it. You two are miserable and making the rest of us miserable in the process."

Rose folded her arms, lips pressing into a thin line. She looked like she wanted to argue, but Blythe wasn't done. "When you decide on your relationship status, then I'll unlock the door."

Rose let out a sharp laugh, completely humorless. "That's ridiculous."

Blythe shrugged, already backing toward the door. "Maybe. But I have zero interest in watching you two tiptoe around each other all afternoon. So figure it out."

With that, she turned and walked away, leaving us trapped together.

The lock clicked.

Rose exhaled, pinching the bridge of her nose. "Unbelievable."

I leaned against the wall, arms crossed. "Could be worse."

Her eyes snapped to mine. "How?"

I smirked, knowing it would only piss her off more. "Could be locked in here without me."

Her nostrils flared. "At the current moment, I'd prefer that."

I nodded, letting her have that one. I deserved it.

Silence stretched between us. I watched as she shifted her weight, arms still crossed like she needed to physically hold herself together.

Finally, I sighed. "Look, Rose—"

"Don't," she cut in. "I don't want to hear another half-assed apology or an excuse. If you have something real to say, say it. Otherwise, save it."

Her voice didn't waver, but there was something raw in her expression, something unguarded that made my chest ache.

I pushed off the wall, taking a slow step closer. "I know I hurt you."

Her jaw tightened, but she didn't look away.

I swallowed hard. "And I hate myself for it."

Her lips parted slightly, like she wanted to say something, but she stayed silent.

For the first time all day, she was actually looking at me.

And now that I had her attention, I wasn't about to waste it.

Rose held my gaze, her expression unreadable, but I could see the way her fingers curled tightly into her sleeves—like she was bracing herself.

I took another step closer, careful, measured. "I don't expect you to forgive me."

She let out a sharp exhale. "Good. Because I don't."

That stung more than it should have.

I nodded slowly, forcing myself to stay steady. "But I need you to know that what happened. When I agreed to go out with Marie again…"

Rose's arms tightened around herself. "You told me you weren't going to see her again. That she wasn't your type."

"I panicked."

She let out a sharp breath. "Yeah. You've mentioned that. Repeatedly."

"I don't do well in high-pressure situations."

Her eyes flashed. "That's such bullshit, Wells."

Her voice was raised now, the frustration in it slicing right through me.

I exhaled, rubbing a hand over my face. "I should've just been honest with her. I just… I don't like hurting people."

Rose let out a humorless laugh, turning her gaze toward the window. "Well, congratulations. You might not have hurt Marie, but you sure as hell hurt *me*."

My chest tightened. It physically hurt hearing that.

She looked back at me, her expression cold, controlled. "Whatever this was," she said, motioning between us, "it's done. I'm strictly your employee now. No more movie nights. No more post-sex cuddles. At the end of the day, I will eat dinner with you and then spend the rest of the time in my room."

I stared at her, my pulse hammering in my ears. "You don't mean that."

Her expression didn't waver. "I do."

"No, you don't." I took a step closer, my voice lower now, more desperate than I wanted it to be. "Rose, don't switch this off like it was nothing."

She let out a slow breath, shaking her head. "Maybe you can't. But I have to."

The finality in her voice hit me like a gut punch.

I opened my mouth, ready to say something, anything to make her see that I hadn't meant to hurt her, that we meant more to me than I'd ever let on.

But she was already moving.

She crossed the room, reaching for the doorknob. It didn't budge. She exhaled sharply and knocked, hard. "Blythe! Open the damn door."

Nothing.

"Blythe," she called again, more forcefully.

Still nothing.

She turned toward me, eyes blazing. "I am not doing this right now."

I rubbed a hand over my jaw. "Sunshine—"

"No." She lifted a hand, stopping me in my tracks. "You don't get to say anything else. You made your choice, Wells."

I swallowed hard. "And what if I made the wrong one?"

Her breath hitched, just slightly, but she caught herself fast.

"Then that's your problem," she said, voice steady. "Not mine."

She knocked on the door again, more aggressively this time. "Blythe, I swear to God—"

Charlie's muffled voice came through from the other side. "She says you need at least five more minutes."

Rose let out a frustrated groan, pressing her forehead against the wood.

I took a slow step forward. "Rose."

She didn't move. Didn't turn.

"Tell me what I need to do to fix this." My voice was quiet, but the weight behind it was heavy.

She turned slowly, her eyes locking onto mine. For the first time during this conversation, she didn't look just angry—she looked wrecked.

"You can't fix everything, Wells."

Her voice was so quiet, so tired, that it almost undid me.

She shook her head once, then looked away.

And for the first time, I wondered if I had already lost her.

CHAPTER 58

SAY DON'T GO

Rose

THE WALLS FELT LIKE THEY WERE CLOSING IN.

I crossed my arms tightly over my chest, my breath shallow as I forced myself to focus on anything but the man standing a few feet away. The air between us was thick, suffocating.

I didn't want to hear another excuse. Another half-hearted explanation.

Wells had made his choice. Now, he had to live with it.

I'd promised myself after Thad, after all the hurt and self-doubt, that I would never let someone make me feel like a second option again.

And yet, here I was.

"I'm sorry, Rose." Wells' voice was low, rough with regret.

I squeezed my eyes shut, willing myself not to react. Not to let his voice, his presence, or *him* get under my skin again.

"I mean it," he said, stepping closer. "I know I screwed up. I know I hurt you."

I let out a sharp breath, my hands clenching into fists. "You keep saying that."

"Because it's true."

I snapped my gaze to him. "And what do you want me to do

with that, Wells? Huh? Just accept your apology? Pretend it never happened?"

He shook his head. "No. I just—" He exhaled, his jaw tightening. "I don't want this to be over."

A bitter laugh escaped me. "That's convenient, isn't it?"

His brows pulled together. "Rose—"

"No." I held up a hand, my pulse pounding. "You made your choice, Wells. *You* decided to backtrack on everything you told me." My voice cracked despite my best effort to keep it steady. "You don't get to stand here now and act like you didn't know what you were doing."

His face twisted, like my words physically hurt. *Good.*

"I was scared," he admitted.

I scoffed. "Of what?"

His hands flexed at his sides. "Of wanting this too much."

I blinked, caught off guard.

"Of screwing it up. Of losing you before I even had the chance to—" He dragged a hand through his hair, frustration laced in every movement. "I handled it wrong, Rose. I panicked and I made a mistake. But you have to know that it was never about not wanting you."

I stared at him, my heart aching in a way I hated. Because I did know. I felt it when we were together. But knowing that didn't make it hurt any less.

I swallowed hard, forcing myself to stay firm. "It doesn't change anything."

His breath left him in a slow, measured exhale. "So that's it?"

I hesitated. Just for a second. But a second was all it took.

Wells saw it.

And that terrified me more than anything.

Before I could say anything else, the lock on the door clicked.

Blythe's voice filtered through. "Well? Are you two done being stubborn idiots, or do I need to keep you in there longer?"

I didn't answer. I couldn't.

The door was unlocked, but neither of us moved. I could've walked out.

I *should've* walked out.

But I didn't.

I stood there, arms crossed so tightly it hurt, every muscle in my body tense. Wells took a step closer, and I told myself I wouldn't listen. That I wouldn't let him get to me.

Then he said my name.

Soft. Desperate.

And I felt it.

"Rose," he said again, his voice thick with something I didn't want to name.

I exhaled sharply. "Wells, don't—"

"No." He shook his head. "I have to."

Something in his expression made my stomach flip. It wasn't just regret. It wasn't just an apology.

"You changed everything for me," he said, his voice rough, raw.

I swallowed hard, my heart hammering in my ears. My arms fell to my sides.

"You think you're just my employee? That this was all just some passing thing for me?" He let out a shaky breath. "Rose, I wake up in the morning and the first thing I do is look for you. I go to bed at night thinking about what I'm going to say to make you smile the next day."

I sucked in a breath, caught completely off guard by the honesty in his words.

"You brighten my life," he continued. "You brought meaning back into it, even when I didn't know I needed it."

My chest ached. I wanted to hold onto my anger, to the sharp edges of my hurt, but they were slipping through my fingers like sand.

"I didn't realize how empty things had gotten before you showed up. How much I'd let myself settle into a life that felt dull. And then *you* came along, with your stubbornness and your smart mouth and your ridiculous coffee order, and suddenly my life was in full-color."

A shaky breath left me.

He stepped closer, and I could see it—the raw, unguarded truth in his eyes. "I adore you, Rose. Every single thing about you. I don't care if that scares me. I don't care if I don't deserve you." His voice was barely above a whisper now. "I just don't want to lose you."

Something cracked in me.

I wanted to be strong. I wanted to hold onto my pride.

But Wells had just laid his heart bare in front of me and I felt every word.

I hesitated, my fingers twitching at my sides.

His fingers barely grazed mine before he closed the space between us in one swift step.

Warm, calloused hands cupped my face, tilting my chin up until I had no choice but to look at him. His emerald eyes burned into mine, raw and pleading.

"Sunshine," he murmured, his thumbs brushing against my cheeks, his touch gentle despite the storm raging between us. "If you're going to be anyone's problem, be *mine*."

My breath hitched.

I wanted to shove him away. To keep my pride intact. To tell him that words weren't enough, that he couldn't just say pretty things and expect me to fall back into his arms.

But his touch, his voice, the way he looked at me like I was the only thing in the world that mattered was undoing me.

I gripped his wrists, my fingers curling around them, as if holding on would steady me. As if it would stop the way my heart was slamming against my ribs.

"You don't get to say that now," I whispered, my voice betraying me with the way it wavered.

His gaze softened, but he didn't let go. "I should've said it sooner."

I squeezed my eyes shut. "Wells—"

"I mean it, Rose." His voice was steady, sure. "You're not just some passing thing to me. You *never* were. You're my everything."

I opened my eyes, my resolve splintering.

Because damn him, he meant it. Every word.

My fingers curled tighter around his wrists, my pulse racing beneath my skin. Wells' hands remained on my face, steady and warm, like he was holding me together when I felt like I was unraveling.

I hated how much I wanted to lean into him. How much I wanted to believe him.

But belief meant risk.

And I was so damn scared.

"I don't know how to do this," I admitted, my voice barely above a whisper. "I don't know how to trust that this isn't going to fall apart and leave me feeling like an idiot."

His thumbs traced slow, soothing circles on my cheeks. "Then don't do it alone. Let me prove to you that I'm not going anywhere."

I swallowed hard, emotions thick in my throat. "I don't want to be the one who cares more."

His jaw tensed, like the idea physically hurt him. "Rose, that's not possible." His fingers curled slightly, his touch firm. "I don't want to wake up one day regretting that I didn't fight hard enough for you."

I exhaled shakily, the last of my defenses slipping away.

"What are we, then?" I asked, the question trembling on my lips. "Because I can't do this halfway. I can't be the person who waits around hoping you'll choose me over and over again."

Wells didn't even hesitate. "We're *together*." His voice was steady, certain. "If you'll have me, that's what we are."

A lump formed in my throat.

"I need you to tell Marie," I said softly. "I won't be your secret."

His lips pressed into a firm line, and then he nodded. "I will. Today."

I searched his face, waiting for hesitation, but there was none. He meant it.

Slowly, I let out a breath.

His hands slid down to my jaw, his forehead dipping to rest against mine. "Okay?"

I let my hands move up his arms, gripping his biceps, grounding myself in the warmth of him.

"Yeah," I whispered. "Okay."

Wells let out a slow breath, his forehead still resting against mine. Neither of us moved, like stepping away would break whatever fragile thing had just settled between us.

His hands slid down my arms, fingers brushing against mine before finally lacing them together. "I'll take care of it, Rose." His voice was soft but sure. "I'll tell Marie. I'll do whatever it takes to prove to you that I'm all in."

I searched his face, my heart pounding. "I believe you."

A small, relieved smile flickered across his lips before he pressed them to my forehead, lingering there for just a beat.

I closed my eyes, letting myself soak in the warmth of it, the tenderness. Letting myself believe, just for a moment, that this could work.

Then a loud click snapped us both back to reality.

The door swung open, revealing Blythe standing there with a satisfied look on her face, arms crossed. "Are we good here?"

Wells gave my hands a final squeeze before turning to her. "Yeah, we're good."

Blythe's eyes darted between us before settling on me, her expression softening. "You sure?"

I exhaled, steadying myself before nodding. "Yeah. I think so."

"Good." She grinned, stepping back to let us out. "Because Charlie and I were about five minutes away from blasting country breakup songs until you two figured your shit out."

Wells groaned.

Blythe smirked.

I let out a small, breathy laugh, and for the first time since last night, it didn't feel forced.

Wells kept hold of my hand as we stepped out of the room, his thumb brushing over my knuckles like a silent promise.

CHAPTER 59

DOWN BAD

Wells

As soon as Rose and I stepped out of that damn room, the air felt lighter, like I could finally breathe.

I glanced down at our still-joined hands, her fingers curled loosely around mine. She hadn't pulled away.

But I wasn't about to screw this up again.

Letting go just long enough to grab my phone off the counter, I unlocked it with a swipe and pulled up Marie's number. My thumbs hovered over the keyboard for a beat before I finally typed out the message:

> Wells: Hey, Marie. I won't be able to make dinner. I want to see where this thing with Rose can go.

I stared at the words for half a second longer than I should have.

It sounded weird. Not because I didn't want it to be true, but because I hadn't let myself imagine it could be.

But now? Rose was mine. And I wasn't about to let anything—especially my own stupidity—get in the way of that.

I hit send before I could second-guess it.

Marie's reply came almost immediately.

Marie: Wow. Why did you lead me on?

I sighed, scrubbing a hand over my jaw. I wasn't going to play into whatever passive-aggressive thing this was.

Wells: I panicked when we were on the phone the other day. I'm really sorry.

The typing bubble popped up, then disappeared, then popped up again. Eventually, she just sent:

Marie: I understand. I hope she's everything you want.

I locked my phone and set it down, exhaling hard. Done. Over with. No loose ends.

When I turned back, Rose was watching me, her expression unreadable.

"Well?" she asked.

I crossed the room in a few strides, closing the space between us again. "Handled."

Her lips parted slightly like she wasn't sure whether to believe me or not. "Just like that?"

"Just like that." I reached for her hand again, brushing my thumb over the back of it. "You told me what you needed, and I did it. Because I meant what I said in there, Rose. I'm all in."

Something flickered in her eyes—hesitation, maybe. But it wasn't fear anymore. It was something softer. Something hopeful.

She swallowed hard. "Thank you."

I placed a kiss to her temple.

Just as the moment between us settled, a small, mischievous voice cut through the air.

"Does this mean I get to be the flower girl at your wedding?"

Rose and I both turned to find Wren standing in the doorway, her arms crossed over her chest, eyes alight with curiosity and just a little bit of judgment.

Rose made a choking noise. "What?"

Wren rolled her eyes before pointing between us. "You guys were just in a locked room forever. I heard Mom say it was true love or something like that. So, obviously, you're getting married. And I'm your flower girl." She paused, tapping a finger against her chin. "Or I guess, technically, I could be the ring bearer, but flower girl is the better role."

Rose let out a strangled laugh, covering her mouth. I just shook my head, fighting a grin.

"We literally just became boyfriend and girlfriend," I told Wren, crouching slightly so we were eye level. "We haven't even been to-gether for a full hour."

"Yeah, but dad says when you know, you know," Wren argued, planting her hands on her hips. "And I know you love Rose because you look at her like Granger looks at bacon."

Rose made another weird sound, somewhere between a laugh and a groan.

I dragged a hand down my face. "Okay, first of all, Granger is a dog, Wrenny."

"Exactly." She huffed. "And dogs don't lie."

I opened my mouth, then closed it again. Kid had a point.

Rose finally composed herself enough to crouch down beside me, giving Wren a serious look. "Listen, kiddo, I promise, if there's ever a wedding, you will be the first to know."

Wren narrowed her eyes. "Pinkie promise?"

Rose sighed, holding up her pinkie. Wren latched on immedi-ately, shaking their fingers dramatically before turning back to me. "And you?"

I held up my pinkie with a smirk. "You really think I'd say no to you?"

She grinned, shaking my pinkie with all the strength her little eight-year-old arm could muster. "Nope."

With that, she spun on her heel and marched out of the kitchen, mumbling to herself. "Gotta start working on my petal-throwing form…"

As soon as she was out of earshot, Rose groaned and buried her face in my chest. "We are never going to live that down."

I wrapped my arms around her, pressing a kiss to the top of her head. "Nope."

She tilted her head up, lips twitching. "And you do kind of look at me like Granger looks at bacon."

I grinned. "Damn right I do."

By the time dinner was ready, the whole house smelled like roasted garlic and herbs, and my stomach was growling loud enough for Charlie to give me side-eye.

"Did you even eat today?" he asked, setting a basket of warm rolls on the table.

I shrugged. "Been a busy day."

Blythe snorted as she settled into her seat. "Yeah, locking you two in a room was exhausting for all of us."

Rose, who had been in the middle of scooping mashed potatoes onto her plate, shot her a glare. "You act like you were suffering."

"I was suffering," Blythe shot back, dead serious. "Do you know how stressful it is watching two stubborn people dance around their feelings? I deserve financial compensation."

Charlie reached over and rubbed her back sympathetically. "You did good, babe."

Rose rolled her eyes and focused on her plate, but I caught the faintest hint of pink dusting her cheeks.

Wren, chewing happily on a dinner roll, kicked her feet under the table. "When do I get to start dress shopping for my flower girl dress?"

Rose groaned, dropping her fork. "I promise you'll be the first to know if there's ever a wedding."

Wren beamed. "Yeah, I know. I just wanna be prepared."

I bit back a laugh as Rose glared at me like this was somehow my fault.

"Can you pass the butter, boyfriend?" she said, voice dripping with sarcasm.

I grinned, handing it over. "Anything for you, girlfriend."

Blythe sighed dramatically. "You guys are going to be disgusting with this."

Charlie smirked as he reached for his drink. "Oh, they're *already* disgusting with it."

Rose narrowed her eyes. "We are not disgusting."

"You kinda are," Charlie said with a shrug. "And we've only been here for five minutes. By the end of the night, I bet you two will be making heart eyes at each other over dessert."

Wren perked up. "Ooooh, I say they'll be holding hands again before we even get to dessert."

Rose immediately dropped my hand under the table like it burned her, snatching her glass of water instead. "No one is making bets on us."

Blythe grinned. "Oh, we absolutely are."

Charlie nodded. "I'm giving it ten more minutes before Wells does something stupidly romantic and Rose pretends not to like it."

"I will not pretend," Rose muttered into her glass.

I chuckled, leaning toward her. "So you do like it?"

She shot me a sharp look. "Eat your dinner."

Wren let out a dramatic sigh. "You guys are so slow. If I had a boyfriend, I'd already be married by now."

Charlie nearly choked on his drink, and Blythe slapped a hand over her mouth to keep from laughing.

Rose pinched the bridge of her nose. "You're eight."

Wren shrugged. "And?"

Charlie cleared his throat, giving his daughter a warning look. "Maybe let's not talk about marriage just yet, yeah?"

"Fine," Wren huffed, reaching for another dinner roll. "But when you do get married, I want a sparkly dress. Preferably pink."

Rose groaned again, but I caught the way her lips twitched like she was fighting a smile.

I leaned in close to her ear. "For the record," I murmured, "I don't mind making heart eyes at you over dessert."

She turned just enough to meet my gaze, something warm and

unreadable flickering in her eyes. Then she huffed and stabbed a piece of broccoli. "You're impossible."

I grinned. "And yet, you're stuck with me."

Blythe let out another long-suffering sigh. "Yep. Absolutely disgusting."

Charlie just shook his head, but Wren grinned like she'd already won whatever bet she had going in her head.

And as Rose nudged her foot against mine under the table, I realized that despite everything, this messy, imperfect thing between us was exactly where I wanted to be.

CHAPTER 60

DAYLIGHT

Rose

THE DRIVE HOME WAS QUIET, BUT NOT IN AN UNCOMFORTABLE way like was on our way to dinner. Wells reached for my hand the moment we got in the truck, lacing his fingers through mine, and neither of us let go the entire ride. It felt easy. Natural. Like this was exactly how things were supposed to be.

By the time we pulled up to the house, the sky had started melting into streaks of orange and pink, the last bits of daylight stretching across the horizon. Wells parked the truck, and instead of heading inside, we made our way to the porch.

He dropped down onto the top step, stretching his long legs out, and I settled beside him, tucking my knees up to my chest. The air smelled like fresh hay and the lingering sweetness of honeysuckle, and a cool breeze rolled over us, carrying the sound of distant crickets.

"This might be my favorite part of the day," Wells murmured, his voice low and easy.

I turned my head toward him. "Watching the sunset?"

He shook his head, his gaze still on the horizon. "Being here with you."

Something warm settled in my chest, spreading like the slow

dip of the sun beyond the fields. I didn't say anything, just let the moment settle over us, the quiet carrying more weight than words ever could.

Eventually, the sky faded to a deep blue, the stars blinking awake one by one, and the night air grew cooler. Wells squeezed my hand. "You ready to head in?"

I nodded, letting him pull me to my feet, and without another word, we walked inside together.

Sunlight streamed through the curtains, casting a soft glow over the room as I stretched, warmth pressing against my back. It took me a second to register where I was—Wells' bed, the sheets tangled around my legs, his arm slung lazily over my waist.

I turned my head, finding him still half-asleep, his hair a mess, one cheek smushed against the pillow.

A slow grin spread across my face. "Where's my daily sunflower?"

Wells cracked one eye open, then let out a low groan, running a hand through his hair. "You're a menace, you know that?"

I smirked. "You set the standard. I'm just holding you to it."

He exhaled, rolling onto his back. "Stay here."

Before I could respond, he was up, pulling on a pair of sweats and disappearing out the door. I stretched out in his bed, enjoying the slow, easy morning, listening to the faint sounds of the house waking up: the creak of the floorboards, the distant hum of the coffee maker kicking on.

A few minutes later, Wells returned, one hand tucked behind his back. He climbed onto the bed and pulled out a single, golden sunflower, handing it to me with a lazy grin.

"Your daily delivery," he said.

I took it, twirling the stem between my fingers, my heart doing something ridiculous in my chest. "You're such a sap."

"Yeah, well," he leaned in, pressing a kiss to my forehead, "I think you like it."

Before I could argue—not that I really wanted to—Granger's nails clicked against the hardwood floor outside the room, the rhythmic sound growing louder as he trotted toward us. A second later, his snout nudged the door open, and he sauntered in like he owned the place, tail wagging.

Wells sighed dramatically. "You couldn't give us five more minutes, bud?"

Granger huffed, then hopped up onto the bed like it was his morning routine. He flopped down right between us, stretching out with a satisfied sigh.

I laughed, scratching behind his ears. "Guess he didn't get the memo that this is *our* bed now."

Wells arched a brow. "Oh? *Our* bed?"

Heat bloomed up my neck, but I covered it with a shrug. "I mean... I didn't say I was leaving."

Something shifted in his gaze, something softer, something certain.

"Good," he murmured, reaching over Granger to run a knuckle along my jaw. "Because I don't want you to."

I swallowed, my fingers tightening around the sunflower in my lap.

This thing between us felt steady now. And I realized in that moment that I wasn't scared anymore.

Wells nudged Granger over with a groan, reclaiming his spot beside me. "Come on, let's get some coffee before the whole farm wakes up."

I rolled onto my side, propping myself up on one elbow. "You gonna bring me coffee in bed too?"

He smirked. "Don't push your luck."

I laughed, letting him pull me up and out of bed, the scent of morning coffee, hay, and something that smelled an awful lot like a fresh start filling the air.

Wells tugged me toward the kitchen, our steps easy and

unhurried. The house was still quiet, the kind of peaceful lull that only came in the early morning before the day had a chance to take off running.

As we walked down the hall, Granger followed behind us like he didn't want to be left out of whatever was happening.

The kitchen was already warm with the scent of coffee, and Wells went straight for the pot, pouring two mugs. He slid one toward me before leaning back against the counter, taking a slow sip.

I wrapped my hands around the mug, letting the heat seep into my fingers. "What's the plan for today, boss?"

Wells arched a brow over his mug. "Boss?"

I smirked. "Technically, you're my boss, aren't you?"

He made a face, setting his coffee down. "Yeah, I don't love that."

"Oh? And what would you rather me call you?"

A slow, teasing smile tugged at his lips. "Boyfriend works."

I took a sip of coffee, letting the word settle over me. *Boyfriend.* It was new. It was different. But it felt *right*.

"Boyfriend, huh?" I mused. "You sure you don't want me to ease into it? Maybe start with 'boss' and work my way up?" I offered a wink, knowing exactly what button I was pushing.

Wells set his coffee down with a groan and pushed off the counter, coming around the island toward me. Before I could react, his hands found my waist, and he lifted me onto the counter like it was nothing.

He braced his arms on either side of me, his face hovering just inches from mine. "How about I make you say it?"

My breath caught. "Make me?"

His grin was downright sinful. "Mhm."

Heat bloomed in my stomach, but before I could fire back with some witty response, Granger let out a dramatic sigh from the floor, his tail thumping once as if to remind us he was still very much in the room.

Wells exhaled a laugh, dropping his forehead to my shoulder. "Cockblocked by a dog. Again."

I giggled, running a hand through his messy hair. "I think we'll survive."

He pulled back just enough to press a quick, lazy kiss to my lips.

And just like that, my heart did that ridiculous flip again—the one that told me I was exactly where I was supposed to be.

I let my fingers trail through Wells' hair, memorizing the moment—the weight of his hands on my hips, the warmth of his breath against my skin, the quiet certainty settling in my chest.

This was it.

Not some grand, sweeping declaration. Not some perfectly scripted ending. Just *this*. The two of us, standing in a sunlit kitchen with coffee going cold on the counter and a nosy dog watching our every move.

And I wouldn't change a damn thing.

Wells pulled back just enough to look at me, his thumb brushing absently along the curve of my hip. "What are you thinking about, Sunshine?"

I smiled. "That this feels easy."

His gaze softened. "It's supposed to."

And for the first time in my life, I believed it.

He looked down at me, that easy, lazy smile back in place. "So. What now?"

I thought about it for a second, then shrugged. "Now? Now we feed the horses, drink too much coffee, and argue over what to make for dinner."

He chuckled. "And tomorrow?"

"Tomorrow..." I leaned up, brushing my lips over his. "We do it all over again."

And maybe that was the best kind of love story. The kind that didn't need some big, dramatic ending.

Just two people, choosing each other.

Every single day.

EPILOGUE

FOREVER AND EVER, AMEN

Rose

WOKE UP TO THE SOUND OF BIRDS OUTSIDE THE OPEN WINDOW, the warm summer breeze stirring the curtains. The bed beside me was empty, but that wasn't unusual. Wells had always been an early riser.

Still, I missed the solid weight of him next to me.

A year ago, I had a room across the hall, a place that was mine and mine alone. Now? That space sat empty, untouched. I hadn't slept there in months. At some point, without either of us really acknowledging it, his room became *our* room. His bed became *our* bed. His life became *our* life.

The two of us had become one.

I stretched lazily before slipping out of bed, padding barefoot across the hardwood. The house was quiet, save for the distant sound of something soft and familiar.

Music.

Curious, I made my way to the front door and eased it open, stepping onto the porch.

And there he was.

Wells sat on the porch swing, his back to me, a guitar resting in his lap. His fingers moved effortlessly over the strings, playing a melody that reached deep into my chest and squeezed.

You are my sunshine, my only sunshine…

I stopped in my tracks, my breath catching.

My grandma used to sing that song to me when I was little, her voice soft and soothing as she rocked me to sleep. It was a memory I'd tucked away, one that made my heart ache and swell at the same time.

And now, here was Wells, playing it like he had no idea what it meant to me.

I didn't say anything. Just stood there, watching him, memorizing every detail—the way his shoulders moved as he strummed, the way his head tilted slightly, the way the early morning light touched his skin like it belonged there.

The song came to an end, and he exhaled a small breath, fingers stilling over the strings.

"I know you're there, Sunshine."

A smile tugged at my lips as I stepped forward, slipping my arms around his shoulders from behind, resting my chin on top of his head. "How long did you know?"

"The second you opened the door," he said, reaching up to squeeze my hand. "You have the softest footsteps, but Granger thumped his tail when he saw you."

I chuckled, pressing a kiss to the top of his head. "Traitor."

He turned slightly, looking up at me. "Didn't wake you, did I?"

"No." I glanced at the guitar.

His lips curled into a small smile. "Good."

He set the guitar aside and pulled me around to sit beside him. I leaned into him, letting the warmth of the morning and the steady rhythm of his heart against mine wrap around me.

The morning air was warm, carrying the scent of wildflowers and the promise of a slow summer day.

We sat there in silence for a while, watching the sun climb higher, listening to the world wake up around us. Granger trotted onto the porch, circling twice before settling at our feet with a satisfied sigh.

"Did you really just learn that song for me?" I finally asked, tilting my head to look up at him.

His fingers traced lazy circles on my arm. "Maybe."

I gave him a look.

He smirked. "Alright, yeah. I did."

My heart twisted, full and aching all at once. I reached for his hand, threading my fingers through his. "It was beautiful."

Wells kissed the top of my head. "I wanted to surprise you. Figured if I was going to be completely gone for you, I might as well go all in."

I laughed softly. "Gone for me, huh?"

"Oh, so gone." He nudged my nose with his. "I figured I should make it official."

"Make what official?" I asked, my pulse kicking up just a little.

He pulled back slightly, watching me with that steady gaze of his. "Us." His thumb brushed over my knuckles. "Forever."

A slow warmth spread through me, sinking into my bones.

Wells had never been one for grand gestures or over-the-top declarations. He didn't need them. Because when Wells loved, he loved with his whole damn heart, in quiet, steady ways that seeped into the cracks of my soul.

"Forever sounds nice," I whispered.

His mouth curved into the softest smile. "Yeah?"

I nodded. "Yeah."

We sat like that for a long time, wrapped up in each other, the sun warming our skin, the quiet settling around us like a promise.

"You ready for some chaos this afternoon?" Wells piped up.

"Absolutely. You know Wren is going to be ecstatic to hear we got more goats."

"I guarantee you she's gonna name the rest of them."

The farm was alive with chaos.

Blythe was chasing Wren through the yard, her laughter ringing through the warm summer air, while Charlie held baby Silas in his arms, swaying back and forth as if the tiny boy had any intention of settling down. Granger barked excitedly at the commotion, his tail wagging like a metronome.

It was beautifully messy.

I stood on the porch, watching it all, feeling the warmth of the scene wrap around me like a favorite sweater.

Then Wells appeared at my side, his hand sliding into mine. "Come with me."

I glanced at him, one brow lifted. "Why do I feel like you're up to something?"

His lips twitched. "Because you're smart. Now, come on."

With an amused sigh, I let him lead me off the porch and past the frenzy of family, toward the flower fields that stretched beyond the barn. The wildflowers had taken over, beebalms and asters swaying in the breeze, painting the fields in warm hues.

We walked in silence for a moment before Wells came to a stop in the middle of it all.

I turned to face him. "Okay, Calloway. What's this about?"

His hands found my waist, his thumbs tracing soft circles against my sides. "Do you remember what you told me once?"

I arched a brow. "You're going to have to be more specific."

He exhaled a quiet laugh before meeting my gaze, something steady and sure settling in his eyes. "You told me that sometimes, we're nothing more than collateral damage of a storm that was never meant to touch us."

My breath caught.

Wells lifted a hand, brushing a loose strand of hair from my face. "But, Rose… what if we were meant to survive it? What if every storm we went through led us right here?"

My heart pounded against my ribs as he reached into his pocket and slowly, carefully, sank to one knee.

Everything around us blurred—the distant sound of Wren

giggling, the wind rustling through the trees, the scent of sun-warmed wildflowers.

It was just him. Just *us*.

"I want this," he said, voice steady. "I want this farm with you. I want forever with you. I want kids, even if they turn out half as wild as Wren. I want more animals, even if it means you keep fake-punching me every time I bring one home."

A startled laugh broke from me as I sniffled. "Damn right I will."

His lips curved. "Rose Solace, will you marry me?"

Tears burned behind my eyes, my throat tight.

This man. *This man.*

"Yes," I whispered, barely able to get the word out. "Yes, Wells."

His smile could have powered the entire town.

Wells slipped the ring onto my finger before standing, pulling me flush against him. His lips found mine, slow and sure, and I melted into the kiss, into *him*.

When we finally pulled back, he pressed his forehead to mine. "You are my sunshine, Rose Solace."

My heart clenched, full to the point of bursting. I cupped his face, my thumb sweeping over the scruff of his jaw.

"And you are my home, Wells Calloway."

The moment stretched between us, thick with something unshakable, something permanent.

Wells kissed me again—softer this time, reverent, like he was sealing this promise between us. When he pulled back, his hand found mine, his thumb tracing circles over my newly adorned ring finger.

"Come on, fiancée," he murmured, a smirk tugging at the corner of his lips. "We've got a family to get back to."

The word sent a flutter through my chest. *Fiancée.*

I grinned, squeezing his hand. "They're probably placing bets on whether I said yes."

"Oh, definitely."

Hand in hand, we made our way back toward the house. As soon as we reached the yard, Wren's sharp little voice rang through the air.

"Well?" She stood with her hands on her hips, looking between us expectantly.

I held up my hand, wiggling my fingers to show off the ring.

Wren gasped. "I KNEW IT!" She spun toward Blythe. "Told you!"

Blythe immediately burst into tears and wrapped me in a tight hug. "I'm so happy for you."

Charlie snorted. "I had faith in you, man," he told Wells, clapping him on the back.

Silas let out a happy squeal in his father's arms, and I laughed as Blythe continued to bawl.

"Alright, alright," Wells said, pulling me against his side. "Let's get inside before Wren starts planning the entire wedding tonight."

"Too late!" Wren shot back, already pulling out a notebook.

I turned my face into Wells' chest, laughing against him as his arm tightened around me.

This was everything I never knew I needed.

Love, chaos, family.

A future that stretched wide and endless, rooted in the very soil beneath our feet.

A home, built not just with walls and beams, but with heart and history.

And as Wells pressed a kiss to my temple, murmuring something only meant for me, I knew with certainty—

This was just the beginning.

BONUS EPILOGUE

BEACHIN'

Rose

THE SKY WAS BRUSHED IN PASTELS—PEACH, LAVENDER, A
breath of gold that melted down into the sea like honey on
warm bread. The tide moved slowly and steadily, curling up to
kiss the shore before slipping back, over and over again.

My toes were buried in the soft sand, my skin still sun-drenched
and salty. A breeze played with the loose ends of my hair. My linen
dress fluttered around my calves. And beside me, Wells sat reclined
on our old quilt, his hat pushed back just enough for the evening
light to catch the smile in his eyes.

Wells glanced around the sand, then stood with a small, almost
mischievous smile. "I forgot something in the truck. I'll be right back."

He pressed a kiss on my bare shoulder—slow, warm, and familiar—and the spot where his lips met my skin tingled in the breeze
as he walked away.

I watched him go, his silhouette framed by the golden wash of
late summer light, then turned back to the ocean. The waves rolled
in with lazy confidence, fizzing at the shore before slipping back into
themselves. The air smelled like salt and sunscreen, and the sun, still
generous even this late in the afternoon, poured down over my skin.

I closed my eyes for a moment, letting it all soak in. The day.

This season. This feeling that everything was somehow exactly as it should be.

A few minutes passed, maybe more. Then I heard Wells' footsteps returning.

When I looked up, he was walking towards me, holding something behind his back.

He knelt beside me and with a quiet grin, pulled a single sunflower from behind him.

The stem was wrapped in a bit of twine. The bloom was slightly imperfect—tilted to the side, one petal bent—but it was still unmistakably beautiful.

My breath caught. "A sunflower at the beach?"

"What better way."

My fingers brushed his as I took it from him, cradling it in my lap like it was made of glass.

"This is straight out of a romance novel."

Wells shrugged, but the smile stayed. "I couldn't miss a day."

My eyes met his, and my heart fluttered.

"I will never miss a day, Sunshine."

It was simple—a daily occurrence—but it meant everything to me.

I leaned in and kissed him right there under the wide-open sky. Forever was wrapped up in a large yellow bloom.

I twisted the stem between my fingers. "What should I do with all these sunflowers, cowboy?"

Wells sat down next to me, and his eyes focused on the water. "Build a shrine to me."

I scoffed. "A shrine?"

He bit back a smile. "A tasteful one, obviously."

I nodded seriously. "Maybe I should create a life-sized statue of you made of leaves."

"Now we're talking."

I nudged his arm. "You are ridiculous."

He beamed. "I'm romantic."

"You're both." I paused for a moment. "I really do need to figure out what to do with them. I've got dried up sunflowers in vases all over the house. I don't want to throw them away. They feel like little pieces of the way you love me."

"So keep them." Wells paused. "I actually had an idea I wanted to run by you."

I raised a brow, not sure where he was going to go with this.

"Save the seeds." He spoke up.

"From the flowers?"

He nodded. "Save the seeds, and next spring you can plant them. Turn them into a field. We can have a whole field of sunshine."

I stared at him. My chest swelled. "A field."

Wells shrugged like he hadn't just handed me a vision of our future together wrapped in something impossibly tender. "It was just an idea."

It wasn't just an idea. It was a dream.

"I could plant some around the porch. Let them grow tall and wild."

"You can cut them and sell them at the Solace Blooms storefront you pretend you're not dreaming about."

I turned my head; my eyes were wide. "You think I could do that?"

"I know you can." Wells comforted.

A laugh escaped. "That sounds like heaven. I'll save every seed."

I looked down at the flower in my lap, thinking about the sunlit shop. I imagine helping people who came in, not knowing what they were looking for. I wanted to be part of something that brought a little bit of joy into people's everyday lives.

Wells reached over and grabbed my hand, pressing it against his lips. "That's my girl."

We let the breeze speak for a while. The waves fizzled up and dissolved, exposing some beautiful shells. The sun dipped lower, and the sky became a beautiful rose gold.

"Do you want to go look for seashells?" Wells asked, breaking me out of my trance.

I nodded vigorously. "Like you didn't already know."

"I figured I would ask." Wells stood and extended a hand for me to take.

I slipped my hand into his and let him pull me to my feet. The sand had cooled down, shadows stretching long across it, and the breeze had picked up just enough to tug at the hem of my dress.

We walked toward the edge of the water with our fingers tangled. The tide pulled back slightly and revealed my favorite shells—scallops. I dropped to my knees near a tide pool, laughing as a tiny crab darted sideways under a rock.

Wells crouched down beside me and picked up a scallop shell, brushing the sand from its ridges. "This one is perfect," he said, holding it out to me.

I turned it over in my hands. It was white with pink swirls spiraling inward. "This is beautiful."

"You can add it to your jar on the kitchen windowsill," Wells suggested.

"My jar is overflowing," I said with a grin. "I think it might be time for a second one."

"Or a whole shelf."

"Or maybe a whole wall in the office."

Wells laughed, shaking his head like I was already too far gone. Which, I was.

We wandered further down the shore, stopping to examine each shell. I tucked my favorites into the pocket of my dress.

We were halfway down the shoreline when Wells found a heart-shaped shell, worn that way by time and tides. He didn't say anything, just held it out to me with a quiet smile.

I stared at it for a long moment, then slipped it into my palm and closed my fingers around it. "I'm keeping this one forever."

"I figured you might."

The sky deepened to a dusky indigo, and the moon peeked over the horizon, casting a silver trail across the ocean. Eventually, we turned back, and my pocket was full, but my heart was more full.

As we sat back down on our quilt, Wells looked over at me. "This might have been our best beach day yet."

That's the thing about love like this—it isn't built on grand gestures alone. It's made in the quiet, in the in-between. In seashells and sunflowers. In salt air and soft promises. It's the ordinary days that become the ones you remember forever.

We talked about everything and nothing. What color to paint the back fence. Whether we needed a swing under the oak tree for when Wren came to visit.

Life is mostly made of those little conversations.

Somewhere between a laugh and a lull, Wells said it again. "Marry me next summer."

I smiled so wide it made my cheeks ache. "You already asked me."

He grinned, boyish and sure. "I wanted to hear you say yes again."

I leaned in and kissed him. "A hundred times, yes."

We stayed there a little longer, wrapped in the hush of the evening, before packing up and heading for the truck. The drive home was filled with wind in our hair, bad singing, shared glances, and dreaming out loud.

Somewhere between the sun setting and the stars rising, I couldn't stop thinking about the sunflower in my lap and the others waiting for me at home.

I imagined sitting at the kitchen table—our kitchen table—carefully pulling out the seeds and tucking them into little paper envelopes.

In the spring, I'd press them into the earth beside Wells' hands.

What began as a simple gesture—one bloom, one day—would turn into something bigger. Brighter. A backyard filled with golden faces turned towards the light.

Love is planted with intention. Grown with joy.

Always blooming.

Read Blythe and Charlie's

story

ACKNOWLEDGEMENTS

Ross (Mr. Shelf Love), thank you for introducing me to a slower way of life and for loving me even when I cried over fictional characters as if they were real people.

Stef, my soul sister in every sense of the word. Thank you for loving these characters as fiercely as I do and for always understanding what my heart's trying to say on the page.

Shannon, thank you for showing up exactly when I need you, every single time. Your friendship is one of the biggest blessings.

My incredible Beta Readers—Kaitlyn, Alyssa, Kristen, Lena, Ali, Jessica, Brynn, and Sarah, thank you for helping me shape this story into what it has become. Your insight, encouragement, and enthusiasm mean the world to me.

Danielle, thank you for all the beautiful design work that brought the visuals of this book to life. Working with you is such a pleasure.

Stacey, thank you for putting together the prettiest books. Your care and attention to detail never go unnoticed.

Elena, thank you for helping me finally nail down my brand and making me feel like a professional for the first time in my author career.

And to the readers holding this book in your hands, thank you for taking the time to be a part of the world I created. I am endlessly grateful you're here.

ABOUT THE AUTHOR

Meet Ashley, a coastal Floridian who turns everything into a story. Creepy next-door neighbor? That's a thriller. The ups and downs of corporate life? Perfect rom-com material. Hears a weird sound outside her in-law's house? Another thriller.

She's a Product Owner by day, keeping tasks on track and her team productive. By night, she's scribbling away on random notepads and furiously typing on Word docs, transforming everyday experiences into captivating tales.

Ashley is also a 24-hour dog mom to two adorable rescue pups. Her journey has taken her from the bustling streets of New York to the laid-back charm of the South, each move adding new twists to her life story. She started college with dreams of becoming a NASCAR reporter, so ending up in IT was a plot twist she never saw coming.

Whether managing projects, crafting stories, or spending time with her husband at the beach, Ashley's life is an ever-evolving narrative full of surprises and endless creativity.